The Philosophical Voyager
in a Land Unknown to
the Inhabitants of the Earth

The Philosophical Voyager in a Land Unknown to the Inhabitants of the Earth

by
Monsieur de Listonai

translated, annotated and introduced by
Brian Stableford

A Black Coat Press Book

Visit our website at www.blackcoatpress.com

ISBN 978-1-61227-367-9. First Printing. February 2015. Published by Black Coat Press, an imprint of Hollywood Comics.com, LLC, P.O. Box 17270, Encino, CA 91416. All rights reserved. Except for review purposes, no part of this book may be reproduced or transmitted in any form or by any means, electronic or mechanical, including photocopying, recording, or by any information storage and retrieval system, without permission in writing from the publisher. The stories and characters depicted in this novel are entirely fictional. Printed in the United States of America.

Introduction

Le Voyageur philosophe dans un pais inconnu aux habitans de la terre, signed "Monsieur de Listonai," here translated as *The Philosophical Voyager in a Land Unknown to the Inhabitants of the Earth*, was first published in two volumes in Amsterdam, "at the expense of the editor," in 1761. That, at least, is what the title-page says, although it was not unknown in that era for books refused the official seal of government approval that would allow them to be printed legally in France to employ fictitious places of publication as a mask; Voltaire had done that more than once.

On the other hand, some of the great works of 18th century French literature and philosophy were, indeed, printed in Amsterdam, including the Baron de Montesquieu's *L'Esprit des loix* (1748; tr. as *The Spirit of the Laws*). The latter was immediately placed on the Catholic Church's *Index Librorum Prohibitorum*, lest it encourage those mentally enslaved by idiotic dogma to start thinking for themselves, and "Monsieur de Listonai" doubtless felt suitably honored when his own book was placed on the *Index* too, given that his whole intention was to provoke thought in stagnant minds. That ban placed him in the august company of many of the mid-18th century *philosophes* and *Encyclopedistes*, and such subsequent writers as Louis-Sébatien Mercier, author of the classic futuristic utopia *L'An deux mille quatre cent quarante, rêve s'il en fut jamais* (1770; tr. as *Memoirs of the Year Two Thousand Five Hundred*), of which Listonai's work is an important precursor.

According to the Bibliothèque Nationale's catalogue, "Monsieur de Listonai" was the pseudonym of one Daniel Jost de Villeneuve, who is credited with involvement in two other texts held by the library, one of them an essay on Italian opera, for which three authors are credited, and the other a printed version of an operetta, *Zephir and Fleurette* (1750, by

Charles-François Panard, Pierre Laujon and Charles-Simon Favart), which he did not write, but for whose first publication he paid, apparently because he had modified it slightly when he put on and starred in a production in Besançon in Eastern France. The attribution is based on penciled notes added to manuscripts of two of the works in question, which were taken at face value.

In one sense, the face value in question does not add a great deal to our knowledge of the works, as "Daniel Jost de Villeneuve" seems to have made no significant impression on history, and those penciled notes probably constitute everything known about him, as well as about "Monsieur de Listonai." If his surname really did warrant the supplement "de Villeneuve," it is odd that he does not seem to be recorded in the extensive genealogical records kept by family of the Comtes de Villeneuve, but it might mean no more that the likelihood that he was too distant a relative for them to note. One of the copies of *Le Voyageur philosophe* currently on sale on the world wide web says that he was a "Tuscan Superintendent of Finances," but it is unclear where that information comes from. I shall be content to follow the strategy recommended in the preface to the work itself, of doubting everything in the absence of hard evidence, setting these attributions to one side in favor of the simple admission that we have only one potentially-useful information about the person who wrote *Le Voyageur philosophe*, and that is the fact that he was an actor.

In fact, it would not have been too difficult to draw that inference from the text of the book, given the extent and the nature of the attention paid therein to the theater and the writing of plays. The author's footnotes demonstrate that he was an assiduous student of Horace's *Ars Poetica*, not merely as an enthusiastic Latinist but as someone who was intimately concerned with the problems and methods of dramatic construction. His views on the subject were to be echoed in some detail by Mercier, who also felt strongly that the artifice of poetry was a bad thing, so that modern and future work should be done in prose, and who similarly picked up the idea of "*drame*" [drama] promoted by Denis Diderot as a new theatrical genre that could and ought to break down the artificial barriers imposed by the rigorous division of tragedy and comedy. However, it would have been difficult to conclude on the basis of the text alone that Listonai was an actor, simply because he reveals such a wide range of other interests and concerns, including an intense, if slightly eccentric, interest in Newtonian physics, an even more eccentric interest in natural history, and some highly idiosyncratic views on medicine and hygiene.

In Listonai's day, universal scholars were known, as they are today, as "Renaissance men," and it was universally agreed that their day was past, because the sum of human knowledge was now far too great for anyone to claim, as had once been suggested of Pico della Mirandola, that he knew "everything that could be known and a few other things besides." That did not, however, prevent the *philosophes*, and the *Encyclopedistes* in particular, from being interested in everything, and wanting to know as much about everything as anyone possibly could: an ambition to which Voltaire, at least, came reasonably close. Monsieur de Listonai demonstrates that it was not an ambition confined to scholars, that it was available to any educated man, including actors. There is a sense in which the fact that Listonai did not have the intelligence, let alone the wit and talent, of Voltaire weakened his ability to write a convincing and appealing *conte philosophique*, but there is also a sense in which that very weakness makes his attempt uniquely interesting.

Most of the writers who followed Voltaire's example in penning *contes philosophiques* did so with an agenda that imported a measure of narrow focus into their works, no matter how much they might digress as the Muse moved them. Listonai was preceded into print be Charles-Francois Tiphaigne de le Roche, who similarly sent a protagonist to visit the moon in *Amilec* (1753) and the sequel added to its second edition. He followed those works up a year before the

7

publication of Listonai's volume with the earthbound *Giphantie* (all three works are translated in the Black Coat Press collection *Amilec and Other Satirical Fantasies*).[1] Although Tiphaigne is a far-ranging writer, however, he is anchored on the one hand by his satirical determination to poke fun—in opposition to Voltaire, whom he loathed—and on the other by the fact that he has theories of his own, especially concerning reproductive biology, which he is keen to develop at length. The writers who came after Listonai also tended to have axes to grind, whether they were political theorists like Mercier or practicing experimental scientists like Louis-Guillaume de la Follie, author of *Le Philosophe sans pretention* (1775; tr. as *The Unpretentious Philosopher*).[2] Listonai was, however, just curious, more interested in asking questions than peddling theses, in spite of a couple of bees buzzing around his bonnet. As a result, *Le Voyageur philosophe* not only presents a broad spectrum of interests but does so, for the most part, in a spirit of open-minded curiosity that offers a precious insight into the kind of illumination to which an Enlightenment mind of relatively moderate scope might seek.

Unlike Tiphaigne, Listonai found the serious aspects of Voltaire's philosophy attractive, and the one point on which he differs strenuously from Voltaire is the one point on which Tiphaigne sympathized with him; Listonai claims to disapprove strongly of satire (although it might be noted in this context that *Zephire et Fleurette* is a parody), and might well have disapproved of Voltaire's satires just as much as Tiphaigne's, in spite of their opposite targets. That did not mean that Listonai was not prepared to employ satire as a rhetorical instrument, but he did so in a much more subdued manner than either of his august predecessors.

If that stance seems inconsistent, it is not the only evidence of inconsistency in Listonai's work; for instance, he includes a chapter on the unreliability of reasoning by analo-

[1] Black Coat Press, ISBN 978-1-61227-033-3.
[2] Black Coat Press, ISBN 978-1-61227-136-1.

gy, but is not at all reluctant to reason by analogy himself when it suits him—and to put the icing on the cake, he also includes a sub-chapter on "inconsequentiality" in which he argues, somewhat inconsistently, that much of what passes for inconsistency is not as inconsistent as it seems. He is not afraid of a measure of self-contradiction, being perfectly prepared to alternate the masks he wears, after the fashion he recommends in his prospectus for the actors of the future.

Subdued as Listonai's satirical impulse is, it remains effective enough to put the reader continually in doubt as to how seriously he means what he is saying. Indeed, he uses the dedication of his work to cast doubt on his own intentions by dedicating his work to himself, in fulsome terms that echo and parody the general tone of the unctuous dedications that the poets of the day frequently offered to their patrons. The dedication is, of course, a joke, but it is a pointed one, especially in juxtaposition with the preface that follows it, in which the author anticipates and defends himself against the charge that his work is a complete mess, devoid of any coherent order or "consequentiality." He mounts that defense not on the grounds that it is more orderly or consequential than it seems, but on the grounds that that is the kind of person he is, and so what? And, indeed, it obviously is the kind of person he is, and the disorderliness of his text, no matter how much it might offend lovers of coherence, does have certain virtuous consequences, not only in representing the vagaries of thought in something akin to their natural perversity, but in encouraging him to let rip, both argumentatively and imaginatively, in circumstances where more orderly authors would undoubtedly have exercised more discretion.

One of the effects of Listonai's haphazard mode of composition is to make the text of *Le Voyageur philosophe* into a patchwork whose individual chapters are unlikely to be equally interesting to all readers, with the result that many of them might seem tedious. He admits that blithely when inviting his readers to skip the four chapters that consist entirely of questions, gathering together all those posed in the previous course

9

of the text and adding a few hundred more for good measure—but he also suggests that some readers might find a certain pleasure in the lists, and is not wrong. By way of compensation for the bits that might seem dull, however, the patchwork quality ensures that a few of the chapters are remarkably striking in their boldness and their reach—especially those in which the narrative voice explicitly dons another mask in order to distance itself from the ideas expressed therein.

The text might seem to many readers not to be a work of fiction at all, because there is a sense—perhaps interesting in itself—in which it minimizes the fictionalization of its materials. It contains only two story elements: the narrator's encounter with the strange "ship" that transports him to the moon, and his meeting with Arzame, who takes him through the center of the moon to the side invisible from Earth, where the advanced society of the Selenites is located. Nothing else happens, except that the narrator reports his observations of Selenite society, including a number of verbal relations by Arzame, and the contents of various essays he reads, using the latter methods of indirect narration to displace idea that he does not want to attribute to himself—although, perhaps oddly, he does describe directly, in distinctly satirical terms, his visit to the depository "discovered" by an earlier fictitious visitor to the moon, Astolpho in Ariosto's *Orlando Furioso* (an episode that also had a considerable influence on Tiphaigne's lunar fantasy).

The greatest narrative distance to be found in Listonai's work is imported into the chapter in which the narrator reads a book—unpublished on Earth—written by a French ambassador to Turkey, in which the fictitious ambassador reports an argument offered by a fictitious Turkish philosopher in defense of Despotism as the form of government most conducive to human happiness: an argument calculated to be shocking to the vast majority of liberal *philosophes*, which revels in its own paradoxicality. By far the most interesting chapter of that kind, however, at least from a modern perspective, is the one in which Arzame invites the narrator to imagine what the peo-

10

ple of the 24th century might think of the scientific knowledge current on Earth in the 18th, and how a new member of the Académie des Sciences might summarize the scientific and technological progress of the interim.

Although the chapter in question is not very long, and almost everything it contains has been rendered obsolete by the scientific and technological progress made on Earth since 1761, it offers a uniquely precious insight into the horizons of the 18th century speculative imagination, being far more extravagant, in its fashion, although less detailed, than the vision of 25th century Earth presented in Mercier's futuristic utopia. Given that Mercier must have read *Le Voyageur philosophe*, it seems not unlikely that the chapter in question might have played some part in prompting him to produce his own vision of the future, but he exercised the restraint of earnest conviction, while Listonai, speculating via Arzame, felt free to be as extravagant as he could. The chapter in question is, in consequence, the most spectacular early attempt to put narrative flesh on the idea of progress as it was understood in the Enlightenment, and it remained the boldest and most wide-reaching for at least half a century.

The idea of progress in the sciences and the arts, and the championship of that advancement's likely contribution to human happiness, was not new in 1761, but nor was it very old. The seeds of the idea had been sown in France in the seventeenth century by Bernard le Bovier de Fontenelle, but it was not until the middle of the eighteenth century, in the writings of Voltaire, Diderot and, most particularly, the propagandizing of Turgot and Condorcet, that the idea really took wing. Turgot's work was still esoteric in 1761, however, and Condorcet had not yet published anything substantial, so *Le Voyageur philosophe* is still within the very foundations of the philosophy as it developed in France, and Listonai's chapter of futuristic speculation is at least as astonishing in its enterprise and boldness as Mercier's subsequent account of Paris in the year 2440. By the time it was overtaken, in fact, the idea of progress seems distinctly tarnished to many observers, and many of the visions of technologically-advanced societies produced in the early 19th century took the view that the advancement of technology might detract from the sum of human happiness rather than increasing it—thus assisting Listonai's chapter in remaining highly unusual.

It has to be admitted that that *Le Voyageur philosophe* is not a particularly easy read, disorganized as it is and inordinately cluttered with footnotes, many of which seem to be included solely for the purpose of ostentatiously showing off the author's Classical education. It is, nevertheless, a work that still offers considerable sources of amusement to the modern reader as well as having an undoubted historical importance, and its eccentricities are certainly not without charm. Listonai was no Voltaire, but nor was anyone else, and *Le Voyageur philosophe* is by no means simply a footnote to Voltairean philosophy or a failed *conte philosophique*. It is arguable, in fact, that there is no other work that gives such an accurate account of the intellectual aliment with which the Enlightenment mind was stuffed, and which it was trying so hard to digest profitably.

This translation was made from the copy of the text reproduced on the Bibliothèque Nationale's *gallica* website. Given that the author's footnotes are a significant aspect of the work's remarkable style, I have resisted the temptation to cut those that might well seem superfluous, profuse as they are. I have differentiated them from my own notes by including the prefatory identifier "Author" to them and placing Listonai's notes in quotation marks, expanding the abbreviations to make the references clearer.

My occasional comments on Listonai's notes follow on outside the quotations marks; my approximate translations of Latin phrases are given in square brackets. There are some passages in the original text that remain stubbornly opaque, sometimes because of the author's obsolete terminology, but sometimes because he seems simply to have lost track of what he was trying to say. I have done my best to decipher and infer the intended meanings of his remarks, and can only apologize for instances in which no clear meanings emerge.

Brian Stableford

EPISTLE TO MYSELF

For a long time I thought Philemon the dearest of my friends, almost my only one;[3] I was mistaken; you have always had preference over him.

I also thought that I loved beautiful women for themselves; I have recognized since that, mistaking passion for sentiment, I only saw their charming features, and really loved no one but you.

Let us make no mistake; our true, our only friend, is ourselves: a verity of sentiment, with which everyone is penetrated internally. Some young people hide it from themselves, some fools sense it weakly, but few souls are capable of convincing themselves of it. I confess it all the more frankly because, without fear of being taxed with pride, much less of scorn for everything external to me, I recognize it as a purely natural sentiment, which every organized being experiences mechanically, from the most sublime genius to the animal most limited in its function, from Newton to an oyster.

Why should I blush at recognizing self-love as the motive for all human actions, since, when well-directed, it is the source of all the social virtues, and consequently linked to general wellbeing?[4] Far from seeking to destroy a sentiment

---

[3] Philemon is the addressee of the warmest of St. Paul's epistles included in the New Testament, whose name thus became symbolic of close friendship.

[4] Author: "There are few comparisons a philosopher can make as fortunate as that between self-esteem and natural heat. No other two principles of action can resemble one another more; each in its order, they are equally necessary. One is the primal mechanism of all physical movement, the other the perpetual motive of all moral actions. They both act with a confident uniformity, although we do not sense them. If the excess of one or the other breaks the equilibrium, they become harmful,

inherent in the nature of every thinking being, necessary and good in its principle, only harmful by virtue of abuse that one can make of it, it is necessary, on the contrary to furnish it with aliments appropriate to its maintenance, for our own wellbeing and to maintain delicacy in others.

If self-love is both useful and dangerous, like reason and the passions, it is, like them, a gift of Heaven, which, its employment being in our hands, enables us to regulate the usage to our advantage and the advantage of our peers.[5] It alone, by imprinting in the soul the desire for public esteem, can put a brake on vicious penchants, subdue unruly passions, purify reason, give rise to the love of glory, pity and disinterest, and bring each member of society to collaborate in the happiness of all.[6]

Receive, my dear self, this confession as a pledge of my gratitude for the attachment that you have testified to me, since I began to breathe, the zeal with which you have accom-

---

useful as they are, one corrupting the best qualities of the soul, the other consuming the most necessary particles of life."

[5] Author: "*Qui sibi amicus est, scito hunc amicum omnibus esse*; Seneca Epistle VI." [You may be sure that one who is a friend to himself is a friend to all] Listonai lifted the quote from Michel de Montaigne's *Essais*, from which he borrowed many other quotes, frequently reproducing errors made by Montaigne, so he undoubtedly exaggerates his own acquaintance with the original texts.

[6] Author: "Self-love, a man of intelligence has said, is a pure passion, from which all the others are born. Well-directed, it is the mainspring and life of the moral world, as motion is the soul of the physical world. It is a passion whose center is everywhere, and circumference nowhere." The "man of intelligence" is probably Jean-Jacques Rousseau, although Rousseau was careful to distinguish "*amour de soi*"—primitive self-love—from "*amour-propre*" [usually translated as self-esteem], which is the conventional phrase that Listonai uses, making no such distinction.

panied me through the turbulence of the world, in affairs and in retreat, in fortune and in disgrace. Accept, too, the fruit of my leisure. To whom, in fact, could I dedicate with more reason the relation of a Voyage that you have been kind enough to make with me, a work that you have imagined, counseled, dictated and written yourself, which I have only attempted in order to flatter your self-esteem, even when I thought I was only working for your instruction, and the pleasure of the public, and in whose success or failure you will share.

At least, in dedicating it to you, more fortunate than Tasso, Ariosto, Theodorus Gaza and many others, I can dispense with piling up here those fastidious and mercenary[7] eulogies which, in every Dedicatory Epistle, debase the protector and the protégé alike. I shall therefore content myself with supposing your virtues rather than praising them. I shall say nothing about your intelligence, except that it will appear singular to some and unhinged to others, but just to those which are analogous to yours.[8]

What shall I say about your style? Everyone has his own, as everyone has his character, from which style takes its tincture. Yours is perhaps too opposed to hindrance; I believe it, however, to be more sturdy than diffuse, more correct than negligent, more rapid than loose, and generally more bright than dark. Your taste for making lists[9] will doubtless find critics. In vain will you claim the support of Cicero; it is a weakness that perhaps only belongs to him. As for qualities of the

---

[7] Author: "….*nec nota potentum munera*. Aeneid Book XII lines 519-20." [Of the responsibilities of powerful men].

[8] Author: "The Epistle, a man of good sense has said, is a chord that only vibrates in unison. In general, we esteem in others our own penchants, our own tastes and our own image."

[9] Author: "An aspect of rhetoric, the property of which is to resemble, in a harmonious style, a sequence of striking features, with the effect of convincing and seducing the mind, almost without giving it time to recognize the fact."

heart...oh, I blossom!...usage authorizes me to accord them to you in the highest degree.

You have always been the unique confidant of my secret thoughts; I have nothing but praise for your discretion.[10] It is not the same with your advice; I have sometimes gone wrong by following it in stormy times, when the human heart is too much the slave of the passions to be able to give and receive sagacity. In a more mature era, I have received excellent advice, of which I have made little use, because it pleased events and circumstances to suspend it or to deflect it; but how many obligations do I not have to you, as well as to my temperament?[11]

I can say without conceit that our union has been unalterable, that our penchants and our tastes have been constantly uniform. Can there, in fact, be anything more united than two beings who have only one soul between them, moved by the same springs, served by the same reason and consequently victim to the same passions? The union between the soul and the body is less intimate, since, being so often in opposition, enslaved to one another although independent, they experience an embarrassment, a continual tyranny over which reason does not always triumph.[12]

A vain objection might be made to me that a man is always at odds with himself. It is one of those foolishly consecrated Maxims, one of those superstitiously revered Axioms, whose examination demonstrates its falsity. A man cannot

---

[10] Author: "*It is necessary to lend to others, but to give to oneself.* Montaigne."

[11] Author: "How many proud individuals, and how many imbeciles, stupidly take vanity from virtues that they only owe to a fortunate organism!

[12] Author: "*....quid enim ratione timemus aut cupimus? Quid tam dextro pede concipis, ut te conatus non poeniteat, votique peracti?* Juvenal Satire X. lines 4-5." [...For what, with reason, do we fear or desire? What do you contrive so favorably as not to repent of the undertaking and your desire?]

want and not want at the same time, just as he cannot have two ideas at the same time. The almost imperceptible passage from one act of will to another makes him confuse the past with the present and mistake the rapid succession of several ideas for the work of a single instant. I have no reproach to make to you of any contradiction to me, or misunderstanding between us.

But what do I not owe you, my dear Self? It is you who, since my earliest youth, has directed my taste toward the study of the Ancients, of philosophy and mathematics, in order to give me a foundation of taste, enlightenment and ineffable verities, and only to judge subsequently for myself. *Amicus Plato, sed magis amica veritas.*[13]

It is You, again, who have taught me to challenge principles of education, as variable as climates, in order to make use of my reason against the host of prejudices that afflict understanding, because it is easier to rebel against imperfections at first than to uproot them when one has become accustomed to respect them.[14] What is more ridiculous, and even more dangerous or harmful to the progress of reason than that implicit obedience of the disciples of Pythagoras in believing blindly what the master has said?—a submission worthy of a slave, not the disciple of a Philosopher.

It is you who have made me sense the necessity of Voyaging, in order to learn to know people, to compare the mores of different lands, analyze their customs, research the spirit of their laws, weigh national prejudices, distinguish truth from plausibility, and accustom myself to supposing everything to be possible, but only to yield to evidence.

I hold with you:

---

[13] A maxim attributed to Plato's great rival Aristotle: "Plato is my friend but the truth is a better one."

[14] Author: "One can only make sure of the route that leads to the truth when one knows the things that are distant from it. Those who obey without reflection all the impressions of education are necessarily false in intelligence and incapable of reform."

That the more one learns, the more aware one is of how much still remains to be learned, and, the path of the senses being too narrow to lead us to the truth,[15] it is necessary to doubt with wisdom before seating one's judgment;

That one is only as happy as one imagines oneself to be, and that there is no condition or situation in which one cannot fabricate a kind of happiness;

That a man is almost always the artisan of his good fortune or his misfortune, that hazard has much less influence on events than one thinks, and that after having exhausted the hones means of contributing to his own felicity, the wise man ought to yield without a murmur to the accidents that prevent him from attaining it;

That one ought to support, with patience, all the evils attached to the human condition, the majority of which nevertheless only reside in opinion,[16] and that one can diminish their intensity by casting one's eyes upon beings more unfortunate than oneself.

Finally, my dear Self, it is you who, in allowing me to regret the happy simplicity[17] in which our first ancestors lived peacefully, by virtue of the ignorance of so much knowledge that now torments us, have taught me to draw more from the state of society in its established form, and instructed me in the duties of the citizen, which consist of respecting Religion, Laws and Government, and not allowing entry into one's soul of any interest that might harm the public interest; serving one's fellows, cherishing virtue equally in all conditions, detesting vices, excusing faults, lending oneself to weakness, bemoaning prejudices and laughing secretly at ridiculousness.

---

[15] Author: "*Quae sunt tantae animi angustiae*. Cicero, De Natura Deorum, Book I, Chapter 31." [What an excess of narrow-mindedness this is.]

[16] Author: "*One often has a stone in one's soul before having it in the kidneys*. Montaigne."

[17] Author: "*...aevo rarissima nostro. Simplicitas....* Ovid, Ara Amatoria, Book I." [A great rarity nowadays: Simplicity]

In our intimacy—a situation so irksome for the majority of humans, in which one seeks, without being able to find, or which one flees, without being able to separate oneself—in those moments as redoubtable for the ignorant as they are delightful for those who make an aliment of reflection, I am convinced that one can avoid the deadly malady of the soul known as ennui,[18] warding it off by means of solid reading and useful occupations that one can and even ought to sacrifice a few moments to commerce with the world; but that, without affecting misanthropy, it is sometimes better to live alone and independently than in the midst of frivolous, dangerous or tyrannical societies; in other words, to exist in oneself so far as it is possible.

Finally, to ensure a species of felicity, it is necessary to honor the Great from afar, to regard children as people, to flee the tiresome and retrench oneself in the class of the middle order.

Without adieu, my dear Self, conserve the tender amity for me that has cost me so little to acquire, but which I have always enjoyed fully under the name of self-esteem. Our property having always been held in common, without altercation, I shall never be suspected with interest in your regard, and, far from coveting your inheritance, I wish you, on the contrary, the longest life, exempt from dolor and ennui, and until age extinguishes all sensibility in me, or some accident deprives me of reason, count on the sincere attachment and inviolable fidelity of another

Yourself.

---

[18] Author: "Ennui is not thinking, or not feeling, as one would wish—which comes to the same thing, with regard to the effect. It is most frequently a matter of being occupied continually with the same thoughts, or always experiencing the same sensations—for apathy is an aspect of reason. Ennui and disgust are always born of uniformity. A philosopher knows nothing of ennui but the name."

THE PHILOSOPHICAL VOYAGER
IN A LAND UNKNOWN TO
THE INHABITANTS OF THE EARTH

PRELIMINARY DISCOURSE

Every voyager is a liar: a saying attributed to Strabo, an ancient voyager and a celebrated geographer for his time. The author of *Telemaque* has said with reason that every poet is mad, Bossuet that every historian is an impostor, Sully that every politician is a knave, Newton that every physicist is a visionary, etc.

That proverb, repeated for seventeen centuries, accredited by prejudice, has become an axiom for limited minds, which decorate with the beautiful name of Universe[19] this molecule of mire, soaked in water and enveloped in air, on which the King of animals crawls and agitates proudly, restricting the entire World to the portion of that little whole to which Nature seems to have nailed human beings and riveted their understanding, as if they ought never to surpass its limits.

The demi-Savant rises up imperiously against everything that is not confined by the narrow circle of his ideas; the fool—who is almost synonymous with him—stiffens stupidly against anything that attacks common notions or destroys fashionable opinions and habitual prejudices, the favorite materials of his philosophy; as if all that is possible were not believable, or ignorance of a fact were a plausible reason for

---

[19] Author: "One continually hears talk of *the greatest Monarch in the world* or *the most beautiful realm in the Universe*. An exact poet has said of Alexander: Master of the entire world, he found it too narrow."

denying its possibility.[20] People cry out against the convenient genies with which Romances are stuffed, who build sumptuous palaces in a trice, transform stones into humans, humans into animals and animals into plants; the likes of Orpheus and Amphion seem fabulous beings, and like likes of Hercules and Achilles heroes fabricated by the imagination in order to recreate or distract attention from the heroism of others.

The marvels of Nature, as sensible in their effects as they are incomprehensible in their causes, forced peoples in centuries more enlightened, morally as well as physical, to have recourse to beings more powerful than them, in order to attribute to them all the phenomena they could not explain. In the same way, in our day, theoretical philosophers freely create fluids to shore up their reasoning and render reason to everything that that is beyond the range of the human mind. If one takes the trouble to consider the great events on which the annals of Empires are filled, those pretended chimeras of genies and enchanters are found realized.

Would the astonishing facts regarding those superior beings, who are merely allegorical for us, have seemed to the Ancients, for whom superstition had made them articles of belief, any more marvelous than the revolutions, caused by real geniuses in the sciences, mores and politics? What do fabulous heroes offer that is more surprising than the extraordinary men who have changed the face of Empires: Lycurgus, Alexander, Caesar, Mohammed, Genghis Khan, Descartes, Newton, and Tsar Peter? If the simple lights of reason were the only rules of judgment, many peoples, some of which still exist, who live peacefully in natural law without any notion of what happens elsewhere, would be ill-founded in subjecting our histories to the same judgments to which we subject fables.

---

[20] Author: "It is for want of experience that people have regarded as fables an infinity of facts that Pliny reports and which are confirmed every day by the observations of Naturalists."

Those imaginary palaces built of precious stones, resplendent with gold, to which a sweep of a magic wand gives birth in Romances, only inspire pity for the starveling imagination that expands into the impossible; one is even tempted to place in the ranks of those brilliant chimeras the Gardens of Semiramis, the Colossus of Rhodes, the Temple of Ephesus, etc. But would the descriptions of the gardens of Marly, and the Louvre find any less incredulity among the inhabitants of Monoemugi?[21]

If someone were suddenly transported to a distant region—on the planet Mercury, for example—where the order of things down here[22] was reversed, where Nature is miserly with what she lavishes hereabouts and spreads profusely what she only accords to us parsimoniously, and where, in consequence, quarries and mountains only produce the substance of gold, and sand that of precious stones, would not that utterly-terrestrial individual be indignant to see huts constructed, fortifications formed and public highways paved therewith, and, on the contrary, to see the palaces of the Great and public edifices built of wood, stone and earth, covered by thatch, with furniture of lead or iron, jewels of marble glass, clay and so on? But his surprise would soon cease if, disengaged from his terrestrial prejudices, he recalled that all matter is one, mud as well as diamond, and that because human beings, by virtue of

---

[21] Author: "I assume that my readers are too knowledgeable in geography, and the interests of the Powers, to have to tell them that Monoemugi is a celebrated Empire in Africa between Zanguebar and Macoco, of which the capital, Mahola, is almost as superb as the least of our market towns." The probably-mythical empire in question, also known as Monemuge, is shown on 16th century maps of Africa compiled by Portuguese mariners, based on hearsay.

[22] Author: "I say down here, but I could equally say up here, for I do not know in truth which it is; I could even affirm that it is neither one nor the other, infinite space having neither a center nor a circumference."

the corruption of mind, only regulate their tastes of preference by reason of the rarity of things or the difficulty of obtaining them,[23] one would necessarily disdain on Mercury that which is sought out on Earth, and esteem that which is scorned here.

A feeble soul ought not to persuade itself that it is a strong soul. Would it not be more reasonable to familiarize oneself with ideas of possibility with regard to all that is unknown to us or appears incomprehensible to us, than to rise up superbly against everything that bears the imprint of chimera or paradox[24]—which is, more often than not, an effect of our ignorance or imbecility?

A man who has only ever seen streams would mistake the Danube for an Ocean A man who has only seen violets or daisies would marvel at the sight of a redcurrant bush, which he would subsequently consider to be a dwarf tree on encountering an oak or a pine. A tuna would appear exceedingly large to a man who had only ever fished up shrimp, but what is a tuna by comparison with a shark, a hundred-foot whale, a kraken or other animals even more monstrous, which are forced by their enormous weight to crawl in the utmost depths of the sea? Are the Spaniards not giants to the Laplanders? Mounted on horses, did they not appear to be Centaurs to the Mexicans?

Can one be easily persuaded that there is a tree in China that yields suet, another that furnishes wax; that there is one that bears fruit on one side for six months of the year and on the other for the next six months; that there are forests of a single tree; that there are forests of floating trees on the sea,

---

[23] Author: "*Quod licet, ingratum est; quod non licet, acrius urit*, Ovid. Ars Amatoria Book II." [We take no pleasure in licit joys; what is forbidden is more keenly sought.]

[24] Author: "A strange opinion or unexpected proposition is commonly called a paradox, when its sole fault is usually to shock established ideas; let us rather say that it is almost always a verity that destroys received prejudices."

which tempests tear up with their roots? All of that, for being extraordinary, is nonetheless true.

What repugnance one feels in believing that there are, in certain countries, Cyclopes, and in others men with three eyes; others who have two pupils in each eye; others who have no necks and who have eyes on their shoulders; others who have only one leg but are nevertheless swift runners; others, finally, who have no mouth, flat faces, two holes instead of a nose, who live entirely on odors and perish of bad ones, etc., etc., etc. All of that is, however, attested by serious authors, notably by Pliny, Book VII, chapter 2.

Believing everything and believing nothing are two equally absurd extremities, which have the same source: lack of examination. Whoever believes everything takes the slightest glimmer for enlightenment; whoever doubts everything takes the slightest cloud for veritable obscurity.

Blind credulity, says an estimable author, is the portion of the ignorant; stubborn incredulity that of demi-Savants; methodical doubt that of Sages. In human knowledge, the Philosopher demonstrates what he can, believes in what he has demonstrated, rejects what he finds repugnant and suspends his judgment on all the rest.

The marvelous might astonish us but it ought not to revolt us; it is necessary, before denying, to have learned to distinguish the impossible from the unexpected, and the methods of Nature for common opinion. It is also necessary, in order to judge the supernatural, to know the natural. The ignorant man is always struck by prodigies that are only, for the Philosopher, the very simple effects of philosophical causes unknown to the vulgar.[25]

Even the most palpable things can induce error in accordance with the point of view from which they are consid-

_____

[25] Author: "Such as, for example, eclipses, thunder, earthquakes, etc."

ered. From the foot of a cedar the tree appears very tall, but it is only a bramble in the plain from the height of a mountain.[26]

It is the same in the moral context; in judging, we are always too close to ourselves and too far away from others; the only person able to differentiate what comes from nature from what comes from education would be one who was a spectator and not an inhabitant of the Universe.

One can only protect oneself from a prejudice or cure oneself of it by giving the soul a tranquil seat, which allows reason to act in the silence of the passions. In general, to find the truth, it is always necessary to turn one's back on the multitude; common opinions are, as a rule, sound opinions, provided that one turns them upside-down.

The objective of voyages being, as Montaigne says, to rub and file the mind against others, one ought, in truth, to be wary of relationships with those unenlightened voyagers who do not take time to examine in depth the laws, habits, customs and mores of a land through which they rush precipitately, only pausing at the surface of things; they judge indiscreetly the character of an entire Nation by trivial adventures occurring in a hostelry, a public square or a coterie; they mistake an extraordinary event for a custom, a unique abuse for a law, and, stupidly comparing the persons of high status in one land with the populace of another, they delight in depicting objects in bizarre colors, which overturn the idea one has of them. There is in each Nation only a number of people chosen as

---

[26] Author: "The highest mountain on Earth is prodigiously great by comparison with a grain of sand, but less so than a human being from the viewpoint of a microscopic animal. That same mountain is very small compared to the entire mass of the globe, which is itself merely an imperceptible point in space. *Omnia cum coelo, terraque, marique, Nihil sint ad summum summai totius omnem.* Lucretius, De Rerum Natura Book VI. lines 678-679." [The Entire Heavens, sea and land, are nothing compared with the greatest sum of all.] Quoted by Montaigne.

representative, the people there are not understood, by magnifying everything to a greater or lesser extent, one makes them
a class apart.

One is more suspicious by prejudice than by reason of
the majority of relationships, and one lends oneself more easily to historians whose narrations are filled with actions and
events incredible to weak souls than to the extraordinary tales
of the voyagers most suspected of bad faith.[27]

The Voyager only differs from the historian in that the
latter ought not to omit anything striking and interesting that
happened under the reign of a Prince or in the duration off an
Empire, whereas the voyager ought only to present chosen,
true facts that are in contrast with the maxims, ideas, customs
and habits of the lands about which he is writing; his employment is, therefore, in communicating useful discoveries, tacitly to indicate to the Reader specifics against national prejudices, the cure for which depends on comparison and reflection.

I confess that there is sometimes indiscretion in recount-
ing certain facts of which one has even been the witness, because they are so opposed to common ideas and notions that
they are more shocking than persuasive. That is because, for
the majority of people, prejudice obfuscates reflection; because they seek to refute an argument rather than allowing
themselves to be convinced by it; and they commonly read a
new work less with a view to instruction than to judge it;[28] and
finally, because for people fed on prejudice, it is a crime to be
enlightened.

From the vicissitude of ideas and opinions that succeed
one another in the human mind, however, the conviction of

---

[27] Author: "What scorn would not be attracted by a traveler
who cited, as a witness, a Horatius Cocles defending alone the
passage of a bridge against an entire army?"

[28] Author: "*Indignor quicquam reprebendi, non quia crasse,
compositum, illepideve putetur sed quia nuper*. Horace. Epistle II." [I get indignant when people criticize a composition for
not being dull or insipid.]

their instability should not be drawn; and, without excepting the majority of positive laws, almost everything ought to be recognized in the class of prejudices[29] that are destroyed by age, study, circumstances and reflection, or replaced by others.

Where is the sincere man who dares to deny that, at an advanced age, in which the heart is disengaged from the passions and the mind enlightened by experience, fortunately or unfortunately acquired at the expense of sensibility to pleasure, he sees things with another eye, and does not confide in them the fire of a seething youth; that in his regard all objects, moral as well as physical, change their aspect although they remain constantly the same, and that at fifty years of age he will willingly make the reformation of the laws that he would have instituted at twenty-five; and that, finally, his manner of seeing does not necessarily follow that of sense—which is to say that change operates successively in the animal economy; that, the perpetual victim of his reflections, his meditations and the inconstancy of human things, he only approves today what he will criticize tomorrow; with the result that, floating incessantly on the ocean of his ideas, he can never seat one except on the debris of another;[30] that, continually changing

---

[29] Author: "Prejudice is the great enemy of the truth, and, in consequence, of the man who can only render himself happy by the knowledge of the truth. That enemy obsesses us from birth, or, rather, seems to be born within us; our first glances are undermined by error. As our faculties develop, prejudice subjugates them and fortifies itself with them. Examples, communication and education serve as means to perpetuate the contagion, sometimes making war in order to triumph over us more surely. There are no forms that it does not take in order to subjugate or seduce us, and never is it more terrible than when it produces itself in respected guise. Even so, it harms the truth less by the lies that it accredits than by the vices that it introduces into the manner of reasoning."

[30] Author: "*Sic volvenda aetas commutat tempora rerum quod suit in pretio, fit nullo denique honore, Pro aluid succedit.*

tastes, studies, opinions, occupations and pleasures, always seduced by new illusions and searching everywhere for happiness and the truth, he does not encounter them anywhere?[31]

Where do the planets move in their periodic course? Is it in the void? What is the force that retains them in their orbit without slowing their velocity and prevents them from falling into one another? What makes them gravitate around a common center? Is it attraction, impulsion? Is it a matter of proceeding to the decomposition of bodies, of ideas? Will there be an analysis? Will there be a synthesis? A few laws of motion are known, but motion itself is inconceivable; a few fluids are know, which are insufficient to demonstrate the workings of the mechanism of the World. Others are gratuitously supposed. Perhaps there are a thousand that are unsuspected, for lack of an extra sense, just as there are no colors in Nature for the blind man, or sonorous bodies for the deaf. A few properties of matter have been discovered, which serve as support for edifying brilliant systems, which the slightest objection might cause to collapse. The most enlightened observer can scarcely lift a corner of the veil with which Nature covers herself, and

---

Lucretius Book V line 1275-7. *Quod petiit spernit; repetit quod nuper omisit. aestuat et uitae dicsoienit ordine toto*. Horace. Epistle I line 98." [So revolving age changes the circumstances of things, and what was of value ends up dishonored (Lucretius); He despises what he sought and seeks what he threw away; he fluctuates and is always inconsistent (Horace)] Quoted by Montaigne.

[31] Author: "*Numquam ita quisquam bene subducta ratione ad uitam fuit, Quin res aetas, usus semper aliquid adportet novi, Aliquid moneat; ut illa, quae te scisse credas, nescias, Et, quase tibi putaris prima, in experiundo ut repudies*. Terence. Adelphi. Act V. Scene IV." [No one has ever had life so well worked out but that that business, age and experience forever brings something new or issues warnings; so you find yourself ignorant of what you thought you understood, and reject on experiment what you thought most important.]

as there are few verities susceptible to geometric demonstration, even among those that are the most universally accepted, sublime human knowledge is almost always is has to be content with the probable, at which it still arrives by the way of doubt. What temerity there is, therefore, in wanting to sound the depths of an abyss whose rim is unknown![32]

Others in despair of being able to be certain of any object throw themselves into absolute Pyrrhonism,[33] a worse infirmity than self-conscious ignorance:[34] *Nothing is certain. Nothing is evident. There is no substance or movement. Pain is not an evil. The Universe can be nothing but a phenomenon, etc.* Always short of or beyond the target, the human mind, instead of making itself a rampart against the assaults of presumption, would rather deny everything than examine anything; any singular idea is suspect to it, any extraordinary fact revolting. It is in vain that it is continually deprived of the idea of the impos-

---

[32] Author: *Quo diversus abis!* Virgil, Aeneid Book V line 165." [Whither does thou wander?] Quoted by Montaigne.

[33] Pyrrho of Elis, who lived in the 4th century B.C., gave his name to a school of skepticism which claimed that nothing can be known for certain, although the school was only founded in the 2nd century A.D. by Sextus Empiricus.

[34] Author: "Only methodical doubt can lead us to verity; it differs essentially from Pyrrhonism, which is nothing but the despair of a feeble mind that has been able to put itself above prejudice, but which, not having the courage to seek the truth, makes vain efforts to annihilate it. Philosophical doubt, by contrast, is the first effort of a generous soul that wants to cast off the yoke of error, and the first step that leads to certainty. The Pyrrhonians, in affirming that nothing is certain, are the most decisive of all Philosophers, for it is necessary to have examined everything in order to determine in an absolute fashion that everything is uncertain."

sible by continual discoveries; it incessantly rises up against the possibility of things it does not know.[35]

Imagine that in a country, such as there are several on the earth, where the inhabitants have no notion of the arts and sciences, where the great effort of human industry is limited to the invention of a crude plow, a European were to present himself who said:

That with the aid of a small instrument one can measure with as much certainty as facility the diameter, the solidity and respective distances of heavenly bodies;

That with characters traced on the bark of a tree, crushed rags or animal skins one can depict thought, give it existence, conserve with those who lives thousands of years before us, transmit our thoughts to the remotest posterity and communicate our ideas to someone on the far side of the globe;

That one can take a hundred copies of a composition in less time than one could transcribe only one, spread its productions to the ends of the earth, instruct the inhabitants and profit rapidly from their illumination;

That with dots placed on lines one can render sensible all the inflections of the throat and have a tune executed in several parts by a considerable number of voices and instruments, in harmony and in the same temporal measure;

That with other hieroglyphs one can trace in a few lines a ballet or a quadrille varied by a thousand figures and have them executed with accuracy a hundred leagues away;

That one can measure by means of a machine, with the utmost precision, the time whose duration can only be regulated imperfectly otherwise;

Know by means of another instrument the degrees of cold and heat and compare them in various seasons;

---

[35] Author: "*Nihil sciri siquis putat, id quoque nescit an sciri possit, quoniam nihil scire fatetur*. Lucretius Book IV line 471." [If a man believes that nothing is known, he does not know even that, because he admits that he knows nothing.]

Distinguish by means of another the variations of the atmosphere and anticipate reliably wind, rain, fair weather, storms, etc.;

That one can substitute with molten sand for weakness of sight and discover objects imperceptible to or beyond the range of sight;

Master the elements by rendering air, water, earth and fire slaves to our needs, our desires and our pleasures, create fire, weigh air, etc.;

That one can anatomize and divide a ray of sunlight whose diameter is unimaginable and which has a length of thirty-three million leagues but weighs less than a grain;

And finally, informed them of the surprising effects of the ardent mirror, the pneumatic machine, the electric machine, the camera obscura, etc., which produce marvels without number.

Those peoples would undoubtedly treat the European as an imbecile, a lunatic or an imposter, whereas witnesses indifferent to these prodigies of human industry because they are habituated to having them before their eyes,[36] rise up against any novelty—which, I repeat, ought to lead us to suppose that anything is possible.

For how many centuries did humans live in the midst of fire without suspecting its existence, and march disdainfully over salt, cotton and sand, before imagining that the first relieves the insipidity of aliments and prevents their corruption, that the second can serve for our furnishings and garments, and that the last was the material of glass, from which we have obtained so many utilities and pleasures? How many things are perhaps under our eyes whose properties and advantages we do not suspect? For how long was the art of making oil,

---

[36] Author: *"Nil adeo magnum, nec tam mirabile quicquam Principio, quod non minuant mirarier omnes Paulatim. Lucretius Book II line 1027."* [There is nothing, however great and amazing it seemed at first sight, that people do not begin to look at with less amazement.]

wax and suet in usage before anyone imagined making use of them for lighting the darkness by means of lamps—which is to say, drawing the principal utility therefrom? Who knew what the horse-chestnut tree would one day produce? How long did it take to cease scorning the oak fungus appropriate to stop hemorrhages?[37]

Today, when, with the aid of a thousand discoveries, we are enlightened by the same philosophy that only marches with the torch of experience, can we believe that there was a time when people recklessly interrogated the Divinity by the ordeals of water, fire and single combat, and that, scorning reason, the fortunes and lives of citizens were judged by such strange means?

That countries were populated by knights errant?

That knaves, charlatans and physicians were burned as witches?

That among enlightened and civilized people like the Romans, people claimed to read the future by inspecting the entrails of worthless animals?

That in the glorious century of Athens, the model of all those that followed, *mathematician* and *magician* were synonymous terms, and that Pythagoras and Anaxagoras were punished by prison and exile for having dared to suggest that the moon was eclipsed by the shadow of the earth?

That great men[38] have been persecuted for having maintained the antipodes and the movement of the earth?

That respectable assemblies composed of the elite of the human species have declared painting and sculpture to be idolatrous arts?[39]

---

[37] Author: "The ancient Greeks erected a statue to the man who found the secret of mixing water with wine. Paris owes one to the man who invented the raft and another to the one who imagined the Languedoc canal."

[38] Author: "Vigile, Galileo." The former reference is to Vergilius of Salzburg (c700-784), a.k.a. St. Virgil the Geometer

Ought we to be astonished that those peoples, deaf to so many verities, had a blind faith in judiciary astrology,[40] when in the midst of so much enlightenment, ignorant people—who exist in all conditions—still regard as supernatural accidents the majority of phenomena that are merely consequences of the order established in Nature and the laws according to which everything acts and moves? If there was a time when an eclipse threw consternation into all minds, when thunder was a sign of the wrath of Jupiter, a tempest a mark of Neptune's anger, how many people are there still today who regard a comet as a prognostication of the death of great men, an aurora borealis as an indication of universal conflagration, earthquakes as presages of imminent destruction, and all strange accidents as signs of celestial vengeance?

Every century, therefore, has had its manner of seeing; ours is appropriate to it; the ones that succeed it will have their own.

All these different ways of seeing, whose effect is the same in the moral sphere as the physical, originate from the disposition of organs, the degrees of light that illuminate an object, its distance from the eye and the environment in which one sees it.

---

[39] Author: "Council held at Constantinople in 754. In 1611 Vatan, a man of quality, was accused of magic because he printed his commentary on the tenth book of Euclid's Elements." The second reference is mysterious, but Christopher Clavius published a version of Euclid in 1611-12.

[40] Author: "It is not astonishing, says Pliny, that magic has seduced so many minds, since, having taken its source in medicine, it has borrowed the force of superstitions and that it has supported itself on mathematics; it is the only art that that has combined the three most imperious powers. Can we doubt, however, that it is to the frivolous art of wanting to read the destinies of humans in the Heavens that astronomy owes its greatest progress?"

An object seen distinctly in the light is perceived feebly in shadow and ceases to exist for the eye in darkness, without it being annihilated.[41]

Thus, Geometry is fully lit; Metaphysics, Politics, Medicine and Civil Law are in shadow; and certain sciences are in the darkness, like Astrology, the Cabala, Alchemy, etc.

In the moral sphere, as in physics, the soul only perceives through the intermediary of the senses; the imperfections of those senses, the accidents to which they are subject, the privations of some, passions, habits and prejudices are as many obstacles to the clarity of vision, which necessarily give rise to different ways of seeing things; it is therefore necessary to pity and not blame those who, by virtue of a particular disposition of mind, struck by admiration for one science, art, or profession, testify indifference or scorn for all the others; thus one deplores the misfortune of someone born deaf or blind, who does not complain about his misfortune.

Minds not being, and unable to be, in unison, whether they are right or wrong, whether they are to be pitied or not, I ought not to ask that they add faith to my narration, even less to flatter myself that my work will be to everyone's taste, inasmuch as I am only writing for a minority of people.

I am not writing for the fop (he is too futile), for the pedant (he is too punctilious), for amiable women (application harms their embonpoint), for the grammarian (he scarcely occupies himself with things); I am only writing for a small number of philosophical minds of any sex, any age or any condition who are curious to learn and to purify their judgment by curing their prejudices, only loving and respiring the truth in all their speech and all their actions.

I have spent the greater part of my life traveling; I have employed my leisure in reflection and meditating on the re-

---

[41] Author: "...*Nec morti esse locum*.... Virgil. Georgics IV line 225." [Death is not the place.]

flections of others;[42] I offer here an ample substance to nourish minds of the same temper as mine.

Of all my travels the only one that appeared to me to merit being written is the one that I made to the part of the moon unknown to Selenographers, which bears the name of America. I am undertaking the narration with all the more complaisance because no inhabitant of the earth has been there, and no geographer has made a map; it is, therefore, an unknown country. Let no one imagine, however, that the certainty of not being able to be contradicted by any eye-witness will enable me to hazard marvelous and incredible things. I love the truth too much. The country of which I have to speak is not one of those ideal republics in which people live without magistrates, laws, physicians and leaders; it has a monarchical government, in my opinion the most perfect of all governments, in which authority resides in one person alone, the pretentions of the great reduced to meriting the favor of a Prince, and where the people live under the protection of laws. I only report that which relates to, but contrasts with, our mores. What point is there in exhausting the imagination with regard to the origins and the advantages of that which might be, which has probably not been, which is not and which perhaps never will be?

I have rejected any means of surprising Readers by means of a title calculated to pique their subtle curiosity, which has produced the debit of many bad books; I respect the public too much to seek to seduce it; sincerity engages me, on the contrary, to warn Readers avid for novelty that they will not be able to shop for it in my work.

The man who sees, tranquilly, a stone falling in a line perpendicular to the center of the earth as a perfectly natural thing, without thinking that with regard to his antipodes it is falling from down to up, and that it would also be possible for it to fall vertically or horizontally, is not my Reader.

---

[42] Author: "*Sit mihi fas audita loqui....*" Virgil. Aeneid. Book VI, line 260." [It is my right to speak and be heard.]

The man who does not know or is not astonished that some parts of his body obey his will whereas others refuse it, ought to limit himself to making use alternately of one and the other, as necessary, and moving according to laws that he does not suspect, instead of wasting his time reading.

Those who, by a sublime effort of reasoning and sagacity deny that the earth rotates because they do not sense any movement and always find themselves on their feet, who doubt the existence of the air because they can neither see not smell it, but who believe firmly on the authority of their nurse that colors are in objects, properties in bodies, etc.—that extensive class of Beings indifferent to everything that surrounds them; in other words, those Automata endowed with reason who only make mechanical use of it—can be assured that I am writing for others than them.

In the number of those who claim or believe that they think, the man who only looks in books for new ideas, and who is not inclined to take for such those that are presented in a new light, or clad in the tone of the century, can renounce forever the reading of the moderns.

Those who only demand style from a work—which is to say, words artistically arranged, well-turned phrases, brilliant expressions and lively sallies—can dispense with reading me; I warn them ingenuously that there is no wit in my book: that which is commonly called wit, which everyone understands and defines in his own manner, contains too much of the cleverness whose proscription everything anticipates since the reign of sane philosophy has begin. I flee cleverness for reason; I prefer good thinking by instinct, meditative thinking by taste. I shall even be content to be without wit, if I succeed in saying instructive things clearly and sensibly.

The man who only seeks amusement in a book, and for whom reflection is a burden, morality an aridity, physics a frivolity and introspection a torture, will find more satisfaction in a romance or a tale than in my book.

The man whose mind is disposed in such a manner that any singular idea, or any that upsets common notions, frightens him, and furnishes him with more objections than desire to learn and be enlightened, will do better not to read me; he will spare himself torments or ennui.

But the man who loves to nourish his mind on ideas and knowledge useful to his wellbeing, and whose memory is not prodigious, will recall here with pleasure many things that have escaped him.

Finally, let the man who, being a lover of truth in everything, seeks to learn, without danger, something on which his mind might innocently exercise itself, which his reason ought to reject, but on which his curiosity ought to pause, only judge me after reading me with reflection; attention is a microscope, which assists in discovering marvels in the smallest objects..

If it is with reason that it is claimed that everything has been said, and that it is no longer permissible to write books without declaring oneself to be the compiler or the echo of all that already exists. It is therefore necessary to destroy the presses. But if the manner of presentation, of reassembly, might be useful or agreeable, an author ought to renounce passing for originality and content himself with a praiseworthy design to please, or to instruct a few readers.[43] It is only desirable that he put a little more equity into judgments and that the majority of minds so avid for new ideas do not rise up so heatedly against those who desire to satisfy them, and that one is content only to read in a book what is there, instead of interpreting maliciously, by taking, as the serpent does, poison from flowers from which the bee only extracts honey. There is no action, no human production that malignity, envy and the

---

[43] Author: *"Omne tulit punctum qui miscuit utile dulci, Lectorem delectando, pariterque munende."* Horace." [Who mingles profit with pleasure wins every point, by delighting and instructing the reader at the same time (Ars Poetica line 343)]

spirit of satire cannot abuse. Literary Annals furnish the proof of it.[44]

Let someone find me a book in which everything is no well-placed that it could not be arranged in any other fashion, even recast, without causing a cacophony or contradictions; in which there is no thought that is not clear and precisely accurate; no term for which one could not substitute a more appropriate or more elegant one; no sentiment could not be reasonably refuted or destroyed; no opinion that could opt be treated as a theory, a paradox or a prejudice or interpreted in reverse; and finally, that has no lax, prolix, obscure or ambiguous phrase, nor any fault of language or construction—let someone find me that Phoenix, and I will say that I ought not to write.[45] But when I see that all human production is more or less faulty, that what pleases one person displeases another; that what is popular in one time is unpopular in another, and vice versa; that every intellect has its style, its way of thinking, reasoning, arranging and presenting, I tell myself that I too have mine—which is to say everything that comes or returns into my head, to place it as it comes up, to say things and not words as clearly and as briefly as possible, and to leave thereafter to critical, meticulous and bizarre minds of a different kind than mine the liberty of arguing, qualifying and judging according to their taste or enlightenment; that is the fate of every author who delivers himself to the press.

Anyone who expects to win universal approval knows very little about people; I ought to flatter myself, at least, that my entire work is a tissue of the uncertainty of human knowledge; of the perpetual difficulty in which human beings

---

[44] Author: "*Est natura hominim novitatis avida*. Pliny Historia Naturalis. Book XII, chapter 5." [It is human nature to hunt for novelty.]

[45] Author: "Mildness and indulgence is necessary in society; it is equally necessary in reading. If one wanted perfection in everything one would have no friends and one would read no books."

find themselves, in developing their ideas and seating their judgments; and finally, of the perplexity in which all examination and all meditation throws them, besieged as they are by prejudices that they are not always able to disentangle from the truth.[46]

When one travels in distant countries, everything, including the stones, the animals and the plants, is so different from what one is accustomed to seeing in one's own that the first observations of a voyager regarding the peoples that he passes in review naturally fall on the assembly of bizarre customs, singular laws and ridiculous prejudices that tyrannize them; the fecund comparisons to be made with our own, which give rise to parallels from which a sage and enlightened mind can take all the more profit when they are less to his advantage.

The country most distant from any point on the terrestrial globe is no more than four thousand five hundred leagues distant. I am describing one that is separated by more than ninety thousand leagues by a fluid in which the human body, elastic as it is, cannot rise up to half its height. What differences must there be between the laws, mores and customs of the people who inhabit those two countries? There are, however, only those that opinion has set in place; the same light is common to them both, but one is obsessed with prejudice and the other is almost disengaged therefrom. With a little reflection the Reader will not be embarrassed in judging which of the two might serve as a model for the other.

This discourse, already long enough, could well end here, but I believe that I am still obliged to anticipate a few reproaches that malign criticism might make with regard to lack of correctness in style, prolixity, disorder, plagiarism, singular ideas, contradictions, repetitions, etc.

---

[46] Author: "*Quid verum atque decens curo et rogo, et omnis in hoc sum.* Horace. Book I. Epistle I." [What is true and appropriate is my concern and study, in which I am wholly absorbed.]

I have, as I have already said, read a great deal and re-flected a great deal. The dread of losing the fruit of my obser-vations in old age, when the memory weakens, has led me to collect them for my own usage; I then thought that what I judged useful for myself might appear so to others. I have de-livered my work to the printing press with all the more confi-dence that it will be equally suitable for those whose minds are insufficiently furnished and those who fear the infidelities of their memory.

I have tried, with regard to the narration, to take a middle course between an attitude of humility, which is always sus-pect, and a smug tone, which is always revolting. I become cheerful sometimes, in order to let my nature take flight.

Less sensible to the art of seduction that to the satisfac-tion of persuasion, and less attached to brilliance than to clari-ty, I have sought to place myself judiciously in the middle, where Readers can make use of their intelligence without in-vesting too much of their own.

I will undoubtedly say many things that have been said before, perhaps in the same manner in which they have been written, but who can be sure that all his thoughts belong to him and that he does not often owe them to the honor of a de-fect of memory? No modern author is sheltered from that re-proach or that infirmity; all I dare advance is that anyone who can find the source of everything that I am going to say is cleverer than I am.

If I am accused of appropriating the ideas of others, I have, on the one hand, the excuse that everything has been said, and on the other, that I have illustrious models in litera-ture for examples,[47] with the difference that I am only offering

----

[47] Author: "The Discourse of Monsieur Gresset on the recep-tion of Monsieur Boissy into the Académie Française is taken almost word for word from Monsieur Marmontel's article on 'Comedy' in the *Encyclopédie*. Metastasio has covered him-self with glory in his dramatic works by copying in servile fashion from Corneille, Racine, Crébillon, Campistron, Vol-

ideas, as an extract of my memory confused with my imagination, with which I have rendered myself familiar to the point that I can no longer distinguish them from those that have emerged from my own brain. In any case, what does it matter to readers whether what I have written is the fruit of my memory, my judgment or my imagination, provided that it presents them with substance appropriate to exercise their minds and provoke reflections? Even if I only have the merit of reassembling, in a small space, the greater part of that which might be agreeable and useful in an immense number of volumes, would that be so very little? I might be, if you wish, a literary gardener who has put to work the admirable art of grafting. That art has produced such good things in agriculture that one could, in my opinion, apply it successfully to literature; any author can graft on the branches that suit him, provided that he furnishes the trunk—and that, I believe I have done.

The benevolent Reader will give me credit for my cares; the Savant will find interesting ideas in my work, the Ignoramus means of exciting him to study, the Jurisconsultant a few judicious reflections, the Honest Man principles of delicate probity, the Citizen a patriotic zeal, the Philosopher a confident love of truth and humanity, the Theologian a respectful silence on matters of an order superior to reasoning. If I have

---

taire, etc. Any folio volume would be reduced to a thin pamphlet if one only conserved what was truly knew therein! Even *L'Esprit des Lois*, that masterpiece of the genius of our century for its depth and sagacity, would experience a terrible diminution." The principal references are to the dramatist Jean-Baptiste-Louis Gresset (1709-1777), the poet Louis de Boissy (1694-1758), the historian Jean-François Marmontel (1723-1799). The classic treatise on *De l'esprit des Loix* [The Spirit of the Laws] (1748), published anonymously in Amsterdam, like the present volume, was the work of the Baron de Montesquieu.

their approval, my aim is fulfilled; I have attained the goal that I set myself.

In offering this ingenuous exposition of the motives that led me to take up the pen, and the nature of the materials that I have employed, I am not enveloping myself in false modesty; I dare to flatter myself, however, that new ideas will be found in my work; I only desire that they do not appear too singular, unless thinking differently from the multitude and thinking rightly are synonymous terms—which I do not believe to have been absolutely proven.

I expect that a few people, to whom education and habit have given reasoning a different inclination than my own, might object to a few of my ideas; I shall only response that I depicted, so far as I can see, objects on which it is permissible to differ, and that if I have criticized abuses and prejudices, it is only with a view to the happiness of humankind.

To encourage morality, combat prejudices and destroy opinion, say those as indifferent to the progress of the human mind as they are insensible to the happiness of society, is a waste to time. Where do so many declarations, reflections and satires lead? Have they achieved any reforms in mores, opinion and the ridiculous? Morality is boring; criticism makes one feel ill, satire is revolting. To which I respond that healthy criticism has not entirely purged style and true comedy has not extinguished everything ridiculous; if Montaigne, La Bruyere, Locke, Pascal and La Rochefoucauld have not taught all people to read within themselves, they have sown seeds that have fructified in many hearts; and, self-esteem having an exceedingly hard shell, it is only by dint of pointing out its errors and depicting its ridiculousness forcefully, of incessantly battering it with the same words, that one can hope to succeed in making a deep and durable impression on it.

People might perhaps be alarmed by the considerable number of questions, as many of morality as of physics and metaphysics, that will be found in this work. I confess my whimsy in presenting them and using means more appropriate to enlighten the mind than simple reflections, which only leave a temporary impression. Reflections ordinarily take on a magisterial tone that indisposes Readers. Questions, on the other hand, which seem to consult them, and do indeed consult them, attract them without violence. Perhaps there are too many; I am sorry about that. I would have tripled the number if I had not restrained myself; the Reader may pass over them if they are deemed to be boring.

The desire to instruct myself and to encounter the truth everywhere has always led me to ask myself questions things that were evident to others, and I have so often made discoveries by that method that if I have followed my penchant, this Book would have been composed entirely of questions. That manner of writing might seem absurd at first, and singular thereafter, and then more appropriate to exercise reflection, to do justice to intelligence and dissipate the phantoms of the imagination. One can only attain the truth by the path of doubt.[48]

Others will perhaps complain that I have presented as questions some matters on which conjectures have been hazarded that pass for solutions. In spite of the authority of various celebrated authors, however, I believe them still to be questions. They have been discussed but not resolved. I respect great men, but I do not defer blindly to their opinions; in the same way, I do not judge the bounty of opinions by the length of time that they have reigned.[49]

I shall conclude this Discourse with a few questions whose solution will only appear in a century less enslaved to methods and precepts than ours, and which will serve as a passport to the form of this work. I anticipate a number of the questions that I have to propose thereafter.

---

[48] Author: "*Quale per incertam lunam sub luce maligna Est iter in sylvis....* Virgil, Aeneid VI, 270." [A faint shadow of uncertain light, like a lamp going out.]

[49] Author: "*Tuo tibi judicio est untendum.* Cicero. Tusculanae Disputationes. Book II. Chapter 26." [You must use your own judgment on yourself.]

Are order and arrangement so necessary in works of the intellect that one cannot free oneself from them without wounding reason or convention?

Are the majority of principles, rules and methods established by grandmasters in the art so infallible that one cannot deviate from them successfully?

Is blind submission to rules and established precepts always a certain proof of their excellence? Is it not rather the effect of a superstitious veneration or antiquity, which puts shackles on genius and hardly retains the moderns in slavery?

Except for the moral verities that one can only develop in consequence of deductive reasoning and geometric verities at which one can only arrive by enchained demonstrations, what works ought to be submitted to rules and precepts that an author cannot infringe with impunity without offending reason or judgment?

Of what importance is order in works of the intellect that treat different subjects? Are there not excellent endeavors in any genre that could be entirely dissolved or inverted without the pleasure of reading them being diminished? For example Montaigne, Bayle, La Bruyere, *L'Esprit des Lois*, etc.

Does one read all books in order to retain them, and place them methodically in the mind that contains them? Is that even possible, when one passes successively from an essay on morals to a drama, from a romance to a treatise in philosophy, from a fable to a history? Do readings succeed one another with any more order than the events of life, ideas and the course of the imagination? Is not a bizarre mixture of treading necessary in order to extend enlightenment, vary ideas and pleasures, and deflect the spirit of ennui into which monotonous studies throw one?[50]

---

[50] Author: "Most readers are comparable to flies that race away from a pot of jam to throw themselves avidly on to excrement and finish their meal with the same appetite with which they began it—which is why so many bad books are published."

Does not the reading that provides the supplements of conversation follow the same irregular march? And is not conversation a tissue of arguments, thoughts and reflections that pass agreeably and without design from one subject-matter to another? Are not the most charming the most varied, and are they anything other than uninterrupted collections of words? Is there any conversation more insipid than one in which a number of intelligent people all find themselves speaking in the same manner?

Finally, is the memory less furnished with thoughts and reflections that launch it into conversations than with oratorical or academic discourses in which reason is more symmetrical? I appeal to experience.

Why, then, should I subject myself to the fatiguing rules of logic that it pleased Aristotle to impose upon me? Have I made a pact with him that holds me in dependency? I only use his system in order not to cover the truth and to protect me from sophism; his authority does not serve to support me or to guide me. There has been no fixed system to which all parties are enchained since the formation of the Universe. If at times I go wrong it is always in good faith; if I sometimes fall into contradiction, that often depends on the angle from which things are presented, either as assertions or as questions. In any case, I let my pen flow; it chooses the route that pleases it, makes an effort or stops at its whim. I do not write, I converse—or, rather, I converse by writing.

Here, at any rate, is material enough, without what follows, to exercise the pens of certain journalists whose sublime talent consists of mutilating any production, in order to render he shreds ridiculous or reprehensible: to dissect the words, count the whos, the whats, the fors, the yeses, the buts etc., cite as linguistic faults errors of impression, substitute opinions with those they refuse and crown the analysis of books, which they have often not read, with a tirade of insults and flat and indecent jokes, which serve equally for all works that they have an interest in tearing apart.[51] One could compare the carping critic to a judge who had formed the iniquitous resolution to send everyone that entered his tribunal to the gibbet.[52]

How glorious it is for certain mediocre authors to find themselves confounded with the likes of Montesquieu, Fontenelle, La Mothe, Voltaire, Marivaux, Boissy, Piron, Destouches, Terrasson, Condillac, Maupertuis, Rousseau, d'Alembert, Diderot and so many Encyclopedists! But what a misfortune too for those who recognize themselves to be inferior to those famous men, that these frail monuments of criticism—or, rather, literary satire—have only an ephemeral literary vogue! The titles of their works and their names might have pierced the darkness of forgetfulness and succeeded, at least by that oblique path, in reaching posterity.

Oh, what a noble, worthy profession is that of the literary artisan, an apprentice architect, an ignoramus in painting, for whom the higher sciences are an algebra, philosophy an enigma and the arts a grimoire, but who nevertheless has the temerity to analyze everything, to talk about everything and to judge everything. *Vade retro Cerberus*, black smoke of literature, whose mind is nothing but an impure exhalation of malevolence, and who only enjoys impunity in the shadow of the scorn that good writers feel for his venomous features. A mastiff does not deign to respond to the yapping of a lap-dog. The gnat, by virtue of its extreme smallness, escapes the resentment of the lion that it has bitten.

Aquila non capit Muscas….[53]

---

[51] Author: "…*Donec jam saevus apertam in rabiem coepit verti jocus, et per honestas ire domos impune minax*….. Horace, Book II, Epistle I." [Cruel wit soon turned to open rage, and dared to engage the noblest families.]

[52] Author: "…*Quod nec Jovis ira, nec ignis, Nec poterit ferrum, nec edax abolere vetustas*. Ovid. Metamorphoses, Book I. line 871." [Which neither the rage of Jupiter, nor fire, nor iron, nor consuming age can destroy.]

[53] An eagle does not catch flies.

I will doubtless be suspected, after that sortie, of begging for the suffrage of those microscopic critics, inept wasps[54] following the Parnassus, who seem, in the eyes of the ignorant multitude, apt to decide the merit of authors. I would blush at their bastardized eulogies; I am only ambitious for the esteem of honest men and sage minds who think for themselves, who will judge me more on the intention than on the style and plan of my work; I shall receive their criticism with gratitude.

---

[54] Author: *"Wasps makes their nests, which are of mud, in high places; as for hornets, they make their in holes or underground.* Pliny Historia Naturalis. Volume I. Chap. 21. *Wild hornets only live two years.* Ibid."

Chapter I
Relation of the Voyage

Although the objective of any philosopher who travels is principally to instruct himself regarding the laws, mores, politics, habits, customs and prejudices of the Nations that he passes in review, each one nevertheless has a determining taste the bring him to pause particularly on the things that affect him more.[55] The Naturalist seeks out preferentially metals, minerals, shells, gums and insects; the Botanist plants, flowers, seeds and pollens; the Antiquary monuments, medallions and statues; the Erudite manuscripts and inscriptions; the Astronomer new stars. Purely curious minds cast a distracted eye over all these things, but everyone has their mania; mine is Cataracts. The philosophical mind has, I believe, directed the greater part of my research, but I have no neglected any opportunity to visit, curiously, all the waterfalls of that particle of matter that we call the Known World—from which one can conclude that I have covered a lot of ground.

I have examined with care the cataracts of the Nile, the Rhine, the Danube, the Vologda, the Zaire, the Albania, the Torne, etc., etc. and I am in a position to give exact descriptions of them someday, but all those waterfalls, as well as a thousand others, are mere cascades by comparison with that of the Niagara—or Nicagara, as some say—which is the most considerable that Nature has placed on our little planet. I had been traveling the seas for five years; the vessel on which I was a passenger, after having tried in vain on several occasions to disembark in the Austral lands and find a passage to China via the North, dropped anchor at the mouth of the river

---

[55] Author: "*Quisque suos patimur manes*. Virgil. Aeneid. Book VI. line 746." [Each of us suffers his own spirits.]

51

Niagara[56] in Canada in order to take on supplies. I seized with ardor such a favorable opportunity to go to see the famous Cataract and to verify what the Baron de Lahontan and Père Charlevoix had reported of it.[57]

Two intrepid Savages offered to take me up the river in a little canoe made of animal hides sown together with reeds, but as the navigation is perilous and the round journey to the cataract considerable, I preferred to travel over land. I separated from my companions, none of whom wanted to share my curiosity, having agreed that if I did not return within a specified time they would re-embark without me. I set out with a guide, who, after having taken me through forests and the immense wilderness, finally brought me to the bank of the river six miles from the place where the superb cataract is precipitated. I got into a skiff and rolled gaily over the foaming waters, in order to consider the admirable object from all points of view.

What an enchanting spectacle for a lover of cataracts! After having delighted myself with the sight of a thousand rainbows, whose colors diversified as I changed place,[58] the aqueous meteoric phenomenon being caused by droplets of water distributed in the air, which separate the colors of the light. After being delightfully frightened by the terrible din that the falling waters make when they break upon the rocks, and having enjoyed the sight of the perilous leaps that enor-

---

[56] The author inserts a note here regarding his use of the word *fleuve* [river]: "Others would perhaps call it's a *rivière*, with reason, but as Scholars are not in accord as to the name that the watercourse ought to bear, where or not it communicates with the sea, that name sounds better in my ear." English does not make the distinction to which the note refers.

[57] The references are to Louis-Armand de Lom d'Arce, Baron de Lahontan (1666-c1715) and Pierre de Charlevoix, S.J. (1682-1761)

[58] Author: "Everyone knows that no two people see exactly the same rainbow."

mous fish make, I approached the cataract closely enough to be able to measure its breadth, with precaution, which I found to be seven hundred and forty-two fathoms, three feet and nine inches, and its height, of three hundred and forty-four feet seven inches and eight lines, from which I concluded that Baron de Lahontan had taken the dimensions from too far away, and that Père Charlevoix had only seen the cataract in profile.

I then went up to the summit of the mountain in order to contemplate the source of the indescribable pleasure that I had just savored. It was necessary, in order to reach it, for me to climb three very steep slopes, through a dense but transparent mist, which extends for two leagues around and communicates with the clouds.

In spite of the fatigues that I had endured, my first concern—for I have always had, as an ultimate goal, the good of humankind—was to calculate with the utmost exactitude the quantity of cubic feet of water that, assuming the flow to be uniform, that impetuous torrent unleashes in a century, its movement, its force, its velocity, the resistances, etc., and all the precisions that give weight to an observation.

Thus absorbed in profound calculations, and my head encumbered with physico-metaphysico-chimerical projects, I was approaching the end of my operation when I was suddenly distracted by a confused murmur of voices, which I judged to be close at hand. Imagine my astonishment in a place where I believed myself to be entirely alone; I was almost tempted to believe, since voyagers have seen flying fish, that I was in a republic of talking fish.

Struck by that marvelous idea, I advanced with long strides toward the place from which the sounds were coming, but I was greatly surprised to find a vessel there of singular structure, the mobiles base of which was alternately assuming a concave and convex form. The framework was made of cork, the masts of reeds, the sails of a metallic tissue and superior in delicacy to the fabrics women by the industrious inhabitants of our gardens, and the rigging formed by the filaments known as maidenhair.[59] The crew had enormous fans for oars and an immense kite for an anchor, with a tail as long as that of a comet of the sixth class, laden with countless blisters.

A considerable number of individuals, the greater number of the fair sex, were embarking gaily for the land that sometimes substitutes benignly for the absence of the Sun above the earth, and which is known in astronomical and vulgar language as the Moon.

I hastened to follow that joyful band, and I had scarcely entered the vessel when the pilot, taking advantage of a thick mist on which the vessel was floating, raised anchor and set sail.

The navigation was so easy, thanks to a wind blowing vertically from the earth, that, having passed through the tempest that rises in the median region, we found ourselves within the confines of the atmosphere in three seconds and seven terces. There the physicist passengers, after having compared their different estimates, firmly decided on their basis that we had already covered eighteen leagues, at twenty-five to the degree. We also traversed nearly two hundred leagues of aurora borealis, after which the helmsman ordered the cessation of any superfluous maneuver, distorting and dangerous at the point of passing into the heart of the void.[60]

---

[59] I have given the conventional translation of "chevelure de Venus" [maidenhair] on all three occasions when it is used in the text, but I am not at all sure what the author means by it; he does not seem to be referring to the fern of that name, nor to the colored veins in certain minerals to which some 19th century texts apply the term. I cannot locate any other uses to support the faint suspicion, derived from context, that it might refer to threads of spider-silk.

[60] Author: "That name is conventionally given to the extremely rarefied air that offers no sensible resistance, which a vacuum pump cannot purge entirely, and which, under the name of Ether, entirely fills all the interstices of matter. Skillful physicists have calculated with precision that such air is seven hun-

Our vessel, agitated by several fairly violent shocks caused by the obstinate and perpetual combat between centripetal and centrifugal forces, suffered an oscillatory vibration that disquieted the pilot cruelly until, finally, by dint of tacking back and forth and heaving to, a thrust of the tiller administered horizontally having taken us away at a fortunate tangent, we felt ourselves attracted, by an invincible force, is direct proportion to the mass and the inverse square of the distance: a force as real as unknown, which, increasing prodigiously, threatened to break us at the point of contact. The skill of our pilot, however, an intrepid calculator of the infinite, having enabled us to traverse the x and y of the hyperborean region, avoid the Carpathos and double the Taurus, we finally landed in Palestine, dropping anchor at the foot of Mont Sinai.[61] We contemplated at leisure its two peaks, the marvel of Arabia Petraea, although it was about midnight, because we had a full earth.

Delighted to find myself in a land that I had so ardently desired to know other than through my telescope and the maps of my imagination, I brightened in advance in the seductive pleasure of making surprising discoveries, to enrich our globe on my return and enjoy in my homeland a role all the more important because I could pronounce assertively,[62] having

---

dred thousand times thinner that the air we breathe, in the same way that the upper region of the atmosphere in a hundred million times rarer than gold."

[61] Johannes Hevelius (1611-1687), the great pioneer of lunar cartography, assuming that the crater nowadays known as Tycho was a volcano, called it Mont Sinai, knowing that the etymological derivation of the word Sinai relates it to a Babylonian moon-god. Similarly, Montes Carpatos and Montes Taurus were names credited to lunar features at an early stage, and are still retained. Calling the area around the lunar Mount Sinai "Palestine" and likening the surrounding landscape to Arabia Petraea are, however, whimsical embellishments.

[62] Author: "A new word, but significant."

seen with my own eyes, touched with my own hands, heard with my own ears and decided with my own judgment.

Alas, though, there is a long distance between imagination and reality. I cannot express the extent of my chagrin, my confusion and my regret when, after having traveled the different climates, frequented the Courts, visited the Scholars, the Philosophers, the Antiquaries, the Controversialists, etc., I realized that I had undertaken a futile voyage; that the Moon, as a satellite of the Earth, to which it is enslaved by the laws of gravitation and perhaps by the continual aspect of its face, necessarily has the same laws, the same tastes, the same habits, the same prejudices—in brief, that everything there was the same as among us.[63]

I found there, in truth, profound Geometers and Astronomers as knowledgeable with regard to the particularities of our globe as we are, who have fixed its distance from theirs at ninety thousand leagues, its diameter at 2890, assuring by the degrees of the Meridian, which they have measured scrupulously, that it is a spheroid flattened at the poles.

Their Lunar map contains a Mediterranean Sea, a Black Sea, a Peloponnese, a Sicily, a Palestine, and Apennine range, etc.

The capitals of the various Kingdoms that I visited were inundated with cabriolets, their theaters resembled prisons, and one saw superb promenades there abandoned as rubbish dump; sumptuous houses masked by hovels; houses on bridges; noxious markets, narrow and devoid of access; tortuous back-streets, cluttered and dirty; few drinking-fountains;

---

[63] Author: "I flatter myself that my Readers will dispense with my telling them how I learned the language of the inhabitants of the Moon in so short a time, in order to be able to converse with them. It is a mercy that they grant to so many travelers of the World, who have spoken boldly about the laws, the mores and politics of different peoples that they have only perceived. Besides, it is usual to credit all voyagers with the gift of tongues; it puts Readers at their ease."

sellers of fashions; opulent restaurateurs; bookshops; artists living in poverty. Admirable discoveries had been made there, of which ignorance, prejudice or superstition did not permit the usage, but in recompense, many newspapers were overflowing with projects and theories devoid of execution.

As despairing of the lack of success of my enterprise as an Alchemist who lacks the final procedure for desulfurizing gold, and tormented by the desire to return to the Earth in order to hide my shame and resentment, I was wandering unknown roads when I finally found myself lost in a dark forest, overwhelmed by lassitude and ready to succumb to the ennui of existence...when I perceived a venerable old man at the foot of a cedar, whose appearance struck me with respect and admiration.[64]

I approached him with the natural confidence of the unhappy. He welcomed me gently.

"Tell me," he said to me, "the reason for the sadness painted on your face; perhaps I can contribute to its dissipation."

I satisfied him, and after having listened attentively to the story of my adventure, he said: "Like you, I am a stranger in these parts, although an inhabitant of the moon, of the hemisphere opposite to the one where we are meeting: a land from which the Earth cannot be seen at all, and which we call America. Our continent is separated from this one by immense seas, the coasts of which are bordered by sheer and inaccessible rocks preventing, so to speak, all communication between these peoples and us. Industry and courage, however, would have triumphed over those obstacles, if not for the fact that there is a traditional antipathy between them and us, which I can only attribute to the difference of tastes and opinions that has separated us for a long time: a barbaric but powerful motive, scornful of reason and common interest, harmful to the

---

[64] Author: "These venerable old men are always appropriate to the consolation of voyagers in unknown lands, or in embarrassing situations."

progress of human knowledge, dividing respectable nations everywhere, which ought only to form a single republic of brothers. It is quite similar to what is observed among you between the Spaniards and the Portuguese, the French and the English, the Austrians and the Prussians, the Savoyards and the Piedmontese, prudes and pretty women, the J...s and the M...s, etc."

"How is it," I said to him, in surprise, "that you, who have probably never left the Moon, are so well-informed about what is happening on Earth?"

"You will know one day, my son," he replied. "In the meantime, I shall inform you on the subject of my coming to this hemisphere, and the means I employed to get here. I have spent my entire life in the study of philosophy, morality and the higher sciences. Dazzled by the degree of perfection that they have attained among us, the desire to spread my enlightenment, combined with the love of the truth that guides true philosophers, caused me to hope that I might acquire useful knowledge in a land with which communication had once been established, and the mores and habits of which more than one vague tradition remains.

"As Nature seems to have forbidden all communication between the two continents via the surface of the Moon, I sought a route through the center, in order to reach our antipodes. Equipped with Salamander skins and asbestos blankets coated with a varnish impenetrable to fire, I boldly traversed the nucleus of our globe, where the central fire conserves a heat capable of consuming any other substance, and I arrived without accident in this hemisphere.

"Like you I have traveled all its countries fruitlessly, and I am returning, desolate, only to have found, in general, false minds, a captious metaphysics, a murky jurisprudence, a superstitious physics, a limited geography, a conjectural medicine, overlong studies, imperfect arts, sciences in infancy, theories, uncertainties, vanity, poverty and prejudice everywhere.

"In this society I have found nothing but authors who write for the sake of ostentation, orators who play with the truth, philosophers enveloped in tenebrous theories, lax moralities, base courtiers, ignorant protectors, pitiless rich people, indolent beggars, fine police regulations fallen into disuse, sage laws eluded and without execution, etc. What can I tell you, in sum, except that, impatient to return to my homeland. I am taking away nothing from these sad places but the satisfaction of having observed the stars that rotate in this part of the sky, which I had never seen—which is something, after all, for the progress of our astronomy."

Pushed less by a motive of curiosity as by a secret bond that linked me to the venerable old man, I begged him to permit me to accompany him. He did not have to be pressed.

"Come, my son," he said, embracing me. "Come to America; you will find there a World worthy of you. Curiosity is a virtue, when it has no other objective than the desire to enlighten and be useful to one's homeland."

Having both made provision of the vestments necessary to make our voyage without risk, we abandoned those ignorant people without regret. We launched ourselves into a profound volcano, and found ourselves transferred in a matter of seconds, traveling in a straight line—for the Moon is a perfect sphere—to the antipodes, which the vulgar people of the land we were quitting do not suspect any more than the Rhetor de Tagaste, whom their Doctors anathematize as the son of Polychrony.[65]

In two days we arrived, via broad and comfortable iron roads bordered with useful trees, at Selenopolis, the capital of the empire where the sage Arzame maintained his abode.

---

[65] The Numidian city of Tagaste was the birthplace of St. Augustine of Hippo, who is presumably the "rhetor" obliquely indicated. *Polychrone* [Polychrony] was once used in French to indicate someone capable of what would nowadays be called "multitasking," but it would have been anachronistic to use that word in the translation.

Chapter II
A Succinct Description of Selenopolis

The boundary of that City, situated three leagues from the sea, with which it communicates via a grand canal, is a perfect square, each side of which is twenty-four stadia long. The main street, called the Imperial, which traverses the city along one of its diameters, is terminated by two triumphal arches, of simple architecture but noble and majestic, which sale the entrances. It is aligned, like all the other streets, twenty-four fathoms wide, not counting the porticos that are twenty-four feet wide by thirty high, forming two parallel galleries where pedestrians go under cover and walk comfortably over large squares of Captschust.[66]

Private houses built with regular facades are intermingled with sumptuous edifices: temples, palaces, fountains, gymnasia, guard-rooms, etc., each of which has its particular symmetry, avoiding the monotony that excessive uniformity always produces.[67]

That long street is cut in the middle by a vast square, where eight streets intersect, which end in other magnificent squares, similar in design but not as large.

The Imperial Square is formed by six blocks of isolated buildings, of superb architecture, differing according to their purpose. On one of the sides stands the Emperor's palace, distinguished from the other buildings by a richer colonnade and pavilions that enhance its majesty, covered with laminae of azured bronze with gold seams.

Opposite, one sees the arsenal, built in a different style, but of the same height as far as the entablement—as are the other four edifices, all of them terminated by a balustrade or-

---

[66] Author: "A species of marble much harder than ours."

[67] Author: "As in the façade of the Château of Versailles facing the gardens."

namented with statues and trophies, which represent the attributes appropriate to each one. Of the latter four, one is occupied by the courts of justice, another by the city corps; the academies hold their assemblies in the third, and the fourth contains a theater of superb structure.

The center of the square is decorated with an equestrian statue of the reigning Prince. It is not ridiculously perched on a pedestal that is the commencement of a column, because one cannot conceive that a horse can climb, and how, in a galloping pose, it could take a stride without breaking its legs or its back.

The effigy represents a warrior hero afflicted by his inability to procure a durable peace for his subjects except at the price of their blood; he is trampling underfoot a host of fallen enemies, who, in the midst of the horrors of death, are still looking at him with admiration.

The love of peoples dictates that the representation of a reigning prince should always be before the eyes in the most eminent place in the city. In every new reign the old statue was transferred into a circus designed for that purpose, where the simulacra of all the sovereigns who had worked for the happiness of their subjects were assembled. Enormous expenses were thus avoided at each new coronation in the formation of new square and new edifices in a city, where all the land was employed and built up in the most convenient form.

Each of the eight streets of the square corresponded with a square variously ornamented with pyramids, obelisks, statues of good princes, trophies of great captains and monuments raised to the memory of men celebrated in the sciences and the arts.

Two of these squares were concave; they were filled with water; they served as promenades for riding on horseback or in carriages on summer evenings.

All the houses built in marble, stone or brick and vaulted at the summit were, so to speak, safe from conflagration, and to facilitate the entry and emergence of carriages, the principal door set in the middle of the vestibule opened both outwards and inwards.

Pure water was brought in abundance into the city by aqueducts. Every house had a reservoir on the roof that distributed water to all the floors; well-to-do people had bathrooms, and the voluptuous had water jets installed in the downstairs rooms, where they took their meals in summer.

A portion of the waters passed into all the streets; a slight slope aided their flow, and to maintain its cleanliness, every house had its ditch into which excrement could be thrown, which was carried to the sea by subterranean conduits wide enough to be visited and unblocked if necessary. In addition, to facilitate the relief of the pressing necessities of the human body and avoid the infection of the streets, care had been taken to place public redoubts in various quarters of the city, which running water cleans naturally.

The public markets were vast and concave; in the middle was a large sewer into which water released from fountains drew and precipitated ordure every day, in order not to leave any vestige capable of corrupting the air.

To maintain the cleanliness that is conducive to health, vast and comfortable public baths had been established, maintained at the expense of the State for the service of individuals who were not able to procure them at home. The baths designed for women were separated from those for men; fresh and pure water ran there without intermission. They were not opened before sunrise and closed immediately after sunset.

Abattoirs were not tolerated within the city, nor were dyers, tanners or firework-manufacturers. The powder-magazines and other combustible materials for the arsenal were situated a long distance from the city.

Sepulchers were situated outside the city in order to prevent the accidents that the corruption of cadavers causes in the air, in spite of the earth covering them.

The infirmary hospitals were also placed at some distance from the city, in good air; they were buildings more vast than superb, in which every room had a ventilator that contin-

62

ually renewed its air. There were only a few hospices in various quarters of the city, which served as depositories for urgent accidents. The hospitals of invalids, orphans, incurables, the inane, imbeciles, the sluggish and people leading bad lives and houses of forced restraint were situated in the remotest provinces of the Empire.

Finally, one saw vast and comfortable barracks on the ramparts, to which all the soldiers retired during the night.

I learned all these details as I went along, which offer eulogies to a sage government and an attentive policing, as well as many others that I shall pass over in silence, because I shall have occasion to talk about them more amply in the chapter on habits, customs, etc. Thus, I flatter myself that the enlightened Reader will be content to traverse the city with the same rapidity that I did, impatient as I was to find myself alone with Arzame in order to converse about more interesting matters. For a curious voyager, no object is indifferent—rural areas, edifices, monuments, etc.—and he does not disdain to cast an eye over the physical features of a land, but only pauses in relation to the laws, mores and practices of those who inhabit it.

My guide, or rather my Mentor, perceiving my haste, said to me, laughing: "I see that it is time to spare you the sight of magnificences that might dazzle you; nothing is more appropriate for that than a philosopher's retreat."

He led me into a small house where he resided, on the ramparts of the city. Everything there was elegant in its simplicity. An admirable view, only limited by the horizon, left uncovered a quarter of the celestial vault; a limpid stream bathed the walls of a little garden garnished with flowers, fruits and the rarest simples.

The necessary purity, cleanliness and comfort were encountered everywhere; a small rectangular room, each angle of which corresponded to one of the four cardinal winds, served as a bedroom; a room of the same form and size contained a library consisting of fewer than a hundred volumes, which nevertheless contained everything that it is possible to know—

which is to say, the essentials of everything written since the creation.

A slightly larger room was filled with instruments of physics, mathematics and astronomy, the majority of which were unknown to me. Of those that we employ I only found the proportional compass of Juste Brigge falsely attributed to Galileo,[68] the armillary sphere of Archimedes, the quarter-circle, the directional compass whose true inventor is the Neapolitan Flavio Gioia,[69] Newton's telescope, the microscope, the barometer, Fahrenheit's thermometer, the aerometer, the pyrometer, the pendulum clock, the T-square, the protractor, Wolf's anemometer,[70] Boyle's pneumatic machine, Huygens' micrometer, the gnomon, the graphometer, the planisphere, the nocturlabe,[71] the camera obscura, the electric machine, the prism and the ardent mirror. All the other instruments were either simplified or of new invention, as useful as they were curious. A small stairway led from that room to a tower, where Arzame made his astronomical observations.

---

[68] The claim that Juste Brigge invented the "Compas de proportion" is made in Alexandre Savérien's *Dictionnaire universal de mathematique et de physique* (1753), where the present author presumably fund it. Savérien says that he got the information from one Levin Huls, who is equally obscure.

[69] Flavio Gioia or Gioha probably never existed, but was invented by Italians in order to claim the invention of the compass (whose use actually predated his supposed fourteenth-century career by several centuries).

[70] The inventor of the anemometer was Leon Alberti (1404-1472); this reference is to an improved model credited to the German philosopher Christian Wolff, whose name was rendered Chrétien Wolf in the *Encyclopédie*, from which Listonai doubtless took this datum.

[71] A nocturlabe, sometimes known simply as a nocturnal, is an instrument used to determine local time by measuring the relative positions of two stars in the night sky.

I noticed with pleasure, but without surprise, that the construction of the house had carefully avoided all arched, circular, octagonal, elliptical and similar forms; all the rooms, doors, windows and fireplaces were at right angles. That confirmed me in the opinion, which I had held for a long time, that the rectangular form is suitable to everything that is at rest, as the spherical figure is appropriate to everything that is in motion.

Arzame's study became the center of the World for me; our conversations revolved around physics, morality and natural history; the simplest matters gave rise to short but luminous dissertations, which held me in a kind of enchantment; I observed in the philosopher's reflections a sagacity, a profundity and a sublimity of ideas that surpassed the range of the human mind; it was as if I were surrounded by transparent clouds, only allowing me to glimpse the light at a great distance, sometimes causing me to despair of grasping it; but Arzame's discourses, always accompanied by the modesty that attracts and the eloquent simplicity that seduces, instead of casting me into depression, only served to excite my curiosity.

"Please," I said to him one day, with a vivacity that made him smile, "complete my enlightenment, or leave me in my ignorance; I am in a violent state; there is certainly something extraordinary, not to say supernatural, that causes me to feel penetrated by everything you tell me, without my being able to understand it perfectly. Instruct me, tell me by what prodigy the Selenites are so superior to the inhabitants of the Earth and why I find everything here in a different order from what happens among us, although the foundation of things and ideas is the same."

"Know first," Arzame said to me, "that by virtue of a prerogative whose cause and origin we do not know, we have in this hemisphere an intimate knowledge of everything that happens on Earth, perhaps to compensate us for being deprived of its sight and its light.

"We have a secret commerce with you, in which you always furnish us without receiving anything in exchange; it is by that means that we have appropriated the best discoveries that you have made in the sciences and the arts. We also have the art of reading in the soul, which renders us participants in your ideas, your reflections, your mediations...you're blushing! Don't be frightened, my friend; that faculty is purely passive and can only be exercised to our profit. We can converse with you, but, not being able to reveal anything, no disorder can result therefrom on the Earth—insensate projects, and extravagant but hidden ideas remain in the most profound secrecy.

"You know now that when you form some project full of inconveniences, objections and obstacles, which you try to smooth over, working on the decomposition of complicated ideas, you are in error in thinking that you are going astray alone and without witnesses. The objections that you raise, the contradictions that you suffer and the difficulties you encounter internally are suggested to you by the inhabitants of the Moon, who play the part in your regard of the demon of Socrates.

"I will even confess to you that, as benevolent friends, we sometimes take pleasure in nourishing within you chimerical hopes that relieve real pains, aiding you in the construction of castles in the air and in the playful dreams known as inconsequential thoughts.

"In spite of that advantage," Arzame continued, "we would be no more advanced than you in the quarrying of knowledge but for a memorable event that changed the face of science and government among us: the revolution is not very old; it owes its success purely to the love of science, philosophy and the truth, and the stubborn desire to penetrate as far as the human mind can go.

"Would you believe that the young people of my time were only spurred on to shine by sophistical arguments; they claimed that a grain of sand is a heap, that a drop of water is an ocean, that a weight of one grain flattens a mountain, etc.[72] Heads filled with Pythagorean numbers, Platonic ideas and Aristotelian forms, they did nothing but disputed entities, quiddities, ecceities, universals and categories; they only sought admiration in their conversations by means of standard rhetorical passages, enigmas and burlesque; they only calculated with their fingers, only measured with their arms; they only learned history from romances and tragedies; they only studied antiquity in modern books; the spectacle of Nature had nothing of the marvelous for them, its phenomena nothing interesting, but they had complete faith in judicial astrology; conversation was nothing but a tissue of adventures, fashions, etc.; the wisest among them occupied themselves by turns with toys, boxes of candy, chatter, marbles, puppets, grotesques, etc.

"However, minds were enlightened, the sciences flourished, the arts were improved and advantage was taken of the discoveries made by terrestrial geniuses of the first order; that was already a great deal of verity, but we were still servile imitators when a celebrated chemist endowed with a penetrating mind of superior genius, sensing the insufficiency of our enlightenment and the scant progress promised by the human mind limited to the five senses known to us, worked for a long time on means of procuring us a sixth.

"After having assembled a prodigious quantity of materials to complete his chemical operation, but fruitlessly, he imagined substituted superhuman means for limited minds. He evoked the shade of the great Newton, which appeared to him and said: 'Since you feel that you have sufficient courage to carry out a project that I sketched out, but which a life that was too short, although laborious, did not permit me to com-

---

[72] Author: "*Subtilius est contempsisse quam solvere*. Seneca, Epistle 49." [(why waste time with questions) in which there is more subtlety is scorning than solving?]

67

plete:[73] decompose the spirits of Homer, Aristotle, Plato, Pythagoras, Hippocrates, Bacon, Galileo, Descartes, Locke, Boerhaave, Pascal, Leibnitz and Montesquieu; then burn all their writings and nourish yourself on the ashes they produce.'

"The chemist followed the method indicated by the great man, but nothing resulted therefrom. Having perceived, however, that in the mixture of spirits he had forgotten that of Newton, who had not named himself out of modesty, he recommenced the operation, adding in the spirit of Newton, and the experiment succeeded.

"The first concern of the chemist, to whom we have erected statues, was to communicate his discovery. A celestial fire penetrated all minds; enlightenment was spread universally; but in the progression of studies, without the help of which the eyes see almost nothing in Nature, the ear is only weakly affected by music, poetry, eloquence, etc.

"By the development of the seed of a sixth sense, famous problems were resolved at a stroke: the squaring of the circle, the duplication of the cube, the trisection of an angle, the equation of the parabola with a straight line. That pleased the speculative geometers, but humanity derived real advantages from the discovery of the longitude and the application of the electrical machine[74] to the human body; was finally convinced, without a murmur, that the philosopher's stone, the universal medicine and perpetual motion are pure chimeras and that the primordial causes of all the phenomena of Nature will remain forever unknown to Mortals.

"The elevation of liquids in capillary tubes and sap in plants, and the generation of the tides, were soon no longer

---

[73] Author: "He lived with a sound mind until the age of 87." Newton was actually 84 when he died.

[74] It is possible that the "electrical machine" that Listonai has in mind is the one invented by Otto von Guericke in the seventeenth century to produce static electricity, but is more likely to be the "Leyden jar" invented to store static electricity in 1745.

mysterious; but the generation of living beings and the laws of the union of the soul with the body will always remain in an impenetrable obscurity.[75]

"Success was achieved in giving more plausible definitions—but whose accuracy is not without objections—to matter, movement, time, space, duration, instinct, infinity, etc. and drawing probable lines of separation between the extremes; from which nevertheless flowed and infinity of physical and moral knowledge with which any sage mind ought to be content.

"That, in brief," Arzame continued, "is what was produced among us by the acquisition of a sixth sense. What will happen in future if we succeed in discovering a seventh? Perhaps we will then be able to pass on to theories for explaining the mechanism of Nature."

By way of conclusion, Arzame added: "To judge by the degree to which the sciences have attained on Earth, and by the progress that has been made in a century, I have no doubt that they will soon arrive at the point that they have presently attained among us. What can we not expect from confident labor animated by the noble love of the truth? One Newton more—perhaps he has already been born!—might complete the work. It is unfortunate that we do not have the faculty of communicating our discoveries to you with the same facility with which we profit from yours, but on your return you will be able to substitute for our impotence."

"I promise to do that," I said, enthusiastically, "if you help me to collect all that with which I propose to enrich our globe and do not weary of my questions." I added, however: "But is the acquisition that you have made of a sixth sense so general that all minds are enlightened to the same degree? Are

---

[75] Author: "*Rerum natura nullam nobis dedit cognitionem finium*. Cicero. Academica. Book IV. Ch. 29." [Nature has granted us no knowledge of the end of things.] Quoted by Montaigne.

geometry, physics, astronomy and chemistry exempt from vulgar prejudice?"

"No," he said. "Enlightenment is propagated by reason of study, education and the disposition of organs, from which the difference of minds results; but it influences everyone to some extent. A Nation has a dominant character that is not general; it only acquires superiority over another because the great men at the head of the government and the philosophers gradually draw the people to their way of thinking and reasoning; the knowledge and mores of geniuses made to govern and enlighten insinuate by degrees even into the lowest conditions.

"A great political Prince, for example, issues fewer decrees than another; he anticipates necessity by reforming mores and abuses without his subjects even perceiving it.[76] He flatters the self-esteem of some by distinctions that stimulate competition; he attaches shame to that which is contrary to public wellbeing, ridicule to ruinous fashions and extravagant habits; he accords honorable privileges to commerce, agriculture and useful arts; and the State gradually takes on the form that he wishes to give it. The people, who ordinarily neither use nor abuse intelligence, are ever ready to yield to the impressions one wants them to take, provided that one does not collide too rudely in the beginning with favorite prejudices, and does not advertise reform. When one recalls that Lycurgus succeeded in persuading the Spartans to renounce the property of their wealth, nothing seems impossible of execution. One can, by subjugating the imagination, inspire zeal, honor and

---

[76] Author: "*Imperiti enim judicant et qui frequenter in hoc ipsum fallendi sunt, ne errent.* Quintillius Instititione Oratoria. Book II. Ch. 17." [Those who judge are inexperienced; they must be deceived to stop them going wrong.] Quoted by Montaigne.

virtue even in mercenary conditions. It is thus that Caesar's legions were composed at two quaquischs[77] per day.

"It only requires a small number of geniuses to enlighten an entire Nation. The usage of the sixth sense was at first the sole prerogative of the portion of privileged individuals always occupied in the search for the truth, the only objective of whose work is the happiness of humankind. Reciprocal need, the imperceptible chain that links all humans, soon transmitted it throughout society, and the philosophical mind reached all the orders; the government worked successfully to suppress abuses, and education took a new form, to which it was principally attached. The prejudice of the first ideas is the source is the source of all mental maladies; once receives them mechanically and, in becoming familiar with them one believes that those notions were born with us.

"Knowledge eventually multiplied, mores were refined, the study of Nature became a general appetite and enlightenment spread through all minds to such an extent that even the people are now sufficiently learned to commence to see in Nature things as they really are and not as they appear to our deceptive senses—which is to say they are much more advanced than many proud individuals on Earth who, in the shadow of a very imperfect education, estimate themselves to be far superior o the vulgar, although they speak their own language rather poorly and do not know the first thing about physics.

"You will not be astonished, therefore," Arzame concluded, "when you find laborers and artisans here instructed in several principles serving as the basis of human knowledge, and giving the explanation of a prodigious number of phenomena that are obscure for those who only vegetate and burden the earth with the weight of their existence. At least it results from these primal notions that the people acquire me-

---

[77] Author: "A monetary unit equivalent to two French sols and six deniers." Arzame is presumably supposed to be using a Selenite term.

chanically by usage, as with the language of the land, a mental disposition to embrace useful projects in agriculture and the arts, against which ignorance always stiffens to the point of refusing to attempt the slightest experiments."

N.B. An idea will be found in the next two chapters of the knowledge, physical as well as metaphysical, familiar to the Selenite people, which will be an algebra for many good minds that preside among us in particular societies. When I say "an idea" of the knowledge, etc., it is because I am only really giving a sketch; enlightened Minds will conceive without difficulty that I could double, triple or multiply it tenfold without exhausting it.

Chapter III
Physical Knowledge Within the Scope of the People

A few universally recognized general principles of meta-physics, combined with the observations of the most profound Physicists, had become the basis of the education of youth and the common sources from which reasoning was drawn, and experiments on the phenomena of Nature. A curious epidemic had taken possession of all minds; even the people familiar with the ideas of beauty and truth were insensibly disabused of a thousand prejudices previously adopted even by people of an elevated rank. Nothing was more common in that class of once profoundly ignorant individuals than the knowledge:

That the great agent of Nature is fire.[78]

That fire is an element and not an incomprehensible effect of movement, which can only give activity, and that, like substance, it has weight.

That it is distributed everywhere in equal quantity, except in animate bodies.

That the Nature of fire, like the other elements, is to tend to equilibrium, from which results the maintenance and conservation of the Universe; and that consequently, in an equivalent air, marble is no colder than wool, the difference of sensation that one experiences only coming from the fact that one touches the more compact body at more points than the less dense one; thus, a file or a wool-carder is less cold to the touch than a bar of brute iron, and the latter less than polished steel.

---

[78] Listonai still subscribes to the thesis of the four "elements" inherited from Greek philosophy, although he obviously has doubts about its propriety, which he voices several time. He is not, however, a subscriber to the phlogiston theory of combustion, which guided the deductions of Guillaume de la Follie's "unpretentious philosopher" in his scientific romance of 1775.

That we are surrounded by fire in a sufficient quantity to cause a universal conflagration at any movement; hence, the World subsists by virtue of a kind of miracle.

That in order to maintain fire, igneous matter, air and water are required, and that in the absence of one of these three things, fire disappears.

That fire and flame have weight, that smoke is a commencement of fire and flame of burning smoke.

That one of the great properties of fire is to dilate bodies, and that, in consequence, everything is greater in Nature in summer than in winter—humans, house, etc.—and that a bar of iron swells and elongates sensibly in fire, and resumes its original condition when it cools.

That what makes known the sensation of heat is not dependent in any fashion on the degree of fire, heat being only the proportion or difference that exists between the fire of the external object and that or the organ.

That heat in animate bodies, as in those that are not, is only the effect of the agitation of their parts, effectuated by means of the fire contained in each body, which produces in the soul the idea of warmth.

That there is a fire that gives the idea of light without heat, and another that gives the idea of heat without light; that if movement expels the fire of bodies in a straight line it gives rise in us to the idea of light, and that if it only expelled in an irregular manner, the idea will be born in us of heat.

That a cold body that is in contact with another does not cool it, but, on the contrary, warms up at the expense of the other, as happens in artificial ice; in the same way, a furry garment only maintains the natural heat of the animate body, and prevents it from heating the ambient air; since cold, being nothing but the expression of less heat, cannot act upon the body, which might lose its natural heat in that way, finally losing all its movement for lack of sufficient fire to maintain it.

That, cold being nothing but the sentiment excited in us by the diminution of the heat that our body experiences, boiling water, very hot by comparison with the human body, is cold relative to molten iron, which has almost no heat compared to an iron within two degrees of the sun, which is a thousand times greater.

That the greatest heat is not produced by the greatest proximity of the sun to the earth, not the greatest cold by its greatest distance, since the middle of winter the sun is a million leagues closer to the Earth than in the middle of summer. That paradox disappears if one observes that the greatest heat is produced by the perpendicular fall of rays of sunlight upon the Earth, which they only strike obliquely in winter. That is rendered sensible by approaching a finger to a candle to within a fraction of an inch almost without feeling the heat, while one cannot hold it four inches above it without being burned.

That black bodies heat up easily because they have more pores than others; they absorb more rays; white bodies, on the contrary, warm up with difficulty because they reflect more rays than they absorb; and thus by gradation from the darkest to the brightest. Of two marbles, one white and one black, exposed to the sun, the former will scarcely be warmed when the latter is burning hot.

That air is a light, fluid, transparent substance capable of compression and dilatation, which envelops the terrestrial globe to a height of eighteen or twenty leagues, which weighs upon the earth, with which it turns, in which all animals breaths in and out, and without which they cannot survive.

That its elasticity is prodigious, since it can be compressed into a space five hundred and fifty thousand times less than in its natural state, such as it surrounds us, and that it can be dilated in a space eight hundred and twenty thousand times more extensive than when it is compressed.

That a column of air weighs as much as thirty-two feet of water or twenty-eight inches of mercury; that with a base of one square foot, a column of air weighs one thousand seven hundred and twenty-eight pounds, and that consequently, a man sustains the weight and effort of twenty-five thousand nine hundred pounds in proportion to his surface, which is commonly fifteen square feet, the Air pressing in all directions.

That the Air we breathe must be fourteen thousand times denser than that at the upper extreme of the atmosphere, and seventy thousand times less rare than the Ether.

That we swim in the atmosphere like fish in the sea.

That Air laden with clouds, although apparently heavier, is nevertheless lighter than in serene weather; because the pores dilate, one senses a languor that seems a heaviness, whereas in serene weather the heavier air presses upon the body and gives more activity to the circulation of the blood and the humors, which makes one feel lighter, although then sustaining a greater weight of atmosphere.

That without the pressure of the atmosphere, one could not draw water with a pump, a straw or a siphon; a child cold not suckle, a horse or a stork could not drink, a man could not smoke or take snuff, swallow a fresh egg, etc. It is thus that a louse or a mosquito drinks the blood of animals; their proboscis doubles served as the model of the siphon.

That all the effects that the Ancients attributed to the horror of Nature for a void are uniquely due to the pressure of the atmosphere.

That without the Air sonorous bodies would not render any sound.

That the Air is at one degree equal to the temperature when water begins to freeze or ice begins to melt.

That with respect to the Nature, the substance and the number of the parts of the atmosphere, we know nothing about it except by conjecture.

That the Air cooperates with the operation of the senses in such a way that on the summits of the highest mountains, where it is rare, the sensations of hearing and smell are considerably weakened, and that the drugs that are most in favor, like pepper, salt, ginger and wine spirit are almost tasteless there.

That in a profound cave the Air is no colder in the middle of summer than in the heart of winter, and that it is even a degree warmer; that the sensations we experience there in different seasons are only relative to the temperature of the air from which we have come, in order to breathe a similar one. It is for that reason that if one plunges one hand into cold water and the other into warm water in similar air, when one takes them out, the one that was in the warm water experiences a sensation of cold, and the one that was in cold water a sensation of warmth; because all heat is insensible to us unless the bodies acting upon our senses have a greater degree of heat than that or our organs.

That all bodies have an atmosphere formed by particles that evaporate or are exhaled continually.

That the Earth has its atmosphere in which all meteors[79] are formed, and that subterranean heat, that of the sun and the breath of reflected winds as are many causes that can collaborate in the elevation of vapors and exhalations in its atmosphere.

If in the morning insensible vapors fall that make sensible drops in combining on plants, leaves and flowers, that is dew; hence one can see that it does not fall from the sky, but that it rises from the earth, to which it falls back.

If the coldness of the air freezes the dew slightly, that is frost.

---

[79] Author: "Although clouds generally produce very useful effects, they also cause a few very dangerous ones; they often combine the rays of sunlight like concave lenses and mirrors, and occasion streaks of intense heat; that is what we call sunstroke; the plants on which they fall are desiccated, cooked and burned; the sun, after having been obscured for a long time and suddenly revealed, sometimes produces the same effect." By "meteor" the author does not mean a "falling star" (which he does not believe to be extraterrestrial bodies) but an atmospheric phenomenon of some kind—which, by virtue of the same etymology, we would still call a "meteorological phenomenon."

An accumulation of vapors and exhalations, departed from moist places and retained close to the earth's surface by their weight, is fog.

Certain nitrous and sulfurous salts that fog allows to flow over plants are niello.

Gross exhalations in combination form the white threads known as maidenhair.

When a cloud grows by the combination of vapors, its weight increases and it can no longer conserve equilibrium with the air, is condenses and falls as rain; the higher from which it falls the larger the drops are, which happens more frequently in summer than winter because then the heat raises the clouds higher than in winter.

A frozen cloud, which falls by virtue of its own weight and is dissipated by the wind, produces snow.

A rain that falls in warm weather, suddenly obscured by a cloud or struck by a violent wind, which freezes, is hail.

Fog that freezes near the ground forms black ice.

When the sun and the moon are pale, when the stars are shining brightly, when doors make more noise than usual, when ants stop work, when swallows skim the ground in flight, when stones sweat, when flames rise with difficulty or flicker, when an iris can be seen around the light of a candle, when cats rub their heads with their paws and lick the rest of their bodies, and when bees does not go out, those are all certain signs of rain.

Swollen exhalations obscure the sun and moon and alter their color; they intercept the rays of the stars; they cause wood to expand by fill its interstices.

Humidity renders the roads impractical to ants.

Swallows fly more heavily and seek the insects that the humidity causes to descend closer to the ground.

Humidity form drops of water on stone.

It resists the elevation of a flame, which seems to skip, because the exhalation is heavier than air, which forms a kind of iris around its light, as around the moon.

Cats favor humidity, which expands over their fur.

Humidity renders the collection of wax and honey more difficult for bees.

That thunder is the effect of an assembly of sulfurous, bituminous and oleaginous substances risen into the middle region, which, dilated by fermentation, break the walls of the clouds that concentrate them, and cause noise by their explosion, which, like an echo, is multiplied as many times as it strikes different bodies.

That the lightning that precedes the thunderclap, because light is propagated infinitely faster than sound, is the glare of the inflamed matter.[80]

That volcanoes, which launch flames or from which lava flows, and earthquakes, are perfectly natural effects of the rarefaction of solid matter melted by the central fire, where filtered waters are reduced to vapors in an enclosure that can no longer contain them; in such a way that its sometimes only requires one stone detached from a rock in a cavity to fall upon another and produce a spark to set fire to the sulfurous and bituminous materials with which the interior of the earth is filled; or for waters rarefied by the violent action of fire, which can no longer be contained in the space that encloses them, to smash the walls of their prison with such violence that the repercussion makes itself felt from one extremity of the globe to the other.

That winds have various causes, independent of many others that are unknown.

Wind is only an effect of agitated air, which causes an effect on an organ and is only manifest when the equilibrium is disturbed; which happens principally by virtue of the action of the sun, when it is perpendicular to the equator and it rare-

---

[80] Listonai might seem slightly behind the times in not realizing that lightning is an electrical phenomenon, given that Benjamin Franklin had already invented the lightning rod in 1749, but Franklin's work was not widely publicized in Europe until Joseph Priestley published his *History of Electricity* in 1767, six years after the publication of the present work.

fies the air to such an extent that the surrounding air, being denser, comes from all directions, even from a long distance, to fill the void that is formed there.

It makes itself felt when the vapors that form the clouds, accumulating in great quantity, breaking the equilibrium of the atmosphere, fall by virtue of their weight and cause and agitation to the parts that surround them.

Volcanoes, which heat up and boil the filtered waters accumulated in the interior of the earth, form vapors that, no longer being containable in the spaces where they are imprisoned, rise up and emerge violently through fissures, caverns and other openings, like an aeolipile over a fire.

The winds, like earthquakes, are more frequent over the sea and over certain lakes because cavities are in greater quantity there than on the continents.

The position of mountains contributes a great deal to the formation of winds, because the air that is squeezed there, acquiring force and rigidity, expands over the plains with impetuosity.

That the petrifactions drawn from the sea, known by the name of madrepores, are only stony bodies formed in the water by worms called polyps; their tubes or cells are the dwellings and work of the animals, which reside therein.

That there are no falling stars, and that the little luminous globes that move through the atmosphere and are seen to fall in flames are only an accumulation of very volatile camphor, sulfur, clay and niter, which enter into effervescence by virtue of mixture with igneous materials that they encounter, and which fall by virtue of their weight in a viscous matter that can be collected.

That no lightning stones fall, but that lightning can detach stones from a tower or a rock and drag them a long way by the violence of its action, or calcinate materials on the ground, which the vulgar suppose to have fallen from the atmosphere.

That water, as well as air, is an element, in accordance with vulgar opinion; it is, however, a transparent fluid that has no odor, not color, nor taste, the natural state of which is ice, and which only becomes liquid by virtue of the action of the heat of the sun or the central fire.

That like all liquids, water always tends to level off, and that in any detour its makes in its course, whether rising or descending, it always rises as high as its source, abstraction made of resistances.

That it always freezes from the center to the circumference, and unfreezes from the circumference to the center.

That water, which has nineteen times less matter—or, to put it another way, has thirty eight times more pores—than gold, cannot be compressed, while gold can be compressed.

That the winds transport over high mountains the clouds that form lakes there, the majority the sources of rivers, which, following the inclination of the terrain, transport the waters to the sea, from which they then return over the land by evaporation.

That springs have no other origin.

That a lake formed on a high mountain is the produce of the flow of waters assembled over even higher mountains, even at prodigious distances, from which they descend along a slope through cavities, which communicate with the basin in which they accumulate.

That the waters that flow from these lakes and filter through the earth and rocks go to form springs at considerable distances, which flow or dry up in proportion to the quantity of ran that falls on the land.

That these springs are cold, warm, mineral, salty or colored in accordance with the substances that they encounter in the bosom of the earth, with which they are impregnated, or by the fermentation they experience.

That there are not only wells of fresh water on the edges of the sea, but springs of fresh water, and even warm water, in the sea.

That water is, with air, the alimentation of all vegetables, and that the earth is only their matrix.

That water can only dissolve a determined quantity of salt, about the thirtieth part of its weight.

That all vegetation ceases at the degree of temperature at which water begins to freeze.

That the freezing point is the extreme point of vegetation in the direction of cold, and that although a few plants, like moss, hay grass, etc. survive it, they do not vegetate during that time.

That molten wax, which is a vegetable substance, has, when it floats in warm water, the exact degree of heat for the opposite point of vegetation in the direction of cold, above which plants perish instead of vegetating.

That the heat of a plant only being that of the air that surrounds it, which in summer is between thirty and thirty-five degrees above freezing point, is always less than that of a man, which is 54°, his blood being 64° and his urine 58°.

That as vegetables lack the powerful unknown machine that in animals, by its contractions, drives the blood through the arteries, Nature has supplied their roots, through which sap rises, with a cover that is a very narrow sheath of a thick and tight tissue, which ensures that nothing can enter except that which can pass through the pores of leaves by way of transpiration, the only route that the excrements of vegetables can take.

That vegetables take in much air by day, which they return at night.

That rain makes sap rise, like the dew, because it diminishes the transpiration of the plant.

That plants enclose a considerable quantity of air; the air in an oak, Pliny says, it makes up almost a third of its weight.

That no terrestrial vegetable or animal can be produced, live or grow without air; that eggs cannot hatch or seeds germinate in the void; that without air there is no corruption or putrefaction; that air thus vivifies and destroys everything; that like water it only owes its fluidity to fire, otherwise the entire atmosphere would harden into solid and impenetrable matter.

That a plant transpires seventeen times more than a man, because it has a surface proportionately greater, and that trees only transpire and draw in proportion to their leaves.

That the sunflower and other tall plants with a weak stem always incline toward the sun because the curvature is greater on the side of the greater transpiration.

That gum, which is a malady of trees and causes the neighboring parts to perish, does not cause any damage to the fruits.

That the mushroom and the truffle are not plants, because they have neither roots nor seeds.

That corruption and putrefaction cannot produce any living being, that they no more engender insects and worms than carrion engenders crows.

That some places are only preserved from birds, insects and other harmful animals by natural and antipathetic causes, like certain odors in wood and the materials of edifices, encounters with hostile winds, etc.—simple phenomena that superstition has often attributed to supernatural causes.

That caterpillars, spiders and many other disgusting insects are not venomous, since several animals live on them and we ourselves swallow millions of imperceptible ones every day.

That nettles only inflame the skin, like caterpillars and other reputedly venomous animals, because they leave a sharp point in the skin that tears it; the caterpillar only produces the same effect as the nettle because a few fragments of exceedingly stiff hair penetrate the flesh and interrupt the continuity of the parts like a splinter.

That coral is not a marine plant, that it belongs to the animal kingdom, as do the sponge, the starfish, the polyp, etc., all composing insects of the sea.

That there are no witches but individuals who, having particular items of knowledge in physics and chemistry, impose them on ignorant vulgarity, presenting perfectly natural effects as phenomena.

That there are no days or months consistently lucky or unlucky.

That when the sun sets and one can still see a part of its disk, or when it begins to appear on the horizon, it is then 18 degrees or 450 leagues below it; the refraction of the rays makes the star appear where it is not, in the same way that a stick appears broken in water, or that when filling a basin with water at the bottom in which there is a coin that one cannot perceive, each of the spectators will discover it, but not in the same place—which is to say that one does not see its at first where it is, and that subsequently one sees it where it is not.

That the sun's rays only illuminate the earth by a double reflection—which is to say, after being deflected twice, once on the ground and once in the atmosphere; if there were no atmosphere there would no more brightness at midday than in a field at midnight by the light of a torch.

That one of the most astonishing phenomena of light is that is reflected from bodies without touching their surface.

Newton

That if one could illuminate an object seen in a telescope, as one does an object seen in a microscope, instead of the thousand times that the longest telescope magnifies it, one would be able to magnify it millions of times, as one does with a microscope.

That the tissue of various colors disposed in an arc in the clouds, which is known as a rainbow or Iris, is the effect of sunlight refracted by raindrops, a phenomenon that the spectator observes at an angle of 41 or 42 degrees when, with his back turned to the sun, he is placed between the star and the cloud. That the meteor in question is not, physically speaking, the sign of any fortunate or unfortunate event; and that, the sun's rays being refracted differently according to the position of spectators, no two of them see exactly the same rainbow.

That one can make a rainbow in a room if, having attached a black curtain to a wall expose to the sun, one disperses droplets of water between the curtain and the spectator.[81]

That the movement of light is, straight since, if one makes holes in the doors of two diametrically opposite doors of a room, the light traverses the two holes to depict an object in the second room without illuminating the first.

That except for Comets, which follow, in their periodic courses, parabolic or hyperbolic lines, all the planets describe ellipses in their orbits around the sun, of which it occupies one of the focal points.

That every body in motion tends to describe a straight line, and to describe it unless some obstacle deflects it; that for the same reason every body that rotates around a center makes an effort to draw away from it, because the further away it is, the more the line its describes approaches a straight line.

That because the earth turns on its axis in twenty-four hours, every point of the globe on the line of the equator travels a distance of more than three hundred and fifty leagues in an hour.

That the distance the earth travels in its orbit is approximately a hundred million leagues in a year.

That the velocity of a cannonball, which travels six hundred feet in a second or six thousand fathoms in a minute, is less than half that of the diurnal movement of the earth, and that the cannonball traveling 144 leagues in an hour, or 3,456 leagues in a day, would take approximately twenty five years to reach the sun.

---

[81] Author: "In double rainbows the colors are inverted because the rays that enter the droplets of water from above and emerge below; they have the contrary effect in the second, entering from below. The meteor presents a rainbow to the eye of the spectator because the rays form a cone, of which the cloud is the base and the summit. We would see the entire circle if we were higher above the horizon."

That sound has approximately double the velocity of a cannonball, since it travels at 1,142 feet in one second.

That wind weakens sound but does not slow down its progress—which is to say that its undulations of propagation in all directions have the same velocity in more or less agitated air, but that a violent wind can carry the sound further than a feeble wind, and that the intensity of the sound is less in winter than in summer.

But that all these velocities are nothing compared with that of light, which, traveling 66,000 leagues in a second, travels about four million leagues in a minute, since it travels from the sun to the earth in seven or eight minutes, which is demonstrated by the immersion and emersion of the satellites of Jupiter.

Huygens.

That there is a sufficiently exact relationship between lights and sound, as between the primitive colors and the notes of music, but that the great Pythagoras' harmony of the celestial spheres is a brilliant chimera.

That the ear has ten thousand times more acuity in distinguishing sounds than sight has in discerning colors.

There is no absolute point of cold, grandeur, smallness or lightness.

That absolute cold, night, shadow, obscurity, darkness, opacity, nothingness, etc. are purely negative entities, cold being merely less heat, shadow and darkness less light, opacity a composite of transparencies and nothingness a deprivation of everything.

That the griffin, the chimera, the siren, the faun, the satyr, harpies, the phoenix, the hippogriff, the centaur, the sphinx, the amphisbaena, etc. are purely imaginary fabulous beasts, but that the hydra with several heads has an example in a freshwater polyp.

That the interpretation of dreams is a stupidity, the art of reading the lines of hands a puerility and the curiosity of penetrating the future a temeritous impiety.

That children who are born in the eighth month of pregnancy live all the more surely because they are more fully formed than those who come into the world in the seventh.

That ants make no provisions for winter, and in consequences do not sever seeds of grain in order to conserve them; that they live, huddled in the earth during the cold, like bears under the snow, entirely on their own substance.[82]

That comets are globes—perhaps inhabited, like the earth—that have no influence on sublunary bodies; that they no more indicate the death of great men than the birth of petty ones, who are beings equal in the order of Nature. That in truth, comets could cause considerable disorder in the systems of the World if their route were not prescribed in space like that of other heavenly bodies; finally, that their beard, their long hair or their enormous tail is nothing frightening, but only a streak of light that accompanies them,[83] drawn by the atmosphere of the sun.

That what are called the cravings of pregnant women, of which children seem to bear the marks, have no reality, in spite of all the prodigies reported in that regard; that the creature in the mother's womb has no relation with her except the nourishment that she furnishes it; that the mother, with regard to the child, is similar to the earth that offers a matrix to plants, which take their nourishment from fluids filtered through their pores; that the placenta on which the fetus repos-

---

[82] Author: "Swallows hide under the ice in winter by huddling together; they remain asleep in this fashion until spring reanimates them. *Philosophical Transactions of the Royal Society,* 1713." The bizarre thesis that swallows hibernate under water, allegedly based of empirical observation, was frequently cited in the *Transactions* during the 18th century and much discussed by the earnest members of the Society.

[83] Author: "The passage of comets only caused terror, like the aurora borealis, in times of ignorance, when stupidity was such that enlightened charlatans enriched themselves by selling remedies against the influences of eclipses and comets."

es is like the nest of a swallow attached to a wall, which has no action upon it; that it is incontestable that, the will having no effect on a foreign body, the imagination alone, fertile in visions, finds relationships between intellectual and material faculties, and expands to fix the causes of perfectly natural accidents with the same sagacity that it encounters castles and animals in clouds and figures in pyrites, marbles and stalactites etc., which are not really there.

That sneezes are of the number of sinister omens the illusion of which has been dissipated for centuries.

That the barn owl, the short-eared owl, the long-eared owl and other nocturnal animals have nothing sinister about them but a taste for cadaveric vapors and an unpleasant cry to which obscurity adds something lugubrious and alarming.

That it does not rain blood, not wool, nor stones, etc., but that supposed rains of blood are only colored by insects of that color lifted from lakes by high winds, and that wool and stones are transported from violent winds from one place to another.

That the piercing powers of sight that are said to penetrate several feet underground and discover sources of water and metals must be placed in the ranks of beautiful chimeras, as well as the property of divinatory wands to identify thieves and murderers.

That in the torrid zone, the nights are as cold as in temperate climates, and that there are, as in Siberia, mountains there that have been capped with snow since the creation.

That black color in human skin is purely the effect of climate, since negroes are born white.

That in the countries situated in the middle of Europe, the most intense frost does not penetrate the earth to a depth greater than two feet, while in the northern lands this side of the polar circle it penetrates to six or even ten feet.

That by virtue of insensible respiration and transpiration, a well-constituted human body exhales four pounds weight of aliments in twenty-four hours without dampening the underwear, and that those four pounds could fill a vast space, the vapors being so dense that rays of sunlight could not penetrate it.

That a man who is awake transpires less than half as much as one who is tranquilly asleep.

That disturbed sleep diminishes natural transpiration by more than five ounces.

That a ball pushed against another communicates the movement it loses when it is halted by the resistance of the impact.

That when a musket shot strikes steel, it detaches particles by the violence of the impact that catch fire and fall in fusion, in little hollow globules that can be collected on a piece of paper.

That a ball of ivory or some other elastic substance that falls on an anvil is flattened, as well as the plane on to which it falls, and is separated from it by the bound that the reciprocal elasticity of the two bodies causes, each suddenly resuming its natural form.

That a bell that one rings is alternately elongated at the place struck by the clapper and immediately reestablished in its original state.

That an iron ball or a stone launched against a rock vibrates even in its slightest part.

That the lightest metal weighs twice as much as the heaviest of other substances.

That rising ground, even conical in form, does not provide a greater extent for sowing or planting than the surface of its base.[84]

That by the natural law of equilibrium that applies to all bodies, if a man extends one arm in the course of a moment, the other rises as a counterweight without reflection playing any part therein; that a man going uphill leans forward and a

---

[84] Author: "Take an object of conical form and fix pins to it perpendicularly, whose points touch the bottom; it will be seen that one cannot enter one more than can be contained by the circular space that it its base."

man going down leans backwards; that men and pregnant women hold themselves straighter than others; that a man walking in a straight line leans his body alternately, with each stride, to the right and the left; that a perching bird sleeping on one leg inclines its head in the opposite direction to the raised leg; that a quadruped gallops without moving from right to left—which a biped cannot do—because it always has for a point of support the left foreleg and the right hind leg, the center of gravity being in the diagonal.

That women, like men, have twenty-four ribs, twelve on each side, of which seven large ones connect to the sternum and five do not.

That cochineal is found in the worm that is the larva of a bug of the Indies, which establishes its dwelling for preference in the tree known as the Indian fig.

That moles are not blind; they have eyes, but so small that one might think that Nature has only given them as much sight as is necessary in order not to dread the light.

That crystals, precious stones and diamonds are composed of quartz, spath and salt; that they are not waters congealed inside mountains but in origin particles of clay or sand linked by salts and oils, which are more or less transparent in accordance with their more or less direct pores allowing the passage of more or less light; thus, the same substance, differently disposed, forms graphite and diamond.

That nacre is a species of oyster, from inside which pearls are taken, which are only found in those that are unhealthy, and which are probably formed of the same manner as stones in the kidney or bladder of an unhealthy man.[85]

That humans who eat all sorts of aliments and the ox that only loves of grass have blood of an almost identical nature.

---

[85] Author: "Why does the same thing not happen in the reasonable animals? The sight of an advantage would soothe humans in the cruel pains they experience in submitting to the cutting."

90

That there is very little difference between the bile of a human and that of a sheep.

That pigeons have gall, and they are more choleric than many other animals.

That in animals, agility diminishes in proportion to their greater strength, and vice versa.

That of all the birds of the day, the cock and the nightingale are the only ones that sing during the night.

That the longevity granted to deer, crows etc., is a puerility; that of all the animals, humans are the most long-lived.

That nothing ferments or rots in the void.

That a bat is not a bird even though it can fly, but a quadruped animal, since it has four feet, is viviparous and has neither a beak nor feathers.[86]

That the swallow and numerous other birds of passage do not cross the sea in order to go live in milder climates, but retire in winter to the interior of the earth, and some to the depths of the waters.

That a cord composed of several threads supports a lesser weight than the same threads combined without being twisted.

That a thread of silk of perfectly equal thickness throughout its length can sustain an immense weight without breaking, since it has no reason to break at one point rather than another. It is thus that nerves, muscles, fibers and capillary vessels in the human body resist prodigious efforts without breaking.

That the finest hair is a sheath that contains several of them.

That a tooth is a composite of a million channels and hollow fibers in which animal spirits circulate.

That there is nothing opaque in Nature; that metals, minerals and vegetables reduced to thin fibers are transparent, as are living bodies—of which once can easily be convinced by holding a finger up to the light; although very thick, it is trans-

---

[86] Author: "This animal has a delicious flesh on the Île de Bourbon, like the ortolan of Europe."

parent. Everything opaque is merely an assembly of transparent layers.

That someone born blind cannot see any object or image in a dream, but can only dream of touching them, having no other knowledge of objects than by touch, in dreams as while awake.

That all known bodies are porous; that gold, even the most compact, only dissolves because it has pores; that with a good microscope one can count more than five million pores in a square inch of carbon.

That matter is both infinitely divisible and indivisible, being metaphysically divisible and physically indivisible.

Matter is infinitely divisible metaphysically,[87] since any number that one can conceive can be reduced to half, to a quarter, an eighth, a sixteenth, a thirty-second, etc., to infinity, and for any portion of matter, which always has a length, width and depth and cannot be annihilated by an extreme separation, one can similarly conceive a division of the same gradation, to infinity. That if the imagination is forced to stop on the way, divisibility is no less possible beyond that point, although there is no longer any means of rendering the idea sensible, in the same way that terms are lacking to express a unity with a thousand zeros, which can easily be represented on paper.

Matter is physically indivisible to infinity because at a certain point of the smallness of its particles, instruments are lacking for taking the division any further; it is nevertheless so prodigious in certain experiments that it far surpasses human ideas.

---

[87] Author: "Infinity is the negation of finity, as immensity is the negation of measure etc. One can prove the infinite divisibility of matter by the fecundity of the authors producing new books—which is to say, fractions of matter only appropriate to increasing the surface area of libraries without adding to their substance."

A grain of beaten gold, extended over fifty square feet, gives two million visible particles.

An ingot of forty-five marcs of silver twenty-two inches long, gilded with an ounce of gold, can be stretched by a wire-maker to a length of two hundred and twenty-two leagues, still golden, without the silver appearing; if that wire were flattened to double its width, its two surfaces would cover a surface area of an arpent.

The same wire being stretched to a length of two hundred and twenty-two leagues, one can dissolve the silver in hydrochloric acid in such a manner that a tube of pure gold will remain, empty along its entire length.

A grain of red copper dissolved in spirit of ammoniac salt and mixed with three pounds two ounces of water tints all the water contained in approximately 10,500 cubic inches, each one of which gives two hundred and sixty million visible particles, so that a single grain of copper has been divided into 2,268,000,000,000 visible particles.

All of that is still nothing by comparison with the divisibility of the matter emitted by odorant substances. An ounce of musk exhales a very powerful odor, filling considerable spaces for entire years, without any sensible loss of weight: an odor so penetrating that it stops, puts to sleep and renders motionless serpents of enormous size.

Finally, living animals have been discovered by means of the microscope seven million times smaller than the smallest animals perceptible by sight.[88] How can the imagination not be alarmed when one thinks that these animals have eyes, feet, intestines, veins, arteries, a heart and blood, and that the blood in question has corpuscles? In view of such prodigies, can one

---

[88] Author: "Leeuwehoek, Hartsoeker, Musschenbroek, Needham, Boyle, Nieuwentyd, Lieberkuhn, Malpighi, Grew, Linnaeus, etc." I have corrected the spelling of two of the names in this list of early microscopists, but cannot identify the one misrendered "Nieuwentyd."

refuse to agree that the finite cannot be comprehended, nor the infinite conceived, even by abstraction?

That six people can arrange themselves around a table in 720 different ways, eight in 5,040, nine in 362,880 and ten in 3,628,800 ways without the same configuration being repeated.

That all the inhabitants of Paris, who number 700,000, could walk in the superb garden of the Tuileries without touching one another.

That the 900,000,000 people supposed to be on the earth could be contained in a space of two square leagues.

That by means of facts ascertained in various lands with exactitude, one finds that a ninth more males are born than females, that generations are thirty years, that the common[89] life of a human being is twenty years; it is on this principle that life annuities have been established at double the value of perpetual income.

That the walnut tree is no more exceptionally subject to lightning than the fig is exempt from it.

That the scales of the epidermis are the excretory canals of the glands of the skin, as is evident in fish.

That in a cuticular scale there are about five hundred excretory canals; that a grain of sand can cover 250 of these scales, and inconsequence, 125,000 pores or orifices through which daily transpiration takes place.

That by virtue of the circulation of the blood, carried from the heart to all the parts of the body by the arteries and brought back by the veins, the auricle or left cavity of the heart, with contains two ounces of blood, empties itself at each systole and is refilled with new blood, so that 120 ounces of blood pass through the heart in a minute, 7,200, or 450 pounds, in an hour, and 10,800 pounds in twenty-four hours; thus, the total mass of the blood, estimated at around twenty-four pounds, passes through the heart 450 times a day.

---

[89] I have transcribed the word "common" directly, although we would now say "average," or, more accurately, "mean."

That it is only certain parts of the body that can procure us pleasures, but that all of them, with the exception of the hair and nails, can experience pain.

That an arrow shot from a bow is not detached from the string until the latter has resumed its natural state.

That fire follets are subtle exhalations in flame, which only lead abstracted or fearful travelers astray because they precede them and are continually pushed forward by the air agitated by the body as it moves.

That a feather, a leaf of gold and a lead pellet fall with an equal velocity in the void, by virtue of the force that attracts all bodies to the center of the earth, but that in air, water or mercury, their fall is unequal by reason of the density of the milieu, their specific weight and their surface area.

That one can by analogy believe that the stars are as many suns, each of which has, like ours, a vortex and planets that rotate around them; and that between two stars, which seem to the eye to be ten fathoms distant from one another, might by twelve hundred million leagues apart, so prodigious is their distance from the earth. The opinion that they are as many suns is supported by the fact that, scintillating, which planets do not do, they have their own light.

That the duration of human life, like that of all animals, is proportional to the duration of growth, being six or seven times as long.

That the sea loses from its surface in twelve hours, by evaporation, a tenth of a inch, and that it would soon dry up if the vapors that the wind transport over the land were not returned to it by rivers.

That the north wind is very keen principally because it blows in a direct line and not in all direction, as from the south; it is thus that the air that, emerging from the lungs, blows both cold and warm, warm when one opens the mouth, cold when one closes it.

That, all matter being calcinable or vitrifiable, marl and stone, clay and pebble are the two extremes of those two classes and the bases of all mixtures, and that the substances of one class can never acquire the nature and properties of the other: an invincible argument against the transmutation of metals.

That is the fall of heavy bodies toward the center of the earth, the accelerated movement or the speed increases in relation to the odd numbers: 1, 3, 5, 7 etc., and consequently, a man weighing 140 pounds falling from the top of a high tower, is smashed, as if he weighed several thousand times more at the end of his fall, but that all the speed gained is lost by the slightest repercussion, so that if he collides with something even feebly one foot from the earth, he will fall without doing himself the slightest harm, in the same way that a ball rolling down an inclined plane acquires much more weight by its speed, but only as much the weight on the last step of a staircase as it acquired in falling from the first to the second.

That, each corpuscle of blood being composed of six globules, and each of the latter of six other globules, each of six others again, each corpuscle is composed of two hundred and sixty sanguine globules.

That the deteriorations and exfoliations experienced by stones, buildings and marbles exposed to the air are not, as the vulgar are persuaded, caused by the impressions of the Moon but by the continual action of the air and the exhalations from which no sublunary body is exempt.

That the opinion that causes fruits to be regarded as the source of epidemic diseases that often occur in autumn is a popular error, reiterated observations having recognized that they are neither more dangerous nor more common in years abundant in fruits of every species than in the rarest ones.

That it is reckless to attribute diseases of livestock to maleficent magic or those of children to fascinations; that beverages which enable the sight in dreams of objects of desire, accidents of impotence, etc., do not do so by any supernatural cause; and that all these pretended enchantments experienced by ardent or distorted imaginations originate from natural causes unknown to those who are their object, and that the majority owe their effect to fear and to traps set for ignorance, superstition or credulity.

That the Moon has no influence on the growth of hair, the plentitude of oysters, crayfish, mussels, the marrow of bones, the success of what one sows or plants, etc. In order to rid oneself of this common error it is sufficient to observe that rays of moonlight assembled at the focal point of an ardent mirror do not produce any sensible heat.

Finally, that the barometer is not an instrument that serves to measure the degrees of weight of the atmosphere, but the degrees of its spring or elasticity.

General Observation

If one added to this extract of the physical knowledge within the range of the Selenite People that of more enlightened individuals, it would give rise to volumes; but it is sufficient to say, in concluding this chapter, that there are so few true physicists on Earth that some deny the possibility of finding salt in pure water; others are surprised that plants grow and multiply on tiles although they only receive air and rainwater for nourishment, etc.

If they wish to be disabused or enlightened, let them study, dissect, compose, analyze, extract, purify, combine and finally examine Beings from the moment of their initial development, their progress and their variations until their decrepitude; let them compare the degree of development and destruction, and the diversity of substances that enter into the compounds that, although emerging from the same source and proceeding on the same principle, acquire an innumerable quantity of forms. They will convince themselves, by repeated experiments and consequent meditations, that corruption is the first degree of all generations, that water contains earth, fire and air, that earth contains air, water and fire, etc.; that all these things are confused and alternately dominant; that water produces stones wood, flesh, bone, fruits etc.

That a loss of equilibrium by virtue of the excess of one element over the others changes disposition, form, color, consistency, virtue and properties.

That all things are not precisely today what they were yesterday, and that tomorrow they will not be what they presently are.

That their economy varies perpetually, that it vanishes, and that every element and the elementary matter that constitutes it returns to their common origin, reuniting by various sorts of modulations to edify other Beings, that a new mixture, in accordance with the quality of the attraction and the matrix, is assembled and proportioned.

Finally, that the salt of Nature unknown in the schools, although there is nothing more commonplace and universal, contains the soul, the body and the animal and vegetable spirit of all material Beings, and is susceptible of all sorts of forms.

Chapter IV
Metaphysical Knowledge Within the Scope of the People

The Selenite people know distinctly:

That the five senses are, properly speaking, only one sense, that of touch, which is continually alert to the instruction of other senses.

That the four senses of sight, hearing, smell and taste are only modifications of the general sensation of touch, since we cannot sense impressions of any external object unless that object strikes some part of our individual, either directly or through the mediation of some intermediary fluid.

That intelligence is, ultimately, nothing but an abstract touch.

That nothing reaches the soul except by the intermediary of the senses.[90]

That because nothing reaches the soul that is not distorted by the intermediary of the senses, the soul, in continuous uncertainty, can only judge anything sanely with extreme circumspection.

That it is from the soul that all sentiments come, but that it is via the organs that all the objects that excite them pass.

That there is no relation between the operations of the senses;[91] that they cannot lend one another help or relief; that

---

[90] Author: "Our senses are the unique way by which we can communicate with all of Nature; there is a milieu interpolated between our soul and the physical World: a milieu through which the images of things, or, rather, the shadows projected on our interior senses, necessarily pass. It is necessary, to purify that milieu, to set aside everything that might distort the primitive images or tint them with strange colors, or at least to be able to recognize, or even rectify, the distortions to which they are subjected in passing."

one of them cannot perceive faults that another commits; that they often, in fact, contradict one another—as for example, a painting that is flat to the touch but seems elevated to the sight; musk simultaneously excites a sensation agreeable to the soul via smell and unpleasant via taste; one can see in water or in a mirror objects that are not there.

That the soul is deceived by the senses, when a square tower appears round at a certain distance; that it judges nonexistent or vanished something which, by virtue of its extreme smallness, is only invisible; that often, by virtue of preoccupation, one does not see the objects at which the eye is staring; that two parallel rows of trees of the same height seem to diminish and draw closer together at the extremity of an avenue, and the Moon sits on their summit.

That if we know an object through one sense, the others have no purchase on it.[92]

That the senses, in their turn, are deceived by the soul and confused by the passions; thus it is that a lover finds in the object of his tenderness features of delicacy, grace and pleasure that do not exist for other eyes; that hatred finds in another features of ugliness and deformity that are not there; that a jealous woman remarks in a rival a gauche appearance, and indecent bearing, a limited intelligence, an exaggerated age and a thousand other faults that are multiplied and augmented in proportion to the advantages that her rival has over her.

---

[91] Author: "...*scorsum quoique potestas divisa est: sua vis quoique est...*." Lucretius, Book IV, line 491." [Each sense has its function and its own faculties.]

[92] Author: "*An poterunt oculos aures reprehendere? An aureis tactus? an hunc porro tactum sapor arguet oris? An confutabunt nares, oculive revincent?* Lucretius, Book IV, line 488." [Do you say that the ears can correct the eyes, and be corrected by touch? That taste, smell or sight can save is from the surprises of touch?]

That a sad or cheerful disposition of the soul obscures or embellishes all objects, which remain constantly in the same state.

That the soul, confused by anticipation, often deceives itself in intellectual matters; thus is it that one undervalues a good book by an author without reputation, while, on the contrary, the name of a celebrated author blinds us to stupidities, and that one sometimes sees an anonymous drama succeed, which fails as soon as its author is known.

That the first movements of passions are in Nature, that they are all good in their essence, and only become criminal by virtue of abuses that are made of them.

That nothing comes from nothing; thus, since the commencement of the World, when everything was created at the same time, every birth has only been a new modification of matter, a perpetual reproduction that emerges from and invisible state after having perished in appearance; in other terms, that nothing is born that has not already existed in one form or another.[93]

That sensations are not in the objects that occasion them; that harmony is not in the harpsichord but in the soul.

That the idea of happiness is equally present to all minds and the desire to procure it equally keen in all hearts. The objects of pleasure and pain, always the same, only change in the manner of envisaging them, in accordance with different sorts of intelligences, characters and temperaments, or the aspects in which they are presented. Death, considered commonly as the greatest of evils, is a good and an object of desire to someone suffering cruelly, so the idea of death is a matter of temperament.

That a man can only produce, and cannot create anything; that he cannot imagine anything that does not have its type in Nature, of which the most perfect imitation is still a crude sketch of art.

---

[93] Author: "...*sic rerum summa novatur.*" Lucretius, Book II, line 74." [The sum of things is ever being renewed.]

That it follows that a man cannot create—which is today, imagine—something that does not have a resemblance to known objects, and that he cannot discover other faculties than those we find within ourselves, that it is impossible to extend our conjectures beyond the ideas that come to us via sensation and reflection.

That the limits of understanding are such that the mind cannot conceive either the infinite divisibility of matter, although demonstrated, now how to visualize, as one distinguishes colors, odors, sounds, the weight of objects, the organization of animals, the laws of the union of the soul with the body, etc., all natural truths that are around and within us.. That in addition, our understanding is such as it needs to be, relative to the ends for which we are destined and the sensations given to us, more to contribute to the conservation of our being than to acquire knowledge that, if it is often mistaken, is nevertheless sufficient to our needs.[94]

That time is neither a body not a substance, but only the flight of things that we conceive, since, if nothing existed, there would be no time.

That, as Nature always tends to equilibrium, nothing is fortuitous, everything being planned, including hazard itself.[95]

That corruption, which is only a negative being, is not the principle of any generation, but only the occasion of a change of form in matter by the dissolution of the continuity of its parts; that when one burns wood, nothing perishes; the most subtle part rises up and flies away as smoke, the greasy

---

[94] Author: "*Non emin me Deus ista scire, sed his tantum modo uti voluit.* Cicero De Divinatione, Book I, Section 35" [God has not willed me to know the cause, but only that I should use the means he has provided.]

[95] Author: "Hazard is a word devoid of meaning, which only serves to express a combination of events or accidents that favors or disrupts human projects. It is a chimerical entity to which one often attributes effects whose causes are unknown."

part attaches to the chimney and forms soot, the grossest part, which one calls ash, falls by virtue of its own weight.

That movement, which is nothing real, does not comprise anything more than the repositioning of one body relative to another body.[96]

That all that is known of movement, and that movement itself, subject to known laws, is the space traversed and the time employed in traversing it.

That the metaphysical causes of movement are unknown, that which is called cause only being so improperly, and often an effect, from which other effects result.

That generation and corruption are the two extreme terms of movement, and rarefaction and condensation the two median terms.

That the most marvelous phenomenon in Nature is movement, without which the Universe would be torpid and plunged into an eternal lethargy, or a uniformity, worse than Chaos.

That all the favorite idols of understanding, domestic or foreign, which the unenlightened human mind seizes with so much passion are merely family errors, or natural to our species, such as the habit of judging all objects by the relationship that they have to us or external objects—which is to say, the prejudices of the Nation, society or education.

That one learns to see, hear and judge distances by touch and by habit, as one learns to read, write and calculate by study, but that it is very difficult to learn to see well and understand well.

That we relate to objects at the extremity of straight rays that affect us, which determines that the object furthest away from us is not at a greater distance in the eye than the nearest; that it only becomes sensible to the organ of sight when the rays that emanate from it are painted on the retina or the cho-

---

[96] Author: "Movement born of the rupture of perfect equilibrium and repositioning comes from the restabilization of that same equilibrium."

roid—which is to say, when they strike the back of the eye, where sensation begins and ends, however far away the object might be; and thus, without the experience of touch, and the habit that is the mechanical study teaching us to judge distances, we could not distinguish any. It is in that manner, for instance, that the Moon, which appears very distant at the zenith, seems to us to be touching the crown of a tree at the end of an avenue; that, although one sees a horse as nearly the same size sat a distance of a hundred feet as at ten, the eye nevertheless sees it ten times smaller; that one therefore does not really see anything in Nature in the manner in which things exist there, of one can be persuaded by considering that one sees objects doubly, from the right and the left, all of them inverted; that although the eye believes that it can see a quarter of the sky though a hole made by a pin in a piece of paper, it can only see one point in space distinctly and all the others confusedly; and finally, that one only sees with one eye, and that while one is seeing the other is resting.[97]

That colors are not in objects; that there is nothing colored in Nature but the rays of the sun or suns, and that all other bodies only reflect them in the greater or lesser quantity, in accordance with the contexture of their pores, and the location of the organ, since no two people see exactly the same rainbow; that in consequence the sky is not blue, snow is not while, sulfur is not yellow, grass is not green, etc., and that the transmutations produced by the mixture of several colors are not real, but only such by virtue of errors of sight, which the microscope corrects by allowing the mixed or crushed colors to be distinguished.

That aliments have no taste and flowers no odor; that fire is not hot, etc.[98]

---

[97] Author: "Argus did not see objects more multiplied than Polyphemus."

[98] Author: "If taste were a property of aliments, the same foodstuffs would be appetizing, sweet, bitter, savory or insipid for all stomachs, as stone is hard o every touch. If colors were in

That people finally, without being scholarly, reason sufficiently to sense that a theory is required in order to imagine things nearly as they are in the World; the manner in which they move; how heavenly bodies are sustained in space without points of support and persevere constantly in their periodic courses without colliding with one another or falling upon one another. Drawn by the suffrage of Philosophers, the Vulgar have a superficial but sufficient idea of Newton's Theory. Scantly sensible as the effects of impulsion on matter are in the operations of art, we do not confuse them with the springs employed by nature, which we content ourselves with supposing. In that case we find nothing more probable nor les subject to objections than attraction, the force of which seems to be manifest throughout Nature and from which stem the most sensible effects and the most luminous consequences.

We sense nevertheless that there will always be voids between the most closely linked theories; but if we reflect on the

---

objects, they would strike sight in darkness as in light. If odor were a property of odorous objects, it would strike the organ to the same degree in high places as in low ones, which is not the case. Fire does not burn, it only contrives an interruption and disruption of the continuity of the parts that it tears, which causes the pain; it does not contain the consuming quality and more than a needle entering the flesh has any innate principle of pain.

"One can say that fire actually warms, shines and burns everywhere, and in another sense, that it does not warm, shine and burn anywhere. The contradictory expressions "everywhere" and "nowhere" come to the same thing, for to feel heat everywhere signifies that one does not feel it at all; it is only the change that it sensible to us. If there were no variation in the Atmosphere, or if air were not susceptible to dilatation or contraction, we would not suspect its existence, as we only sense that which compresses us violently, when our body emerges from its natural state by the rarefaction or condensation of the same air."

imperfection of the instrument with which we form them, the weakness of our minds and the limits of our intelligence, we will rather be astonished by what we have discovered than what remains hidden from us. Thus I will confess to you in good faith that until a new theory has destroyed attraction as completely as it has annihilated vortices, which I do not affirm to be impossible—or, rather, until it pleases Nature to show itself to discovery, which I dare not hope—we shall hold on to the greatest probability that we can receive.

Chapter V
The Vanity of Nations

Nothing was more delightful for me than the frequent conversations I had with Arzame.

"If there is a people," I said to him one day, "in what we improperly call the Universe—which is to say, in the little vortex of the Earth, from which we still have the injustice of expecting the Moon—who can reasonably draw vanity from its superiority, it is undoubtedly that of the Selenites; I would like to know its origin."

"Oh," Arzame replied, "spare me, I beg you, from satisfying you on that subject. In all the prejudices that remain to us—for there is no humankind that has dispensed with them entirely—that one, I dare say, plays no part. Our self-esteem does not go so far as to fabricate an origin in the midst of the profound darkness that surrounds the truth.

"In any case, when one recalls that almost all great empires must owe their foundations to bands of brigands, scoundrels and outlaws, who, in order to assure themselves of impunity, have been driven to crime, murder and rapine to establish colonies in distant climates, one finds that it is dangerous to dig into remote times,[99] and that it is wiser to enjoy the mildness of a policed government than to seek subjects of shame and confusion in an obscure or fabulous source. How many illustrious Houses would blush to have as a root-stock, vile, mercenary and barbaric souls? There are no Kings who, in going back to the source with which they decorate their genealogy, would not find that they had slaves for ancestors, nor slaves who could not count Sovereigns among theirs. It is more glorious to be the sons of one's own endeavors—which is to say, the first rather than the last of one's race.

---

[99] Author: "All great Empires have begun with hamlets, and Maritime Powers with fishing boats."

"Whoever has no other merit than to count a long sequence of noble ancestors can be compared to an old man in infancy, who had once done great things; that vast gallery ornamented by the portraits of those who preceded him and made him illustrious, which he displays with so much ostentation, is merely a monument that deposes against him.[100]

"Boasting about the nobility of one's ancestors, a sane man has said, is seeking in the roots of trees the flowers and fruits that the branches ought to bear. A stream is often limpid at its source, which is turbulent and becomes miry in its flow. True nobility is personal. It consists in the practice of honor, virtue and good deeds. Instead of going astray in the immensity of time, we hold to those maxims and find them god."

"I wish to Heaven," I exclaimed, "that all the peoples of Earth were as wise, and that vain titles would go up in smoke! But the malady of all Nations is to have an ancient origin, to invent and adopt the most absurd fables to support it, and often to find, in languages that have no analogy with one another, coincidences of names to demonstrate it.

"The Greeks were so vain in respect of their own antiquity that the Athenians would rather have descended from the ants of the forest of Arcadia than recognize themselves as a people foreign to Attica.[101]

"The Thessalians were obstinate in the same folly, honoring the insects and worshiping them as their true ancestors.

"That mania for antiquity extends to the capitals of subaltern cities, market towns, villages and hamlets. Several

---

[100] Author: *"Nam genus, et proavos, et quae non secimus ipsi. Vix ea nostra voco...."* Ovid. Metamorphoses. XIII." [Birth, ancestry and what we have not done ourselves, I would not call our own.]

[101] The eponymous ancestor of the Myrmidons was said to be the son of Zeus and Euymedusa, conceived when their former turned them both into ants—a whimsy based on the etymology of the name Myrmidon, which could be construed as "ant-man."

towns imperiously dispute eminence over one another, whose proud inhabitants can only offer as evidence of their superiority the sad advantage of existing on sheer mountains, which can only be reached by climbing rugged paths; tottering towers ready to bury them beneath their ruins; buildings in which they are exposed to all the vicissitudes of the seasons; an arid soil that refuses them the primary necessities of life; real misfortunes for which they believe themselves to be compensated by the chimerical glory of having served as the birthplace of great men in arms, science and the arts—which is to say, geniuses who have had the good sense to desert the walls that saw them born in order to draw knowledge from foreign wells and lay the foundations of their elevation in countries less ancient but more fortunate.

"It is also the mania of all men to draw vanity from a thousand things with which they are only relatively connected. People glorify themselves in belonging to a Nation that exceeds others in its opulence and the number of its inhabitants, in having rich parents, elevated in dignity. They boast pompously of a superiority that is only owed to the form of government, to the constitution of the State, to the education that influences their character and politics, whose art is put to the profit of the passions—an art that renders entire peoples brave, full of honor and frankness, while it renders others timid, superstitious, effeminate and pusillanimous. Is not regarding these advantages as gifts of nature akin to being proud of having being born in a mild climate, of having fertile soil, of breathing salubrious air, of not being born blind, or deformed, etc. Who could doubt that a Sybarite raised in Sparta would have been disinterested, sober and intrepid, whereas a Spartan nourished in Sybaris would have been soft, effeminate and avid for pleasures?

"That phantom of the imagination is nevertheless very real, in that it excites emulation in indolent souls. For some, it is a branch of patriotism, which produces heroic actions, striking virtues, with leads to the sustenance of an acquired reputation, to share the honor attached to a nation by glorious deeds of which one believes oneself to be the heir. It is a species of patrimony, in which self-esteem invites one to contrive an increase, and which one transfers by example to one's descendants.

"Why is it necessary for an opinion that is the source of private virtues and the glory of a State, to engender at the same time the national hatreds that, gripping the minds of very individual in an enemy or rival country, puts humanity to shame? The good people of all Nations are made to love and esteem one another. Differences of government, mores, customs and beliefs, and even wars, are not obstacles to that natural sentiment, which ought to link all human beings.[102] Antipathy is a miserable prejudice of birth or education, which would have a contrary effect in an opposite climate, and which judgment ought to redress in favor of individual merit. It is necessary to leave those hatreds of rivalry to the unreasoning people; they often take the place of zeal for public welfare.

"By virtue of nurturing a prejudice, like that of the excellence of the mores, taste or genius of one's homeland, one becomes so convinced of it that one can no longer distinguish it from reason. The Greeks,[103] that people so polite and en-

---

[102] Author: "*Tros Rutulusve fuat, nullo discrimine habebo.* Virgil, Aeneid. Book X. line 108." [Trojans and Rutulians are the same to me.]

[103] Author: "The Greeks had the vanity of claiming to be the inventors of all the sciences and all the arts, which they had only improved after receiving them from Barbarians. Tatian the Assyrian told them in a malignly extended discourse that they had originated nothing. 'What among you,' he said to them, 'is the science that does not take its origin from Abroad. You are not unaware that the art of explaining dreams comes from Italy; that the Carians are reputed to be the first to predict the future by the various situations of the planets, that the Phrygians and Isaurians made use, for that, of the flight of birds and the Cypriots of the fuming entrails of slaughtered animals; you also know that the Chaldeans invented astrono-

lightened, treated all the other nations as barbarians, which similarly called them barbarians. Who was right?

"Barbarism, among peoples, only signifies, strictly speaking, a difference of customs and education.[104] Conceit and ignorance honor one another reciprocally with the same titles. In some countries geometry, astronomy and mathematics are considered to be barbaric sciences, as we improperly call 'wild' the fruits that Nature produces without cultivation; while that denomination only suits those whose natural quality we have altered by artifice.[105]

"We freely apply the epithet of savage to those nations that follow, in everything, the simple impulsion of Nature, in

---

my and the Persians magic, the Egyptians geometry, and that the Phoenicians, by a rare good fortune, invented letters and navigation. You owe the first elements of poetry and all your ceremonies to Orpheus; you have borrowed the manner of writing history from the Egyptians; the sweet chords of music from Marsyas and Olympus; the chorus of flutes from the Phrygians; the warrior trumpets from the Tyrrhenians; the Cyclopes have taught you the art of forging iron and an illustrious queen of Persia the rules of epistolary style, etc. Of what are you so proud?' How many vain and superb peoples could be humiliated by similar reproaches?" The quotation is from the early Christian writer Tatian (c120-c180 A.D.), whose *Oratio ad Graecos* [Address to the Greeks] chided them for their paganism.

[104] Author: "Anarcharsis, having come from Scythia to Athens in order to learn the laws and maxims of Solon, was treated as a barbarian by a young Greek. 'Of what are you proud?' replied Anarcharsis, coldly. 'I only appear in your country as you would appear in mine.'"

[105] Author: "It is necessary to agree, however, that although the strawberries of the woods and a few other fruits are more flavorsome than those of our gardens, industry has rendered others more agreeable by means of scions, grafting and cultivation."

111

which lying horrifies, raw judgment is superior to our sanest politics, and which, in sum, have no need of laws, engineers or physicians; we deplore their poverty and yet our poets only find in their condition the model of a perfect felicity. The true savages are those who have disfigured Nature in claiming to reform her, and who have travestied the sentiments of humanity, which inspire us, and, by dint of a refinement foreign to the naivety of its principles, give entry to all the vices that trouble, corrupt and dishonor the state of society.

"Is it not, again, that vanity which provokes, in certain peoples, disputes of the glory of having been the inventors of gunpowder, the compass, the printing press, the telescope, the microscope, etc? If all those discoveries have a favorable aspect for the civil estate, several of them also have an aspect as disadvantageous as it is deadly for humanity.

"If gunpowder renders wars less long because people can kill one another more promptly, and less murderous, because there are fewer battles, it also ensures that there are no more impregnable places—which is to say that there are no longer any shelters against violence and injustice, and that between individuals there is no longer any shelter from vengeance and temerity.

"If the compass has enriched botany, medicine, astronomy and natural history, if it has united entire peoples separated by immense spaces to make, so to speak, the entire earth into one society ready to lend aid to one another and communicate reciprocally the wealth that Nature has dispersed and accorded to a few countries to the deprivation of others, it has also caused the barbaric destruction of one of the most beautiful parts of the World unfortunately rich in a metal that is the object of the avidity of all the others. The compass has extended commerce, but it has suggested new ideas of sensuality to us, deadly to health; it has multiplied our needs—in other terms, has procured us remedies for maladies that we did not have. It has increased the insatiable thirst for wealth, the poisonous source of the corruption of mores; it has brought to a peak a destructive lust; it has, finally, transferred from one hemisphere to the other a frightful malady, unknown before that marvelous discovery—a malady that has long been the scourge of the human species in Europe, or the instrument of vengeance for the extermination of the Americans.[106]

"If the printing press renders us contemporary with the remotest centuries, if it has transmitted to us for our instruction the ideas and knowledge of the illustrious men who have preceded us, their heroic actions and virtues as models, the science and the arts cultivated before us for our utility, it has also immortalized the stupidities of men, which Nature seemed to have taken care to render temporary; it has conserved the memory of shameful deeds, of atrocious crimes, of which it would have been better to be ignorant; it has occasioned indecent and scandalous literary wars; it has multiplied and eternalized works dangerous to mores, capable of tormenting future races, which would have perished with their authors; it has perpetuated satires and libels that have unjustly defamed respectable man and entire families; revealed mysteries that ought to have remained buried in eternal obscurity. In sum, it has perpetuated more errors than truth, and caused so many disorders in the moral system that the question of whether the admirable discovery, so greatly celebrated, of the pointing press has done more good than harm will probably remain in the ranks of insoluble problems. *Adhuc sub judice lis est.*[107]

"If the microscope has revealed to us, in terms of marvels imperceptible to our eyes, a new World, it has also humiliated our pride and punished our curiosity but concentrating our admiration on objects that were previously judged vile and despicable; it has rendered hideous the beauty that attracted and united all our affections. The most beautiful woman regarded through that instrument only displays a skin eaten away by vermin, covered in coarse scales, rugosities and scars, the sketch of a cadaver. The most beautiful diamond only of-

---

[106] Syphilis.
[107] The case is still before the judge—i.e., not yet settled.

fers facets poorly dressed and asymmetrical; in the most beautiful features of a painting, one sees nothing but a confused mixture of discordant colors; in the most superb cloth, nothing but a mass of threads bristling with oakum; in the most delicate aliments and the most sensual preparations nothing but disgusting animal dens; in the air, nothing but devouring insects that we breathe in by millions, to hasten our destruction.

"Was it, then, so desirable to see in Nature things as they really are? That benevolent mother had disposed our eyes to deceive us delightfully, and to satisfy our needs in an agreeable manner, and cleverly present beauty to us where it was not, and where it was more important for us to encounter it. Our imprudent curiosity has destroyed an ever-flattering illusion often preferable to the physical reality; it only remains to us to numb our pain and blind ourselves to our misery by agitation and torment—feeble compensation for what we have lost by the fatal discoveries from which we stupidly obtain so much vanity.

"Optical devices, fortunately, have thus far been limited in their effect to the physical; beware that industry does not invent a moral microscope that can represent human sentiments and character accurately and unmask hypocrisy. People would no longer be able to tolerate their fellows and society would collapse.

"How ought one to regard those sumptuous monuments to human pride designed to perpetuate their existence through centuries after they have ceased to be,[108] in which they once represented themselves, as the Emperor Hadrian built the

---

[108] Author: "...*Nunc levior cippus non imprimit ossa? Laudant conivae, nunc non e manibus illis, nunc non e tumulo fortunataque favilla nascentur violae?* Persius Satire I. lines 38-40." [Does not a lighter hillock now mark his bones? The guests praise: now will not violets spring forth from those manes, from that tomb?]

Mole Hadriana[109] for his sepulcher? When, among princes who vowed humility, Julius II constructed the vastest temple that ever existed to serve as a mausoleum;[110] when the Kings of Egypt employed millions of men to erect enormous pyramids, which, by virtue of their structure, braved the fury and the ravages of time, in order to enclose a little ash[111] therein; when one recalls that Alexander consented that Mount Athos serve as his statue; when Semiramis saw her own executed of Mont Bagistant,[112] a steep rock seventeen stades in perpendicular height and full of inequalities, which it was first necessary to smooth, and that she be placed in the middle of a hundred guards; and when one considers, finally, with a philosophical eye, that these destructible monuments to vanity, already consumed by time, will one day perish with the memory of those who had them erected, perhaps one can conceive the pride of humans in a momentary passage on a globe that is merely a dot in the Universe.

The richness of tombs, one sage of Antiquity has said, does not dazzle the gods.[113]

---

[109] Author: "Today the Castel Sant'Angelo in Rome. *In the extreme care men take to extend their being they have provided for all the pieces; for bodies, sepulchres; for names, glory.* Montaigne."

[110] That was the original intention of the pope in question, but he changed his mind, much to Michelangelo's chagrin,

[111] Author: "*Quid brevi fortes jaculamur aevo Multa?* Horace, Ode XVI." [Why tease ourselves with so many projects in so short a life?] Quoted by Montaigne.

[112] The reference is to a huge rectangular carving, the Farhadtarash, on Mount Behistan or Bagistan, which, like many mysterious monuments in the region, was associated by legend-mongers with the mythical queen of Nineveh, Semiramis, especially by Greek historians.

[113] Author: "If there is a madness in wanting to live after death, it lies in neglecting one's mores for the sake of one's reputation; and if it is true that to seek to survive by striking

"If all the men who have lived had had a tomb—I do not say a temple—it would have been necessary, with time, in order to find land to cultivate, to overturn those sterile monuments and stir the ashes of the dead in order to nourish the living.

"The more modest and wiser Sovereigns of today are content with a vault common to their family, many do without mausolea, urns, simulacras, sarcophagi, and cenotaphs. Titus, Trajan, the Antonines, Louis XII, Henri IV and Louis XV will doubtless live on longer than those vestiges of grandeur, magnificence and weakness. Hearts are archives that do not perish."

"Your manner of thinking," I said to Arzame, "appears to me to be so just and sane that I have no doubt that it has its source in the first principles of education. I would be glad to be informed regarding the form given to that received by the young Selenite."

"I shall satisfy you," said Arzame, "in another conversation."

---

actions of honor and virtue, is a madness, it can pass for wisdom in this world, by dint of the good that the example and the lessons procure the human race in inspiring it to virtue. The folly has this aspect too, that it is universal and has nothing ridiculous about it."

Chapter VI
On Education

"The education of youth being the most important object of legislation," Arzame said to me, "since it influences all the actions of life, and is the source of the happiness or unhappiness of individual people and society in general, the Prince, occupied as a father of a family with the felicity of his people, has not neglected anything to ensure that children receive a good education, and that they suckle with their milk principles tending to form good, faithful and useful subjects.[114]

"On the plan drawn up by the Prince, the first cares of parents have for their objective the temperament, which alone makes the difference between human beings.

"Children are raised harshly from the cradle, a time when nature yields to all sorts of impressions; they are exposed naked to the ardor of the sun and the insults of the seasons; they are often plunged into cold baths.

"The body, thus tempered from the most tender infancy, finds itself exempt in consequence from the thousand evils to which delicacy is subject, while the contrary practices protecting children from those discomforts ensure that they can no longer support any of them at a more advanced age.[115]

---

[114] Author: "...*Ingenuas didicisse fidelitur artes emollit mores, nec sinit esse feros*. Ovid, Epistulae ex Ponto." [To have learned the liberal arts faithfully softens manners and prevents them from being harsh.]

[115] Author: "*Udum et molle lutum es, nunc nunc properandus et acri fingendus sine fine rota*.... Persius, Satire III, line 2." [You are but soft moist clay now, thus to be formed instantly and incessantly by the glowing wheel.]

"One keeps them thus until the age of three when one begins to dress them lightly and without ligatures.[116]

"The body becomes accustomed, by necessity, to the rudest exercise and the most difficult labor. Frugality augments strength, temperance maintains it. To prepare youth in advance to all the unfortunate accidents of the climate is to diminish their intensity when they experience them; it is to protect them from the deadly impressions that the elements cause in weak constitutions, and save them from the thousand accidents to which the body is subject, more by the softness of education than by temperament. Nature has constructed all beings to live in the fluid that surrounds them; is it not stupid to withdraw them from it by precautions, of which one can avoid the necessity? Medicine, that science more rational than conclusive, the principles of which are vague, the progress uncertain and the method equivocal—a science more apt to produce maladies than cure them—has little to do for hardened bodies accustomed early on to brave its remedies or do without them.

"Scarcely have children begun to articulate a few sounds than one only leaves them in the presence of people who speak the language of their country purely.

"Until the age of five, when they enter gymnasia, they only learn to read and write, and domestic education consists of inspiring them to sentiments of mildness, modesty, docility, sincerity and respect for their fathers and mothers. Obedience is a duty, respect a tribute to the authors of their birth, of which we collect, in our turn, the rewards. Both are in Nature; the first kings took paternal authority for the model of their government; and although, according to the language of ingratitude, it seems that we owe nothing to those who have given us being, that they have only been blind agents of the

---

[116] Author: "One observes on the Earth that in the countries where there are neither swaddling-clothes nor ligatures, the people are naturally better made, better conformed and less subject to the deformities so common in Europe."

system of the World, mechanical instruments in the order of Nature, and that our existence is a pure effect of hazard or pleasure, are we not indebted nevertheless to our fathers and mothers, for the care that they have devoted to us in our infancy and our education, the comforts of which they have deprived themselves in order to support our needs, their endeavors to procure us a fortunate situation, and their patience in tolerating our faults? Gratitude is a weak tribute for such benefits; only love and respect can acquit them. One cannot, therefore, imprint those sentiments in the hearts of children too early or with too much faith; they contribute to happiness throughout their lives. One cannot be a good citizen if one has not learned first to be a tender and respectful son.

"No dolls are given to children; three-dimensional geometrical figures are substituted, capable of pricking their curiosity, which accustom them mechanically to reasoning, before the age that is called that of reason, which ordinarily only comes so late because its development has been slowed down by bad education. To occupy them with trifles is to prolong their infancy instead of hastening the use of reason in them.

"As it requires more effort to destroy a prejudice than to secure it, and it is better to direct habit that to wait to correct faults by the labor of reason, which easily breaks against the reef of the passions, far from inspiring fears in children, the panic terrors of specters, phantoms, shades, goblins, etc., which are difficult to efface from the imagination because the soul struck by the extraordinary always retains the impression into maturity, one only introduces such notions as chimeras, in order to acquaint them with their extravagance and illusion.

"On the contrary, one only amuses them with truths, and one only talks to them with reason; their games embody instruction; they are diverted with conjuring tricks, which are explained to them afterwards, in order to deflect them at any early age from dangerous impressions that leave in the mind the frivolous ideas of magic, enchantment, etc. If their attention is drawn to singular things, it is to teach them that the mechanism of phenomena is in Nature, and the marvelous in knavery and mystery, which charlatans cultivate. Children become, so to speak, philosophers, at an age when dolls are ordinarily an object of confidence and occupation.

"Shame is attached to hand games, diversions so base for well-born individuals, whose consequences are sometimes so dire.

"Children are brought up to use both hands, a resource when, by accident, one is deprived of the functions of the right hand; to affect to employ that one for preference is a puerile prejudice; there is no left and right in Nature.

"The opinion of the Selenites being that public education is preferable to domestic education, the latter having advanced the age of reason, children, entire public gymnasia at the age of five in order to begin their studies; it is the same for girls as for boys. They are founded for all the classes of citizens, in which all children are brought up relative to their condition.

"The schools, which everywhere else are places pernicious to health because of the corrupt air breathed after an hour of being enclosed there in, have spacious rooms in which the air is renewed continually.

"At the head of these schools are wise individuals charged with informing youth by their speech, their writings and their example. The most celebrated scholars and philosophers make it a glory to contribute gratis to public education, regarding it as a traffic unworthy of virtue to put wisdom in shackles and to extract a tribute from their enlightenment, the usage of which belongs to the fatherland.

"Except for the class of artisans, in which one works principally to formulate mores, to extend natural enlightenment to a certain point and to inspire them to attachment and fidelity to the Sovereign, consideration for the Great, pity for the unfortunate, love for the fatherland and a taste for the professions of their fathers, education is the same for all the rest, free one day to choose an estate in conformity with their inclination or talent, which are assisted to develop but not forced.

"In accordance with the principles of Religion and the duties that it imposes in a gentle manner toward the State, society and oneself, the study of Morality and Logic is the basis of all instruction. It is judged that it is first necessary to form mores, to be a good citizen, to think accurately and reason solidly, to attract the esteem and confidence of one's compatriots and to speak one's native language purely, in order to add amenity and pleasure to all conversations. Subsequently one learns to calculate and measure with exactitude; immediately after comes the explanation of the celestial sphere and experimental physics, which, in extending the views of the mind, set limits to curiosity. Finally, the young receive a slight grounding in history, geography and natural history. In hours of recreation the mind is left free to relax by means of metaphysical subtleties, algebraic demonstrations, electrical experiments and the study of foreign languages.[117]

"Instead of sacrificing a considerable time—the most precious of life—as was once done, to learning dead languages or things that reason and better-formed judgment will soon be in the necessity of forgetting, young people, by a contrary method of study, find themselves at the age of ten instructed in everything that might be useful in the course of their lives, whatever estate they might choose. Two years is then employed in giving them an idea of the laws, politics, drawing, music and the arts in general.

"Two further years, finally, are devoted to exercises appropriate to form the body, increasing strength and giving it agility, like dancing, arms and gymnastic. Thus, at fourteen,

---

[117] Author: "...*Ludus animo debet aliquando dari, ad cognitandum melior ut redeat tibi.* Phaedrus, Fabularum Aesopiarum Book III fable 14. 'Clarke is a greater metaphysician than Newton,' said an abstract mind one day. 'That might be the case,' replied a philosopher, coldly, 'but it is as if you were saying that one plays better with a balloon than the other; prick one of those bladders and it contains nothing but wind.'" [The quotation translates as "Relaxation should occasionally be given to the mind, the better to equip it when toil is resumed."]

everyone following a taste, penchant or talent, embraces an estate—for idleness is regarded as a vice and a scorn of duties to society—a choice that is almost always fortunate, when it is determined by natural instinct, a guide even more reliable than reason itself.

"Although the principal goal of government is to form honest and useful citizens, one does not neglect the inspiration of youth to the art of pleasure, distanced from the baseness of flattery, so necessary to elevate the charms of civil life.

"With a few differences relative to the constitution and functions appropriate to each individual sex, the education of women is the same as that for men. The abuse of the ignorance in which girls were once brought up, relative to matters of which the usage and property are common to the human race, has been realized. It has proved, by communicating to them the enlightenment of which a false and miserable prejudice had long deprived them, that careers in the arts and sciences have been extended to them, and that society has gained from it, without the domestic economy assigned to that beautiful half of society losing out. One could say that they receive an education mid-way between those of Sultanas and Amazons; so that, the distinction between the sexes no longer consisting of anything but the division of cares and labor in proportion to strength and delicacy, a number of females, who had been excluded by base jealousy and ingrate politics from councils and academies, in which they nevertheless presided secretly, were soon seen taking part there, as they do today, with faces uncovered, to their ornament and glory.

"An excellent education is the source of all virtues, just as its neglect is the seed of all vices.[118] In a natural goodness

---

[118] Author: "*Doctrina sed vim promovet insitam, rectique cultus, pectara roborant: utcumque defecere mores, dedecorant bene nata culpae. Horace. Book IV. Ode IV."* [Instruction improves the innate powers (of the mind) and good discipline strengthens the heart. When art has not aided in forming mores, vice often dishonors the gifts of nature.]

(and that is in greater number than the clinical annals affect to publish) it fructifies fortunately; at the least it combats vicious penchants and suspends their deadly effects, even if it does not triumph completely. Humans all have in the heart a principle of justice, which protects the civil estate from the greater part of the violence to which the human species is exposed. To convince oneself that humans are less wicked than unfortunate, and that their inclinations almost all have their root is good or bad education,[119] it is sufficient to consider that entire States are populated by just and virtuous hearts; that people become benevolent in society; that dissolute soldiers only need to pass into better disciplined corps suddenly to acquire their spirit and maxims; that when the passions are deadened, the heart soon returns from its deviations; that there is no real peace for vice and that even scoundrels are never exempt from remorse.

"We have recognized," Arzame continued, "the injustice and danger of imprisoning young people in houses of correction or force for human weaknesses occasioned by bad company or pernicious examples, almost always drawn from domestic circumstances. Young people, susceptible to all sorts of impressions, are all too frequently victims of corrupt models that they have before their eyes. It is inconsiderate to put a stain on their reputation by punishing their errors as crimes, with too much severity, and that kind of punishment ordinarily has no other effect than to rob them, in those retreats, the residue of innocence that they bring into them.

"To facilitate the advancement and progress of studies, we have found means, not of donating memory—for all humans are born with a sufficient proportion of that faculty, which only needs exercise in order to extend its properties and order to collect its fruits—but of preventing its weakening, which follows a deregulated usage of reading as well as the occupations of an agitated life. The manner of its maintenance

---

[119] Author: "The figure, Aristotle says, is in the block; the sculptor has only to reveal it."

has been reduced to principles, by placing methodically in the brain that which can naturally be retained there. The materials can only be linked together and acquire some solidly there if judgment and reflection dispose of them in such a manner that one study is not harmed by another. It is necessary, for that effect, to reverse the order that is seen in plants, and to hasten to gather the fruits before ornamenting it with flowers.

"It has also been found to be good to accustom children to meditate instead of studying aloud, for it has been observed that by pronouncing the words one retains little more than the sounds, while a torrent of ideas runs continually. In silence, attention develops thought, which appear obscure at first, and which, embarrassed with sounds, will always remain so in the mind. One grasps what one reads better than what one hears read. The chain of reasoning is uninterrupted by distractions, and more vivid and durable impressions remain of it.

"The necessity of knowing the language well is of great importance in all conditions. The abuse of a term obscures an idea, and from the obscurity of ideas a thousand evils are born for the heart and the mind. How many cruel wars, ruinous lawsuits and individual animosities must owe their origins to an ambiguous term or a shady expression differently interpreted in laws, treaties, contracts and testaments?

"One of the principal objects of education is instruction in the maternal language. It is necessary in all the circumstances of life, while the usage of dead or foreign languages[120] is very rare; it can even substitute for the other, since almost all of the best that the Ancients and enlightened nations have written has been elegantly translated.

"More attentive than you to guard against inconveniences that might be born of ignorance of the mother tongue, we bring up children from the cradle, as I have said, to speak

---

[120] Author: "One ought only to learn foreign languages that might be useful relative to the profession one chooses—which is to say, those of Nations from which one might seek instruction, or with which one might trade or enter into war."

purely. They learn good terminology as easily as bad. Scarcely are they able to link meanings than one does not tolerate the use of careless phrases or vicious expressions; also, one does not hear among us the words devoid of sense that are continually repeated in your conversations, not the base and corrupt terms in the speech of well-born individuals, such as one observes all the time among you."

"You surprise me," I said to Arzame, with a kind of vehemence. "Well brought-up people, among us, speak purely; women, without study, even set the tone for scholars and wits."

"That may be," replied Arzame coldly, "but your opinion is a prejudice nevertheless. It is the effect of the scant attention that you bring to listening as well as to speaking, of the distracted habit of hearing what people mean rather than what they say, and finally, of dispensing with studying a language that you think you possess, because it is spoken mechanically and well enough within the walls that have seen you born, and because you have academies and a reasonable dose of vanity.

"Make no mistake, though, my friend: the knowledge of all the turns and delicacies, of the true significance of the words of one's own language is not acquired by simple communication or by the rapid reading of novels, but by profound study and usage, and continual observation of oneself. I repeat it to you after long experience, and I maintain that even in your capital, with the exception of the healthiest part of the people of the Court and men of letters whom study has preserved more than others from contagion, there is not one whose familiar style is not infected by corrupted terms, trivial phrases and defective expressions that degrade discourse.

"Lend an attentive ear to the majority of conversations and you will easily agree that, if one removed from them the words as frequently repeated as they are unnecessary to the liaison of the discourse, almost nothing essential would remain. Observe, I beg you, that the people and artisans are not irrelevant to this matter. The frequent *he saids* and *she saids* that make one sick, the padding with which sentences are unnecessarily stuffed: *certainly...I assure you...by the way...finally...of course...do you know?...*etc.; the term *thing*, so improper and so wearying, to substitute for nouns that abstraction or vivacity prevents from coming to mind: 'give me that *thing*,' 'I've discovered this *thing*' etc.—a base term, always ridiculous, often indecent, which says anything one wants it to, but expresses nothing.

"I shall not attack here the errors of usage of which examination makes their defectiveness felt, and of which it would perhaps not be indifferent if the language were purged, such as calling an infamous penalty *honorable amends* or saying of something irrational, an entity that does not exist, that it *stands to reason*; of saying *hands tied behind the back* when, if they were tied the other way around, one would not say *behind the breast* or *behind the stomach*; *a horse of a different color, a hobby-horse, a horse shod in silver*; a beautiful color *rose, fire,* or *cherry...the majority of men are inconstant* when one ought strictly speaking, to say *is inconstant*.[121] *If I go to the country tomorrow* or *I will go if I can*, where the *if,* which is a dubitative conjunction, ought to indicate the future; *an event occurred...to link, unite, join, reunite together*, which are pleonasms; *there wasn't a living soul*, as if there were dead souls; *I saw it with my own eyes*, as if, physically, one could see with someone else's eyes; a *well-placed* heart...a *well-born* or *well-made* soul, etc.[122] Terms of movement employed

---

[121] Author: "One claims in vain in this case that the sound, rather than the words, is the principle rule of constitution—a feeble excuse for a voluntary error."

[122] The list goes on to cite half a dozen further idiosyncrasies, all unique to French, for which it is impossible to find English equivalents, although a sensitive pedant would have no difficulty drawing up an entirely different set of peculiarities of common English usage. The more general examples cited in the next paragraph also include several inapplicable to English, some of which I have omitted; it would be inappropriate to substitute similar complaints sometimes made of English

in repose…even absurdities that habit has consecrated and are employed by good authors have been accepted and even respected, in spite of the protests of reason.

"There are even various errors of meaning, faults of construction and grammar from which your best authors are not exempt, such as applying the same case to two verbs that require different ones, giving the same preposition to two verbs that require different ones, giving the same adjective to two substantives of different kinds, and so on, some of which faults are almost universal in the best-written books.

"As for the poets to whom, by virtue of prejudice, you believe with Despreaux that you are indebted for the perfection of your language, but have, on the contrary, disfigured it, and the most correct of whom cannot stand up to the slightest analysis without being constantly caught at fault, you owe them indulgence for the sacrifice they have made of reason to rhyme, in order to please you in cadence, and the hindrances in which your ear has judged it appropriate to imprison their judgment.

"You doubtless also require," Arzame added, in concluding his observations, "that I cite you some you the corrupted words by which my ears have often been wounded in the familiar style and conversation of people who are reputed to speak well."[123]

---

usage (splitting infinitives, ending sentences with prepositions, etc.), which have no application in French.

[123] The author concludes the chapter with a table listing more than a hundred French words and phrases whose spelling or gender has allegedly been corrupted, including some unique to the 18th century that are no longer seen today and some where the modified form has been so solidly established by usage that the Académie has admitted them to its official dictionary, while his preferred alternative has vanished. He also adds his own footnote: "Wounded self-esteem will rise up in vain against the justice of these observations, which do not concern either the people or the lower middle class, for whom it is suf-

Chapter VII
The Condition of Literature Among the Selenites

On the incontestable principle that difficulty adds nothing to the merit of a good book, except in complications—
laborious research in history, antiquity, chronology, etc.—in
which genius plays no part, the disputes and conflicts animated between rhyme and reason have terminated quite naturally
in favor of the latter, which no longer writes except in prose,
the natural style of common sense. Rhyme, like fiefs and duels, owes its origin to barbarity. It is the prerogative of an enlightened century to banish it from the empire of Letters. The
Selenites no longer employ it, except in the principles of a few
sciences for the use of children, to imprint them on the
memory with more facility.

They came to regard as a waste the precious fraction of
time vainly expended in racking the brain to find and couple
rhymes, with the idea of rendering thought more brilliant that
ought only to satisfy the intelligence, the heart and reason, and
which more often led to the distortion or travesty of the natural, accuracy, meaning and verity. In addition, the inversion of
speech-patterns that is part of the merit of poetic language
seemed as opposed to veritable construction as an edifice
would seem strange whose cellars were placed under the roof

---

ficient to make themselves understood; they come directly
from the best-educated individuals of the highest status. What
would ensue if one analyzed the construction of sentences?
What gibberish, what chaos, would one not be able to record
in a conversation of people of intelligence, enough to make
one blush? There are no Pyrrhonians on this matter except
those who have never picked up a pen; let them try to write as
they speak and then read objectively, and they will soon be
disabused. That is, after the reflective reading of good authors,
the only means of improving familiar style."

and grain-lofts in the foundations, or a ship whose oars were set on the poop deck and its sails in the depths of the hold. What disorder cannot be generated by the reversal of the order of words, when one remembers that there are some Latin or Italian lines of six words that can be switched around in seven hundred and twenty ways?

The philosophical mind, which only admits that which bears the stamp of clarity and verity, had dealt a fatal blow to rhyme, which is merely a seductive game, an abuse of intelligence, verse being itself merely an ornamentation of thought, not an art of better speech. It is not the language of Nature; a peasant sometimes expresses himself well without study; with difficult labor, a poet often reasons very poorly; bad notions are passed off under the varnish of striking rhyme, which weaken the good and often leave nothing in the mind but words.

The necessity of subjecting a true and precise thought to the tyranny of rhyme, producing the inconvenience of twisting it,[124] recasting it and removing from it the simplicity and verity that constitute its character, inevitably has the result that the most brilliant and most exact verification is, in the best authors, full of equivocation, and faults of language, meaning and construction, in which the mind is tortured and genius shackled, giving birth to nothing but embryos and monsters. A scrupulous analysis of the most celebrated works of poetry has demonstrated that truth, disabused the ears and dissipated the seductive charm of consonance.

The proscription of rhyme initially offended the vanity of a few young men who believed themselves to be favored by

---

[124] Author: "*Aut qui non verba rebus aptant, sed res extrinsecus arcesset, quibus verba conveniant.* Quintillian. Book VIII chapter III." [Who do not fit words to the subject, but look for things from the purpose to fit the words.] The misquotation (*Aut* is not in the original, *aptant* should be *aptabit* and *quibus* should be followed by *haec*) is copied from Montaigne.

129

the heavens with a superior gift, which they called poetic enthusiasm, divine fire, etc., but they soon recognized the abuse of a practice harmful to the progress of reason, and how much more sensible it is to nourish the intelligence with thoughts than the ear with sounds.[125] So the production was soon seen of admirable works in every genre, the accuracy, clarity, precision, number and energy of which charmed all good minds. Thus, instead of striving stupidly to put *Telemaque, L'Avare, Cenie, L'Oracle* and *Le Pupille* in verse, they would have preferred to translate *L'Henriade*, the *Ars poetica, Cinna, Athalie, Le Misanthrope*, etc. into prose. Only La Fontaine, by virtue of a unique naturalness, would have remained in possession of rhyme.

Versifying the dramatic poem is one of the strangest manias. In fact, is it not very singular that a poet should take the trouble to rhyme a play, when the great artistry of the actor in the performance consists of causing the line, rhyme and scansion to disappear?

If the first books were written in verse before prose was in usage, as some claim, it was doubtless with a view to aiding the memory in the study of laws, philosophy, theology, medicine, etc., but after the principles of sciences were established, that method became superfluous.

Poetry is a gift that the heavens distribute; versification is a purely mechanical artistry in the arrangement of the parts of a machine whose inventor is the poet. The disposition of letters to compose words and words to link phrases is a task of maneuvering, which only constructs to the Architect's design.

Rhymed poetry is therefore, merely an arrangement of words and almost always a disordering of things, which each poet disposes in his manner.

One arranges the first line, which, by virtue of the habit of assembling words, always comes quite easily; he then

---

[125] Author: "*Plus sonat quam valet*. Seneca, Epistle 40." [More sound than sense] Again, from Montaigne, cited on the same page as the previous quotation.

searches his thoughts in order to link it to what ought to follow.

Another commences with the second line and relies on hazard to link it with the first, with the result that he often does not say what he would like to say, and says what he does not want to say.

Another fragments or elongates a finished meaning in order to conclude his scansion, removing a necessary word or inserting an unnecessary epithet, sometimes succeeding in rendering his work obscure or saying in two lines what could be expressed in one.

One supposed favorite of Apollo possessed by Metromania, who is uniquely sensible to snoring, first places a rich rhyme, which waits for something to come to fill the scansion; epithets present themselves in a host, as necessary, to complete it; the most accurate yields its place to the one that best fits the frame, the meaning follows suit, altered if that is what the case requires. If he means "the summit of the rock," he says, emphatically "the rigid summit of the glowering rock," and the enthusiastic imbecile applauds himself for having ingeniously followed the rules, contriving twelve feet that do not support a body. Hence the prodigious number of discordant notes in the works of the best poets, because, in the heat of composition, they are often less occupied with thoughts than with the words that serve for their enunciation.

Versification, whatever its partisans say, is nothing, properly speaking, but the art of mounting words, of making a simple thought pass for a fine one, a common one for new, and pillaging with impunity, without appearing to be a plagiarist. Thus, with the art of twisting a line, one can easily produce a thousand epigrams without having given birth to a thought.[126]

---

[126] Author: "Pierre Corneille, powerful versifier as he was, ceded with difficulty to the public taste for rhymed dramas. 'I shall soon finish *Rodogune*,' he said. 'I only have the verse to make.' At least he fitted the verses to the play; it seems, on the

The constraint of versification extinguishes the fire of the enthusiasm; forced to linger for a long time on the same thought and to exercise patience, genius wearies and becomes drowsy. If, by chance, while searching for a rhyme, one finds an idea, one often renounces employing a vivid, delicate or sublime thought for want of embedding it in the limits of the verse, or making it ring with the tinkle of rhyme.

Rhymed poetry would doubtless hold sway over poetic prose if it could charm the mind and the ear equally, but is inferior to it in that it can scarcely content the latter except that the expense of the former. To savor prose only requires sentiment; to be flattered by verse requires habituation. Thus, rhyme is not natural.

If one simply reflects on the cold meaning, one will be convinced that rhymed verses do not even have a serious appearance, and that habit alone prevents one from sensing their absurdity or barbarity.

In prose, the essential thing is depth, in verse, it is style. Prose therefore requires more thought and intelligence than verse, where mediocrity hides beneath the varnish of rhyme. The versifier is often an unintelligent Artist, who does not seek to please so much as to deduce, or to charm so much as to dazzle with a false brilliance that deflects attention to the surface from the ingrate foundation of the work.

The desire to shine in a career that not everyone can follow animates young people, who soon weary of the pursuit and blush at being so fatigued without having achieved anything.[127] To write in verse is to consume a great deal of time in composing a work, which cannot please everyone, since, being unable to go abroad except in translation, it always loses

---

contrary, that plays are nowadays fitted to the verses, that they are filled with sententious maxims, already widespread in works of morality and politics, which only cost the author the difficulty of rhyming them."

[127] Author: "*One can play the fool almost everywhere else, but not in poetry.* Montaigne."

much of its freshness, its force and its color, while the orator can retain all his grace in making the transition. Thus, it is the case that well-made dramas are welcomed in all nations, but that critical or satirical plays only please those who have the originals before their eyes. Like the ephemera, the works of the day only last a day.

It is rare that poetry progresses with reason; it sacrifices too much intelligence,[128] only consisting in the cadence of repeated sounds; a good thought is no more piquant for being rhymed; it is often only stilted, forced, made ridiculous or obscure. Doubtless it seems more elevated in its mounting, but can one believe that it marches more surely?

Difficulty vanquished is the apparent merit of rhymed poetry; anagrams, acrostics and *bouts-rimes*[129] have the same advantage, but the victory often costs very dear and is never complete.

Poetry is for the soul, versification for the ear.

The abuses of poetry are innumerable. It has been seen to spread superstition over the earth and place crime in the heavens.

An epigram has often blackened the name of irreproachable individuals and cost the life or public esteem of illustrious authors.

The ridiculousness of a prosaic versification, which is precisely that of a failed enterprise, had been sensed; but no one stupidly criticized, in prose, the arrangement of words that is called verse, when it was found there naturally; the best prose is perhaps that in which it is most frequently found.

It was agreed, in spite of the general prejudice, that far from owing to poets the improvement of languages, they had,

---

[128] Author: "*Scribendi recte, sapere est et principium et sons.* Horace. Ars Poetica, line 309. [Knowledge is the foundation and source of good writing.]

[129] The term *bout-rime* [literally, end-rhyme] is derived from a kind of poetic game where a poet is given a set of rhymed words and required to improvise a verse to fit them.

on the contrary, mutilated them, by dint of dissecting them, and that their progress was owed to good authors in prose.

Criticism being more harmful than advantageous to the progress of Literature, when it is not confined by the limits of reason and equity, a tribunal of taste had been established, composed of wise and enlightened individuals, which had the right to pronounce in sovereign terms on all literary disputes. Works were examined there with care before their printing was permitted. It was not sufficient that they contained nothing contrary to religion, mores and government; it was also necessary that they be judged good and that they contain new and useful ideas; otherwise, they did not pass. If the production was only one of pure pleasure, written in a vivid, concise and brilliant style, the tribunal pronounced that it was "good for the temporary relaxation of the mind."

To protect against the consequences of literary disputes, which degenerate too frequently into indecency and invectives dishonoring to men of letters, the contenders were obliged, before entering the lists, to establish clearly the question that was being put to the academy. That precaution strangled the majority at birth. Accord is often achieved as soon as the contenders understand one another. In dissertations of physics on phenomena, there was a similar obligation to establish the facts before submitting it to discussion. That often avoided the imbecility of searching, like Democritus,[130] for a cause where there is none. To proceed differently is to compose remedies for imaginary ailments or institute laws to reform non-existent abuses.

Everyone was left at liberty to give definitions of metaphysical entities according to his taste or pleasure, and even of

---

[130] Author: "It is known that he wanted to know why figs that had been served to him had a scent of honey, and became angry with his maidservant, who told him, naively, that she had put them in a jar that contained honey. He was annoyed that she had robbed him of the satisfaction of finding a cause of a non-existent phenomenon."

racking his brains to discover sources and fix origins in human understanding, except for going innocently astray; those kinds of works, indifferent in themselves, serve for recreation. For example, two thousand different definitions of mind had been offered, all contradictory and all exact.

Thus, with everything resident in opinion, good minds were content to enjoy and to sense, abandoning speculation on matters that have no absolute utility—such as mathematics— to those invalids overburdened by leisure, who are ignorant of the art of filling it and cannot concentrate on subjects capable of demonstration..

The field was open to criticism, but the petty masters of that art were objects of greater scorn than those indefinable individuals who sow ennui and disgust in society. As for the brigands of literature, they were treated as pirates.

Journalists and professional critics, submissive by their status to the authority of the tribunal of taste, were obliged to sustain their censure there and to make authentic reparation to authors attacked by the iniquitous darts of envy, malignity or suggestion.

It had been projected for a long time to reduce the number of newspapers, without regard to commerce in paper, ink and printing, in order to save the time and faculties of those whom the epidemic ruined via the purchase of those mostly estimable works. To put a stop to their multiplication it was ruled that no journalist could treat matters for which another had been made responsible. It was demanded, moreover, that each remained within the bounds of his talent.

Thus, a certain periodical publisher, a bold champion who produced a sheet under his name every ten days, was limited to simple literature, with an express prohibition on touching, in any manner whatsoever, on the sciences and the arts, on which he had abusively arrogated the right to discourse with the same ineptitude with which his predecessor had spo-

135

ken about the philosophy of Newton[131] *non sacra profanis.* His work, thus reduced to the sixth part, was tolerated for the service of the province, but moderation in his writing was imposed on him at the same time, along with fidelity to his citations, circumspection toward celebrated authors and impartiality in his judgments, and he was forbidden to indulge in wordplay, offensive sallies, and bitter mockery. His little work, which had already alienated good minds, then denuded of the ingredients that had caused the ignorant, idle and malign multitude to seek it out, became so insipid that it even disgusted feeble minds and naturally fell into oblivion.[132]

---

[131] Author: "See *Observations sur les écrits modernes* by the Abbé des Fontaines, vol. XV p.49. You will see there, with disgust, that Newton is not a philosopher, and not a geometer, observer and calculator; that Newtonism is a bad physics reproved by all the good philosophers in Europe; that the terms *void, absolute gravitation* and *attraction* are a miserable jargon of vile peripateticism proscribed in all the schools of Europe. On p.76 of the same volume, analyzing *Les élémens de la philosophie de Newton* by Monsieur Voltaire, the journalist says with the same sagacity that it is only necessary to recall the mind to the great principles of clear ideas to have a sovereign scorn for the physics that has dazzled Monsieur Voltaire *et al.* He doubtless finds those clear ideas in vortices, and the horror of Nature for the void, which appear to him to be demonstrated; he applauds himself for being a composite of Monads; he would doubtless, with the same accuracy of mind, have degraded the music of the village soothsayer by comparison with the celebrated plainsong of Proserpine. May he have for adversaries everyone under the age of thirty who is breathing." The ingrate Pierre Desfontaines (1685-1745) turned on Voltaire after the latter had helped him, attacking his dramatic works fiercely and starting an exchange of satirical gibes that he was bound to lose. The periodical cited ran to 35 volumes.
[132] Author: "If the sheep-like readers of that periodical work want to have an accurate idea of its intrinsic merit, let them

Another very estimable and well-regarded journalist was required to remove from his collection—for he only put into it endless eulogies—the enigmas, logogriphs and a few insipid tales, and to tighten the fugitive part; but on the representation he made that the fragmentation of his work was due to the variety of its composite materials and the eccentricity of his readers' tastes, he was permitted without any consequence, to insert those trivia, one condition that, since the reign of rondeaux, ballads, sonnets and triolets was over, he put into it, like his predecessors, anagrams, proverbs, bout-rimes, acrostics and rebuses.[133]

---

merely read the *Revue des feuilles de Mr. F.* of the Academies of Angers, Montauban and Nancy, and several others of the year 1756 and the *Observateur littéraire*, a sage and judicious periodical work, of the year 1762, volume I, letter II, p. 40, and they will be convinced that in order to obtain any advantage from the author's judgments it is necessary to take them in reverse—which is to say, to purchase the works he tears apart and reject the majority of those he praises." Mr. F. was Élie Catherine Fréron (1719-1776), a contributor to the Desfontaines periodical cited above and publisher of the *Année Littéraire*, of which Listonai speaks scathingly elsewhere; he was the most vociferous enemy of the Enlightenment *philosophes*; like Desfontaines he was particularly aggressive in attacking Voltaire, who naturally replied in kind, lampooning him in several works. It appears to be Fréron who coined the term *roman scientifique*, applying it to the theory of gravity.

[133] Author: "It has been learned since this ruling that the periodical had been sagely confined to enlightened criticism full of intelligence, as distant by character from insipidity as from bitterness in its judgments, designed to give that work all the luster of which it is susceptible, and which will doubtless suppress the knick-knacks that disfigured it."

Two other newspapers of an excessively similar contexture were combined into one, and several were entirely suppressed.

The tribunal of taste, the depository of the glory of the Nation, was careful to ensure that no work appeared capable of tarnishing it. To obviate from the start the inconveniences of the vanity of writing, young men gripped by that desire had to pass an examination on all sorts of subjects, and the genre of writing for which they were judges appropriate was prescribed to them. One who had a penchant for writing history was restricted to composing novels, another to knitting socks instead of buskins,[134] and another, whose preformation had inclined him to write in slack, bombastic and obscure verse, constrained to put dramas into clear prose. Another, who projected and epic poem, was limited to vaudeville, and a great number were condemned to eternal silence. Everyone, placed in his sphere, thus treated successfully material that he would not have chosen, whereas he would have failed in those to which be brought more inclination than talent.

With regard to certain genres in the sciences and the arts, however, which had been thoroughly sounded, and in which, all possible calculations having been extracted, nothing remained to do for the mind and the imagination, it was only permitted to extract, carefully and tastefully, maxims and principal percepts. Thus, immense volumes, the majority of which were repeated under different names, had been recast as very brief compilations.

These abridgements were known as the elixir, or the quintessence, of the principles and rules of a science or an art.

And, as it is insane to invest intelligence or seek to invent with respect to exhausted materials, one is limited there

---

[134] In spite of having his tribunal of taste ban other people's wordplay, the author was not about to give up on it entirely, but the long-established metaphorical usage that equated the French *brodequin* [sock] with comedy and *cothurne* [buskin] with tragedy does not translate into English.

to knowing the enlightenment of others, and to exercise one's intelligence and talents on subjects that have not yet been treated, or have not attained the level of perfection. So one no longer sees presses groaning under the weight of so many poetic plays, histories of philosophy, discourses on poetry, mythology, the elements of sciences, etc.

As it is rare for an athlete, in the heat of combat, to be able to judge the moment when his strength begins to run out, the tribunal of taste imposed silence on an author when age began to enervate his genius, in order to preserve him, in spite of himself, with all his glory.[135]

For the same reason, the printing was not permitted of plays that owed their success in the theater entirely to the talent of the actors.

The sciences having become too extensive, with regard to the multiplicity of discoveries that had been made in the course of the centuries and especially in the recent revolution, universal knowledge was not require of any man, especially in history, physics and chronology. A man of letters was one who, with a smattering of all human knowledge, was profound in the part that he cultivated for preference, with a reliable taste and always guided by the philosophical spirit.

By virtue of the taste for healthy criticism, universally spread, everyone contributed to animate nascent talents instead of discouraging them by excessively bitter censure or insipid mockery. Criticism, welcomed as mild and useful instruction, directed the young, who received it with less chagrin than gratitude.

Anyone who wanted to embark on a dramatic career had to furnish three plays within a limited period. The failure of a

---

[135] Author: "...*neque semper arcum tendit Apollo.* Horace, Book II, Ode X. ...*tenet insanabile multos scribendi cacoethes et agro in corde senescit.* Juvenal, Satire VII, line 51." [Nor does Apollo always keep his bow drawn. (Horace); An incurable itch for scribbling affects many, and grows old in their sick hearts. (Juvenal)]

first tragedy, in which veritable beauties were found, earned the author a pension, half of which was withdrawn if the second had no success. He lost the other half if the third failed, after which he was forbidden to work for the theater again.

The pension was doubled for comedies of character in five acts and quadrupled for operas, each by reason of the difficulty of success.

Under the protection of enlightened Maecenases, sheltered from impassioned criticism, it did not take long for geniuses full of a noble ardor to reach the summit of Parnassus; those weak at their dawn, whom bitter censure might have stifled, eclipsed their rivals in their noon.

It was by such means that competition and the love of glory, which did not exclude personal interest, extended the career of talents, that taste was purified, and the Nation procured pleasures as well as collecting immortal laurels.

Chapter VIII
The Customs, Practices and Opinions of the Selenites

The philosophical mind, in extending careers in the Science and the Arts, had brought about a fortunate change in mores, which influenced all estates, conditions and societies.

A taste for agriculture and commerce, too long neglected and even scorned, had gripped all minds. The honors accorded by the Sovereign to all those who distinguished themselves in those two professions, which form the basis of the felicity of an Empire and the two columns on which the political edifice rests, had annihilated the fatal prejudice that had kept them subjugated in shameful obscurity. Far from blushing, people gloried in contributing, by such praiseworthy means, to the welfare of the Fatherland.

Humanity had become a virtue natural to all highly-placed individuals. Respect for and submission to the orders of the Prince, the image of Sovereign Intelligence on earth, was so profoundly engraved in all hearts that the life of Monarchs as secure against the deadliest accidents. They went abroad without guards and without the apparatus that, in its origins, testifies less to the grandeur as to mistrust of those who govern. The love of subjects for the father of the homeland had destroyed the seeds of civil war.

Duels, whose fury had only been diminished by the most rigorous decrees, became entirely extinct with the aid of the light of philosophy; it was generally recognized that a subject should only employ his arms in the service of his Prince and his Fatherland, and leave to the Law the care of avenging insults and injuries.

The frightful Tribunals originally established to conserve the purity of mores and religion, not to tyrannize thought, reason and humanity, having become purely political, were sagely restricted solely to punishing scandal, in accordance with the spirit of their first institution.

The chimerical power of prohibitions extended over States and Sovereigns who only owed their temporal power to the Supreme Being; that odious and tyrannical right, which, sustained by superstition, had shaken Monarchies and caused the shedding of rivers of blood, was no longer regarded with anything but horror and scorn by subjects irrevocable linked to their Prince by an oath of fidelity, and attached to their common father by a sentiment of love and gratitude.

The young no longer made a trophy of attacking and maltreating those whom the Minister established for their own defense and public safety.

Philosophical thinking had necessarily rendered the Nation more serious, but without it losing the amiable gaiety that is not incompatible with reason. Thus, rendezvous in gambling houses and taverns had been abandoned, quite naturally; lewd songs, equivocal conversation, pungency, wordplay, insipid compliments and the poetic and the burlesque had been banished from the table.

The vigilance and attention of the Government in procuring public safety, comfort, ease and the free exercise of industry was recognized throughout the Empire.

All the major roads were bordered with doubt rows of useful trees, and the sea coast planted with woods appropriate to the construction of ships and edifices.

Commerce had been considerably augmented, and the abundance it procured throughout the Empire enhanced by multiplying the canals connecting the great rivers, and large ironclad roads, solidly constructed and carefully maintained. At every mile, one found a quadrangular pyramid, each angle of which corresponded to one of the four cardinal winds, with inscriptions engraved in the bronze that indicated the routes and marked the exact distances from one place to another and the relationship to the Capital to the nearest ten miles. There was a clock on the apex of the pyramid which only had to be wound twice a year, and one found stone bridges wherever necessity required one.

To maintain an exact communication and facilitate traveling throughout the extent of the Realm, comfortable carriages and diligences had been established at State expense on all the major roads, which served initially to carry mail, and in which everyone could purchase seats at a moderate price and go to the extremes of the Empire, or for shorter distances at a proportionate fee.

The cares of the Government had long provided for all the needs of travelers, but the laws of hospitality, which the archives only find in hearts, and whose beneficence had returned to common practice, had naturally destroyed those mercenary refuges stabled by interest in cities, which disputed enviously the privilege of entertaining guests. Great and wealthy individuals had founded hospices open gratuitously in remote or solitary places, in which Nature had not provided soil appropriate to the settlement of inhabitants.

The greatest advantage procured by the art of hydraulics, which the Selenites possessed to a superior degree, is that all the regions were transected by canals more elevated than cultivated land and sustained by dykes. Those canals communicated with rivers that kept them filled with water, which was distributed to the land in accordance with need. By that means, pasturage was always abundant and there was never any famine caused by drought.

To encourage talents and virtues useful to the State, statues, columns and pyramids were erected to all those who distinguished themselves in the military, high employments or public responsibilities, but people were content to honor the memory of good men at their death by funeral orations, for the instruction of others. Monuments reserved for glory and striking actions, to stimulate emulation and contribute to the public good had been displaced in favor of simple civil virtues, which were honored in silence and only caused admiration in a corrupt century. That would have been to praise a man for not committing crimes. The greatest proof of widespread depravity is the decoration with the name of virtue of that which is merely the accomplishment of one's duties.

In Generals and Ministers, incapacities or faults due to inexperience were excused, and, far from being severely punished, were regarded as instructive lessons for the future.

A masterpiece in the Arts or a useful discovery in the Sciences was never without recompense; it was often accompanied by crowns and other glorious distinctions, more flattering for superior geniuses than the rewards themselves.

That authors of satires and defamatory lampoons, however, were dishonored and rigorously punished as murderers and poisoners, all the more dangerous because their profession is more enveloped with darkness.

They were prizes founded by the academies for poetry, physics and eloquence, because people need those relaxations, which always produce public benefits in well-made souls, but the most considerable were destined for research and discoveries useful to the State—which is to say, to the cultivator who secured the most abundant harvest, for the artisan who took industry furthest, for the artist who invented the simplest machine, for the entrepreneur of a manufacture, for the author of a new branch of commerce. The mechanical arts were considered the equals of the liberal arts, because men occupied in making us fortunate were esteemed as much, if not more so, than men who work to make us think that we are.

One practice that merited imitation by all sane peoples is that every ten years, a number of chosen subjects were sent to travel in foreign lands, in order to collect there anything that was good and useful to the State and public welfare. These men had to be more than fifty years old, clear-minded and ornamented with knowledge, especially of the laws of their country. With good eyes, one can always see in voyages things that others do not see, or see poorly—which comes to the same thing.

These philosophical bees, who leave themselves, so to speak, in their own country and only take their intelligence abroad,[136] always come back laden with a precious booty of ideas and useful discoveries appropriate to cure the mind of the host of nationalistic prejudices that custom, to the shame of reason, consecrates and perpetuates, all the more so as habit prevents them from being perceived.

A practice perhaps even more important, with regard to the consequences that could result from it, is that the reigning Prince, to capture the affection and attachment of his people more fully, had made a law requiring him only to take a spouse among his own subjects. According to him, beauty, combined with merit and virtue, was required, as well as birthplace, in order to reach the throne that illustrates all who approach it. That politics wards off the inconveniences that arise from foreign alliances in exposing peoples to the risk of passing one day under foreign domination or undertaking wars in which the State would not take part if the honor of a Nation did not require it to embrace the quarrel of a Prince to whom it was linked by the imaginary ties of blood—ties often deadly, always demanded and broken with the same facility by individual interests.

The views of all the Princes being turned toward commerce and the population, the canals and highways facilitating the transportation of merchandise and foodstuffs had, as I have said, been multiplied by the Selenites. The goods in question were subjected to low taxes, which did not excite fraud, from which those of primary necessity were exempted; only objects of luxury were surcharged, and industry, in complete liberty, obtained exemptions but never exclusive privileges.

Exports were exempt from all duties; those on imports were fairly high, but were only paid on entry to the Realm. The multiplicity of excise duties between provinces is odious and unjust between subjects obedient to the same sovereign, and an obstruction to the circulation of internal commerce, whose liberty produces abundance in all the parts of the State.

---

[136] Author: "...*Mens sine pondere ludit*. Petronius. Satyricon chapter IV." [The unburdened mind is playful.]

Credit being the soul of commerce, the engine of fortunes and the resources of the State, laws had sagely provided everything that could maintain confidence and ensure the strength of creditors. Usurers were punished severely but lending was not suppressed; on the contrary, contracts in which the strength of the borrower was better than that of the lender were regarded as an open door to industry.

It had been attempted so many times, ineffectively, to favor population growth by granting exemptions to those who contributed a large number of citizens to the State, that it was decided to do away with them entirely; but by means of singular protections and effective aid accorded to agriculture, laborers had been naturally stimulated to regard a large number of children as a real asset and necessary to cultivation. There were only privileges attached to the status of women who were breast-feeding their children.

No means had been neglected that might increase the population. Among others, there was one day of the year indicated for marriages, when all the young people of both sexes to be married assembled in a place designated for the ceremony. The bachelors gave an account of their wealth, and were the divided into three classes: the rich, those of mediocre fortune and the poor. Three classes were similarly formed of the young women: the beautiful, the passable and the ugly. The beautiful were allocated to the rich, who paid a certain sum in order to have them, the less beautiful to the less rich, who paid nothing, and the ugly to the poor, to whom the sums paid by the rich were distributed. That custom procured a large number of marriages that would otherwise not have taken place; but as the poor were always in greater quantity than the rich, the Government subsidized in various ways the establishment of those who remained unmarried for lack of the means of subsistence.[137]

---

[137] Author: "That custom subsists, it is said, among the Chinese."

Firstly, when events demanded public rejoicing, such as the marriages of Princes or the reestablishment of their health, instead of those transient feasts that require excessive expenditure and the memory of which vanishes with the pleasure they provide, those expenses were diverted into the establishment of young poor people, whose marriages were celebrated with considerable pomp, which provided diversions all the more agreeable because the wellbeing of the people was their object and the wealth of the State their fruit. The Nobility and rich individuals imitated the example of the Court. The capture of an important place, however, a complete victory obtained at the price of the blood of faithful citizens, deadly effects of an unfortunate necessity, only ever occasioned dolorous rejoicing, indecently mingling laughter and tears; they were postponed until the peace, a time in which all hearts could participate in public delight.

Secondly, in order to favor marriages and population growth—which, for reasons whose revelation decorum does not permit, was not always a consequence thereof—the State took charge of the fate and education of children exceeding the number of those that individuals had the means to nourish and raise, and had them adopted by well-to-do people who lacked posterity.

Thirdly and lastly, the excessive sums that ostentation and vanity had previously sacrificed to the pomp of funerals were employed for similar measures, by means of a tax proportionate to the wealth of people who died. They were content to cremate the dead modestly and thus to return bodies to the earth with the same simplicity that it had produced them, and the Government, which until then had taken charge of the funerals of celebrated men who had died without fortunes, only occupied itself henceforth with the establishment of their children.

These various means of favoring marriages, combined with the interests of the population, had inspired such an aversion to celibacy, the gulf that, in some States, buries future families at the expense of the prosperity of the State, that those

147

who died celibate at a certain age were stigmatized, and solemnly married after their death in reparation of the outrage they had committed against Nature and society during their lifetime.[138]

To ward off the deadly effects produced in the conjugal couple by disgust, inconstancy, the pretended incompatibility of humors, and to avoid the indecency of divorce, no surer means had been found than to authorize it.[139] A man born to liberty persists constantly in an estate in which he is not constrained to remain; the faculty of breaking an engagement is often sufficient to deflect the very desire. The pleasures of amity, natural between the two sexes, balance out the difficulties that are inseparable therefrom, and lead to respective considerations that prevent discord and maintain the union. That law, which caused some disorder at the time of its initiation, was recognized so wise consequently that there was no example of anyone claiming the privilege.[140]

Many other accessory means had also contributed indirectly to population.

Among other regulations, investment in individual life annuities was prohibited, under very heavy penalties, the least

---

[138] Author: "Lycurgus notes the infamy of celibates. There was even a particular solemnity in Lacedaemon in which women led them, stark naked, to the feet of altars and insisted that they make honorable amends to Nature, which they accompanied with a severe correction."

[139] Author: "*Sic visum Veneri: cui placet impares formas, atque animos sub juga ahenea saevo mittere cum joco.* Horace. Book I. Ode XXXIII. [Such is the will of Venus, whose pleasure it is in cruel sport to subject ill-matched persons and tempers to her yoke.]

[140] Author: "Impotence and adultery can be the only causes of divorce today. It is quite ridiculous, Milton says on this subject, that more regard is given to the most sensual and coarse aspects of marriage than to the incompatibility of humors and minds, from which so many disorders are born."

of which was deprivation of income to the profit of the treasury. That strange manner of placing funds is harmful to commerce, to the cultivation of lands and circulation, and appropriate to increase cupidity, maintain idleness, slow down industry and, at length, to destroy population. The State only made use of those mortal resources regretfully. In cases of extreme need, the only people permitted to invest their wealth in that manner were those who, deprived of talent of health, had not sufficient to live in accordance with their status, or who, without direct posterity, and having no relative in indigence, wanted to procure more ease. As only living for oneself is an unnatural sentiment, which, from the Prince to the least of his subjects, would soon annihilate any harmonious system within the State, one could not, in the capacity of usufructuary, engage one's patrimony, which belongs by right to those who survive us. By virtue of that sage regulation, one no longer saw, as among us, to the shame of all human sentiment, fathers responsible for families who have lived in luxury, leaving to their children only the inheritance of contracts without incomes and movable property often absorbed by debts.

The right of primogeniture had only been retained with regard to the Sovereign, because welfare and security, which depends on the power of the Prince, would have exposed the subjects to the risk of the horrors of civil wars by virtue of the division of the Royal Domains. It had been wisely abolished among the subjects as an unjust prerogative opposed to the law of Nature, which does not disinherit anyone; because it is a source of jealousies, murmurs; because, contrary to population, it harms the establishment of several individuals by the elevation of one alone to the prejudice of the others; and because it constrains those to whom birth gives an equal right to paternal succession to remain limbs useless to the support of the Republic.

As a consequence of this principle, it was forbidden to make a will to the prejudice of descendant and ascendant lines of the first degree, except to use the right of substitution, an act of prudence, in the case that the bad conduct of an heir is

149

recognized, but unjust and tyrannical when it extends across generations that do not yet exist. One could only leave aliments to those who consumed their youth in someone's service, and make a few modest legacies in the form of marks of amity or gratitude from one's acquisitions or savings; patrimonial property passed by right to those to whom it ought to belong by order of succession. Legacies are not always the price of service; they are often the recompense for a lax servitude, and almost always monuments to vanity and shameful marks of the weakness of the testator.

In times of war, commerce was free between the belligerent Nations. They were content, following the narrow regulations of the unfortunate law of war, only to attack soldiers; they did not touch ships' crews. In sieges, they only attached fortifications. The ravaging of lands and the burning of buildings were regarded with horror. That was to render an evil judged necessary as least catastrophic as possible. If wars lasted a long time, because the resources to sustain them were greater, they were also less ruinous and less disastrous for the peoples. But the custom widely established between Princes of commencing where they would eventually finish—which is to say, of preceding hostilities with conferences—prevented many wars and rendered those which were inevitable less frequent.

Princes respected one another in declarations of war. The declarations, always succinct, simply contained an exposition of the rights, grievances and motives for taking up arms, one which basis, without expanding into reproaches and insults unworthy of Majesty, the Sovereigns demanded, on the justice of their claims, the protection of the Supreme Being.

The frightful maxim of certain policed Nations, which admits the right of people to put a price on an enemy's head, revolts humanity. It is only tolerable against a rebel subject or a traitor to the fatherland, monsters already condemned by the law, and in which cases reason and the interest of public safety permit deliverance by the most violent means.

Annalists and Journalists, wisely contained within the limits of respect owed to all Sovereigns, were not free in times of war to attack their sacred person by means of indecent articles, odious imputations and atrocious calumnies[141] that in calmer times would lead to shame and repentance. Insults add nothing to rights, invectives degrade them. The soldier, animated solely by love of the fatherland and the defense of its Master, was not excited to a brutal and obstinate fury, but only to sustain, by valor, the justice of the common cause: a motive more powerful than vengeance to carry out glorious actions against Nations enemy for the moment, with whom amity would be sought as soon as the respective rights were clarified and everyone would be constrained to respect the peace. May Heaven ensure that the wise principles of the Selenites will one day illuminate the hearts of all the Peoples of the Earth.

To accustom the people only to make rumors public with a certain degree of credence, a gazette was distributed at the end of every year of all the false news that had been spread during the interim.

A principle of justice and equity had given rise to the establishment of a proportionate taxation, which, in times of peace formed the greater part of public revenue. Every possessor of real estate was subject to it, without any privilege being able to exempt him; only industry was respected, all the more justly because it augmented its produce indirectly. In times of war, a tax of a fiftieth, a twentieth or a tenth was imposed on the net product of real estate, in accordance with the needs of the State. The collection of these impositions was made with the greatest economy. They were the most equitable, the most just and the least subject to constraint, when the proprietor has the choice of paying in cash or kind. A proportionate division does not trample anyone and does not excite murmurs; the true citizen ought only to consider himself more fortunate than

---

[141] Author: "Between individuals, the calumniator was condemned to the same punishment to which the accused would have been subject had the accusation been found to be true."

another to the extent that he can contribute more than him to the necessities of the State.

When needs increased, Lotteries were held, in which free will collaborated with a view to its own interest. Finally, in cases of urgent necessity, borrowing at interest was the last resort, because, although it was the charge least onerous for the State, it was ruinous for families. The odious monopoly on the diminution or augmentation of cash money, which had shored up tottering finances for such a long time and dealt mortal blows to commerce, had fortunately been proscribed, abandoned forever.

The establishment of a common system of weights and measures, applied to currency, which had been blocked by a thousand obstacles for centuries, was finally achieved when, after having balanced the inconveniences against the advantages, the necessity was felt of sacrificing individual interests to the general interest.

Moneyed metals only being the sign of wealth, they no longer had legal or ideal value. Payment and receipts were made on the basis of weight, which established real exchange values, which naturally followed those of foodstuffs, since the abundance of certain foodstuffs relative to the hunger of others necessarily demanded a greater weight of materials in one time than another; coins, in consequence, had no arbitrary value, but only an imprint designating their weight. The representative wealth of a State could only be augmented or diminished by the abundance or rarity of staple foods. A prince is only richer in semblance in having an income of a hundred millions at fifty livres per marc than in having two millions at twenty sols. If that manner of evaluating metals had been established in all times, one would be enlightened on many points of history obscured by calculations that have no point of reference. One would doubtless find a parity between the moderate sums with which innumerable armies were maintained and the enormous expenses made in our day to raise small ones; and political economics, which is always occupied in searching in the past for the causes of the vices of a present

152

government, would be freed from many chimeras based on false comparisons.

They were not stupidly prejudiced against what are called elsewhere "proposers of projects."

Projects

Every limited mind imagines that everything is perfected: sciences, arts, the language, etc., although the degree of excellence is only found in the works of Nature. That opinion spreads a kind of scorn for theoretical minds.[142]

The philosopher sees, everywhere, more things to do than have been done. If he is at the head of the government, he welcomes generously all the projects that are presented to him, and takes advantage of those that are good, relative to circumstances, in which he finds what can be found. One such project caused the splendor of a State, or saved it from ruination, which was so simple that one could not imagine how it had not occurred simultaneously to all minds capable of thinking. The motive force that gives rise to them is, in truth, often the effect of chance, sometimes a dream, commonly an effort of indigence, rarely that of glory, always that of an individual interest that flows back to the general, because there are fewer generous souls than mercenary ones—but whatever the source of a good action might be, it is always estimable when the State and humankind obtain benefits from it.

In the conviction that there few projects, however singular and however subject to inconveniences they may seem,[143]

---

[142] Author: "It is important to distinguish *l'esprit systématique* [a theoretical mind] from *l'esprit de système* [a hidebound mind, or pig-headedness]"

[143] Author: "A man who was ill in hospital in Madrid proposed to the King of Spain that Lent be converted into an obligatory fast, on bread and water for one day per week, to which all subjects ought to be subjected between the ages of 14 and 60, and that all the expenditure that would have been made that

that do not contain a few principles of utility, they were generally received generously. An idiot sometimes offers good advice.

Their authors were allowed to defend them against objections, the inventor of a welcome project was always recompensed in proportion to the utility that it procured. Small
acknowledgements were even accorded to the authors of projects that were good in their essence but unformed, or unsus-
ceptible to execution at the time, but promised objects of utility in circumstances to come.

Thus were crowned the merits of invention, which is not
always the gift of great men at the head of affairs, in whom
wisdom, prudence and the love of public welfare are qualities
preferable to creative genius. How many great Princes, and
renowned Ministers, only endowed with weak judgment and
exquisite tact, have enjoyed the most striking reputation without ever having imagined anything?

The offices of Ministers are filed with projects presented
all the time, which, covered in dust, languish along with the
memories of their authors in shameful forgetfulness. What a
seed-bed a Statesman and zealous citizen might find who sacrificed a few minutes each day to reviewing them! What an
ample crop might be within arm's reach, for the reform of

---

day be evaluated in cash, which, could, by setting a tax-rate
for contributors, amounting to less than half a real per head, or
five French sols, raise for three million individuals 750,000
reals per week, less parish expenses, and that the produce
could be used for the relief of the poor and the maintenance of
hospitals for the sick and the invalid.

"That fast, offered to Heaven, would have been salutary for
the health of the soul and the body, by virtue of the good effect of dieting, would have produced a considerable sum destined for useful purposes, raised in an almost imperceptible
manner, but there is so little appetite for good things that the
proposal only appeared ridiculous and provoked nothing but
laughter."

abuses, the glory of his Sovereign and the prosperity of his State!

When one recalls that one owes to fortunate hazard the most sublime discoveries, and observations of genius distant from affairs or dead in obscurity, and that advantages obtained from them, perhaps one ought not to neglect any useful projects, no matter what hand offers them.[144]

---

[144] Author: "The greatest events in political theory, and the most celebrated discoveries in physics, mechanics, etc., are due, for the most part, to chance, or—which ought to humiliate the human mind—have only had for causes the smallest objects, which became great by virtue of meditation and the philosophical mind.

"Galileo and all philosophers before him attributed the ascension of water in pumps to the imaginary horror of Nature for the void. On the observation, which he made during maneuvers in the gardens of Florence, that the water stopped at a height of thirty feet, he investigated the cause of the phenomenon and discovered the weight of the air, which he had not suspected. He learned that a column of air had a weight equal to the water, which rises in a tube of any diameter. Pascal, by his experiments at the Puy de Dôme, and Torricelli subsequently demonstrated the truth of it. What a host of discoveries that principle has since produced!

"An apple fallen from a tree snatched Newton from his reverie. He meditated on the cause of that fall in a line perpendicular to the center of the Earth; he judged that anybody abandoned to itself might be attracted and driven toward the earth. A thousand sublime calculations confirming his opinion, he drew consequences from it that became the materials with which he fabricated his sublime—I would willingly say the true—theory of the Universe; Nature surprised becomes his confidant; he perceives the orbit of the earth without measuring it; the cause of gravitation is no longer a mystery, that of the tides follows; he knows the orbits of the planets, their density, their distance, their respective force; he calculates the return of comets almost as easily, and eclipses; by lifting a part of the veil with which Nature covers herself he encourages posterity to rip it away entirely."

"The properties of the magnet only offered, for centuries, subjects of amusement; a Genius composed the compass. With that instrument, the sea was immediately traversed with more boldness and security, no longer hugging the coast, and its bounds prodigiously extended. Christopher Columbus, with the aid of that instrument, judged on the shape of the earth that one could find a route to China between the tropics; he searched for it and discovered the Lucayan islands, for which he was not searching; he discovered America, for the good or ill fortune of Europe.

"Spectacles were invented several centuries ago to aid the weakness of sight without anyone imagining the effect of the multiplication of lenses. The children of a lens-grinder of Middelburg, playing with his lenses, sometimes perceived far away, sometimes close at hand; the rumor spread as a pleasing fact; people laughed at it, women amused themselves with it, the Great found diversion in it. The news reaches Galileo three hundred leagues away and strikes him as a philosopher; he draws consequences from it and comes after several experiments to form telescopes, with which he sees the phases of Mars, enriches Jupiter with satellites and confirms the theory of Copernicus. The knowledge of objects too distant to see leads to research on those that escape sight by their enormous smallness and gives birth to the microscope. The universe is enlarged, veritable new worlds are discovered. Navigation is improved, occult qualities disappear and Atheism is reduced to dust.

"Everyone knows that when sailors cook fish on the sea shore a violent fire melts morsels of niter and manifests the nature of glass, of which industry and philosophical genius compose, many centuries later, spectacles, mirrors, telescopes, microscopes, etc.

The sage measures taken by the government to accustom beggars to work, without violence, the help accorded to the cultivator, the shame and scorn attached to idleness had reduced the number of the unfortunate and the crimes to which

---

"That the invention of the leaven that causes dough to ferment, gives it more lightness and renders it easier to digest, was due to the economy of a woman who, wanting to make use of the remains of old dough, mixed it with new, from which resulted by chance, contrary to her expectation, that which the chemist had not yet invented.

"That it was a goat that gave the idea of pruning vines; that animal having browed a stock, it was noticed that it gave more fruit than usual the following year.

"That painting owes its birth to the departure of a regretted lover, whose profile was drawn on the wall by his mistress to conserve a few features during his absence.

"That the invention of printing is owed to a soldier, and that of gunpowder to a monk.

"That an Indian, wanting to climb a rock covered in trees and bushes, attached himself to a branch emerging from a fissure in the rock; when the branch was torn away the Indian immediately saw something shiny, which was the origin of the rich mine of Potosi.

"That a laborer wanting to surround his land with a fence, to render it more solid, encased the inferior extremity of the stakes in trunks of buried ivy; those stakes having fused with the ivy were only one body and became tall trees, which gave birth to the admirable invention of the graft.

"Who would believe that the discovery of metals was due to fires and earthquakes, that by the conflagration of a forest and the violence of the fire, which melted the metal, iron was discovered by the ancients on Mount Ida, and that it was to the eruptions of volcanoes that we owe the invention of metallurgy?"

indigence and idleness give rise. The sagacity that prevents evils is far superior to the art that finds remedies for them.

The number of invalids in the hospitals diminished significantly because the maladies to which idleness, slovenliness and dissolute conduct give rise were eclipsed by work and exercise.

In the persuasion that poverty is a vice and that only the idle lack bread, the race of professional beggars, whom nothing could stimulate to work, had been extirpated by imprisoning them in places where they were forced to labor in accordance with their strength or aptitude, and where they could only enjoy the few privileges procured by their assiduity and their industry.

Except for Regicide, parricide and crime of high treason, the death penalty was not pronounced on anyone; it was believed that malefactors could be punished more sensibly by employing them in forced labor, on land, in galleys, in mines and other burdensome tasks useful to the society whose order and security they had troubled. Scoundrels are more rigorously punished by the loss of their liberty and subjection to work than by an accident that terminates their pains by a leap from life to death.[145]

Although the country was full of mines abundant in all kinds of metals, only criminals were employed therein; people disdained to work there by repugnance and had a horror of sacrificing subjects more usefully occupied in the cultivation of the land in order to extract metals absolutely useless in themselves, which are merely the symbols of wealth and the esteem of which diminishes with their abundance; since, having only an ideal value and the price of foodstuffs rises by reason of their mass, their quantity only produces an imaginary opulence for the State, and the work of the mines a real loss of citizens.

---

[145] Author: "*What determines that the death of a criminal is licit in a society is that the law that condemns him has been made in his favor*. Montesquieu."

158

On the principle of Natural Law that for the maintenance of order and public safety no crime ought to remain unpunished, all sanctuaries in which a malefactor could escape the severity of the law had been closed.[146] None was granted in foreign States to those guilty of theft, murder, abduction, rape, poisoning, lèse-Majesté, etc. Refuge was only given to those who had been discovered in unfortunate encounters or implicated in deplorable affairs in which premeditated design had played no part. Criminals were returned to the requisition of Princes who had the right to have them punished. That reciprocal convention prevented many disorders and misdeeds previously multiplied by the hope of impunity.

The Question, that torment which is an affair of temperament, which a vigorous scoundrel can endure or an innocent person of delicate constitution succumb,[147] that torture justly considered as an act of inhumanity, had been abolished and reserved for criminals already condemned from whom it was desired to extract a confession of their accomplices. So many precipitate judgments, and rehabilitated memoirs had given the lie to the certainty of discovering crimes by such cruel means that it was inconceivable that such a barbaric practice had continued to be admitted long after the primitive centuries. Can a hundred semi-proofs be equivalent to one evident proof? The torment is certain, the crime is not. What is more precious than the blood of a citizen? Ought not probability take its place except in cases where the risk of error is not con-

---

[146] Author: "It was forbidden in Rome to snatch from the altar those who had taken refuge there, but provided that they were not touched, all sorts of stratagems and artifices could be used to make them perish. The mother of Pausanias Lacedaemonius brought the first stone to wall up the shelter in which her son had taken refuge"

[147] Author: "*Etiam innocentes cogit mentiri dolor.* Pubilius Syrus, Mimes, line 191." [Pain forces even innocents to lie.] Cited by Montaigne.

siderable? Is it not better to risk setting twenty guilty men free than to punish an innocent one?

Whatever the origin of slavery was among different peoples, whether the law emerged from a foundation of humanity or cruelty, it is nonetheless contrary to Nature, which causes all men to be born equal. Uniquely founded on force, it degrades humanity; it supposes at the least a harsh and pitiless Master and excessively unhappy subjects. In contrast to Monarchical Government, in that it debases human nature, brutes are made in Despotism. That odious law was soon abolished among the Selenites, gripped with horror for everything bearing the imprint of barbarity and inhumanity.

The Law of Escheat, and those pertaining to debris and shipwreck, etc, so contrary to humanity and hospitality, were rejected and suppressed as vestiges of ancient barbarity.

For fear of debasing the noblest of professions, soldiers were not mistreated; they were only punished by the privation or suspension of their functions and the privileges attached to the honorable title of defender of the fatherland.

The love of liberty is so strongly imprinted in all hearts, and inconstancy so natural to the human condition, that the accidents that result therefrom bear with them a kind of excuse. On that wise consideration, deserters were not rigorously punished, but chastised by prison and the stigma to ignominy until they had repaired their cowardice by some striking action. If they fled armed, they were treated as thieves, and anyone recaptured, after having gone over to the enemy camp, was punished as a traitor to the fatherland.

The innocent children of a guilty party were not punished either in their person, as veritable criminals, nor in the wealth that they obtained from patrimony, their labor or their industry; they were merely declared unable to succeed to wealth and advantages that their father had acquired by entitlement of grace, such as pensions, honors, dignities, nobility, privilege, etc.

Opprobrium and punishments of infamy did not rebound unjustly on the family of a man who had been punished.

Crimes are personal, as are shameful actions. On the contrary, the relatives of the criminal were congratulated on being delivered of a corrupt member, a subject unworthy of society.

The patriotic concerns of the Government in maintaining fortunes against the dangerous and deadly abuses of gambling had given rise to laws that were executed without remission against those who abandoned themselves to games of chance.

Gaming

Gambling is commonly a war between friends, from which compassion is banished, in which people have no scruple about despoiling one another reciprocally. It is difficult for good faith to reign when interest commands and trickery is permitted, when science or conspiracy give some advantages over others that expel equity.

The gambling of commerce and society were tolerated as relaxations, but persons of delicate probity abstained from them because they consumed precious time better employed in useful or pleasant occupations and are, as has been said, a perpetual traffic in subtlety and perfidy, in which one profits from the ignorance or distraction of others. larceny, of which one ordinarily has no conscience, and corruption being such that one goes so far as to esteem the skill of someone who plays what one calls "a good game."

Strictly speaking, it is only games of exercise, spurred by slight interest, that can merit universal approval. Games of chance, in which science and skill play no part, or equality of strength is established between the players, supposing the necessity of games, would be the most legitimate if they were not also the most dangerous.

As a diversion, gambling is perhaps permissible; as an occupation, it is shameful; as commerce, it is odious and despicable. It has sometimes been the source of the most abominable actions; it has occasioned prostitution, the ruin of families, the loss of honor, theft, murder and suicide; but as the maxims of Government tended les to punish than to correct by mild and sensible means, those who were convicted of having delivered themselves to games of chance were sentenced for a first offense to render the sums that they had won to the profit of hospitals for the insane and imbeciles. In cases of recidivism, they were defamed, as well as having to pay gambling debts in full.[148]

There were among the Selenites a considerable number of practices and customs that, although not all being of absolute importance, were nonetheless respectable. I shall transcribe here those that are traced in my memory.

Etiquette

The Etiquette established in the Courts, and, following their example, in the cities, the sumptuous tyrant that exercises is empire even in the lowest conditions, which presides on Councils, enters into Treaties, Negotiations and Contracts, which substitutes for the respect that pride secretly refuses to one's superiors and harshly demands of one's inferiors—that vain ceremonial, in sum—had been banished from all estates as an obstacle to the expedition and success of business and a hindrance to the concord and agreeability of society.

Respect no longer being considered as anything but the prize of merit, and founded on the esteem that is stolen from us when respect for the position is no longer distinguished from respect for the person, Etiquette no longer appeared to be anything but an inconvenience, a shadow of natural homage owing nothing to reflection.

Etiquette is the slavery of Princes; they command everything else, but they obey Etiquette. The Doge of Venice purchases the shadow of sovereign power at the price of his liber-

---

[148] Author: "Gambling was unknown among the ancients, even in Greece. Might it be because they had little communication with women?"

ty, and on condition that his children and brothers are excluded from the principal responsibilities of the State. He cannot open any letter, make or receive any individual visit, except with the permission of the Senate and in the presence of honorable spies who never quit him. Can one not say that, a prisoner in Venice, and even in his own palace, his dignity as Doge being for life, he does not emerge from captivity until the end of his days?

The King of Loango in Africa, it is said, takes his meals in two different houses; he eats in one and drinks in the other. Can one imagine the reason for such a bizarre subjection?

With what compassionate eyes one ought to envisage that enslavement to strange etiquettes! In observing them too exactly, Princes have been allowed to perish while hunting or at sea, in the midst of people appointed to serve them, because only an officer had the right to help them, and none was present.

Can one learn without shivering with horror that a zealous subject was condemned to death because, in order to save her from a conflagration, he had exposed a Queen in her nightgown?[149]

The most singular of all the Etiquettes of fabulous times is that men were admitted to the beds of Goddesses, but could not eat with them.

We regard with pity certain practices of peoples distant from us; would they not render the same, with interest, if they knew about the thousand puerilities to which we are scrupulously attached?—among others, the election of those domestic Kings whose domain is limited by the circumference of a table and have no other authority than of conferring charges without exercise and ordering toasts. Would they not take us for lunatics if they learned that a splendid and delicate table is served to Great Men for some time after their death, and that

---

[149] Author: "Spanish Etiquette holds as a maxim that austere decency is part of public mores, and that is why the Court is feverishly attached to it."

they are continually interrogated as to the state of their health. What would they think of those pious promenades, in which mitered holy men are surrounded by masquerades and indecent flagellations? Finally, what would they say about the festivals of fools, of which vestiges still remain, and of which mere accounts give rise to horror? Would they judge them as favorably as we do, in the sublimity of our enlightenment?

The taste for sciences and true philosophy, combined with the study of Nature, had produced this good among the Selenites that they had no more Atheists. They were too enlightened to be Atheists at heart, and feared scorn and ridicule too much to be Atheists by intellect.

It was not permitted to employ indifferently such terms as lot, destiny, hazard, fatality, etc. Every oath that was not authorized by the judge was a blasphemy or a profanation.

On the principle that there is, in morality, only God who can serve as a model for humans, and in art only Nature, no attempt was made in paintings to represent the Eternal Father, Angels and all celestial substances in corporeal forms. The Deity was supposed behind a cloud from which resplendent rays emerged, a feeble sketch of the light that surrounds the Eternal Being. It would have been an impious extravagance to attribute a human face thereto, to suppose a sex and features altered by time. It was regarded as an absurdity to pretend to offer to the eyes, under material colors, that which cannot be painted. People were wisely content to recognize the Essence, the infinite Bounty and Power of the Supreme Being in everything that exists and manifests grandeur, instead confiding the expression recklessly to the weakness of the brush.

As for the azure vault, the stars and the planets, painters were free to represent them in the forms and colors in which they appear to sight, thus to trace metaphysical beings by means of emblems and attributes, until the imagination found itself blocked, as in the representation of an echo.

Judiciary astrology, the composition of talismans, the occult virtue of numbers, the art of interpreting dreams, the secret of transmutation, were arts and sciences so sovereignly scorned that adepts were sent, straight away, to hospitals of the insane and impostors.

They had suppressed the public displays of rope-dancers, who only procured an insensate, even inhuman pleasure, because it arises less from admiration of dexterity than the peril run by the dancer, the leaper or the acrobat. Combats of ferocious beasts had also been forbidden, which could only familiarize people with the sight of bloodshed.

Court jesters had been banned; only true sages were tolerated there, of a natural joviality, who, with the liberty of speech, acquired the right to instruct without offending with the witty remarks that serious minds do not permit themselves. The number of those Aesops was very small, for it requires a great deal of intelligence and wisdom to play that part and conserve the art of pleasing.

When there was a question of erecting a monument or a public building, everyone was admitted to the competition without distinction, free to furnish plans and ideas. The author of the project selected was recompensed by a medal of great value and publicly crowned. It sometimes happened, to the great astonishment of celebrated artists, that the crown was stolen from them by simple amateurs, to whom they could not refuse their praise.

In order to avoid the deadly effects of seduction, anyone who was convicted of having offered a present to a Minister or a Magistrate was punished as guilty of *lèse-équité*. If the present was accepted the corrupted individual was demoted and subjected to the infamy attached to the corruptor, but no such case had every happened within human memory.

All solicitation was considered as an insult to virtue, a doubt outraging the discernment of the benefactor or the integrity of a judge, and presents as iniquitous instruments of corruption. To express what we understand by the words *grace, favor, benefit* and *protection*, the Selenite language only contained the term *justice*, in which was understood that of *equity*. The most ignorant man of the basest extraction, with talents and virtue, could aspire to the most eminent positions. Hence the laudable competition to succeed, and the useful and equitable employment of so many geniuses who would otherwise, stifled by the prejudice of birth, have been lost to the State. Hence the signal services rendered by the likes of Aesop,[150] Rose, Faber, Jean Bart, Duguay-Trouin, Vauban, Catinat, Ximenes, Peretti and a thousand others.

Only dangerous or furious lunatics were imprisoned. Often, by depriving of liberty those whose minds are deranged, one renders them more furious; by contrast, leaving them free in society to enjoy the advantages of madness contributes to their happiness. In what estate of life does one not sometimes feel envious of a felicity sheltered from evils, which the derangement of reason often reveals to us? To possess, without cares, immense treasures, to govern vast empires without anxiety, to command the entire world without fear of revolt; is not enjoying everything without difficulty, without cares, without disgust, realizing the imagination? What is there more fortunate in sanity, which is similarly the work of opinion? One is only as fortunate or unfortunate as ne believes oneself to be, as long as the delirium does not end.

As drunkenness, in attacking the faculties of the body, enervates those of the soul, drunkards are taken away, no matter what their quality or condition might be; they are released subsequently, after they have been made to drink a beverage that gives them a permanent disgust and aversion for all liq-

---

[150] Author: *"The Athenians once erected a statue to honor Aesop because of his genius, and placed the figure of that Slave on a base of eternal duration, in order to inform everyone that the career of honor is open to all, and that glory is the price of virtue and not of birth.* Phaedrus, Fabulae Aesopii, Book II, in the Epilogue." The others cited in the list of individuals who rose from humble beginnings to glory of a sort include two famous French privateers, two Maréchals de France and a Spanish Inquisitor; "Peretti" might or might not be the Venetian Battista Peretti, but cannot be the 16th-century cardinal of that name.

uors capable of harming health, weakening the brain and deranging reason. That is called returning men to themselves; they are thus cured without perceiving it. It would have been desirable to find as many antipathetic remedies against the vices of society, such as hatred, slander, indiscretion, ingratitude, the abuse of intelligence, etc., but these specifics are only found in the study and practice of sane philosophy, which, unfortunately, few temperaments are disposed to put to use.

That blind passion known as avarice, whose effects are incomprehensible for those not tainted by it, which causes a man to deprive himself of everything in order to lack nothing, to possess less wealth than if he had none, and, always indigent in the bosom of opulence, to mistake for real wealth that which is only the means of acquiring it,[151] to render him a slave to prodigality, forever enriched by his treasures and forever impoverished by his desires, so that he finally savors only possible pleasure; that shameful passion born less from a thirst for wealth, which is cupidity, as from the insensate satisfaction of nourishing himself on the sight of it, had given rise to the establishment of public Guardians who, taking over the administration of the wealth of these imbeciles, forced them to contribute to the good of the State by the enjoyment of the commodities of life. However, to compensate those whose infirmity was more in the eyes than in the heart, they were taken for a walk every day in the Royal Treasury, of which they were accorded visual possession. There, they contemplated at their ease the color, hardness and quantity of those cherished metals, until, recovered from their lethargy or cured of their madness, they consented to live as human beings and citizens.

As for the miserly money-lender, he was punished as an extortionist.

---

[151] Author: "Lucilius makes fun of a certain miser who, by testament, instituted himself as his own heir."

If there are noble faults, as there are excusable ones, prodigality can be placed in the rank of virtues under the name of generosity, as avarice can be covered by that of thrift, but every excess is a vice that a well-policed government has the right to suppress. It is on that principle that the State, as attentive to prevent dissipation as to favor circulation and entertain equilibrium in fortunes, had submitted the prodigal, as well as the miserly,[152] to the inspection of public Guardians, who, in order to extract them from their derangement, caused them to experience for a while the horrors of the situation by which they were inevitably menaced, exposing to their eyes the frightful image of the crimes to which despair leads. Having become sage by means of these striking lessons, in time, the resumed the administration of their wealth, frightened by the evils and reefs to which virtue is exposed when, one finds oneself precipitated from the heights of fortune into the abyss of frightful poverty.

Suicide, considered as an act of weakness rather than of strength of mind, was apparently authorized by the laws, but only after one had obtained permission to deliver oneself from a burden judged to be unbearable, and had passed certain tests, which had gradually extinguished that frenzy and dissipated that delirium, which insensate sages have recklessly called a remedy for the maladies of the soul. The petitioner, after having listed the motives leading him to withdraw from society, was put in the hands of philosophers and physicians, who, by means of mild remedies and solid arguments,[153] freed him

---

[152] Author: "There is no absolute avarice or prodigality; there is no miser who does not have his generosity nor prodigal who does not have his meanness, just as there is no fool devoid of finesse or intelligent man devoid of stupidity; the extremities touch one another."

[153] Author: "...*mentem sanari, corpus ut aegrum, cernimus, et flecti medicina posse videmus*. Lucretius. Book III line 510." [We see the spirit cure itself like a sick body, and reestablish itself with the help of medicine.] Quoted by Montaigne.

from the vapors and illusions that were numbing the animal spirits, and always sent him back covered in shame for having planned, by a reckless act, to abridge the days whose term, which is neither at the disposal nor in the knowledge of the creature, belongs one to the one who determines them.

No witches are burned, to the shame of judgment and reason.[154] It should never have been done anywhere, since, if the accused were truly magicians, they would have eluded torture by the force of their arts, and the judges ought to have feared their resentment, while if they were not, they were punished unjustly; therefore, they only merited being ridiculed for their weakness, or corrected for their trickery.

To avoid disorder and confusion in genealogies, family names were always joined with that of the fief from which it was obtained; the vanity of parvenus was doubtless offended by that, but ranks no longer being confused by the usurpation of an illustrious name grafted on to a plebeian or city-dwelling family, genealogical trees were drawn up without error and the aristocracy enjoyed, without pride or disturbance, the consideration due to noble birth, which added to the merit and virtue of those who sustained its brilliance.

Fathers and children did not have the stupid vanity of treating one another as strangers with the cold and indifferent forms of address "Monsieur" and "Monseigneur," instead of "Father" and "Son," which inspire union and confidence, and enliven between them the tender sentiments of Nature.

When abuses are necessary and one cannot destroy them without danger, it is better to submit them to laws than to abandon them to their own disorder. When one cannot extirpate a vice, it is at least necessary to subjugate it. On the basis of these maxims, in order to preserve the honor of virtuous women from violence and brutality, prostitutes were tolerated, but their estate was subjected to so much opprobrium and hu-

---

[154] Author: "The Emperor Claudius condemned a Roman knight to death who carried a serpent's egg in his bosom in order to enchant his judges."

miliating subjections that the Government was fully justified in the sad and unfortunate necessity of supporting a lesser evil in order to avoid more considerable ones. Those infamous individuals, excluded from civil life and deprived of the advantages of society, could not have any communication, even between themselves, and were ignominiously punished at the slightest sign of disorder or scandal; they were also subjected to a tax whose product was scrupulously applied to the maintenance of those who abandoned the detestable profession.

Various useful academies had been established, among others one of commerce, one of agriculture, one of morality and one of politics. In the last-named, human beings, their passions and their enlightenment were studied, carefully and with accurate calculation. Only the examination of the past, in combination with the present, can lead to an anticipation of the future. It is the unique branch of judiciary astrology whose usage is permissible, and which time can justify.

Conferences were held frequently in each academy, in which so-called prejudices were debated in an adversarial manner, as a means of ensuring the destruction of the errors and vulgar opinions that debase the human mind, degrading the noble faculty of thought and harming felicity; but certain prejudices were allowed voluntarily to subsist, which, subject to slight inconveniences, were in many respects useful to the good of the State and the happiness of individuals, such as honor, bravery, the dread of opprobrium, politeness, certain etiquettes, etc.

No subject was able to engage his liberty until he reached the age at which the law authorized him to dispose of his wealth.[155]

I shall conclude this chapter with the description of an allegorical Temple of Truth, erected by the reigning Emperor, in

---

[155] Author: "That has often been said and cannot be repeated too often."

recognition of the inestimable advantages that had been obtained for his happiness and that of his people by opening free access to his throne to it.

The Temple of Truth

Poets have lodged Truth in the depths of an abyss inaccessible to the human mind; that is a hyperbole; it could more justifiably be placed in an arid desert surrounded by monsters that forbid its approach—the passions, self-interest, flattery and prejudices—and which it is necessary to vanquish in order to grasp it.

Entirely enveloped by clouds s the Truth is, when one seeks it with a veritable desire to find it, one encounters it, inasmuch as it is human intelligence to know it, but always sufficient to its needs.

On that principle, generally admitted, the Selenites had erected a temple to Truth simple in its structure but noble, in which, to remove any suspicion of Idolatry, there was no worship. It was, among those wise people, like the simulacra that represent among us virtues designed by the attributes that accompany them, which are admired without being honored. The edifice was situated in the middle of a dense wood distant from the Court and cities, an abode appropriate to meditation and recollection. The statues with which it was decorated, made by the most skillful artists, represented on one side hatred, jealousy, envy, flattery, satire, ambition, idolatry and superstition, enchained and tormented by the furies, and on the other, justice, candor, disinterest, submission to the Prince, respect for the laws, amity and benevolence, crowned with flowers by the Muses.

In the depths of the Temple, one saw on an altar, majestically elevated, the Truth, covered by a light veil. That metaphysical being, considered as an emanation of the Supreme Being, attracted people of a mild and sensible nature, lovers of the truth disposed to its knowledge. They went in with the desire to find it and rarely came out without being fully satis-

171

fied, if, before going in, they had stripped themselves of the passions and the deceptive usage of the senses. They breathed a pure and tranquil air there, but sufficiently agitated to remove from the sanctuary those tyrants and vanquishers of mortal weakness, errors, opinions and prejudices.

That Temple was, on a large scale, the emblem of the study of a true Philosopher.

VOLUME TWO

Chapter 1
Laws and Jurisprudence

There had been a time when the Judges in the first resort were required to sustain at their own expense the appeals against their sentences and to pay the costs if their verdicts were quashed at the final jurisdiction.

At another time Advocates had been forbidden to declaim and to precede their arguments with exordia and perorations, and to preserve the Judges from the seduction of the gestures and graces of the orator, they made their pleas in the dark.

Afterwards it had been attempted, but in vain, to put a time limit on the judgment of trials.

Respect for ancient laws had then been taken to the extreme that it was only permitted to any subject to propose new ones with a rope around his neck, in order that he might be strangled on the spot if they were not unanimously accepted. It had been recognized since, however, that such a strange maxim only put a brake on the multiplicity of the laws, which became an obstacle to the establishment of those that became successively necessary by virtue of the vicissitudes of circumstance.

In a more enlightened time, those puerile and extravagant practices, impossible of execution, were naturally dissipated to give way to wiser regulations, but Jurisprudence only took on a regular and stable form truly useful to the general good when, in order to remedy the abuses of chicanery and villainy that the fury of procedure caused, they had begun by establishing a Court of Arbiters chosen from among the most celebrated Jurisconsultants, and that no trial was permitted to begin

173

until the contestations had been brought to their tribunal and means of conciliation had been judged impracticable.

On the incontestable maxim that, whatever the laws are, it is necessary to obey them and to regard them as the public conscience, to which each individual must conform, but that they ought to be clear and precise, a general Code of laws and customs was drawn up, taken from the immense labyrinth of those that subsisted before, the majority in contradiction, often equivocal or unintelligible, for which a long life scarcely sufficed to make a superficial acquaintance, penetrate the meaning and decipher the spirit.[156]

That Code, drafted in clear, laconic terms and in the language of the country, was sheltered from any interpretation, and the Judges were obliged to observe it to the letter; after which, all commentaries were burned,[157] as well as all the glosses, thus reducing the laws to a small number of volumes, of which the brief and facile study within the scope of everyone became part of education and enabled everyone to form a summary judgment themselves.

In order to ensure the unshakable consistency of the new Code, the majority of ancient laws, dictated by ignorance to savage authority, had been reformed on those of nature—or, rather, only those were conserved that were in conformity with them[158]—but those laws were distinguished from police regulations, which were only affirmative and which, without alter-

---

[156] Author: "*Ut olim flagittis, sic nunc legibus laboramus*, Tacitus, Annals, Book III, chapter 25" [Once we suffered from our vices; today we suffer from our laws.] Misquoted by Montaigne—*flagittis* ought to be *vitiis*—but subsequently quoted correctly by Blaise Pascal in his *Pensées*.

[157] Author: "The Commentators on all sorts of works had been so great in number as to count between fourteen and fifteen thousand on the works of Aristotle."

[158] Author: "*Nunquam aliud Natura, aliud sapientia dixit.* Juvenal, Satire XIV." [Never does Nature say one thing and wisdom another.]

ing the constitution of the Government, are necessarily subject to variation as mores and tastes change.

The respective knowledge of the rights of each individual, acquired with sufficient facility, obviated an infinity of foolish and unjust pretentions. That enlightenment, combined with the authority that the arbiters had to conciliate the interests of parties, before permitting juridical contest, had considerably diminished the number of advocates, destroyed the monster of chicanery all the way to the roots and extirpated forever the population, as innumerable as they were dangerous, of solicitors, bailiffs, sergeants, recorders and other vampires who, to the shame of reason, drew their subsistence with impunity from the weakness, ignorance and perversity of the human mind.[159]

The execution of the law, to the letter, is the only means of ensuring public tranquility and the stability of fortunes. How great, on the contrary, is the misfortune of peoples among whom, by virtue of a fatal prejudice, the Law is interpreted arbitrarily?[160] Thanks to the feeble light of reason, their honor, their fortune, their status and their very life, continually in peril, often depends on a passionate motive, hazard or the distorted organization of a brain.[161] How many unfortunates

---

[159] Author: "Tribunals have been compared to thorny bushes in which a ewe seeks refuge from wolves but can only emerge after leaving a portion of her fleece behind."

[160] Author: "Of three persons who see an anamorphosis—that is to say, a grooved picture that represents three different subjects--the one placed to the right says that it a lion, the one to the left that it is Venus; and one facing says that they are both wrong and that it is a forest. That is the image of the opinions of Judges on the Law; it appears in accordance with the direction from which one envisages it. Woe betide anyone whose life or fortune depends on human judgments!"

[161] Author: "*Veri juris, germanaeque justitia: solidam et expressam effigiem nullam tenemus; umbra et imaginibus utimur*. Cicero, De Officiis, Book III chapter XVII." [We have

175

have been condemned who would have been sent away absolved if fever had surprised two of the Judges who were inclined to rigor!

As it is not given to human intelligence to anticipate all possible cases,[162] however, nor to express itself in an uninterpretable manner, a Court of Equity had been established to temper the severity of the letter of the law in circumstances demanding that rigor be set aside. That establishment, adding compassion for human weakness to the satisfaction of justice, appeared so admirable that it was incontinently imitated by all the peoples who acquired cognizance of it.

Although believing themselves sufficiently furnished with good laws to ensure the felicity of peoples, they had not taken superstition so far as to forbid the right to create new ones, but that was always undertaken with extreme circumspection and when the necessity had been judged absolute, all the Orders of the State having been consulted. One naturally rises up against any novelty, but what is in usage today was new yesterday.[163] What Legislator can boast of having foreseen everything? The laws, which have acquired degrees of force by their antiquity, were new in the time that they were given. If people had thought then as they do at present, they would not have been received.

If, to support a rule that one wants to establish, one sometimes has need to seek examples in the past, reason dic-

---

no solid and express effigies of true law and genuine justice, but we employ shadows and images to represent them.]

[162] Author: "To provide for all needs the number of laws would be infinite, and those same laws subject to countless interpretations, so accidents could be multiplied to infinity."

[163] Author: "*Quod si tam Graecis novitas invisa fuisset quam nobis; quid nunc esset vestus? aut quid haberet quod legeret, tereretque viritim publicus usus?* Horace. Ad Augustus Book II Epistle I." [If an unseen novelty had been the same to the Greeks as us, would it now be old? Or would it be decided individually in terms of public utility?]

tates that one should prepare similar aid for posterity when present welfare requires it. Times change, mores and tastes change with them, to the extent of sometimes astonishing those who have quit them in order to embrace the new. New laws are, therefore, necessary from time to time, which will one day become respectable by virtue of their antiquity. It is the duty of a great genius to work, along the way, for the happiness of future centuries, as it is of a good citizen to form solid establishments and to sow the woods that will become forests for his descendants. Where would we be if, throughout the centuries, men had only thought, written and lived for themselves, if they had only built life? Where would the Sciences and the Arts be? The World would not yet have reached its adolescence. How could we be as advanced as we are if our ancestors had not conceived the admirable and courageous project of an Encyclopedia, reprinted every hundred years with the augmentation of the discoveries made in the course of the century? How many treasures that we enjoy placidly today would have been lost? What honors should we not award to the inventor of a work so useful to humankind?

I cannot refuse my eulogies to an infinity of sage rules that a purified taste and an enlightened reason had introduced for general wellbeing. A substantial fraction of them have already been found in the chapter on practices, customs opinions, etc. I shall content myself with simply adding the following:

That, as experience had shown that human conventions are always easy to evade by dishonest dealers, who take their warrant from the obscurity or ambiguity of terms, when it was a matter of establishing a law or making a treaty, the Jurisconsultants and Politicians, far from relying on their own enlightenment, exposed them beforehand to the examination of the most subtle critics and grammarians, in order to make sure that the expressions, in being just and clear, were sheltered from any malign or captious interpretation.

That there were no honoraria attached to the functions of the Tribunals but only to marks of distinction. Honors, which are mere smoke for common souls, are for beneficent spirits and true citizens, even for philosophers, a kind of sensuality.

That positions in the Judiciary were not venal, but the prize of merit and virtue.

That it was not the custom to be appointed to one before the age of forty, or to continue in its exercise after that of seventy. Before forty, the mind has not acquired enough enlightenment and experience to fulfill such delicate functions; at seventy, it lacks vigor. Youth is prey to passions, old age to seduction.

Finally, to avoid the inconveniences of the partiality that every man has, instinctively, for his birthplace, no one could be a Judge, Intendant or Governor in the province, much less the city, in which he had been born.

Chapter II
On Medicine

Medicine, which is, among ignorant peoples, only a practice of experience reduced to precepts, without any knowledge of anatomy, knows few maladies but cures them promptly. Among enlightened peoples, it is only a conjectural science, which sometimes aids Nature but often destroys her efforts.

That useful science, which has for its object the discipline most interesting to humans of repair and conservation, had reached its highest degree of perfection among the Selenites.

Freed from the pompous confusion of terms as obscure as they were shiny that had previously accompanied it and contained a small number of reliable principles, medicine, which is the art of adding and removing, was reduced to observation—which is to say, to allowing Nature to act, sometimes assisting her but never pressing her.

A small number of celebrated men, all equally versed in anatomy, botany and chemistry, composed the School of Medicine. They were full of scorn for the ostentatious talent that claims to submit the human body to geometry, and which, reducing everything to calculation, including the movement of solids and fluids, the majority of which are supposed and unknown, leads the sick recklessly to death by demonstration. All the physicians spread through the rest of Europe emerged from that school.

A considerable honorarium attached to the maintenance of citizens devoted to the service of humankind dispensed them from receiving any retribution from the Public.

They possessed the direction of a complete pharmacy, maintained at the expense of the Prince. It was renewed every year, and furnished abundantly for the needs of the capital and the surrounding areas. Every province had a similar one in its principal city, where the more distant came to obtain their provisions.

On the incontestable principle that Nature tends to equilibrium in all things, and consequently seeks to repair herself, in conformity with the laws of animal economy, a very discreet use was made of drugs, which, in any case, rendered her efforts vain when, at the same time as healing the patient, she had to combat the remedies opposing her operations.[164]

Although physicians had been reduced to a small number throughout the Empire, they were nevertheless sufficient; they even had little to do, since that respectable Body, full of zeal for humanity, had carefully composed a little book, which contained the most experimented remedies, the simplest and most useful for all kinds of accidents and maladies—remedies that always ought to be employed soberly in the case that Nature had need of assistance—clearly indicating their usage; which, with the study of one's own temperament, rest and a dietary regime, if required, enabled everyone, almost invariably, to do without the assistance of the Faculty.

That book, which, in spite of the variety and multiplicity of ills to which the human body seems to be subject, was a small volume, had been extracted from the books of Solomon on the properties of plants, the original of which was to found in the cabinet of things lost on the earth. And it was astonishing to recognize that the most scornful plants, which every country produces, contain the same virtues as those that were once sought, at great expense, in the most distant lands, Nature, that benevolent mother, having dispersed in all climates those appropriate to the maladies that reign there. Prior to that discovery, all remedies had only been palliatives, with the exception of quinine, opium, emetic and mercury, the only ones then capable of operating cures virtuously.

---

[164] Author: "...*exsuperat magis, aegrescitque medendo*. Virgil, Aeneid. Book XII line 46." [He swells up more and grows more distempered by medicine.]

The discovery was not disdained, however, of certain specific simples and compounds that fortunate hazard sometimes procures, rather than the most difficult study and research, and when the utility of a remedy was recognized by the Faculty, the inventor was always recompensed in accordance with its importance and amply compensated by the State for the privilege, which he was not allowed to retain to himself, the secret immediately being made public. It was thus that empiricism had long disappeared of its own accord, like any profession devoid of exercise.

To give to the few remedies that were in usage the virtue that often only operates on the body relative to the disposition of the soul, one ordinarily began by treating the maladies of the mind that oppose their efficacy, recalling gaiety by means of innocent amusements and fortifying the constitution by moderate exercise. By that method, the disappearance was seen, in a short time, of hysterical and hypochondriac affections, obstructions and melancholies etc.

A sage ordinance of the Prince had abolished the dangerous usage of copper for domestic water pipes and other vessels and utensils used in the preparation of aliments. The same province the possessed the mines had solicited the prohibition, by a generous sacrifice of its own interests to the general good.

Without regard to the considerable benefits that the Prince might have obtained from the consumption of tobacco, he had not hesitated to proscribe the usage of that plant before people had contracted the dangerous habit, because of its ammoniac odor and narcotic virtue, because tobacco is harmful to cleanliness, because it occasions superfluous expenditure and causes artisans the loss of the sixth of a day's work, because it produces more harmful effects than salutary ones, in that it damages the memory, dries out the brain and enfeebles the sense of smell. The drug was relegated to the class of remedies.

Almost all human beings bear at birth a principle of death, which is the smallpox, from which few people are ex-

181

empt, and which, by its ravages, harvests a quarter of the human race. Inoculation had scarcely been invented, with the sole aim of saving the beauty of the wreck, than the importance of the discovery for the conservation of the human species was fortunately recognized.[165] In truth, it suffered many contradictions, but, sustained by the eulogies of the Faculty and supported by the example of the Sovereign, who submitted his entire family to it, it soon triumphed over the futile prejudices that opposed its establishment in the capital, from which it is still extending, successfully, into the other parts of the Empire. By means of an exact enumeration, it has been recognized with joy that in less than half a century the number of inhabitants has increased by a tenth, which led the Government to favor the progress of such a salutary and consoling operation, in spite of the puerile objections of those feeble souls and fanatical clairvoyant ever ready to thwart advantageous establishments by interesting Religion in matters that are utterly foreign to it.

To cure that imaginary malady knows as rabies, they began by treating the imagination, after which innocent remedies completed the cure.

By the profound study of Nature, of her progress and her penchant for crises, experience had demonstrated that the maladies incurable in the Middle Ages were a chimera, and a falsification, in which the last resource of ignorant physicians, in overloading the body with remedies, rendered cures impossi-

---

[165] The treatment of smallpox by vaccination was not introduced to Europe until 1798, but reports of the process of inoculation, or variolation, used in the Ottoman Empire were reported to scientific societies in Western Europe early in the 18th century. It involved introducing powder from smallpox scabs into the bodies of healthy individuals (thus enabling at least some of them to form antibodies to dead virus particles without catching the disease).

ble.[166] The cure of the mind often leads to that of the body, if one laves the care of healing to Nature. Botany was perfected by virtue of the careful examination of the conduct of animals, which instinctively seek out in their maladies the remedies appropriate to them. With the aid of those observations, they succeeded in discovering the properties of many plants that had escaped the sagacity of humans. It is thus, it is said, that the discovery was made on earth of cinchona, which is sought by lions subject to intermittent fevers,[167] the dittany with which goats cure their wounds on the island of Candia, and that humans learned bleeding from the hippopotamus, the clyster from the ibis, the siphon from the louse, etc.

Consequential experiments had been carried out on many reputedly harmful plants, which had destroyed the vulgar opinions regarding their supposed dangerous properties, and as there is no useless production in Nature, a few simples, recognized as effectively poisonous, were found, on the contrary, by analysis and experimentation, to be antidotes to various ills, as we have discovered of emetic, opium, hemlock, antimony, arsenic, sublimate, realgar, etc.[168]

It was expressly forbidden, under very severe penalties, either to compose or sell the drugs and ingredients that vanity and corrupted desire was pleased to imagine appropriate to repair the outages of Nature and time upon the skin. The char-

---

[166] This reference is slightly odd; it surely cannot refer to such Medieval ravages as the plague; it probably refers to leprosy, which had become far less common in the 18th century than it had been in earlier eras.

[167] Given that cinchona, or Peruvian bark—the source of quinine—is native to South America, very few lions could actually have found it.

[168] "Sublimate," or "corrosive sublimate," was mercuric chloride, used in the treatment of syphilis; realgar is arsenic sulfide. All the substances cited were thought to have medical value in the mid-18th century, but most have now been relegated once again to the status of dangerous poisons.

183

latan was punished as the author and accomplice of frauds and artifices that women employ with impunity to seduce men; even the fair sex had applauded the care of the Faculty, which had demonstrated that the simplest cosmetics were harmful to health and that the unique art in question operated in direct contact to what was expected of it, only giving at a certain age, when it is useless, a little more glamour at the expense of that which ought to follow—in sum, that any cosmetic is a deceitful mask, which advances the eclipse of natural beauty, and a false charm that only dupes fools.[169]

Regicide, parricide and treason against the fatherland being, in the Constitution of the State, the only crimes punishable by death, in order to purge the land of those execrable monsters, criminals of that species were designated for surgical experiments, from which anatomy had obtained knowledge that the dissection of cadavers and living animals could not procure.[170]

The perfection of medicine among the Selenites only lacks the discovery of the universal remedy, but they were too enlightened to search for it and too wise to struggle against the experience of all the centuries. The human body is a machine in motion, the springs of which must necessarily wear out at length; but that machine, contrary to all those that human industry has invented, tending to repair the disorders that overtake it, it is necessary not to multiply obstacles in order to perpetuate its movement until the term marked for its destruc-

---

[169] Author: "...*tu non inventa reperta luctus eras levior*. Ovid, Metamorphoses Book I; ....*tanti est quaerendi cura decoris*. Juvenal. Satire VI." [My sorrow was lighter when you were lost than now that you are found (Ovid); so great a concern is the quest for beauty (Juvenal)]

[170] Author: "*Omne magnum exemplum habet aliquid ex iniquo, quod contra singulos utilitate publica rependitur.* Tacitus. Annals. Book IV. [Every example of punishment has some injustice in it, but it effect on individuals is balanced by its tendency to promote public good.] Quoted by Montaigne.

tion.[171] The entire art only constitutes the avoidance of too rude a friction, maintaining the free flow of fluids and the flexibility of solids, less by the usage of certain aliments than by the privation of many others.

But the true and unique means that are within our reach and our power to prolong the course of life are frugality, temperance, gaiety, sobriety[172] and useful occupations; they prevent infirmities, exercise dissipates them, moderation in pleasures avoids disgust, bitterness and satiety. Reading is the antidote of ennui and music of melancholy. The physical means of lengthening our being, as Montaigne says, is to acquire in infancy the habit of only giving to sleep exactly what Nature requires of repose to repair the forces expended in wakefulness. The moments that pass in suffering, those which extend in ennui, those which elapse in sleep, species of death counted on the duration of life, are as many deductions from the number of our days.

---

[171] Author: "There are a thousand evident signs of death, and not one of anything that can ensure health and life. Only one road leads us into life; there are a thousand that lead out of it."
[172] Author. "It is really only sober people who can savor the pleasures of the senses in all their excellence."

Chapter III
Fashion

Are garments necessary to human beings? That is a good question; there is reason to believe, however, that if it had been necessary for them to be clad, Nature would have done so, as she provides animals with fur, hide, shells, feathers, scales, etc., and everything necessary to the survival of each living being.[173]

Decency, a term unknown during many centuries of candor, has been able to demand by convention that humans veil certain parts of their bodies, but the care for their own survival demands that they do not deprive others of the benign influences of the element in which they are destined to live. Whatever the motives are that led them to dress themselves, it is certain that thy only owe that practice to the weakness of their temperament, and many infirmities from which the body would be exempt in the open air, among which are principally numbered fluxions, rheumatism, sciatica, gout, catarrh and all the other accidents that originate from a transpiration interrupted by the usage of garments and ligatures, which also give rise to that uncleanliness harmful to the animal economy, from which everybody exposed to the open air is almost always preserved, and against which people can only be protected by repeated cares and continual repair.

Is it credible that it would be impossible for humans to shrug off a yoke so deadly to health, in order to recover their original constitution, if the unfortunate habit—which is not, as is said abusively, a second Nature—did not always triumph

---

[173] Author: *"Proptereaque fere res omnes aut corio funt, Aut seta aut conchis, aut callo, aut cortice testae.* Lucretius. Book IV, line 933. [And for that reason nearly all things are clothed with skin, or hair, or shell, or bark, or some such thing.] Quoted by Montaigne.

with impunity over reflection? The famous Tsar Peter, that creative genius of our century, who pushed experimentation to the point of forcing his sailors only to drink sea water, of which they all died, omitted to attempt this one, which was far less dangerous. Success might perhaps have justified the enterprise; it would have been appropriate to give that example to the rest of the earth.[174]

Is it not an insensate mania to multiply needs, rather than the rigor of the climate, that makes Europeans and the civilized inhabitants of the torrid zone dress themselves, while entire peoples who live in rigorous climates expose their bodies to the inclemency of the air and nevertheless enjoy better health and a longer life than we do?

Is it not by habit rather than by necessity that we cover certain parts of our bodies and leave others uncovered? The most sensitive, like the hands and the face, are exposed; the eyes, so tender, proudly brave the north wind and frosts; a few Cenobites, heads and feet bare, confront them in complete security. Why do men not bare as much of their torso as women, whose complexion is more delicate? The desire to please or seduce in one sex, the continual needs of sight and touch in

---

[174] Author: "I admit that in our present mores, similar propositions can and ought to appear revolting. That is because humans, in the state of society, can only sense the obstacles, which do not exist in a state of Nature. So I am only claiming, in making the real inconveniences of clothing felt, that although it is impossible today to quit it entirely, it would be easy to make some reform from which the human body might obtain many advantages, such as always keeping the head, the chest, the arms and the feet uncovered, of suppressing all ligatures, etc. Varro holds that when we were ordered to keep our heads uncovered in the presence of Gods, Sovereigns and Magistrates, it was done more for our health and to protect us against the insults of time than for the sake of reverence. *Montaigne*."

both, are thus more powerful than the concern of our preserva-
tion, to which everything is sacrificed elsewhere.

In the present state of things—which is to say, with the
deteriorated temperament that our ancestors have transmitted
to us by virtue of the fatal practice of covering ourselves—
propriety has become a subjection, or, to put it another way, a
necessary care, which would only demand simple clothes,
comfortable and a good defense against cold and the inclemency of the seasons, if vanity, which enters into all calculations did not lead humans to combine art with pure need;
hence elegance, and finally refinement, which have engendered fashion.

Fashions, subject to inconstancy by the natural taste that
humans have for variety, renders them slaves to a thousand
false needs; luxury brings them to a peak.

Luxury is still to be defined. Whether it is useful or
harmful in a great Monarchy that collects the commodities of
primary necessity is a question that gives rise to a thousand
paradoxes. The austere Lacedaemon, as Melon says, was no
happier and less flourishing than voluptuous Athens; both
produced great men with entirely opposite mores; Athens even
furnished a greater number than Lacedaemon.[175] According to
some, luxury is sumptuousness in edifices, furniture, carriages,
garments and the table; according to others it is the abuses of
wealth. Moralist chagrin makes it consist of everything that is
not absolute necessity. In that case a garment formed from a
simple animal skin is already a luxury.

---

[175] Author: "The Spartans, so lauded for their austerity while
they observed the laws of Lycurgus religiously, passed to an
opposite extreme after the victories of Lysander, who spread
gold and silver in the Republic, delivering themselves to all
the excesses of luxury and debauchery, to an insatiable cupidity and an extreme avarice, in which they surpassed the Athenians, whose mores had long served them as a contrast. Thus it
is necessary to distinguish the Spartans under Lycurgus from
the Lacedaemonians under Lysander."

Luxury is the most dangerous enemy of population. Arms employed in extracting and maneuvering gold are neglecting the veritable productions of the earth. To sustain ostentation, one refuses the wishes of Nature; one prefers augmenting the number of domestic servants to that one one's descendants; it seems that one destines the few children one has to live one day in servitude.

What is certain is that when luxury has taken rot in an opulent State, it is very difficult to repress. Sumptuary laws only put a temporary brake on it; vanity and industry find a thousand ways to evade them.[176]

To arrest the progress of luxury in the most important items, several pragmatic measures had been tried among the Selenites, some of which had succeeded, principally the one pertaining to meals. Instead of stopping in puerile fashion at fixing the number of dishes and services, the quality of foodstuffs, etc., they had limited the number of persons who could assemble, and prohibited the entry of spices into the Realm, and the usage of spirituous liquors. Within a few years that regulation had caused the disappearance of stomach upsets, headaches, the vapors and other fashionable epidemics, diminished the number of maladies by half, doubled fortunes and exterminated the hungry race of parasites.

As for the fashions of adornment and glamour, the privileges of luxury that exercise a secret empire over the wisest minds, retained by a false decency and the enthusiasm of the multitude, they had only succeeded in destroying them by sti-

---

[176] Author: "The Lex Oppia was the first of the sumptuary laws of Rome, principally regulating the attire of women. The Ladies agreed between themselves no longer to have children until they had obtained the revocation of the law, which was abrogated in spite of the grave and severe speech of Cato in the Senate, twenty years after it had been decreed." The Lex Oppia was, in fact, repealed in 195 B.C. as a result of the pressure of mass demonstrations around the Forum by the matrons of Rome.

fling new fashions at birth. When a young person of whatever condition appeared in public in a brilliant attire of singular taste, it was immediately represented in the theater by a similar outfit, accompanied by all the caricature and ridicule capable of rendering it the object of public mockery, and the eccentric was treated as a foreigner in his native land until he had renounced his frivolity.

After having tried several times, in vain, to submit the entire State to a simple and uniform mode of dress, which is only practicable in a petty republic, they limited themselves to establishing a pragmatic rule for the distinction of ranks, in which there were few classes. Everyone felt that too much subjection to the delirium of mind that the taste for superfluity maintains is only appropriate to produce ridicule or lend a character of inconsistency to an otherwise-respectable Nation; that a rational economy can form the establishment of several children with that superfluity; that it is shameful for a part of the State to live on the follies of another; that luxury only multiplies needs and that the arts of necessity can never have too many arms.

If everything were assessed at its true value, how much luxury, of the frenzy of style and the empire of fashion, would still subsist? Fashions have the singular aspect that whoever presents himself in a new attire appears bizarre, and then turns to ridicule those who continue to wear it once he has abandoned it.[177]

---

[177] Author: "That which one was accustomed to regard as an adornment in good taste appears a ridiculous accoutrement a short while afterwards. Who can observe nowadays, without laughing with pity, that women in their clothing looked like cylinders surmounted by a step pyramid that served as their coiffure, and soon afterwards they diminished their height excessively by submerging themselves in truncated cones of prodigious base without any coiffure at all? That enormous transition took place in a few years."

To what extreme of extravagance can fashion not take its tyranny? There have been epochs in which it has had an influence on health; it was not always seemly to enjoy it, if one did not want to be confused with coarse individuals. At other times, vapors were in fashion; it was in good taste to be sickly, and the care taken to affect it became a real malady, which only lacked a name: a dilapidated stomach, an appearance of emaciation in conjunction with and appearance of high social status, established an evident distinction from the people, too deprived of delicacy, sentiment and fortune to acquire such noble infirmities.

Fashion is contagious; it has, however, such a narrow district that it is foreign everywhere but in the places where it is received. Reason, which ought to exclude it, is not foreign anywhere, except in the majority of verifiers.

Except for human beings, can any species be found in Nature that frivolity nourishes, and over which the negligible has any power?

What virtue, then, do sumptuous garments have, to fascinate both the eyes of those who wear them and those who admire them? Do they cure gout, headaches or the vapors? Are they not, on the contrary, their privileged habitat?[178]

Is not glorifying oneself with a vestment that an animal wore before us, ornamenting ourselves with its skin, a poverty? Is not making an adornment out of what was for the animal only a burden or the production of its excretion pusillanimity?

Is not the bizarrerie of mind that makes one esteem the adornment more than the person, who ought to be the sole

---

[178] Author: "*Nec calidae citius decedunt corpore febres textilibus si in picturis, ostroque rubenti. iacteris, quam si in plebeia veste cubandum est*. Lucretius Book II line 34." [Fevers quit a man no sooner because he is stretched on a couch of rich tapestry than if he is in a coarse blanket.] Quoted by Montaigne.

focus of attention, something to be placed in the ranks of bastardized sensualities?

If a beard is a sign of virility, the privation of which exposes the most handsome human faces to mockery. if it has been placed by Nature on the face along with the eyebrows; if we admire it is some individuals, as in the portraits of our ancestors, and if it is made an ornament among some peoples, why do we remove it today with so much care after having trimmed it artistically in various ways at different times? Is it not a complete outrage that fashion, caprice and opinion are doing to Nature? Can one believe that one is embellishing oneself by disfiguring oneself?

To how many whims has the hair itself been subjected? Sometimes long, sometimes short; curly, flat, shaven in part or in total, powdered, dyed or perfumed, plaited, pigtailed or pouched, etc., it has been subjected to all possible metamorphoses.

Over what does fashion not extend its tyrannical empire, even at the expense of our commodities?[179] What is this mania for walking in an unnatural fashion, with artificial heels, which only serve to constrain the position of the body, hasten lassitude and render falls more frequent? Do people think that they are substituting for an omission of Nature? Is not a taller stature an advantage for their eyes alone, the illusion of which is dissipated when everyone raises themselves up in the same way? Have people of short stature the stupid vanity of elevating themselves artificially? Would they deem themselves more considerable and more respectable mounted on stilts? The pedestal is not part of the statue. Undoubtedly, they should only think themselves ridiculous. Are humans sufficiently devoid of judgment to think themselves estimable only in pro-

---

[179] Author: "…*usus, Quem penes arbitrium est, et jus, et norma*…." Horace. Ars Poetica, line 72." [The will of custom, in the power of whose judgment is the law and standard of the language.]

portion to their height?[180] Would it not be more flattering only to be measured by the heart? Can they be proud with regard to a pygmy if they are humiliated by the sight of a giant?

Let us recreate, momentarily, by the analysis of accoutrement, the cherished object of the complaisance of the animal *par excellence*, which enjoys the privileges and inconveniences of clothing exclusively. Let us see what advantages it has obtained from the necessity it has imposed on itself of being dressed, and with what industry it has substituted for the avarice or neglect of Nature in its regard. I shall pass over the subjection of edifying and destroying its work every day, in order to reconstruct it the following day—difficult work, augmented by virtue of the quantity of pieces making up the harness.

First of all, I see it inconvenienced by the rounded, squared or pointed shoes, in which the foot, which has none of those shapes, cannot be at ease.

Then I see it tottering in a stance inclined by means of a pedestal, which, raising the level of one of the extremities of that shoe, renders the foot less capable of governing the weight that it supports.

Finally, I see the entire body garroted by ligatures, which impede the circulation of fluids, retard growth and hinder respiration.

If one transported to a land of savages an assortment of the headwear of European women, would they not consign them to the category of bizarre curiosities, without any of them being able to imagine or conceive their usage? Would it not be for their philosophers—for there are some among them, if many of them are not[181]—an insoluble problem?

---

[180] Author: "*Homunculi quanti estis?*...." Plautus. Rudens, Act I Scene II line 60." [What is it, little man?]

[181] Author: "Diogenes was asked why, ignorant as he was, he mingled with philosophers. 'I'm a better philosopher for it,' he replied."

Would not the clothing of a man, although less complicated than that of women, not similarly be an enigma for those
good people, capable or tormenting their best minds? Would it
be an absurdity to presume that, if one invited them to try to
place each item of that attire on their own person, one would
put the underpants on his head in the form of a hood, another
the shirt on top of the jacket? Another might think that the
undershirt, the shirt, the waistcoat, the jerkin, the frock-coat
and the overcoat were enough to dress six people, since a single thick or furry garment could take the place of the whole set
to protect against the presumed insults of the air. They would
find them too heavy for summer, too light for winter, and obstacles to running. Some would mistake stockings for gloves,
collars or bracelets, buckles for head ornaments, an old-
fashioned wig for a cushion and a modern one for a fly-
swatter. With a little more knowledge of the employment of
all those garments they would find the sleeves of the coat too
short and too narrow, those of the shirt too broad and too long,
the coat-tails superfluous, as well as the pleats, the belt too
tight, the trimmings as extravagant as uncomfortable; they
would get rid of the buttons that do not correspond to the but-
tonholes. Instead of putting the hat under the arm or in the
pocket they would doubtless have the good sense to place it on
the head, after having flattened it.

After a reflective examination of all the part forming that
machine, what idea, do you think, would the savages form of
the judgment of peoples who voluntarily subject their bodies
to the yoke of such a complicated apparatus,[182] the arrangement of which must cost considerable time taken from fishing
or hunting? They would certainly not imagine that the machine was in usage in a land swarming with mechanicians and

---

[182] Author: "The savage, far from bemoaning his nudity,
would be more like to say, like an Ancient who found himself
at a fairground where curiosity-seekers assembled, coveting a
thousand rare things, *quam multis rebus non egeo*!" [How
many things do I not want!]

geometers. Perhaps reflection would lead them to condemn the malefactors among them to dress in the French fashion for life.

But what would be their astonishment if they learned that the art of sporting all these superfluities took the place of merit in some and almost of virtue in others, and that consideration attached more to them than the person within? Would there be any torture more cruel for those simple people than to be condemned to assist in the dressing of a contemporary dandy?

Chapter IV
The Theater

One of the six isolated blocks of buildings that formed the decoration of the Imperial palace was, as I have already said, destined for the Theater. A superb vestibule served as its entrance. The hall was elliptical in form, with an aisle along its major axis, decorated with tiers and a beautiful colonnade; it was the most noble design, capable of containing the largest number of people in the smallest space, and the most susceptible to a delightful view, in which every spectator enjoys the illusion without hindrance, and the audience becomes a magnificent spectacle in itself. The spacious theater in which operas, comedies, balls and concerts were presented alternately, was maintained at the Emperor's expense. Entrance was free to all, and everyone was seated in accordance with their rank.

The building, constructed entirely in stone, was fireproof. Broad stairways led to wide, well-lit corridors, by means of which everyone could reach their seats without inconvenience.

Sheet-metal partitions, artistically disposed, diminished the depths of the lodges and the apparent extent of the hall when it was deemed appropriate, and the air was continually renewed by means of four ventilators.[183]

---

[183] Author: "Air filled with animal exhalations, particularly those that are corrupted, has often caused pestilential fevers throughout a country. The exhalations of human bodies are subject to corruption. Water in which one bathes acquires, by virtue of the sojourn, a cadaverous odor. It has been demonstrated that fewer than 3,000 people, placed in the extent of an arpent of land, would form there by their own respiration, in 34 days, an atmosphere about 71 feet high, which, if not dissipated by the wind, would rapidly become pestilential. One can judge on that basis that in places where a large number of

The Theater, ornamented with superb decorations, was reserved for the stage; the spectators did not indecently diminish the space necessary to the actors and dancers. None of the pleasure of being able to see and savor the charm of the performance was sacrificed to the stupid vanity of disturbing the effect in order to make a spectacle of oneself.

All the spectators were seated. The practice of making honest folk stand up, exposing them to weariness and collapse, or being stifled by tumultuous waves that disturb the spectacle and cause pleasure to degenerate into torment, was considered barbaric.

The orchestra, placed in the wings of the stage, was not visible. After the overture, it was only employed in plays in which there were entr'actes—for many authors were not subservient to that routine—to advertise the reigning mood of the following act, by means of characteristic music, touching, lugubrious, pathetic or frightening, always adapted to the situations or the dominant passions, in order not to distract the spectator from involvement, which can only be interrupted at the expense of pleasure. The music of the orchestra, composed for each play and forming part of the subject, kept the soul attached to it, instead of drawing it away with insensate distractions, as happens elsewhere, by intruding jigs and tambourines haphazardly into the course of a conspiracy, sarabands and bagpipes in the midst of the horrors of war; fanfares amid moaning and weeping, villanelles and gavottes in the preparations for a frightful sacrifice, etc.

After pathetic dramas, they did not put on, ridiculously, exodes, Atellan farces, satires or pantomimes to dissipate the

---

people are assembled, as at spectacles, the air becomes filled in a short time by animal exhalations that are very dangerous by virtue of their rapid corruption; after an hour, one is no longer breathing anything but human exhalations; one is admitting infected air into one's lungs expelled from a thousand chests, along with all the corpuscles that can be extracted from those chests, often corrupted."

presumed sadness that tragic subjects cast into the soul, because, in sum, either the pleasure that one obtains from being saddened in insensate, or the illusion cannot last too long; force destroys the impressions so suddenly that the soul, in being freed therefrom, seems to be accusing itself of a error, from which it is seeking to escape by extravagance.

They had sagely banned from the theater parody, farce and burlesque, amusements unworthy of a sane mind and only appropriate they give delight to truly vulgar lower orders. Tragicomedy was regarded as monstrous in its essence, only fit to please hermaphrodite minds.

Many of our theatrical works were performed there successfully. In the repertoire of dramas, which were put on alternately with those of the Greeks,[184] there were eight by Corneille the elder and two by the younger. All of Racine was performed except for *Alexandre, La Thebaïde, Bérénice, Esther* and *Les Plaideurs*; of Campistron, *Andronic*;[185] of Crebillon, *Electre* and *Rhadamiste*;[186] almost all of Voltaire and a few detached pieces, such as *Venceslas, Médée, Pénélope, Manlius, Arie et Pétus, Cléopâtre, Inès, Gustave,*

---

[184] Author: "Greece was the cradle and throne of epic art and dramatic art. Tragedy owes its birth to the poems of the *Iliad* and the *Odyssey*, as comedy owes its own to the *Margites* of Homer." Although Aristotle attributed the comic mock-epic *Margites* to Homer it is unlikely to be the work of the author of the *Iliad*. Most of the work has been lost, only being known directly via a few fragments.

[185] Jean Galbert de Campistron (1656-1723), the author of *Andronic* (1685), is virtually forgotten today, except perhaps for *Acis et Galatée*, which was set to music by Jean-Baptiste Lully.

[186] Prosper Crébillon (1674-1762) was regarded as Voltaire's great rival as a dramatist; *Electre* (1708) and *Rhadamiste et Zénobie* (1711) were renowned for their melodramatic violence.

Denis-le-Tiran, Les Troyennes, Didon, Iphigénie en Tauride, Hipermnestre, etc., etc., etc.[187]

With regard to comedy, although Molière was recognized as a great man even in his least productions, only eight of his most celebrated plays were presented, esteemed in the following order: *Le Misanthrope, Tartuffe, Les Femmes savantes, L'Avare, L'École des Maris, L'Ecole des Femmes*,[188] *Amphitrion* and *Georges Dandin*; of Regnard, *Le Joueur, Démocrite* and *Les Menechmes*; of Destouches, *Le Philosophe marié* and *Le Glorieux*; a few plays by Boissy, Marivaux and La Chaussée, *La Mère coquette, Le Grondeur, Le Méchant, Le Flatteur* and *La Métromanie*.[189]

---

[187] Venceslas (1647) is by Jean Rotrou; *Médée* (1635) is by Pierre Corneille; Pénélope (1716) is by Abbé Charles-Claude Genest; *Manlius Capitolinus* (1698) is by Antoine de La Fosse; *Arie et Petus, ou Les amours de Néron* (1660) is by Gabriel Gilbert; *La Cléopâtre* (1636) is by Isaac de Benserade; *Ines de Castro* (1723) is by Antoine Houdar de La Motte; *Gustave Vasa* (1733) is by Alexis Piron; *Denis le tyran* (1749) is by Jean-Francois Marmontel (who produced new versions of at least two of the other plays cited); *Les Troyennes* (1751) is by Jean-Baptiste Vivien de Chateaubrun; there is more than one tragedy entitled *Didon*, but the one cited is presumably the one published in 1734 by the Marquis de Pompignan, it cannot be the later one by Marmontel; *Iphigénie en Tauride* (1758) is by Claude Guymond de La Touche; *Hipermnestre* (1716, but not published until long after) is by Charles-Hubert Gervais and Joseph de Lafont.

[188] Author: "They had removed the terms *cocu* et *cocuage*, so frequently employed in those two plays, which had become sufficiently base as to be considered indecent in society." The two terms are equivalent to the English "cuckold" and "cuckoldry."

[189] Jean Regnard was generally reckoned to rank second after Molière in the ranks of late 17th century dramatists. *Le Joueur* was first performed in 1696, *Démocrite amoureux* in 1700 and

Pradon, Montfleury, Hauteroche, Scarron, Champmêlé, Poisson, Le Grand, Dancourt and a hundred others of the same category had been forgotten forever. They could not conceive that there had been a time when authors like those of the ancient Italian theater could contribute to the pleasures of an enlightened people. They could not believe that Pradon's *Phaedre* had competed with Racine's,[190] that *Athalie*, the masterpiece of our theater, had been long ignored, and that *Timocrate* had had eighty performances.[191] Finally, they could not persuade themselves that the Court had been amused by the miserable farces of Gros Guillaume, Gautier Garguille and Guillot Gorju.[192]

They were of the opinion that the rigorous unity of place is an obstacle to the pomp of the spectacle; that the unity of

---

Les Menechmes (1705). *Le Philosophe marié* (1727) by Philippe Destouches was widely suspected to be autobiographical. *La Mère coquette ou Les amants brouillés* (1665) is by Philippe Quinault. *Le Grondeur* (1691) is by Brueys [sic] and Jean Palaprat; *Le Méchant* (1747) is by Jean-Baptiste Gresset; the *Le Flatteur* cited is the 1696 work by Jean-Baptiste Rousseau; *La Métromanie* (1738) is by Alexis Piron.

[190] Racine and his subsequent champion Nicolas Boileau treated Jacques Pradon's work very harshly, especially *Phèdre* (1677), which appeared in the same year as Racine's play of the same title, but bowdlerized the story by refusing to make the eponymous heroine the stepmother of her lover.

[191] *Timocrate* (1656) was by Pierre Corneille's younger brother Thomas. The length of its run made it the biggest hit of the century

[192] Gros-Guillaume (Robert Guérin, 1554-1634) was one of the most famous actors of the 17th century. He formed a famous trio with Gautier-Garguille (Hugues Guéru, c1573-1633) and Turlupin (Henri Legrand, 1587-1637). His successor Guillot-Gorju (Bertrand Hardouin de Saint-Jacques, 1600-1648) was a qualified physician who made something of a specialty of playing comic doctors and apothecaries.

time put too much restriction on the development of ideas and events; that once could exceed the limits prescribed by austere geniuses without wounding propriety, deflecting attention or allowing action to languish; and that overly narrow limits were only suited to painting, which can only render an instant.

Thus, in the performance of tragedies, the Selenites admitted changes of scenery, without infringing too much on the understood rule of unity of place; if, for instance, a play is set in a Sovereign's palace, it is not necessary for the action to take place in a single location within that palace, whose walls enclose reception rooms, galleries, gardens, a temple, an amphitheater, etc., through which the actors may pas successively without, so to speak, leaving the stage. In thus shaking off a prejudice of habit, the precepts of which are found neither in Aristotle nor Horace, but which economy alone has engendered and maintained, the Selenites treated freely and successfully a great number of fine subjects impractical for us, and gave a striking apparatus to their spectacles of which we are deprived by a severity as strange as it is irrational.

What is the point, they said, of submitting authors to rules impossible of execution, which, at the very least, put shackles in genius? Find a drama in which the necessity of confining the action to too narrow a space does not produce absurdities and contradictions, such as weaving a conspiracy in a Sovereign's study, and having guards, confidants and other characters enter it who ought not to have access to it, or holing a secret meeting in a public square, etc. Find those phenomena, they say, and the rule can be admitted, harsh as it is.

As for the unity of time, ought one to protest, say the Selenites again, with reason, when a poet gives a play a duration of several days, or even several months, when he is permitted to execute in two hours what happens in twenty-four? Is one any more plausible, or possible, than the other? Is it reasonable to see in that short interval, as is frequently encountered, night succeeding day and the dawn dissipating the darkness of the night, to give way to a new course of the sun? If, in two hours, one can read an epic poem, which leads rapidly from one extremity of the globe to the other, or a romance that transports the readers from Olympus to the Elysian Fields without troubling the order of ideas or shocking a plausibility that is not being sought, why, in the same space of time, should one be offended by it in dramatic theater, when one lends oneself to it so easily and with so much pleasure in lyrical theater. Are not both of them equally the seat of illusion?

The Selenites, indulgent with regard to the ostentatious precepts of the unity of place and time, did regard as an inviolable rule, unlike the majority of our authors, the unity of action—which is to say, of intrigue in comedy and peril in tragedy—a rule transgressed by our best dramatists, which one cannot set aside without injuring the subject.

They did not admit in dramas the absolute necessity of entr'actes; they used them soberly, and only in cases where it was necessary to suppose time passing in the interval which would have caused the scene to languish had it been represented. What is the point, they said, of dividing a subject into several parts? Why into parts of similar duration, always in odd numbers?[193] A division into five acts—not to displease the Romans, who thought they were outdoing the Greeks— necessarily produces the inconvenience that, in order to fill the prescribed, or habitual, measure the poet is often obliged to have recourse to the padding of incidents and episodes that load the piece with foreign ornaments, since there are really only four necessary phases in a drama: the protase, the epitase, the catastase and the catastrophe; or, in other terms, the exposition, the intrigue, the knot and the denouement. The division of the poem into five acts is, therefore, a false distribution, a deviation from reason, an automaton march that makes it almost impossible to find a play in which the third or the fourth act, which ought to be made into one, is not weakened, lan-

---

[193] Author: "In Madrid, after the death of the great Gustave, King of Sweden, a tragedy was staged in eighty acts, the performance of which lasted a fortnight; the King was in attendance."

guorous or superfluous. Is that division demanded in a History or a Romance? Are those works any less pleasing because they are not intercut with gaps that are unnecessary, or harmful to the continuity of interest that makes reading enjoyable? What pleasure could one take in a conversation or an interesting story in which, interrupting the narration, one was compelled from time to time to go for a walk, or to give a musician time to perform a concerto? On the contrary, what impatience and resentment would it not cause in the souls of those who were taking pleasure in listening?

Great advantage was obtained in the Theater from masks, such as the Greeks admitted to the comic and tragic stages, but far removed from the custom, as extravagant as ridiculous among us, of giving dancers masks in green, blue, red, etc.[194] Actors' masks were formed of extremely delicate skin, almost as fine as the epidermis, in which the head was enclosed exactly, with the exception of the eyes, the mouth and the ears, and on which features and physiognomies were skillfully painted, appropriate to represent truthfully the characters in the play.

With that art they had succeeded in giving performances an air of verity that faces too often belied among us, for want of actors appropriate to render the roles with which they are charged. It was, in consequence, unnecessary to give a young man playing an old man a white beard, moustache and eyebrows, which clash with the eyes and the youthfulness of the face.

Baron could, at seventy-five years of age, decently play the role of the Cid;[195] Mesdemoiselles Gaussin and Grandval

---

[194] Author: "*Personam tragicam forte vulpis viderat. O quanta species, inquit, cerebrum non habet*. Phaedrus, Book I, Fable VII." [A fox happened to see a tragic actor's mask. 'How beautiful,' he said, 'but it has no brains.']

[195] Author: "Pliny says that the actress Luceja played comedy at the age of a hundred." Actually, Pliny claims that she was still active at the age of 112. Listonai's reference is to Michel

were able to render appropriately, at the age of fifty, the roles of Luciade and Charmant;[196] one can only see with difficulty an actress who has not yet attained her fourth lustrum scolding and admonishing a granddaughter of thirty or forty years;[197] a young Sovereign, in love with an ugly and aged Princess, extravagantly praises her charms, graces and youth; an actress representing Agnés or Iphigénie with a highly-colored complexion and a brazen gaze; an actor with a foolish appearance playing the role of a cunning character, and vice versa; another with harsh features and furious eyes boldly playing Egiste, Hippolite, Britannicus, etc.; another with the features of an honest man playing the role of a scoundrel. One only sees with repugnance the same actor ornamented with a scepter and a diadem in the first play wielding a shepherd's crook or a spade in the second, Alexandre becoming Lucas and Tamerlane

---

Boyron (1653-1729), who used the stage name Baron; he became famous acting in Racine's tragedies and Moliére's comedies, and wrote ten comedies of his own; he made a famous return from a 29-year retirement to play Corneille's eponymous hero at the age of 67.

[196] Mademoiselle Gaussin (Jeanne Gaussem, 1711-1767) turned fifty in the same year that *Le Voyageur philosophe* was published; Voltaire and Denis Diderot were among her great admirers. The actor Charles-Francois Racot de Grandval (1710-1784) was her contemporary and a fellow member of the troupe of the Comédie-Française in the late 1750s. Mademoiselle Grandval was younger than fifty when this line was written; hence the reference to her in the next footnote. I cannot identify the play to which reference is made.

[197] The author adds references to "Mademoiselle Camouche" and "Mademoiselle Grandval," the latter being the actress in her thirties or forties. Mademoiselle Camouche's debut at the Comédie Française in 1759, at the age of 17, is noted in Diderot's correspondence; he judged that she had the potential to become a great actress, but she seems to have faded from view very rapidly.

transformed into Blaise, etc. The eyes and mind are impeded in lending credence to the designs of a usurper who wants to invade a throne under the resemblance of the veritable Sovereign, and who pretends to seduce the eyes of an entire people with features that are completely different and would not fool a child.

By contrast, the Amphitrions, the Sosies, the Menechmes, etc. under perfectly identical masks, augment the illusion with all the plausibility to which the fiction is susceptible. In addition, all actresses can be young or pretty, old or ugly, serious or frivolous, in accordance with the needs of the author.

Let no one imagine that, beneath that species of invisible mask, the public is deprived of the pleasure of seeing the passions imprinted, and of recognizing their symptoms and movements, on the faces of the actors. To dissipate that dread or error, it is only necessary to recall that one sees in the Italian theater every day joy, fury, sadness and all other interior agitations painted and faithfully characterized on the monstrous masks of the excellent Arlequin and the admirable Pantalon, which make the pleasure and the delight of the spectacle in question. A skillful actor makes the mask disappear; the mouth and eyes, entirely free, can paint almost alone the vivacity of passions and the sentiments of the soul, the play of muscles and fibers is rendered sensible through such a delicate skin, just as the painting appear in its entirety beneath the varnish. If art can gives soul and movement to the mute and tranquil characters on canvas, what can it not do when it is supported by the voice and gesture? Finally, if it is true that the spectator loses a few nuances in the play of the passions beneath the mask, he is fully compensated by the exact relationship that he encounters between the entire physiognomy and the character that the actor is representing—a correspondence that gives the illusion the tone of verity.

It would be rather singular if, the practices of the Selenites being adopted on Earth, after having taken masks away from the dancers, they were given to the actors. That novelty, which has nothing impossible about it, would only find obstacles in prejudice, always slow to be destroyed, and would perhaps be a sign of the progress of reason and good taste. The use of masks would undoubtedly enrich the theater with pleasures and privileges unknown today. Some jokers might laugh at that singular project, but they could only applaud themselves for having mocked if, after its execution were attempted, success did not justify it.

Ignorance, prejudice and personal interest have, at all times, thwarted the execution, and even the attempt, of wise and useful projects. Perhaps one can form an idea, for example, of the pleasure that the Greeks and Romans experienced in seeing plays performed in which an actor recited while another gesticulated. The idea seems ridiculous; one is even tempted to doubt that it was ever the case, because one cannot imagine that such a procedure that that could have pleased the spectators. We are only criticizing our ignorance. It is sufficient to put a brake on our judgment of that singularity, to know that the fact is attested, and then remarked on, that it is not in Zanzibar or Greenland that the practice was employed but in the centuries of the most sublime knowledge and the most delicate and purified taste, among the most civilized and enlightened people on earth, who left us models of intelligence, taste and sentiment in almost all genres. It is sufficient to know that the practice was only introduced after having long savored recitation almost as we know it; a prejudice very favorable for the opinion and sentiment of those who admire that kind of declamation. Do we understand better how singing and declamation were denoted, as well as the gestures that sustained it, or in what the musical accompaniment that united them consisted? Choreography, invented rediscovered in our day, gives us a slight idea. Once again, it is the height of ignorance to treat as ridiculous or tax with absurdity everything outside the narrow sphere of one's understanding.

I cannot help saying that I see with astonishment that the Selenites have been in possession, for a long time, of a genre of comedy unknown to the ancients, who tended to limit comedy to laughing at the ridiculous. Sound minds gave it at its origin the name of "high comedy," bad jokers called it "tearful comedy"; there was eventual agreement to give it the name of "drama," a rarely used by distinctive term which seems appropriate to designate a genre half way between tragedy and comedy. A monument was erected to the man who had enriched the stage by procuring a new source of pleasures for the public. After having, so to speak, exhausted characters and the ridiculous, instead of descending into feebly tracing imperceptible nuances, as some poets of narrow genius have done, could one imagine anything more agreeable and useful, as a judicious man of genius remarked, than putting conditions and states on the stage? Could one open up a nobler career than to depict the passions and mores of private life, unveil the hidden secrets of the heart and analyze the sentiments while uplifting the soul to the virtue of society?[198]

A host of blind, cold or insensate critics strove in vain to depreciate the advantages of that new richness and to prove to the public that it ought not to savor the pleasure and resent the performance of plays of that kind because Aristotle had judged it bad two thousand years before it was invented. Others, more subtle or more inept—terms that are often synonymous—thought to degrade it by showing that a few subjects of the plays in question had been taken from the Romans, a feeble declamation.[199] Do romancers not take their subjects from

---

[198] Author: "*Interdum speciosa locis, morataque recte fabula, nullius veneris, sine pondere et arte; valdius oblectat populum, meliuscque moratur quam versus inopes rerum nugaeque canorae.* Horace Ars Poetica line 319-322." [Sometimes a story marked by commonplace thoughts and well-drawn characters, though lacking in charms and crudely formed delights the audience and holds their attention better than verses without substance and sonorous trifles.]

[199] Author: "*Creditur, ex medio quia res arcessit, habere saudoris minimum, set habet comoedia tanto plus oneris, quanto veniae minus.* Horace, Book II Epistle I." [Writing on

society? Those among them who are the most successful are the ones who have painted simple nature most accurately, and the most interesting those who have described civil society naively.

This genre of plays, like everything that bears the imprint of novelty, divided opinion for some time, until continual success assigned it a place in the theater among the worthiest compositions; the second generation, the sole infallible judge of productions of the mind, fixed it there indefinitely.

Rigid observers of Tragedy in all the arts of imitation, the Selenites treat subjects exactly in all the historical verity of times, laws, mores, practices, places, costumes, etc. One did not see in their dramas the first Romans making speeches about parricide, against which they had no laws because they did not suspect the possibility of that frightful crime. One did not hear the Greeks reasoning politically on the maxims of Machiavelli. One did not see the Druids honoring their divinities in temples; Roman ladies sitting at a banquet;[200] Alexander laying siege to places with cannon. Scythians, Traces, Parthians, Dacians or Tartars were not given the mores, costumes, politics and frivolous minds of the French. One did not see Ethiopian monarchs with white complexions, Arab princesses primped, powdered and prettified, warrior inhabitants of arid deserts covered in gems and gold embroideries, with superb furniture, Babylonians lodged in palaces in the Corinthian style, dungeons of elegant structure containing prisoners gallantly enchained, etc., etc. etc. etc.

The Selenites could not understand why, in our theater, homicide excites horror but suicide is permitted. Is the stage, they asked, less bloodied by one than the other? Is delicacy

---

vulgar themes is thought to be an easy task; in reality, however, it is much the more onerous toil, as its faults will not be pardoned.]

[200] The younger Cato, afflicted by the poor state of the Republic after the battle of Pharsalis, only ate sitting down thereafter.

less wounded by seeing a Queen stab herself than seeing a courageous Citizen rid his fatherland of a Tyrant, a traitor or a scoundrel? By virtue of that ridiculous distinction, born of a feeble prejudice that one cannot support with even an appearance of reason, of how many striking situations and astonishing *coups-de-théâtre* have we been deprived, which might have produced the most vivid emotions and the most dazzling successes?

By what bizarrerie, they also said, do people inveigh against the honest depiction of passions in the theater and the sage lessons delivered there for the correction of mores, while they honor in painting and statuary indecent works capable of offending modesty and igniting criminal desires?

Opera was the most brilliant spectacle one can imagine. Superb decorations, ingenious machines, characteristic dances, almost always in tableaux, linked to the subject and taken from the action, competing fiercely in bringing out, by flattering all the senses, the magnificence that is the object of that kind of spectacle.

The Poem, always taken from the fable and treated, with regard to the passions, in all its verity,[201] furnished the pomp and the marvelous, which are the essence of that spectacle.

The Recitative, even more distant from song than the declamation, was spoken rapidly; the very brief scenes of sentiment were punctuated with arias sung to delightful music, sustained by harmonies and admirable accompaniments, which, not overburdened with notes, assisted the development of the voice instead of drowning it out. The singing of these arias was not infected with trills, cadences, voice-projections, drawn-out inflections and other ridiculous embellishments, which, being unnatural, are only the product of false taste, uniquely liable to enervate the singing, weigh down the voice, corrupt the melody and numb harmonious ears.

---

[201] Author: "*Ficta voluptatis causa, sint proxima veris*. Horace Ars Poetica line 38." [Fictions meant to please should approximate the truth.]

They made moderate use of choirs, which were often linked to ballets.

Their Actors, great musicians[202] and rigorously subservient to the measure, which is the basis of singing, were able to make themselves heard all the better for projecting their voice less; they had no need to be guided, either by the orchestra or by an imperious scepter, as noisy as it is disagreeable, every musician only being occupied with his own part and no one beating time, even lightly, except for the choir.

As can be judged by the vain efforts of so many celebrated authors to succeed in theatrical lyric poetry, that genre, although inferior to authentic tragedy, is the most difficult of all in which to work, and the Selenites, as sensitive to the beauty of the words as to the excellence of the music, only receiving true pleasure from their harmony, had few poems; but they made up for that sterility by producing the same dramas with different music.

They employed for that purpose the poems of Quinault and La Motte, *Thétis and Pélée, Iphigénie en Tauride, Jephté* and some of our ballets with a few changes in the words; and although they judged the historical subjects inappropriate to the nature of the spectacle, they did not neglect the representation from time to time of Italian Operas, because of the music and the softness of the language. I saw performances of Pergolese's *Olimpiade*, of Vinci's *Artaxerxes*, Bernasconi's *Adrien*, Pulli's *Bérénice*, etc., which were a complete success, although denuded of dances and choirs because they were only given as concerts in action, a genre of spectacle that we lack.

---

[202] Author: "When Darius was defeated by Alexander at the battle of Issus, Parmenion found 329 concubines in the Asiatic Prince's tent who all knew music perfectly and played various instruments, which proves that the Orientals made much of that art, overly neglected in a certain country on earth where the principal academy of music has only produced twenty virtuosos in thirty years."

Free of stupid pride and nationalistic prejudices, the Selenites have the wisdom to take from the world everything that can contribute to their pleasures or their advantage. I was assured that they had only employed in our operas a few orchestral and choral works, our recitations, the majority of our arias and old vaudevilles having been relegated to the class of specifics against insomnia.

The Selenites thought more sanely about actors than many enlightened nations, whose spectacles are always performed delectably. Athens charged them with embassies, Rome degraded them from the rank of citizen; Albion has accorded them a tomb next to Kings, Lutece refuses them a sepulcher.[203]

Far from these excesses, the Selenites did not regard them as Statesmen, but did regard them as citizens. They were not unjust enough to dishonor a useful and agreeable profession, which demands superior talents to render the voices of the finest geniuses and share with them the glories of the sublime arts, the employment of which is to celebrate the striking actions of heroes, excite virtue, inspire a horror of vice, destroy ridiculous things and perhaps contribute to the correction of mores.

In general, they deemed actors to be the equals of painters, musicians and authors, who devote themselves to the in-

---

[203] Author: "Although holding different opinions as to the status of actors, the Greeks and Romans idolized spectacles equally and made immense expenditures for their maintenance. The performances of three tragedies by Sophocles cost the Athenians more than the entire Peloponnesian war. Esopus, a celebrated tragic actor, left his son the equivalent five million in our money, which he had amassed acting. Macrobius says that Rolcius received three hundred thousand livres of public deniers in fees." "Esopus" must be the actor Claudius Aesopus, whose name was thus rendered in Philip Massinger's play *The Roman Actor* (1626), with which Listonai might have been familiar.

211

nocent pleasures of the nation and whose mores are not subjected to analysis when they respect public honesty in their works. They even sought the commerce of those who, having the virtues of society, and with all the more insistence because, commonly more learned than the majority of men, they were better able to manifest the wit and amenity that are the charm of conversations.

They were convinced that the dissolution for which actors were once so much reproached was less a deregulation of the estate than an effect of the vice of opinion, which, in imprinting a kind of stain on an estimable profession, dispenses, so to speak, those who embrace it of the shame that retains those who might claim consideration. For the same reason that nothing is more capable of exciting virtue than the esteem attached to a condition, and that honor, that phantom of the imagination, often gives rise to virtuous actions in corrupt souls, the scorn in which the profession of actor is held is doubtless what draws those who exercise it into depravity. A few excessively severe maxims on the one hand, and others too indulgent in their regard, are equally the source of their disorders. One part of the Nation covers them with opprobrium, the other applauds them; alternately charged with anathemas and eulogies, scourged and protected, their status is indefinable.

A few Rigorists, more zealous than clear-sighted, already internally persuaded of the necessity of the theater and falling back on their prejudice regarding the dangers that one runs there, all the more convinced of the honesty of the maxims that are cited in respect of it, only declaim against the scandal of actresses in public. If, instead of authorizing it, they repressed it severely, they would make acting troupes, if not virtuous companies, at least decent societies, and doubtless there would soon be unanimous accord in rendering them the rights of citizenship that they merit, more justly, than many other professions, which enjoy it too peacefully.[204] The meeting of minds on this matter is doubtless reserved for a philosophical century.

---

[204] Author: "Among others, charlatans, astrologers, usurers, painters, obscene authors and others that one dares not name."

Chapter V
On Despotism

As it is common practice today, in all works of a certain order, to treat the subject of Despotism, I shall speak about it too, but in a fashion so opposed to general ideas that are commonly held that I must expect sharp objections. That is the fate of all those who undertake to destroy ancient prejudices supported by long possession.

In a corner of Arzame's library I found a manuscript entitled *Essai sur le Despotisme*,[205] by a French Minister to the Ottoman Court, a work that has probably not been printed on Earth, and of which this is a summary:

"Things seen at close range present an appearance very different from those that one only perceives at a long distance. The ideas that people have in Europe regarding the nature and effects of despotic Government appear to me to be among the number of those that loose much of their justice when examined in depth.

"When I arrived in Constantinople I expected, on the faith of several celebrated Writers, to find excessively unhappy peoples plunged into barbarity and curbed under the weight of a tyrannical oppression, detesting their existence. Imagine my astonishment when I saw abundance and tranquility reigning everywhere! After having obtained an intimate knowledge of the way of life and thinking of the Ottomans, I found their mores generally pure; in society, mild and moderate men and complaisant women, finding their happiness in submission,

---

[205] Listonai had no way of knowing, of course, that Honoré de Riqueti, Comte de Mirabeau (the son of the Mirabeau subsequently referenced in the text), who was only twelve years old when *Le Voyageur philosophe* was published, would make his debut as a political writer in 1776 with a work bearing this title—but not, of course, reproducing the same argument.

having little enlightenment to verity but an accurate sensibility; gravity in bearing but amity in conversation; little communication but much respect; circumspection without mistrust, candor with friends, humanity for slaves, probity in treaties, good faith in commerce, laws of hospitality in full exercise[206] and, which ensures an imperturbable felicity, a perfect resignation to eternal decrees for all the events of life.

"I thought I was dreaming, so powerful is the effect that first impressions and national prejudices have on the mind, when one of their sages, with whom I conversed freely about my opinions on their laws, their mores, their customs and the form of their Government, said to me one day:

"'If, falling from the sky upon the earth with a profound knowledge of the Nature of all the different Governments established there, I had to make a choice between them of the one I thought most likely to make me happy, I confess frankly that I would be embarrassed; but, whether by virtue of education or habit inclining people naturally to that which surrounds them, or because I am better instructed than others as to our true situation, I believe that I am in a position to prove to you that the constitution of the despotic State is preferable to that of all other Governments, Monarchical, Democratic, Aristocratic, Oligarchical or Mixed, for the good reason that it

---

[206] Author: "The law of hospitality, which extends among the Turks to animals, proves that humanity and charity are the basis of their mores. The Chinese show hospitality to animals but none to humans; they claim that if they are reduced to misery, it is the effect of their idleness or a permission of heaven, whose effects it is not permissible for them to alleviate. In the vicinity of Surate there is a great hospital for animals, and others to nourish importunate little insects, for which charity awaits. Poor people are hired there, who are obliged to allow themselves to be bitten in order to feed the little animals." Listonai obtained the datum about an animal hospital in Surate from John Ovington's *Voyage to Suratt* (1696; French tr. 1725).

makes the greatest number happy, a unique means of judging the bounty of a Government.

"'Do not take my reasoning for a theory,' added Osmali—that was the name of my sage, 'to which our world is inappropriate to give rise, much less for a paradox, the fabrication of which is unknown to our simplicity. What I have to say to you is founded on experience; no one is better placed to judge the degree of its felicity than me.

"'Rid yourself of all prejudice and you will agree with me that one does not have, in Monarchical States, a sufficiently accurate idea of Despotism and its effects on the minds of peoples submissive to it to be able to make, with sagacity, a satire on it or an apology for it.

"'If one considers Governments as religions, you will agree that one instructs oneself in one's own fundamentally, that one is fascinated by its abuses, which do not, in fact, destroy its essence, and that one is content to cast a superficial glance at the others, which one always judges sufficient to affirm oneself in the one that one has received from one's fathers, only considering the absurdities, the vicious and often ridiculous aspects of other Governments, often on the basis of ignorant of suspect critiques. How, then, can one flatter oneself that one is drawing accurate parallels and making equitable judgments?

"'You will not deny that all those who have written thus far on Despotism have only depicted its horrors by copying one another, or to flatter the Government under which they live. An impartial examination of the condition of the peoples who live under the supposed yoke, and a more distinct knowledge of their veritable circumstances, will enable you to estimate the value of the general opinion on the nature of despotic Government.

"'If, without pausing to discuss which is the best form of Government—a problem that will always remain devoid of a solution, *adhuc sub judice lis est*—one can be assured that the that the best one is the one that makes the greatest number happy, and the happiest subject is the one who is content with

216

the Government under which he lives, I do not think that it will be difficult for me to convince you that the peoples born under what you call the yoke of Despotism are, without contradiction, the happiest of all.

"'You will doubtless grant me that custom and habit render men happy in certain conditions and in certain climates that would make other unhappy; that an inhabitant of Siberia would find himself in violent discomfort on the burning sands of Libya, and that a Greenlander would not exchange his ice, north winds and long nights for the serene days and benign sunlight that fertilize the fortunate Kingdom of Naples.

"'You will also grant me, without difficulty, that it is more pleasant to live under the empire of one Despot than under the laws of a hundred or a thousand tyrants, as in Aristocracy and even in Oligarchy; and that internal troubles, engendered by factions and fomented by the spirit of independence, incessantly expose to risk the life and fortune of citizens in a Democracy. Have you not seen, in your lifetime, the Swedes plotting against the Senate to reestablish the Despotism whose mildness they doubtless regretted? And do you not presently see the Danes blessing the felicity of mitigated Despotism?

"'Tranquility of mind is not incompatible with blind obedience. If one does not confuse license with liberty, is not the imaginary liberty on which a few people pride themselves with so much ostentation, a different manner of bearing chains? With a just idea of liberty you will agree that there is no free man anywhere on earth, and that there is no condition in which a man can be free. Did not Diogenes, having been sold, believe himself to be the master of the man who had bought him?

"'On that principle one can affirm that there is no veritably freer man than the one who is able to render himself scornful of all the accidents to which life is subject, or who has enough strength of mind of philosophy to imagine that he is. A Sovereign, the only being whom one can believe to be veritably free, does indeed command his people, but he is sometimes obedient to his enemy, often to etiquette and always to his passions; the scepter cannot preserve him from the bitterness of frosts, or his diadem from the ardor of the sun.

"'The people under the Despot, similar to serfs in Monarchical States, accustomed from infancy to the yoke of servitude and convinced that they could never tempt to shrug it off, except with many risks, seek to savor the placid pleasures of slavery rather than the tumultuous advantages of liberty, which is less of a good in the eyes of the slave, as privation is less of a dolor to a man who believes himself to be free. Habit gives the latter a horror of slavery, just as it makes the slave indifferent to liberty.

"'Enslaved people reason, with regard to a free people, as a poor man with regard to the rich; he adapts tranquilly to his poverty, which he seeks to soften by labor, without thinking of striking out against the injustice of fortune by killing the rich; that is why, in Turkey, people are more tranquil than elsewhere.

"'I am not unaware,' Osmali continued, 'that a blind prejudice sometimes compares us to docile animals harnessed to a plow, which the plowman guides according to his caprice, and which, accustomed to the yoke, offer themselves to it. One might say as much of all people, in general, and because we are less turbulent than elsewhere, there is no necessity to refuse us the usage of thought. Are there not, in Europe, an infinite number of men for whom the faculty of thought is a torture, and judging in accordance with others, a relief? Ignorance and laxity are perhaps the causes of their apathy, but are they any less happy for that?[207] Do they not even have the advantage over those whose unquiet mind and immoderate desire to know everything is incessantly tyrannized by meditation and reflection, and whose judgment is tormented by prej-

---

[207] Author: "*Nil admirari prope res est una, Numici, solaque quae possit facere et servare beatum*. Horace Book I, Epistle VI." [To admire nothing, Numicius, is almost everything, and the only thing that can make and keep us happy.]

udices, which attack understanding, and the circumstances that thwart their theories of happiness?'

"'It is not, therefore, a matter of knowing whether people have reason to be happy, but whether, in fact, they are.

"'Writers, as I have said, servile echoes of those who have compared the different sorts of governments relative to their way of seeing rather than the intimate knowledge of each of them, cried out loud against that arbitrary power, whose will is the only law and who disposes, according to his caprice, of the lives and fortunes of his subjects, as if, because all Sultans are not Tituses or Trajans, they are necessarily Neros or Caligulas. It is, however, a fact that people enjoy life here in security and peace.

"'The Sultan is so scarcely despotic, in relation to the idea that you have of the term, that he cannot touch money; his treasury is separate from the public treasury. He can only demand someone's head with a warrant from the Divan or a fatwa from the Mufti. He is often obliged to consult the political and military estates to declare war or peace. He has no absolute right to dismiss Janissaries. Finally, on his accession to the throne, he swears on the Koran to have the laws observed; if he sometimes fails in his engagements, he has that in common with many Potentates.

"'The Sultan does not have the right to increase taxes, which, moderate throughout the Empire, do not excite fraud: a sage maxim that renders collection easy and prevents the cruel necessity of rigorously punishing an infinity of wretched individuals who can only find their subsistence by avoiding them.

"'Justice is as prompt as it is severe against abductors and oppressors; in addition, the Turks judge summarily and inexpensively, in accordance with common sense and equity, not being prey to the leeches of chicanery or victims of the ruinous form of laws under the weight of which many people more enlightened and civilized than they are groan, who claim to be free.

"'Perhaps there are vices and virtues annexed to certain climates. It is a fact that the Turks, self-interested as they are, almost never commit larceny; idleness does not lead them to gamble, nor to intemperance; very few use the privilege of marrying several wives and enjoying several slaves, even among the most opulent. There is no city in Europe that has fewer prostitutes than Constantinople.

"'The Dogma of fatality established among the Turks makes men resigned to the decrees of the Supreme Being into subjects blindly submissive to the orders of their Sovereign, and intrepid soldiers. Opium disposes them to receive restraint stoically.[208]

"'Medicine, simpler here, and, in consequence more salutary than in the rest of Europe, does not have the deadly talent of fabricating maladies from the simple accidents that Nature dissipates when she is allowed to act. The art of healing, in accordance with the method of our ancient Arabs, is limited here to observation and waiting tranquilly for crises. Our physicians have a sovereign scorn for the ostentatious and murderous art of treating ills mathematically, submitting all the parts of the human body to calculation, as one does eclipses and the periodic courses of the planets. The frequent usage of coffee and opium takes away the ingredients that might be harmful or dangerous, entertains health and alternately gives the body the degree of activity or health that it needs, rendering it alert or torpid at will; that is, so to speak, commanding Nature.

"'Deprived, thanks to the prohibition of printing, of the means to enlighten their minds and corrupt their hearts,[209] are not the Turks, more that the inhabitants of States where license rules in impunity, sheltered from the effects of satire, calumny

---

[208] Author: "*Felices errare suo....*" Lucan, Pharsalia, Book I line 459." [Happy in their error.]

[209] Author: "The Scythians, having taken possession of Athens in the time of the Emperor Claudius II, gathered all the books they could find in order to burn them. They only stopped when someone suggested to them that it was necessary to keep a few in order to weaken the courage of their enemies."

and literary wars, which are sometimes so scandalous? Distanced from the reefs on which the vanity of authorship breaks and preserved from the venom of principle contrary to morality, which so many find minds glory in sowing in feeble hearts, and whose unique fruit is the disturbance of innocence and peace, where can more candor be found, except in your rural regions? Is not that virtue, which civilized people incessantly put in contrast with the dissimulation of Courts, the effect of a submissive ignorance, which makes the felicity of shepherds and agricultural laborers? Cease, then, pitying peoples more content with their lot than you really are with yours.

"'After all these observations, can one still decide that peoples submissive to Despotism are really unfortunate? Should one not, on the contrary, be disabused of that opinion, if one recalls that there are many examples of slaves in Barbary, where despotism is harsher than it is in Turkey, Persia, etc., who, after having groaned for a long time about their fate out of pure patriotic instinct, became so accustomed to it at length that they refused to be redeemed, preferring a mild and tranquil life to the liberty that was offered to them to go and beg in their homeland; that many others, by their regret of having quit a pure sky, overwhelmed by miseries in the bosom of their fatherland, have not refused the eulogies due to the humanity of those barbarians?

"'If one compares the manner in which the Africans use their slaves with that of the Spartans with regard to the Ilotes, one will find those barbarians very humane; it is even more astonishing that the Ilotes were so cruelly treated in the bosom of Greece, whose polite mores have served as an example to posterity. An error common to the majority of Writers is to mistake the errors of a Government for the foundations of its constitution. The authority that is always assumed to be capricious and barbaric in Despotic Government strikes harder when it is exercised against Pachas and Viziers, whom it deprives simultaneously of wealth and life; they are always regarded as sad victims of envy, cupidity and tyranny, a prejudice that ought, as is almost invariable the case, to be set aside.

221

The equitable restitution of wealth extorted in commerce, finance and important employments is almost impossible. Is it, then, a cruelty that the Prince dispossesses an avaricious and extortionist Minister? The practice has a host of examples in more civilized states. In what does it differ from Star Chambers, which authorize the penalties and infamies to which ex-actors and those who infringe the law are condemned? That a Despot increases his treasury by such means at least dispenses him of charging his subjects with new taxes in order to allow unworthy favorites to enjoy the rewards of their rapine and brigandage.

"'How far does the prejudice of enlightened Nations against Despotic Government extend? Is not treating the Turks as imbeciles in the knowledge of the Law confusing ignorance with stupidity? Is it not supposed that our Empire is a machine that is only moved by the springs of the intrigues and the jealousy of the women of the Seraglio? They are apparently judged by what happens everywhere else; there is, however, no country in which women have less empire over men. Hence the accreditation of the fable of Mahomet II cutting off the head of the beautiful Irene.[210] But consult skillful Negotiators, who have dealt with the Viziers—interrogate them yourself—and you will learn, doubtless with extreme surprise, that the politics of the Gate are perhaps the least entangled of all the Courts of Europe; that among the Ottomans, good faith generally reigns; that it is the basis of their treaties, which they ob-

---

[210] The reference is to the Ottoman Sultan Mehmed II (1432-1481), who was said to have killed a Greek captive with whom he had fallen in love in order to regain the respect of the Janissaries and control of his Sultanate; Listonai could not have known when he wrote this that the legend would be the subject of Voltaire's last play, *Irène* (1778), but he might have been aware of the English play *The Tragedy of the Unhappy Fair Irene* (1658) by Gilbert Swinhoe.

serve religiously when they are written in their language;[211] that common sense often works better in its own interest than the most subtle mentality, all the more subject to deception because it thinks itself finer and, working on that presumption, almost always fails in confrontation with simplicity and candor—from which one could conclude that where there is less intelligence there is more judgment, and that too much light dazzles more than it illuminates.[212]

"'You also have unwarranted ideas,' Osmanli said to me, 'about our Seraglios, which you consider as inhuman enclosures in which the more beautiful half of society is unjustly retained in eternal captivity, while the women of the Orient, who know the custom better than you do, yearn for no greater happiness that to be enclosed therein. Does their condition differ very much from that of a courtesan who believes herself

---

[211] Author: "Bajazet II threatening to make war on the Venetians, the Republic sent an ambassador to request peace. The prince granted it, and had the articles delivered to the ambassador in Latin. André Gritti, a Venetian who had lived in Constantinople for a long time, and was not unaware of any of the customs of the Turks, warned the ambassador that they attributed no value to anything not written in their own language. The ambassador did what he could to have the treaty changed into the common language of the country, but to no avail. In fact, as soon as the ambassador had gone, the Turkish fleet set sail for Morea."   The reference is to Andrea Gritti (1455-1538) and Bayezid II (1447-1512), Mehmed II's successor. Listonai obtained the anecdote from Pierre Bayle's *Dictionnaire Historique et critique* (1697).

[212] Author: "One reads in the history of Greece that the ambassadors of Samos, having come to Sparta to persuade King Cleomenes to make war against the tyrant Polycrates, made an eloquent speech. After having let them speak, Cleomenes replied coldly: 'I have forgotten your exordium; I no longer remember the middle; as for your conclusion, I declare that I do not want to do anything.'"

223

to be free because she pledges her liberty voluntarily? Does the solitary free to live in the turbulence of society think himself unfortunate when he renounces it as a matter of taste? Where is the smitten lover who would not prefer captivity with his mistress to liberty without it?

"'Alas, the more one reflects, the more one persuades oneself that slavery is a vague term that everyone translates in his own manner. Is the lot of a European woman, always exposed to peril, whose virtue and decency incessantly combats desires, the victim of the caprices of furies of a jealous husband, racked by domestic cares and concerns, often struggling against ill fortune, although free in appearance, really kinder than that of an Asiatic woman? Is it preferable to the so-called slavery of a Sultana, distanced from opportunities of seduction, who can only obtain the favorable gazes of her lover by her tenderness, her complaisance and the purity of her mores. Who enjoys all the comforts of life peacefully, without chimerical ideas of liberty, from which a fortunate education has preserved her?

"'As for us, the plurality of women saves us from their empire; passions weaken in abundance; pleasures less vivid but sweeter spread a serenity in the soul preferable to the torments fabricated by an ardent imagination. I also think that our climate is a pneumatic machine, which enervates the senses and softens the passions; at least we obtain therefrom the advantage of savoring the charms of repose.

"'That,' Osmanli said to me, concluding his reflections, 'is what I have to say to you to convince you that, although subjects of a Despot, we are happier than you Europeans, or at least that we are intimately convinced of it, which is sufficient for us. I will not go into the religious reasons that do not permit you to admit the greater number of our principles, controversy only being the prerogative of our Doctors. You were born on the Seine and I was born on the Black Sea; that is what establishes our different beliefs, but it ought not prevent men, who are all brothers from one pole to the other, from loving one another and helping one another.'[213]

"I confess that Osmanli's speech, confirmed by the experience that I acquired during my sojourn in Constantinople, gradually destroyed the opinion that I had formed of the sad condition of the subjects of the Despot, and I understood easily, in spite of the prejudices of education, that because knowledge only multiplies the needs of the heart and the mind and diminishes the means of satisfying them, the happiest man on earth is the one who has the fewest desires—in which respect savages are doubtless the happiest of all.

"I am well aware that, departing from opposed principle, the objection might be raised that every thinking being, raised in an enlightened century under a Government that enables the sciences and arts to flourish, proud of his superiority, bemoans, with reason, the stupid barbarity in which the subjects submissive to the Despot are plunged; and that, in comparing the condition of modern Greece with that of ancient Greece, it is dolorous to see ruins, debris and hovels shamefully covering the places once occupied by the celebrated monuments off sculpture and architecture in the beautiful centuries of Athens and Corinth, flocks grazing in the lyceums, gymnasia and hippodromes, and cowherds replacing the likes of Plato, Socrates, Pythagoras, etc.[214]

"A spectacle of human vicissitudes so striking saddens, to the point of tears, an enlightened amateur; but his dolor,

---

[213] Author: "Saladin left by his testament equal distributions of alms to poor Mohammedans, Jews and Christians, wanting to make it understood by that disposition that all men are brothers and that in order to help one another it is unnecessary to inquire as to what they believe, but only what they are suffering."

[214] Author: "...*Videat desertaque regna pastorum et longe saltus lateque vacantis*. Virgil, Georgics Book II, line 476." [After so long he may see the shepherd's realm deserted and the empty meadows wide open.]

purely relative to his knowledge and his tastes, produces no sensation in the peoples who inhabit those desolate climes. Deprived of the enlightenment that increases desires and gives birth to regrets, they are born and die in a lethargy that closes any access to their soul of any dolorous awareness of privations of which they have no idea. For them, a Corinthian capital and a tree trunk serve equally as a table on which to take a frugal meal, which is sufficient to their needs; an Ionic cornice forms, for want of a joist, the step of a stairway; the marble of Paros does not appear more precious than brutal stone; those inscriptions, which have no more significance for them than the knots and tumors of tree-trunks, do not put their imagination to the torture of deciphering the characters and interpreting their meaning. One does not desire what one does not know; one is not curious about that which one does not suspect. Would it not add further to their happiness if it were given to them to sense that their poverty shelters them from the deadly effects of ambition and cupidity felt so cruelly by the Romans, Carthaginians and Mexicans, unfortunately divided by the riches and treasures that caused their total destruction?

"True felicity is only found in the bosom of a mediocrity from which one never emerges, as real misfortune only consists in the loss of a condition whose pleasures one has savored. In the country, rustic occupations take the place of the more vivid pleasures of cities.[215] There, time is spent, here it is killed. Gaiety is only encountered under the humble roofs of cottages, while sadness, anxiety, maladies and ennui afflict the brilliant abodes of palaces.[216]

---

[215] Author: "*Fortunatus et ille Deos qui novit agrestes, Panaq, Sylvanumque senem Nymphasque sorores!* Virgil, Georgics Book II line 493." [Fortunate is the man who has come to know the rural gods, Pan, old Sylvanus and the sister nymphs.]
[216] Author: "Anxiety and inconstancy are, in the majority of men, only the consequence of a false calculation. An exaggerated expectation of the things one desires causes one to experience, as soon as one possesses them, a malaise and disgust

"The shepherd, always singing, is fortunately unaware that there are pompous spectacles in the capital, to which one goes when one has nothing else to do, languidly parading one's face and ennui; academies where envy, intrigue and discord reign, where sages go to spread and collect incense in profusion, to talk eloquently and unreason methodically, bureaux of wit in which common sense is a stranger, mistrust naturalized and conceit prevalent; feasts to which the multitude go in order to gorge themselves on foodstuffs pernicious to the health, where parasites reveal themselves by their damage, fine minds by their deviations and the host in being duped; brilliant festivals at which no one rejoices; promenades where no one walks; balls at which no one dances; operas in which no one sings; in sum, fatiguing and demanding etiquettes, respected and detested by their most zealous partisans.

"Let us agree, then, that true felicity only consists in exemption from dolor, the privation of an unknown wealth and an imaginary evil; that habit renders even the harshest condition supportable, and even pleasant, its rigor only being sensible to someone who recalls having savored a more satisfactory one; that, on the contrary, pretended liberty only procures pleasures inseparable from cares and bitterness, which always lose their realty by possession, never being anything but feeble diversions from dolor; that enlightenment is poisoned by doubt, curiosity by the impotence to satisfy it, enjoyment by monotony or satiety; and that, in the final analysis, liberty and slavery both reside in opinion; and that in consequence, a man born under the empire of Despotism is no more unhappy, and might even be happier, than one born under any other Government.

---

that does not allow us to enjoy anything. One passes on to other objects; thus, life passes from illusion to illusion, exchanging chimeras; that is the sickness of keen and delicate souls."

"To support my reasoning I will advance a strange proposition, paradoxical if you wish, but which I nevertheless believe to be true; it will be my final brush-stroke.

"Making an abstraction of all prejudice of birth, education and habitude, who can deny that a person would be truly happy, whose organs were sufficiently deranged for him to be to take as much pleasure from the lugubrious cry of a barn-owl as the melodious song of a nightingale and in French music as Italian music; to whom a thatched roof appeared as elegant a structure as the peristyle of the Louvre; an inn-sign as well-defined as a painting by Raphael and as well-colored as a painting by Rubens; whose sense of smell was as agreeable affected by fetid matter as the most delicate perfumes; his taste was flattered by insipid aliments as the spiciest; his mind equally satisfied by parades and the French theater, by *La Pucelle* and *La Henriade*, by *Don Japhet* and *La Métromanie*; by *L'Année littéraire* and *L'Esprit des Loix*; who would find, finally, in decrepitude the graces and charms of youth, and in the horrors of solitude the attractive delights of society?

"The joy of such an individual would be as pure as it was tranquil, safe from the cares that thwart pleasures, the troubles of mind that poison them. That kind of impassibility would at least preserve him from all the imaginary ills that give rise to what is known, in good society, as taste, delicacy and sentiment.

"If, therefore—I always return to my principle—true happiness only consists of the absence of dolor, the condition of that presumed unfortunate would undoubtedly be preferable to that of the best-conformed, the most sensible and the most delicate of men.

"Let us rid ourselves, if it is possible, of the common error of appreciating pains and pleasures at the tariff of our tastes and penchants—a rule that is only reliable for our own individuals selves—and we will soon realize that, although so many disorders in the animal economy are not easily found assembled in the same individuals, we have examples of eccentricities before our eyes every day, which do not ensure either the misfortune or the pain of those who are their playthings.

"How many mathematicians have drunk ink or oil without even perceiving it? Tamerlane slaked an ardent thirst deliciously with a little water mixed with mud and blood, which he drank from a skull in the middle of a battle. In how many besieged towns have people devoured rats, scorpions and toads as exquisite foodstuffs? What is chiaroscuro to so many idolaters in painting? Can an impaired brain distinguish the odor of a violet from that of a poppy? For many ears a long-winded monologue by Lully is equivalent to a delightful arietta by Pergolese; all music is similar; for the majority it is merely noise; for the deaf it does not exist.

"How many young men, in the dark, applaud themselves for having enjoyed Venus in the arms of Tisiphone? Ignorance and frivolity put all books at the same level. For a misanthrope, for a betrayed lover, a frightful desert is an enchanter's abode. Pale colors give a sensual tint to ash, plaster and charcoal. We treat as depraved those appetites insensible to the foods that are our delight, and pity those afflicted by them, but we would be far more reserved in our judgments if we were better acquainted with the power of habit, and the singular means that Nature employs to procure us pleasures, which everyone only savors in appearance. It is thus that we judge deplorable the condition of peoples who live under Despotism, sheltered from so many of the agitations that harass Monarchical and Republican brains."

Chapter VI
On Analogy

Does Analogy, the Selenites wonder, delight Nature as much as our ignorance is pleased to suppose? Is it not rather an instrument of thought, more convenient than reliable, for reasoning about everything that is beyond the range of our sight and understanding?

The stars, it is said, scintillate; therefore they are as many suns, like ours, which have their own light and also have planets in their vortex. They are at a distance proportional to their apparent size. Six classes have been established; there might be millions. Sirius, for example, is 27,644 times as distant from us as our own sun; the proof given of that is that, all suns being the same size, the disk of Sirius appears 27,644 times smaller, and it is therefore 27,644 times further away. However, the planets of our vortex are all different sizes; Saturn, more distant from the center than Jupiter, is not as large as that planet; the Earth is 1,170 times smaller than Jupiter, etc. Why should all suns by the same size?[217]

According to the opinion almost generally accepted by virtue of the demonstration given by Römer,[218] light being

---

[217] It is, of course, the case that all stars are not the same size, and that the relationship between their magnitude and their distance is complex, but it was still impossible to measure stellar parallaxes in 1761 and would remain so for nearly eighty years, so the question could not yet be settled.

[218] The Danish astronomer Ole Roemer was working at the Paris Observatoire when his observations of the eclipses of the Jovian satellite Io in 1696 allowed him to conclude that the velocity of light was finite and calculable, although it was Christiaan Huygens who did the necessary arithmetic. The discovery was, however, widely disputed and was by no means universally accepted in 1761.

emanated by the sun, its entire vortex only receives radiance at the expense of the star; why, then, does it not diminish in volume? Why has it not been exhausted? A thousand theories account for that, each more hazardous than the next. Every emanation of a luminous or odiferous body is a particle, which comes to strike the retina or the nervous tufts of the nose, and thus diminishes the volume and weight of the body from with it emanates to that extent. Even musk, an ordinary standard of comparison, diminishes in weight at length; why, then, does the sun not diminish like other bodies? How does it repair its losses?

Is there any analogy in the velocities of different bodies in motion? Is that of light comprehensible? It is astonishing that the Earth travels, in a year, a hundred and ninety-eight million leagues without our sensing the slightest movement; that is certainly something at which to marvel. The Earth, swift as it is, is only a sluggard by comparison with a ray of sunlight, with travels more than four million leagues in a minute—that is what one can call traveling! The speed of a cannonball is almost nothing in comparison, since it required twenty-five years to travel the same distance that a ray of sunlight covers in eight minutes; with a similar speed a man could go around the world seven times in a second.

It is more natural, say some of those who support the movement of the Earth, that it travels 8,700 leagues in twenty-four hours around its own axis, than to say that the sun travels ninety-eight millions leagues in the same interval of time. I agree; in the same way, it is more natural that light should be instantaneous than propagated, although it is not. If we only had that reason for making the Earth rotate, it would be very feeble; for I can as easily conceive that the sun, and even the stars which are four hundred thousand times more distant, rotate around the Earth in twenty-four hours as that rotates on its own axis.

Here is a demonstration. Let us suppose a wheel with spokes a hundred thousand times thinner than a ray of sunlight, extending a hundred million times further than the fixed stars of the sixth magnitude; one would grant me without difficulty that the extremity of a spokes that touches the hub can rotate around the center in a second, and that, consequently, the opposite extremity would turn in the same time, although it is describing a circle whose area is unimaginable, since, in order to calculate the quantity of leagues that the extremity of each spoke would travel in a second, a unity with a thousand zeroes would be insufficient. What difficulty is there, then, in the sun, or even the firmament, rotating rather than the Earth?

Our little planet is inhabited by humans and animals, and charged with plants; thus, by analogy, the other plants are similarly inhabited, covered with animals, waters, forests. Otherwise, what would they be for? To reflect a little light back to us? One perceives on the moon, therefore, by the shadows that the sun causes on its surface, seas, capes, gulfs, promontories, etc. One immediately draws up a topographical chart. Thus far, the analogy holds good, because the Moon, as the satellite of the Earth, is submissive to the same laws of gravitation, motion, etc. And I can confirm it, having the proof before my eyes. But who can be sure that the other planets experience the same conditions, as if it were not possible for an opaque body to have neither water, nor land, nor air, but only matter modified in a manner as impossible to imagine as creation is inconceivable for any created being? Who can doubt, finally, that if the planets are inhabited, it might be by beings of a nature entirely different from ours?

The planet most sensible to our eyes by its apparent size and proximity to the Earth is the one that is slavishly subjected to it, of which at least we know the movements and the irregularities; how dare we, then, judge so imperiously the condition, the density and the nature of all the others?

Independently of the thick veil that envelops, in all beings, the mystery of generation, what analogy can be found in the physical means that various sorts of animals employ to perpetuate their species?

Viviparous animals only engender by coupling.

A male fish does not touch the female; he only fertilizes the eggs that she abandons to the current of the waters. If Platonic love exists anywhere, it is only apparent among the cold inhabitants of the waves, since it is devoid of enjoyment—unless desire obliges it with an enjoyment of which humans have no idea.

A few animals, which have both sexes, like the slug, sometimes couple but also engender without copulation.

The freshwater polyp is so singular in its generation that one cannot discover any part of it that is appropriate to that purpose, and it can be regarded as the last of the animals or the first of the plants. It can, if necessary, realize the fable of the Hydra with several heads, since, by cutting the head of the polyp into a thousand pieces, a thousand perfect heads result.

Analogy founded on the apparent uniformity of the operations of Nature, whose effects are infinitely various, cannot be other than very faulty, since one realizes, at every step one takes in the study of her mechanism, the weakness of human intelligence in distinguishing its true relationships. One finds—or rather, one believes that one finds—analogies in the most disparate things, because, in the operations of Nature, one cannot discern the nuances distinguishing one formation from another. In the system of the Universe everything is doubtless linked in such a way that there are no interstices, except between the creature and the Creator.[219]

Is not analogy more sensible in default with regard to the virtues and properties that one perceives in plants and fluids by way of analysis, when one attributes the same effects to the union of bodies that are similar or homogeneous in appearance? The majority of the most salutary plants give, by that

---

[219] Author: "From the stone to the brute the distance is great, but to our feeble eyes, it is less between the oyster and the ape, and between the ape and the human; it is considerable between the human and celestial substance; it is infinite between the angel and the Supreme Being, but between created beings the gradation is imperceptible."

kind of operation, the same principles as the most venomous. The waters of Forges and those of Passy give the same result by decomposition. The aloe and the opium poppy present the same principles, although one is the corrective of the other. To what, then, is analogy reduced if one can only obtain from bodies by analysis feeble inductions and notions as vague as those that can be obtained of the subject and colors of a painting from its ashes?

Is analogy any more help in medicine? Does it not, on the contrary, expose dangers evident in the relationship one finds between two maladies offering the same symptoms, one caused by indigestion and the other by starvation, which occasion contrary treatments in their cure? To what unfortunate accidents, and to how many fatal consequences, has the poor human body not been exposed by the incapacity of the disciples of Aesculapius who recklessly endeavor to repair it?

There are not on earth two perfectly similar faces or two voices, two blades of grass of the same color, two flowers that have the same scent, two aliments that produce the same taste sensation, two geometrically equal human statures, two identically conformed temperaments, two perfect synonyms in any language, two minds of the same temper, etc. What use, then, is analogy? What does the word signify, except a sterile means of explaining what cannot be demonstrating, which, at the most, spares arguments and puts human pride to the sad necessity of often consenting to the probable for want of certainty, to perpetual conjectures, to a universal "as if"? Analogy is thus, in sum, what the testimony of others is to those who have neither seen nor heard.

Chapter VII
Moral Traits

In a supper that Arzame gave me in the company of friends, amiable philosophers, he proposed, following Plato's example, to examine each of them individually to see whether there was a single one among them who had not merited, at least once in his life, a sentence of death.[220] We all agreed in good faith that none of us ought to have escaped it, and that the most austere philosophy was not exempt from paying a tribute to humanity, not for the odious crimes against which laws prescribe severe measures, but for actions that prejudice depicts as innocent, or that interest and passion seems to justify, but which, being contrary to the laws of exact probity, are nonetheless criminal, even though they remain unpunished.

Crimes are not only actions contrary to the laws, but also to justice. Reprehensible vices are not only those that infect society but also those that trouble or destroy peace and harmony. If the laws have not pronounced against vices, it is because, unable to compel the opposed virtues, they have been obliged to hand over to members of society the right to punish them by means of shame and scorn.

Criminal or shameful actions that go unpunished are much greater in number than is commonly imagined. There is a means as simple as it is infallible of appreciating their merit; it is sufficient imagine oneself in the place of the injured party, with the right and the power to take vengeance. To shed light on my proposal I shall content myself with sketching a few features of unpunished vices that ought to be placed in the ranks of crimes and submitted, like them to the rigor of the laws.

---

[220] Author: "*Ut nemo in sese tentat, descendre nemo*. Persius, Satire IV, line 23." [No one descends into himself (to find the secret imperfections of his mind)]

Although gratitude is not obligatory, because it would have the effect of a contract that would annihilate the gift, ingratitude is nevertheless a shameful vice, born of pride, which tends to destroy any sentiment of benevolence in society; it is baseness in the soul, injustice in the heart and blackness in the mind. Who would ever have the effrontery to admit to ingratitude?

Bigotry tends, by an excess of zeal, to shred another's reputation pitilessly, violate the laws of fraternity and to abandon itself safely and disproportionately to the poisonous inclinations of slander, whose effects are irreparable.[221]

The revelation of a secret is a sacrilege and the unjust employment of a sacred deposit, even with regard to an enemy.

The abuse of a confidence as a result of hazard or indiscretion is a base and shameful crime; to one's own advantage it is a larceny; to the profit of others a perfidy.

A sally, which is always unworthy of the rank of an aristocrat, has often tarnished the reputation or ruined the fortune of a good man.

Indiscretion in a fortunate lover is always a despicable vanity, a stain on probity; it is to repay a benefit with an injury, to do violence to the most cherished wealth of all, reputation; it is to take unworthy pride in an odious vice, which often receives from vengeance the punishment that the laws cannot and ought not to pronounce.

Is not protecting a criminal or a liar, soliciting on his behalf, corrupting judges in his favor an infringement of natural and civil laws, oppressing the innocent by repercussion and rendering oneself guilty of the evil consequences of the unpunished crime?[222]

---

[221] Author: "*Quid de quoque viro et cui dicas, saepe videto.* Horace, Book I, Epistle XVIII." [Be careful what you say about anyone, and to whom.]

[222] Author: "There are singular cases in which the constitution of the Government seems to authorize certain vices and to

To seduce the wife or daughter of a friend is to abuse his confidence cruelly and break the most tender of social bonds, by casting trouble and disorder into the bosom of a family, which one is more obliged than anyone else to respect; not to mince words, it is rascality. Can it be the case that there are countries where the corruption of morals has reached such a level that the frightful crime in question, disguised under the name of gallantry, is treated gently?

To disguise the truth, of which one ought to be the witness, under the envelope of equivocal terms that misrepresent it, is a crime against probity, which neither debates nor deliberates: a crime as black as that of the sycophant, who corrupts the truth in order to excite vice by applauding it.

To abuse the sad situation of a girl in order to ravage her innocence, or the desperation of a woman plunged into poverty in order to dishonor her, and to cast one or the other into disorder, is a brutal cowardice, an unworthy baseness that merits the greatest punishment; to fail subsequently in one's engagements, illicit as they might be in morality, is to add theft to the insult and to declare oneself in shameful infraction

---

extend traps, so to speak, for virtue itself (*Ex senatus-consultis et plebiscitis scelera exercentur*. Seneca, Epistle XXXV. [There is nothing so absurd that some philosopher has not said it.]) An honest man would not render himself accomplice to an unjust act, by soliciting, in favor of a guilty murderer, his relative or ally, if the iniquitous practice of spreading over an entire family the opprobrium that only one of its members did not force him to save himself from the dishonor that will be attached to him. That barbaric custom ought only to take effect in the case of an attempt on the life of a Sovereign. In any other circumstances, the ignominy with which an entire innocent family is covered for the crime of a single individual cannot even be justified by the hereditary glamour that descendants of the nobility draw from their ancestors. That advantage, which only exists in opinion, is really only an imaginary possession, which cannot enter into parallel with a veritable evil."

of the most respected law of society, the promise that is the pledge of faith, and has the value of a contract between men of honor.[223]

The poorly-instructed disciple of Hippocrates who attempts recklessly to treat the human body is nothing but a vile interested party, guilty toward the State of all the homicides that he causes by vanity or incapacity; he is a brigand, who plans a thousand murders in cold blood. The physician who prolongs a malady, which art or Nature, acting alone, could abridge, is committing a species of murder, to which the motive of interest adds further enormity.

---

[223] Author: "Under the command of Septimius Acyndinus at Antioch, an individual who had not brought to the treasury the pound of gold with which he had been taxed was put in prison and the Governor swore that he would be hanged if he did not pay within two days. The unfortunate man's wife was pretty. A gallant offered her the pound of gold if she would spend the night with him. To save her beloved husband's life she promised to accept the offer if her husband, whose life depended on it, consented. The latter thanked her and consented, but the gallant, having satisfied himself, substituted for the promised bag of gold a pound of earth. Having perceived that, the woman demanded justice from the Governor, whose eyes were opened by that accident to the violence of his threat, which had driven those unfortunates to such an extreme remedy. As reparation, he paid the pound of gold himself and awarded the wife the domain from which the earth she found in her purse had been taken. A father of the Church tolerated that action, because the woman, in that encounter, lent her body to her husband, not by reason of the customary desires but the need that he had to live." The anecdote can be found in Voltaire's *Dictionnaire philosophique* (1764), but Listonai could not have seen that (unless he was personally acquainted with Voltaire, which is certainly possible); I have not been able to trace Voltaire's source.

An Advocate who undertake the defense of a case that he recognizes to be bad or unjust commits his honor or his faith; he is planning to deceive either the judge or his client. He is guilty in either case; if he believes that he will lose, he is acting in bad faith; and if he hopes to triumph by virtue of the inattention or incapacity of the judges, he is rendering himself accomplice to a conspiracy.

A Prosecutor who spins out a trial by the iniquitous detours of chicanery is a monster, who is ravaging both allied and enemy territory.

Is not a Magistrate who neglects the investigation of a civil or criminal case the thief of sums that are paid to him unjustly, or guilty of the death of an innocent man? Can one conceive that instead of seeking to obtain with so much ardor the thorny right to judge his fellow, a good man would only ever accept it tremulously?

To defraud Royal rights is to deflect common wealth to one's own profit and to commit an offence against the entire Nation.[224] The tributes that the needs of the State render necessary, and of which the Sovereign only has the administration, are established for justice and equity; they are just, because they are employed for the maintenance of order, tranquility and public safety; they are equitable in that they are distributive; they ought therefore to be faithfully acquitted since they are part of the revenues of the State; it is a contribution that it is only permissible to elude by temperance and frugality. It is in vain that those in infraction think themselves

---

[224] Author: *"Detrahere igitur aliquid alteri, et hominem hominis incommodo suum augere commodum, magis est contra naturam, quam mors, quam paupertas, quam dolor, quam cetera quae possunt aut corpori accidere aut rebus externis.* Cicero. De Officiis, Book II, chapter V." [Therefore, to take anything from another, so that one man increases his own interest to the detriment of another, is more unnatural than death, poverty, grief and other things that happen to the body or externally.]

justified by the pecuniary or afflictive difficulties that they incur; it is always a theft from the mass of the State and its citizens, who, for want of the necessary recovery, are unjustly charged with new impositions.

It would be a good thing, it is true, if the law were sometimes less disproportionate in its pricing; fraud, becoming less lucrative, would excite less avidity; it would be even better if all exclusive privilege were abolished, except for that of the fabrication of money, and if the commerce in a few goods, like salt and tobacco, were freed from certain conditions, which would render to the Domain the equivalent of the profits obtained therefrom. That regulation, whose execution is less difficult than one thinks, which special interests have always thwarted but humanity advised, would save the life and liberty of many unfortunates, and the law would not be cruelly forced often to punish as malefactors and treat as scoundrels people that it cannot regard as wicked.

Chapter VIII
A Gallery of Curiosities and Things Lost on Earth
that are Collected on the Moon

I hastened to render a visit to the curious gallery agreeably described by Ariosto[225] in his admirable *Orlando Furioso*, in which are assembled all the items lost or vanished from the Earth, some never to return and some to reappear under the specious titles of new discoveries, new inventions, new theories, etc.

In a cabinet designed to contain things that are lost to the Earth forever, I saw arranged in order, by emblems, the glory, the dignities, the honors and the plaints of the present, the idolatry of the past and curiosity regarding the future, the jealousy of husbands, the sighs of lovers, oaths of undying mutual lover, the sentiments of actresses, the faith of the prestigious, the fear of death, the good faith of businessmen and treaties, Platonic love, perfect disinterest in friendship, dedicatory verses and epistles made to Great Men, epithalamia, funeral orations, mausolea, apotheoses of the living, etc., etc., etc.

And in addition:

The aerial architecture vulgarly known as the art of building castles in Spain.

The abandonment of wellbeing in the hope of something better.

Sophistic arguments against experience.

The majority of projects useful to the State and humankind called by people in power "the dreams of good citizens."

The despotic power of excommunications against Sovereigns.

The majority of foundations.

Restitutions at the end of life.

---

[225] Author: "Ariosto did not know that the gallery in question is located in the hemisphere of the Moon that was cannot see."

241

The morality of Lovers and theatrical Plays.

Projects to be carried out in old age.

Specific remedies against fear.

The *Dominium maris* of the English.

Eternal declamations against the taste, mores and ridiculousness of one's century.

Love of the Fatherland.

Conjectures regarding future or contingent events.

The majority of periodical works, notably *L'Année Littéraire*.

The felicities that one savors in dreams, the ordinary portion of misers, courtiers, gamblers, protégés, negotiators, politicians, alchemists, etc.

In a room reserved for the library I found, to begin with:

The famous book *Della Opinione, Regina del Mondo*, a work that a few ignorant bibliographers, like Varron, Scaliger, Saumaise, Casaubon, Bayle, Pascal, Pico della Mirandola, and other limited minds of the same stripe deem never to have existed, but which was, however, begun shortly after the Creation and augmented considerably over the centuries as knowledge was multiplied.[226]

Then there was a prodigious heap of manuscripts and scientific books removed from or having gone moldy in the libraries of those who only bought them for reasons of ostentation and never opened them, including:

A complete treatise on the music of the ancients, with several compositions of the best Greek authors and an opera by Orpheus, the recitative of which is as simple as the declamation, and of which no vestige remains on Earth except in Italian opera.

---

[226] The title was cited by Blaise Pascal as a work he knew by the title alone [On Opinion, Queen of the World], but which he would like to see. It did not exist in 1761, but it does now (very nearly) thanks to the recent use of the title by the French journalist Jacques Juillard, which has been translated into Italian.

Three hundred treatises by Epicurus, in which it is demonstrated distinctly that in regarding voluptuousness as the foundation of his philosophy he has been unjustly made into the head of a sect to which he did not belong, since he was, throughout his life, a model of continence, sobriety and all the human virtues.

What was lacking on earth of Cicero's treatise on the Republic, of which only a few fragments survive, and which completes the book of Offices.

The corrections made in Virgil's own hand to the last ten books of the *Aeneid*.[227]

Ten Decads and a half of Titus Livius, forming the hundred and five books that we lack.

An ample treatise on Human Rights, to which no Prince can avoid submitting.

Considerable fragments of the Library of Alexandria.

What is lacking of the treatise of Epicharmus on the nature of things.

The twenty thousand lines that the Druids were oblige to know by heart before being initiated into the mysteries.

Two very exact geographical maps, one of the Austral lands, the other of the interior of Africa.

The books of the celebrated King of Juda suppressed by Ezechias, containing the analysis of all plants, from the cedar to hyssop, and all the properties of terrestrial animals, birds, reptiles, fish, insects, etc., an irreparable loss on Earth for Botany, Medicine and Natural History.[228]

The books of the Sibyls in their entirety.

---

[227] Author: "Everyone knows that the first books of Virgil's *Aeneid* are copied from Homer's *Odyssey* and the last from the *Iliad*."

[228] The Talmud records that the Biblical King Ezechias, or Hezekiah, suppressed a book of "remedies." The Occult Tradition, probably basing the claim on a remark by Josephus, credits the book in question to Solomon.

A treatise on Latin pronunciation composed with care by Cicero and revised by Isocrates.[229]

The manner of writing, by means of simple signs representing words and entire phrases, more rapidly than one can dictate, invented by Ennius, of which we only have very imperfect usage.

Seventy-three tragedies by Euripides, of which the poet only saw five crowned, just as Menander only saw prizes given to eight of the hundred comedies he had composed—proof that in all times, intrigue and jealousy have been obstinate in their opposition to true merit.

A hundred and fourteen tragedies by Sophocles, some of whose subjects, as with Euripides, have been divined and treated with sublimity by the force of modern geniuses who nourished themselves by reading Homer in the original.

The elements of arithmetic for the method of calculation with Roman numerals.

The original Hebrew of *Ecclesiasticus*.

The supplement to the *Satyricon* of Petronius.

The original of the Salic Law.

A little treatise on the tempering of steel appropriate to the sculpting of porphyry.

In a small room, the origins of all useful inventions were found, and all theories, as many of physics as morality, but they deteriorated, weakened or disappeared as they were recovered on Earth under the specious title of "new discoveries."

The mirrors of Archimedes had disappeared.

Encaustic painting had almost disappeared.

The music of the ancients was full of gaps.

The treatises on navigation were entirely crossed out.

The treatises on morality conserved all their freshness and integrity.

---

[229] This reference is odd, given that Isocrates was Greek, and lived two centuries before Cicero.

Those on metaphysics were still present in their entirety.[230]

The treatise on the circulation of the blood had ceased to exist three hundred years ago.

I was assured that there had never been any treatises on chemistry, anatomy or experimental physics, and only a few feeble essays on astronomy, of which only a few fragmentary lines remained.

I saw in an alcove to one side various substances covered in dust, among which I recognized malleable glass, with which vases, statues and items of furniture were made more solid than with metals; specular stones for building temples and transparent palaces; the substance of the Greek fire invented by Callinicus; Tyrian purple, with which the garments of Emperors were dyed, they alone having the right to write in that color; the art of melting stones; inextinguishable lamps, etc., and a thousand other marvelous inventions whose examination I put off until I had more time.

---

[230] Author: "It is a matter here of the works of the Egyptians, from whom the Greeks obtained the most sublime beliefs, of which they only took the part from which the moderns have taken their own intelligence, those ancient Treatises on Metaphysics not having reached us."

Chapter IX
Essay on Animals

"When one considers," Arzame said to me one day, "that in the moral sphere we have no guide but reason, always combated and often vanquished by the passions and by a secret penchant for evil,[231] and that, in physical matters, instinct always guides us to good fortune without opposition, is one not tempted to believe that instinct is a surer guide than reason?

"Should it be the case, then, that one cannot pronounce the words *soul, instinct, matter* and *animals* without frightening the minds of good men? I think, on the contrary, that when one confines oneself within the limits of reason, when one respects established principles, when one accords humans intelligence to the exclusion of animals, one can, without exposing oneself to be taxed with irreligion or materialism, reason with regard the singular phenomena that strike us so evidently in the mechanical conduct of animals and the advantages that they appear to have over us in physical terms; but before pronouncing so imperiously on the preeminence of reason over instinct, would it not be wise to define what Instinct is?"

What, then, is this Instinct, which constantly directs animals toward wellbeing, in relation to that sublime reason, which so frequently deflects human away from it?

In the physical sphere, humans are perhaps unable to produce anything as perfect as the work of pure instinct: to spin like the spider; to build as regularly as the bee, to sing as

---

[231] Author: "We have the liberty of actions, but not that of penchants; thus Zopyrus, a celebrated physiognomist, did not offend Socrates in judging him a vicious character who had been reformed by the study and practice of virtue." Zopyrus the physiognomist offers his opinion of Socrates in a dialogue by Phaedo of Elis, one of the followers of Socrates who was present when he died.

melodiously as the nightingale, etc. All their reason only enables them to render feeble copies of those creatures that they
scorn, in striving to imitate Nature by an industry that always
leaves human production at an extreme distance from its model.

Once the distinction is established between intelligence
and mechanism, one of which is a celestial gift directed toward a superior end and the other a regular movement imprinted on matter in the physical order, would it be a crime to
reason about the marvels that result therefrom?

Do animals have a language? If they have one, is it different for every genus? Do they understand us? Are they capable of reflection and comparison? How far does the faculty
that we call instinct extend? Are those not as many questions,
which will remain undecided, until we know what instinct is,
or what we understand by instinct?

"Instinct," says D. C.,[232] "being nothing but the effect of
habit, is common to humans and animals, with the difference
that animals have instinct without reason and we have instinct
and reason: the instinct that, by habit, makes us feel; and the
reason that enables us judge, by reflection and comparison, of
which animals have less need than us, their instinct being surer; for the habit of seeing, feeling and comparing becomes, in
humans, an instinct that judges, without the help of reflection."

I agree with all that; I even sense that it is with that instinct, which increases by the exercise of things, that a poet
finds, more easily than another, the structure and rhyme of the
verse that is appropriate to him; that a composer encounters
rapidly, and without confusion, a thousand notes of his instrument; that one can read and write without spelling the
words out; that one can sing without learning scales, in tune,

---

[232] Presumably Descartes, tacitly rendered Des Cartes, although it is not obvious why he is reduced to initials, especially
given that the chapter subsequently includes a reference to
"Cartesians."

without beating time, etc. I agree with all that. I sense that I am right, but I am not certain that animals have no equivalent. I cannot conceive how they know all that it is necessary for them to know without having mastered it, while we execute so poorly what we have learned. Their instinct is not habit, since their trials are always masterstrokes. What name should I give, then, to those actions, which seem as if they depart from reflection? To assign one to them would be attempting to translate a book written in a language that has no alphabet.

If animals are exhibiting some reflection when they appear indecisive in their movements, when they study a height that they want to scale, when they measure with their eyes a space that they want to cross, when they turn away from an evident peril, when they set traps for their prey, when they use cunning to surprise it, when they discern the aliments or remedies appropriate to them, when they learn to talk, to dance, to sing, and finally, when they correct certain vices for fear of punishment, can one deny that their instinctive judgment might have a much greater extent than we accord to it? To prove that animals are pure automata, as the Cartesians say, it would be necessary to demonstrate that in their movements they follow the laws of mechanics, which is false. Learned and civilized humans boldly place at the rank of brutes certain stupid people in whom they do not observe any intelligent action, while they are led to credit intelligence to apes, judgment to elephants, etc.

The animals, some say, have no language, because we cannot understand them—a fine solution! What a marvel not to be able to understand them, when we do not understand those of our fellows who speak in a different idiom than ourselves! Would we be justified in claiming that they too only whistle, howl, whinny, coo, etc?

Whatever the nature of animal language might be, it is certain that they understand one another. A dog, by means of sensible signs, can vividly depict pain, joy, jealousy, and its various needs.[233] If we understand those signs, why should not the animals understand them in one another? Whether they have a general language or particular ones for each species, or equivalent signs by which they can communicate their needs, does it not come down to the same thing? What difficulty prevents those that cannot express themselves in articulate sounds from making themselves understood by signs? What more can infants in the cradle do?

Do we not have a mute language, and, in order that we can understand one another, a silence that is sometimes more expressive than speech? Gestures testify admiration and surprise more forcefully than tones of voice; eyes depict the passions more vividly than the sentiments can express them; pantomime[234] is only discourse in action. What prodigious expressions have been seen in the gestures of certain mutes, standing in for the voice that they lack.

One can, therefore, without racking the brain to seek out relationships between two faculties as evidently distinct as mind and matter, reasoning, for the sake of curiosity, on the phenomena of instinct, agree without a murmur that in sharing the gifts of Nature, the animals have been treated more favorably than us, sensing the excellence of our reason and regretting, in silence, that it is not always a guide as sure as instinct.

Might it be the case, one wit has suggested, in jest, by a sublime effort of reason, that the animals have forbidden themselves reason in order to enjoy the effects of their sensations more tranquilly?

---

[233] Author: "*Cum pecudes mutae, cum denique saecla ferarum dissimilis soleany voces variasque ciere, cum metus aut dolor est et cum jam gaudia gliscunt.* Lucretius, Book V, line 1059-61." [Dumb animals, tame and wild alike, routinely emit different sounds when afraid, when in pain and when they are overtaken by gladness.]

[234] Author: "A King from the vicinity of the Black Sea at the Court of Nero questioned him in an excellent pantomime that he used to serve as an interpreter in all languages."

Without reducing humans to pure sensations, of which only the abuse requires condemnation, I cannot deny that if, by their industry, they succeeded in uniting the various advantages that various animals possess individually, it would add considerably to their good fortune.

I have no intention of debating whether everything is good, whether everything that seems bad might be good, or whether that which is good might be better; I shall simply say that everything is doubtless as it has to be, and that the wise man ought to adapt to that which is, but that it is perhaps not illicit to wish that many things were other than they are. I will add that reason ought to destroy pride in weak beings dependent on everything surrounding them; and that, in the end, humans will only be able prove their preeminence over all the other animals in the physical sphere when, with the intelligence with which they are endowed, to the animals' exclusion, they can demonstrate:

That human, like all other animals, are comfortably clad for all seasons;

That, without study and exercise, humans are musicians to compare with the nightingale, weavers like the spider, manipulators like the beaver, architects as elegant as the bee and the wasp, etc.[235]

That human sight is as piercing as that of the eagle and other predators, and the human sense of smell as keen as that of dogs.

That, as in the freshwater polyp, the crayfish, etc., the section of a limb leads to tits replacement by another.

That humans can run as swiftly and indefatigably as the red deer, the reindeer, etc.

That without any knowledge of physics, botany and chemistry, humans can discern the virtue of useful simples and find the remedies for their maladies.

---

[235] Author: "*Without apprenticeship, humans only know how to cry*. Montaigne."

That human excrements smell pleasant, like those of the marten, or have no odor, like those of grazing animals, or are an agreeable aliment, like those of the thrush and woodcock.

That, like the red deer, the crow and certain fish—according to general opinion—humans can live for centuries.

That, like certain migratory animals, humans can follow the course of the sun and cleave through the air in order to reside in the climates that the beneficent star lights and vivifies successively.

That, human nature changing tastes and opinions as the chameleon changes color, humans can, like the chameleon, live on air.[236]

That humans are as constant in love as the roebuck and his mate.

That in other regards they have the virtue of the red deer, the toad, the honest sparrow, etc.

That, armed by nature for their own defense, like the least of the insects, they only make war for their subsistence and self-preservation.

That, indifferent to the past, they enjoy the present honestly and tranquilly, without any fear of future misfortunes that might not occur.

That to the fidelity of the dog, the docility of the horse, the patience of the donkey, the strength of the lions, the prudence of the serpent, humans add the foresight of the ant,[237] the filial recognition of the swan and the maternal tenderness of them all.

That they care less about the esteem of others than their own.

---

[236] Author: "This is founded on vulgar opinion, which makes air the aliment of the chameleon, although it really consists of plants."

[237] Author: "General opinion is being borrowed here regarding the prudence of the serpent and the foresight of the ant, problematic in the first instance and false in the latter."

If, in sum, sharing all these advantages with the animals, as they share the habitation and the wealth of the earth, or, procuring them by means of industry with the gift of intelligence that animals do not have, humans can show themselves always to be excellent in the qualities of the heart, perhaps they will then be entitled to claim sovereignty over the animals and declare with some foundation that animals were all created for human use.

But when I see humans as the prey of ferocious beasts, the victims and nourishment of the smallest insects, the slaves and the tyrants of the animals from which they extort service,[238] with a sight so short, a sense of smell so limited, a power so weak, an industry so far below instinct, perpetual playthings of reason and intelligence, I no longer know, all compensation made and physically speaking, what rank to assign to human being in Nature.

---

[238] Author: "*Beluas a Barbaris propter beneficium consecratas*. Cicero. De Natura Deorum, Book I, section XXXVI." [Beasts are deified by barbarians because of their utility.]

Chapter X
Prejudices Justified

In order to redress, with regard to hazardous judgments, the spirit of youth, which relates everything to the manner of seeing of its own century, a curious book had been composed in which the origin and causes were carefully researched of many bizarre laws, singular customs and extravagant or barbaric practices in honor even in enlightened centuries, and which seem repugnant to the natural sentiments imprinted in all hearts. An attempt had been made to discover their spirit, without being able to refuse to recognize that laws and customs all derive from the diversity of opinions founded on the interest of peoples relative to climate and utility, and always have general utility for their object—and, finally, what appears at first glance to be a strange opinion, an insensate custom or an inhuman action had doubtless been founded on principles of equity, justice and reason. That is why sketched projects are judged are often judged ridiculous, deformed or pernicious, because disgrace, envy or death have robbed their authors of the means of completing them; it is also why praiseworthy actions are often reckless judged to be bad, for want of knowing the motives that occasioned them. Here are a few examples.

Among certain peoples, the children eat their fathers before they reach extreme old age.

Led by a virtue of ignorance, but seduced by an excess of filial tenderness, the children, believed that they were testifying their gratitude toward those from whom they received the light of day, by sparing them the afflictions and infirmities with which Nature overwhelms them in old age. The fathers made it a duty for them, and the children judged that they could not give the authors of their birth a more honorable sepulcher than their own entrails. Besides which, for peoples who are fortunately ignorant, as animals are, of the dangerous art of medicine, there is no veritable malady but old age.

Sacrifices of the leading man of the Republic among several Nations.

The idolaters believed that they were honoring the Divinity in their sacrifices by the oblation of whatever was noblest on the earth,[239] as in a purer morality, people immolate their tastes, their pleasures and their most cherished passions in exchange for real rewards that are promised to us in another life.

The people, in truth, were rather imbecilic in not perceiving that beneath the veil of humility and disinterest, their Pontiffs, not persuaded of the excellence of these devotions, willingly exempted themselves from the honor of the pyre or the sacred knife. We lament the error of those peoples; we deplore their blindness. Those sacrifices, however, might have desolated a few families, but they did not depopulate the earth. The enclosure of the temple was sprinkled with blood, but the earth was not inundated by it; whereas, more enlightened than them, we honor with the ostentatious title of Great Men and Conquerors crueler barbarians who, under the pretext of the defense of the Fatherland, have inhumanly devastated it, have immolated thousands of subjects to the fury of a personal resentment and destroyed entire nations to avenge a slight insult or satisfy a private passion.

To judge something sanely, it is necessary to look at it from all angles. The source of all our errors comes from the

---

[239] Author: "*Ubi iratus Deos timent, qui sic propitios habere merentur?* St. Augustine and Seneca." [How are they afraid of the gods who think to merit favor thus?] Quoted from Seneca by Montaigne—but not, in fact, by St. Augustine, who is cited for a different quotation on the same page of Montaigne's *Essais*.

fact that our passions only allow us to see things from one side, or even make use see things where they are not. When will we abandon the deadly habit of only darting a distracted glance at all objects, or only looking at them in profile?

Indian Women burn themselves on their Husbands' Funeral Pyres.

What a vivid depiction of sentiments of conjugal tenderness among those people is that of the frequent sacrifice of young and beautiful women to the manes of their Husbands![240] These voluntary acts, authorized by custom, which are not prescribed by any law, perhaps less insensate than the maxims of points of honor among us, are merely a heroic fanaticism for depraved mores, an extravagance for cold hearts. It is a delirium for whoever knows the power of time over afflictions, a stupidity for whoever questions the possibility of those afflictions, and a subject of mockery, mingled with compassion, for those who, turning the most sacred of bonds to ridicule, only admit the grandeur of the soul in the vain triumph of accidents born of illicit engagements.

In what do these sacrifices among the Indians differ from the editions of Condrus, Menecea, Curtius, Decius and so many others celebrated among the Ancients? Is love of the Fatherland nobler than conjugal love? Of those passions long eclipsed among us, one is the effect of a sentiment of generosity, subject to misunderstanding, the other is a strict duty, which benevolent Nature seasons with sensuality. Besides which, the dread of being delivered to long regrets without relief, the suffering of evils without remedy, combined with the flattering hope of being promptly reunited with the be-

---

[240] Author: "Politics might have contributed to the custom of certain Asiatic peoples, who require wives to be burned, as a point of honor, on the tombs of their husbands, in order to insure their lives against murder by their wives."

255

loved object, are natural reasons to render life indifferent and to produce a magnanimous resolution.

Gladiatorial Combats constituted the Amusements even of civilized peoples.

The Combats of Gladiators are doubtless repugnant to humanity; hence they can only, in their origin, contribute to the pleasures of a primitive people, in which it is desired to maintain a warrior humor by the habit of seeing the blood of criminals shed publicly in the arena. But that they constituted the delights of civilized Nations, that the Princes, their Courts and the Vestals of Roman witnessed them and applauded them while blushing,[241] along with Senators, Ladies and even Emperors who had fought therein and feverishly solicited the suffrage of the people; that an art was made of that infamous métier and refined in its murderous instruments, who had to make the blood flow more slowly in order to prolong the pleasure of such a barbarous spectacle. All these horrors, the mere recitation of which makes one shiver, would appear to be so many fables and incredible facts if we did not still see, in our own day, persons of both sexes and all conditions running in crowds to executions with all the more urgency if the tortures and the execution are more horrible.[242]

---

[241] Author: "*...consurgit ad ictus, et quoties victor ferrum jugulo inserit, illa delicias ait esse suas, pectusque jacentis Virgo modesta jabet converso pollice rumpi.* Prudentius, Contra symmachum, II, Line 617." [The modest virgin is so delighted with the sport that she applauds the blow, and when the victor sticks his sword in his opponent's throat she says it is her pleasure and turns her thumb to order him to kill the prostrate victim.] Quoted by Montaigne.

[242] The public execution of Robert Damiens, accompanied by blood-curdling tortures, had recently taken place in Paris in March 1757, in the presence of a vast crowd.

Singular Combats authorized by the laws for several centu-ries.

Singular Combats were authorized on the maxim of the point of honor, of which every man of probity is naturally jealous, but which, poorly understood, only serves to prove that the phantom in question is dearer to him than his own life. That principle, justly approved in its origin to excite valor, only becomes dangerous when it degenerates into fury and, by is employed, by a criminal abuse, as a juridical proof, reck-lessly to interrogate the Divinity on the justice of public or individual differences. One owes to the paternal concern of Sovereigns for the conservation of their subjects, and even more to philosophy, which has enlightened them as to their veritable interests, the total extinction of that frenzy, which, for many centuries, had deprived States of so many brave citi-zens destined to defend them.

In some countries, Great Lords have the exclusive right to execute criminals.

Inspired by the horror of crime and the love of virtue, the great Lords of Georgia deem it an honor to be the instruments of punishment of criminals, just as ours go in pursuit of fero-cious beasts for their pleasure. The scoundrels who pitilessly trouble the order of society and shed the blood of their breth-ren cease to be human beings; they were merely monsters, of which it is necessary to purge the earth. By similar deeds Her-cules was deified. What are the great Lords of Georgia doing, as Magistrates, if not serving as the executors of judgments pronounced by just men and protectors of public tranquility? The scorn attached to that ministry, and the idea of homicide, are merely vain prejudices. In olden times Judges executed the condemned themselves.[243] Among the Greeks, far from the office of executioner being infamous, it was one of the respon-

---

[243] Author: "Adrien Beyer, *Journal des Savans*, 1703 p.83."

sibilities of the Magistracy.[244] In our day, in a few policed states, those officers are not stigmatized with infamy; a few even acquire the titles and privileges of Nobility. Deserters, everywhere, are put to death by their comrades. For one's own defense one rids oneself without scruple of a perverse individual who tries to kill us. In war, that scourge of humanity, which concern for public security has consecrated, even authorizes deception in order to defeat the enemy. The difference only consists, therefore, in the manner in which the murder is committed. The effect is the same. Prejudice, always vicious, therefore has the right to justify in oneself what one condemns in others.

The Community of Women is practiced in certain Nations.

In the fortunate ignorance of *yours* and *mine*, humans do not sense any distinction between the goods that Nature presents to them, their intelligence being unable to realize the chimera of opinion that a good that one shares with others, such as the benign influence of the Sun, is diminished in quality and ceases to be a veritable good. Savages, whose mores are closer to the state of Nature, have no idea of that delicacy, the daughter of pride and avarice, which drives civilized peoples to keep watch on the conduct of their companions, and even to deprive them of their liberty, in order to enjoy privately a fidelity of which they still have the injustice of believing themselves to be exempt. True delicacy does not subsist with tyranny; it only has real charms in an engagement in which the rights are reciprocal.

What difference is there between lending one's wife and lending a book, or one's horses, procuring friends the enjoyment of one's table, one's gardens one's gallery, the property and usage nevertheless remaining to the possessor? Is it not more noble, on the contrary, to admit one's intimates to share

---

[244] Author: "Aristotle, Book VI of his *Politics*, final chapter."

one's felicity? What greater mark of urbanity and hospitality is there than to offer, as the subjects of the King of Calicut once did to Foreigners, that which is dearest and most precious to them?

To how many evils and how many crimes that phantom of delicacy exposes us, from which the fortunate Savages are exempt! Cruel jealous does not trouble their repose, the laws do not confer any penalties on abduction, rape, adultery or incest. In the community of women children are placidly born subjects of the Republic; they suppose themselves all to be brothers; no one differs there over the imaginary force of blood; caste ears are not scandalized in Tribunals by shameful petitions for divorce; there is no knowledge of the indecent usage of congress.

How many wars might be avoided by that accord, so much in conformity with the desires of Nature! What union, what peace there might be in the Nation! Thus, stripped of a prejudice as dangerous as it is ridiculous, the wise Cato lent his wife to Hortensius, and the Lacedaemonians, full of love for the Fatherland, while occupied in a long war, detached the most robust young men from their army in order to repair, with their wives, the depopulation that their absence was caus- ing, with the same tranquility of soul that a vigilant landowner repopulated his pools and forests.

In some Nations abstinence from all that has life is recom- mended, and in others, Religion makes it a precept.

The practice of nourishing oneself on the blood and flesh of animals is cruel and barbaric. Who taught us that they were destined for our subsistence and to satisfy our deregulated appetites, when the earth furnishes our true needs abundantly? Do not the strength and the weapons with which Nature has provided the majority of them seem to be signs of prohibition for humans? Do the people who forbid themselves that aliment not dread that the ferocity of certain animals might pass into their hearts with the same facility that their flesh is changed into their own substance?

In the times of darkness when Metempsychosis reigned, and Religion, which, in the absence of the true one, was the most appropriate to regulate mores and put a brake on the passions, the abstinence from all that has life had the effect of a religious worship: abusive, it is true, but natural and human.

A few peoples push the scruple so far as only walking with fly-whisks, in order to move insects out of the way for fear of crushing them. Others contribute to their nourishment, even maintaining hospitals for animals. They consider us to be cruel and tyrannical, who even sometimes take delight, for vengeance, in making them suffer. Without adopting maxims so rigorous, what proof do we have that harmful insects are not necessary on earth? Our intelligence does not extent as far as to be able to judge; perhaps they are as useful, in the order of things, as certain poisons, from which art has extracted remedies salutary against maladies.

On what foundation do we presume the existence of ferocious beasts to be superfluous? Is their ferocity anything but an effect of the natural need that pushes every individual to the conservation of its being, or a force capable of resisting the violence that we employ against them? Do they ever attack, if they are not solicited by hunger? Some allow themselves to be easily tamed; education can render them domestic. Were not lions and tigers seen among the Ancients submissive to the yoke, harnessed to triumphal chariots? What are human beings, deprived of enlightenment and the assistance of society? With reason, of whose usage they ignorant and whose deviations are often so deadly even when they does know it, would it not be wiser to be humble than to attempt to penetrate incomprehensible decrees?

It is said that Plato recommends abstinence from beans.

What subtle dissertations, and what frivolous consequences are drawn from the precept in question, which Plato never proposed, since he ate beans himself! People have racked their brains over an imaginary precept, supposed on the basis of a badly-translated Greek word, and have exhausted themselves searching for the cause of something that has none. Enthusiasm has gone so far as to claim that Timischa,[245] a female follower of the philosopher, was a martyr to her master's opinion, preferring to die rather than reveal the mystery to Dionysius the Tyrant. Was she not rather a victim of forced silence than a discretion that general opinion scarcely accords to her sex?

The Sciences and the Arts have been considered by ignorant Peoples and by enlightened Nations as principles of the destruction of mores and the dissipation of duties to society.

This opinion, discussed with reasons was solid on the part of those who sustain it as those who oppose it, is the subject of a problem that will probably remain forever insoluble, as with everything that, having various faces, cannot only be considered from one angle, at which the mind has been placed by education and circumstance, or riveted by habit and prejudice.

We undoubtedly know a great deal, but—alas!—what is it in comparison with that remains for us to discover? Our weakness at least teaches us that we ought not to criticize excessively the opinion the opinion of those virtuous people who have banished the Science and the Arts from their Republic; ignorance is undoubtedly preferable to the abuse of Science, especially in Medicine.[246] Perhaps in a hundred centuries,

---

[245] This name must be misrendered, but I cannot identify the intended reference. The alleged abstinence from beans was cited by Plato as a Pythagorean principle rather than one he followed himself.

[246] Author: "Medicine was only introduced to Rome six hundred years after its foundation. It was only received in France during the reign of Charles VII."

comparing the discoveries made in the interim with those from which we take so much vanity, people will be astonished, and rightly so, that we have been able to presume ourselves to be so enlightened, with such limited knowledge and insight. If a dozen heads, to whom we owe so much, had been cut off in the flower of youth, we would scarcely be weaned.

Legal Proceedings with regard to the memory of Great Men.

The legal proceedings undertaken with regard to the memory of Great Men among the Egyptians and other Peoples following their example were founded on the incontestable principle that the love of glory is only a virtue insofar as it is united with a desire to contribute to the general good. The passion that can win fame, isolated and detached from motives, precipitates men into scorn, errors, oppositions, deviations and reckless enterprises that trouble the wellbeing and tranquility of States.

Far from lessening the love of glory in well-born souls, the just appreciation of their heroic deeds and striking actions by the severe examination of the motives that produced them put a brake on frantic ambition, inspired scorn for usurped reputations and irrevocably fixed those of true heroes. It was an act of justice for the times, offering precepts of conduct to posterity.[247]

The Daughters of Sparta danced stark naked in public places.

The practice in question, established by a sage legislator, seems offensive to modesty, but among a warrior people whose mores were pure, Lycurgus judged that it was appropriate to preserve young people from the dangerous effects of the

---

[247] Author: "The accusations were received before inhumation. If the deceased was found guilty, he was refused his sepulcher; recognized just, his eulogy was made, in which no mention was made of his family or race."

surprise of the passions, which were weakened by familiarizing them with the objects. In any case, virtue, which reigned in the hearts of those Republicans, knew "that public honesty covered those daughters and disposed eyes to insensibility."[248]

In Sparta, skillful theft was permitted.
In Sybaris it was only tolerated when made with fracture.

It is difficult to imagine how the desire to steal was born in a country where everything was common, and why theft was authorized, if it was not to exercise the agility and necessary as necessary as bodily strength in military labor, since the law that authorized theft punished those who were caught in the act; but one can say that in Lacedaemon, *yours* and *mine* being a crime according to the law of Lycurgus, what we call larceny was in the punishment.

In Sybaris, by contrast, where the people were soft and effeminate, and, in consequence, easy to surprise, it was necessary to inspire precaution against major accidents; thus, theft carried out with skill was punished there grievously, and tolerated with fracture.

---

[248] Author: "The Lacedaemonian women, Plato says, esteeming that they were sufficiently covered by their virtue, did not deign to cover their thighs. *Ille quod obscaenas in aperto corpore partes viderat; in cursu qui fuit, haesit amor.* Ovid, De Remedia Amoris, Book II, line 33. *Nec veneres nostras hoc fallit; quo magis ipsae omnia summopere hos vitae post scenia celant. Quos retinere volunt, adsiristosque esse in amore.* Lucretius, Book IV, line 1180." [Our passion is checked in full flow when the lover sees the obscene parts of his companion's body in full view (Ovid); Of this our ladies are well aware, which makes them carefully remove behind the scenes the defects likely to check the ardor of love. (Lucretius)] Both quoted, consecutively, by Montaigne.

Suicide is permitted or tolerated in the greater part of the known world.

So long as people only knew one, purely human, morality, it was quite natural to think that humans were only held to life insofar as they were attached to it by some agreeable link, and that when, on the contrary, it is overwhelmed by misfortunes and dolors, it is merely perfidious to conserve it out of weakness; that if they come into the world without their consent, they can exile themselves from it, when existence becomes burdensome, as they can deliver themselves of a gangrenous limb in order to save the rest of the body; that, far from troubling the order of Nature, the goal and progress of which were unknown, they were, in terminating their days, only anticipating a consummation that must necessarily arrive sooner or later. It would have been, in truth, more virtuous to wear away the chain than to break it, but true heroes are rare.

In Babylon, as in Lydia and among other Peoples, all Women were ordered, by a law founded on an Oracle, to go once a year to the temple of Venus, in order to prostitute themselves there to Foreigners.

Who would have believed that the law in question, which appears to be so corrupt and infamous, was founded for wise and praiseworthy reasons, with regard to the beliefs of the people who observed it, and that it had been established in order to prevent debauchery and dissolution rather than to favor them? To be less surprised in one's judgment of the custom, however, it is sufficient to consider that it was, among those peoples, among the number of religious ceremonies.

Remember that, in the darkness of Idolatry, the most enlightened peoples, like the Greeks and Romans, admitted malevolent, unjust and cruel Gods, only believing it possible to appease them by means of bloody or violent sacrifices. That is why the Babylonians, the Lydians, etc., were intimately persuaded that the penchant imprinted in creatures that caused the two sexes to seek one another out was troubled and poisoned by the caprices and malignity of a Goddess who excited the female sex to impurity and disorder, and took pleasure in throwing its members into debauchery and corruption.

On that opinion, and with a view to appeasing the bizarre Goddess in question, they had doubtless imagined that species of sacrifice in order to save the virtue of women from disaster, and to redeem their chastity forever by causing them to make a deviation, with which they believed that Venus would be content, and would then leave those victims tranquil for the reminder of their lives. What justifies the motive for those singular sacrifices is that the women prepared themselves for it by means of offerings and prayers, and that the men who contributed to it implored the Goddess in favor of the victim. Finally, what confirms that the intentions were pure and exempt from any sentiment of debauchery and corruption is that the most earnest Historians of those times asserted that, as soon as the women of Babylon had satisfied the obligation imposed on them by the law, whatever approaches were made to them in the future, they were inflexible.

The fabulous centuries were replete with heroes who were glorified by an illegitimate birth that they owed to the Gods; lovers who felt honor-bound to marry maidens that they had seduced; husband who, far from complaining about frequent larcenies, respected the object and fruit of their amours even more. Of what are minds abused by false principles of religion not capable? Are not all these deviations of reason among ancient peoples emblems of what self-interest produces in our day in the most enlightened Nations, and which pique the sentiment called—I have no idea why—delicacy, which only resides in the imagination, since one discovery no trace of it in Nature?

That is enough to put us on our guard against precipitate judgments and teach us that, in order to pronounce sanely on the value of so many bizarre laws, singular customs and strange opinions, which seem to us to have infected the morality of a few ancient peoples, it is necessary to search for the motives and, in order to discover them, to transport oneself into the centuries in which they were revered, instead of vainly relating to a time that did not exist, the events of a time that is no more. To operate differently would be frequently to expose oneself to stoning old opinions with new ones. Prejudices enter into the composition of all ideas and all actions; they move under different faces, circulating in all kinds of forms; that is the sad lot of humankind.

Chapter XI
On Intellectual Attraction
to Serve as a Supplement to the Philosophy of Newton

As usual, I went into Arzame's study without having myself announced, and found him occupied in investigating the properties of a curve with a double curvature.

"Ah," he said, on seeing me, "I shall gladly suspend my operation for a moment; I had destined this morning to release us from the serious matters that we have discussed in recent days, by the reading of a small volume that I've just received—but I'll hand it to you to peruse, while I continue my work.

"We are," he added, "disciples of the great Newton, as you cannot doubt, given the profound study that we have made of the sublime Work of that illustrious philosopher on attraction, which rather merits the name of Discovery, or Theory of the World than that of System, since it demonstrated, we are persuaded, with one of your most amiable Philosophers, that he has established *the facts of Nature*.

"The true physicists among us no longer hesitate to admit the force of attraction throughout Nature, but as yet they only recognize its effects of matter.

"Here is a follower of Newton with a lively and cheerful mind, gripped with the enthusiasm of his disciples, who has taken his discoveries further than his master, in demonstrating the reality of that force over intellectual objects; he has thus succeeded in proving that attraction is a universal principle. This little work can serve as a complement to Newtonian Physics. I'll leave you to enjoy it; I'll rejoin you soon."

I read the pamphlet with a great deal of pleasure and took a few fragments from it, which I shall transcribe.

Attraction and Electricity, the Author says, are the causes of all phenomena, both physical and mental. Attraction is a force, the action of which is known throughout Nature; it not only operates on all material bodies in direct reaction to their mass and inversely to the square of distance between them, but—a verity no less important—it acts in a parallel fashion upon intellectual objects, in accordance with exactly the same laws.

One can suppose that force, he adds, to be the cause of the hardness of bodies, their cohesion, of coagulation, fermentation, effervescence, magnetism, electricity, etc., but it is indubitably the cause of all the intellectual phenomena of which, without admitting that force, it is impossible to give a rational account. It is the cause of memory, in which ideas are attracted one another by virtue of the string conjunction of the idea of the time or place where an event occurred with the event itself, which causes the memory of one necessarily to recall the memory of the other. The name attracts the memory of the thing forcefully, and the thing the name.

The conjunction or disjunction of ideas gives birth to a more or less powerful attraction, as between the subject and the attribute, the negative and the affirmative, the proposition and the argument, the problem and the resolution, etc.; that is what Aristotle was only able to suspect, but that Locke understood very well.

There are ideas that attract one another so powerfully at the point of contact that nothing is capable of parting them, such as *virtue is estimable* and *vice is despicable*. It is not even necessary for the intellect to make any effort to unite them; on the contrary, whatever the condition of the soul and heart might be, it is necessary to recognize their union as unbreakable.

These axioms that are respected in themselves, in ignorance off the causes, such as *everything is greater than its part, two entities equal to a third entity are equal to one another, a container is larger than its contents*, etc., are the effects of attraction-which the Ancients understood without knowing the cause, as Kepler understood the elliptical orbits of the planets, in the same way that people made use of spectacles for several centuries without imagining telescopes, and we now make use of the compass without understanding the cause of magnetism.

Attraction operates to such a degree of force on the knowledge acquired by education, custom and habit that their cohesion is capable of resisting the greatest efforts of reasoning and experience to separate them; that is evidently what convinced vulgar minds that colors are in objects, flavors in fruits, odors in flowers, heat and fire, etc. Attraction is singularly manifest in the phenomena produced by the electricity of words in a long speech learned by heart with difficulty, and of which one cannot recall the first word; once that word is found, it is followed by all the others, because in studying them, those words have often been put in conjunction, with the result that, by reiterated friction, they attract one another strongly, electrification arriving by attrition and heat.

Ideas heated by the imagination, pleasure, dread and desire are electrified, like bodies. Electricity, caused by heat and movement, bring the forces of attraction into play; thus, things that excite within us a keen sentiment of fear, anger, jealousy, vengeance or ardent desire, which is nothing by the agitation of igneous matter, imprint themselves more forcefully on the memory, because ideas heated by passion are more easily electrified than others. That is how the memory of children is inflamed, as well as the vanity of authors, the ambition of Great Men and the cupidity of all men by the hope of obtaining glory, honors and rewards, in illusion or reality.

Probable ideas are to axioms what attraction in bodies distant from one another is to those where there is a point of contact; they have a less powerful attraction in the minds of those who use violence to separate them, but in the brains of weaker minds they acquire a considerable electricity from the proximity of the parts.

The probability of propositions is born from an electrification of ideas, formed by the practice of putting them together, which causes them, in accordance with the nature and disposition of the mind, to acquire different degrees of attraction by virtue of various principles that guide them. The Miser

269

obtains from gold the color and the weight; the Prodigal only esteems it as a means of contenting his passions: the Stoic, only considering the abuses that can be made of it, only sees it as instrument of corruption, a reef for virtue; the Cynic places it in the rank of superfluous possessions, which cannot take the place of any necessary foodstuff; the Alchemist evaporates it with the foolish idea of cause it to vegetate; the Conqueror only desires it in order to buy iron; the Politician employs it sagely as a representative sign, which really augments, up to a certain point, the wealth of a State.

All the actions by which one acquires goods, honors, credit or reputation—an exterior sign of virtue—are founded on probability; thus Logicians ought to apply themselves to producing laws of probability rather than evidence, since much more use is made of the former than the latter and the number of those who learn Geometry is far less than the number of those who apply themselves to purely probable Sciences such as Medicine, Politics, Jurisprudence, Metaphysics, etc.

What contradictions would have opposed anyone who said, a hundred years ago, that a body set in movement relative to itself will continue moving forever; that an infinity can be smaller than another infinity; that Nature is so simple in her methods that she never employs more than the smallest quantity of possible movement;[249] that there are dead forces;[250] that even inertia is a force;[251] that bodies have no other action than to change location; that the Earth moves and is not perfectly spherical; that light is propagated; that the plants travel in ellipses, etc. Today, electrified ideas hold all that to be certain, not because all philosophers are evidently convinced, or even because the majority think so, but because, accustomed to these propositions and believing them to be conceivable, they

---

[249] Author: "Maupertuis."

[250] Author: "De Mairan." i.e. the biologist and astronomer Jean-Jacques d'Ortous de Mairan (1678-1771)

[251] Author: "Newton."

have received them as true, and long usage of the integral and differential calculus in taken as proof.

The force of syllogisms is also born from attraction. Virtue is good; patience is a virtue; therefore patience is good. How could one arrive at that phenomenon is the third idea of virtue, by attracting the two others of patience and good, did not communicate a force to them that attract them violently toward it? That happens, as in bodies, which not only attract others but communicate the attractive force to them, since on sees the third idea joining the first two and uniting them even more narrowly.

Memory is not a faculty, a power of the soul, like respiration, but an effect of habit. Judging is only distinguishing and comparing; hence, no memory, no judgment. One can only make a distinction by associating one idea with another; that cannot happen if one has no memory of the other idea. Without attraction, there would be no memory; without that force, which moves everything, once could only complete a sentence begun by linking the end to the beginning.

The attachment or antipathy that one forms for a Nation, an Order, a Sect or a Society is an effect of the electrification of ideas. On the faith of Historians and Voyagers one imagines that all the people of a Nation have the same character, while one cannot even find two similar individuals in one's own family; one believes in the influence of climate on character, as if it acted upon humans as the soil does on plants. Hence the prejudice, as unjust as it is unreasonable, that prevents people believing in serious, constant Frenchmen who are enemies of frivolity; attentive, cheerful, religious Englishmen attached to their sovereign; sober Germans capable of composing tasteful works; witty and casual Swiss; modest Spaniards peaceful in their amours; generous, brave Italians expect from jealousy and vengeance; and Turks impressed by the excellence of Despotic government. It is only necessary to electrify ideas by means of Voyages to be convinced that attraction acts powerfully between the honest people, scholars and good minds of all Nations, in direct proportion to the mass of their virtues and talents.

It is attraction that gives birth to arithmetical, geometrical and algebraic demonstrations. Proof attracts facts, and facts proof. Attraction also acts by opposition, just as ills, according to Avicenna, are cured by contraries: *contraria contrariis curantur*. The idea of vice attracts that of virtue, which is its antipode, and vice versa. The opinions of two scholars, two men of intelligence, two singular characters electrified in conversation, controversy, and impact, and launching quips that inflame one another, produce, in turn, attachment, obstinacy, bitterness, etc.

Attraction is the cause of analogy and sympathy: it is what causes an inclination toward one competitor rather than another; it is what engages two honest hearts, two men of intelligence, or two scoundrels who encounter one another fortuitously to link themselves narrowly together.

Orators, by their captious discourses, Courtiers, by adulations, Poets, by dedicatory epistles, Protégés, by baseness, and the Great, by vain promises, electrify the ideas of those who are imbecilic enough to listen to them.

Attraction, which is, incontrovertibly, the unique cause of the secret penchant that leads to the two sexes to unite,[252] is

---

[252] Author: "The Gods, says Plato in his *Symposium*, first formed humans round in shape with two bodies and two sexes. That bizarre whole had extraordinary force, which rendered it insolent. The Androgyne resolved to make war on the Gods. In order to weaken it Jupiter ordered Apollo, after having separated the Androgyne into two halves to improve the two half-bodies by extending the skin in order that their entire surface would be covered. Apollo obeyed, and knotted it at the navel. That fable has been ingeniously employed by a celebrated Poet. He attributes, with the ancient philosopher, the penchant that draws the two sexes toward one another to the natural ardor that the two halves of the Androgyne to rejoin, and inconstancy to the difficulty that each half has in finding its fel-

undoubtedly the cause of other surprising effects, which produce the cravings of pregnant women, since, there being no communication between the mother and the fetus, much less between the imagination and the accidents of a foreign body, there is no reason for that to happen otherwise.

There are various degrees of force in different attractions. Strongly electrified eloquence triumphs rapidly over the will and uncertainty of minds. In Philosophy, attraction acts by reason of a compound of stubborn study and a love of the truth. There is a double attraction in the animal endowed with reason, one of which draws him toward vice and the other to virtue. Education and circumstances give him all their activity and energy. Finally, attraction, a force admitted but whose cause is unknown, the agent with which Nature puts everything in motion and holds everything in equilibrium, acts universally.

A fine action attracts admiration; bad deeds attract scorn; mild mores attract esteem; pure mores attract respect; benefits attract gratitude; ingratitude attracts indignation; censure attracts hatred; kindness attracts regard; wealth and noble birth attract consideration; delicate tables attract parasites; glory attracts conquerors; honors attract noble souls; recompenses attract mercenary souls; vice attracts criticism; virtue attracts praise and true philosophy is attracted by the love of truth and virtue.

The Author terminated his essay thus:

"An invincible argument in favor of intellectual attraction is that, in addition to the proofs already established of its existence and universality, there is no other means of giving

---

low. When a woman appears to us to be amiable we immediately take her for the half with which we would have made a whole, but for the insolence of the Androgyne." In fact, in the *Symposium*—the only Platonic dialogue in which all the participants are manifestly drunk—puts this bizarre invention into the mouth of the comedian Aristophanes, to indicate that it is not seriously intended.

an explanation of a thousand metaphysical phenomena, such as memory, will, volition, imagination, the comparison of ideas, reticence, etc. etc., and that the theory—if it is one—satisfies all possible objections."[253]

---

[253] Author: "It would be very singular if this sketch of a theory, which can be seen as pure imaginative play, seduces a few minds. What a Revolution it might cause in the Republic of Thought! What would become then of the sublime abstractions, the profound reasonings, the marvelous conjectures on Being in general into which all matter is separated? The famous Treatises on Metaphysics by Aristotle, Descartes, Malebranche, Clarke, Locke, Leibnitz, Condillac, etc., would return, like vortices, into the chaos from which the greatest efforts of the human mind had drawn them. There is no opinion so absurd that it does not have its sectarians. (*Nihil tam absurdum diction protest, quod non dictum abs aliquot philosophorum.* Cicero, De Divinitas,) After the host of systems that we regard today with pity, and on which fortunes were built in their time, one ought not to despair of anything. But enlightened minds, after having laughed at the idea, will appreciate this theory at its true value; they will see it only as a playful critique of extension that the excessive sectarians of Newton are striving to give to the principle of attraction, very differently from their Master, who spoke of it so modestly that he seemed rather suspicious of it, in spite of the sublime calculations with which he supported his hypothesis."

Chapter XII
Books to Write on Earth

A small portable book had been composed for the use of young Selenites, *Blunders of Humankind*, to serve as a guide and instruction in all aspects life. Its principal contents were:

A sampler of various memorable actions of disinterest, generosity, grandeur of soul and patriotic zeal, with a severe and impartial examination of the motives that had occasioned them, which reduced the truly estimable actions to a very small number.

Examples of men who reached the highest degree of grandeur by vile and rascally actions, who, having been objects of envy and admiration during their lifetime, had become objects of horror and execration after their death, by virtue of the trial to which their memory was subjected.

Modest philosophers who, ignored and confounded with the crowd of idle men during their lifetime, had rendered signal services to their Fatherland via their writings.

Virtuous citizens whose inconsiderate zeal and spirit of fanaticism had caused infinite harm and delivered mortal blows to the causes that they were striving to support.

Examples of men in high positions who, spreading graces and favors with full hands, had never achieved anything except to teach ingrates to measure benefits.

Men who, with infinite intelligence, enlightenment and honesty, had never seen any of their projects succeed, by virtue of their rigidity in refusing to bend to circumstances.

Others whose most honest reflections, most mature reflections, and consummate prudence had never taken any but the worst decisions in business and councils, for want of the sagacity that discovers all the aspects and the accurate sight that embraces all the difficulties.

Others incapable of the slightest planning, whom pure chance and fortunate accidents had always led to their goal without their going astray—perhaps whims of fortune, but considerations appropriate to cure the mind of presumption and submit it to the established order, whose consequences are unknown to it.

Ministers of a genius of the first order, who had had the imbecility to allow themselves to be governed by valets, mistresses and limited courtiers. *Habeo Aspasiam*, said Pericles, *sed Aspasia non habet me.*[254]

Curious remarks on the faults of great Captains, great Ministers, great Magistrates and Authors celebrated for all kinds of subjects.

Clarifications of an infinite number of points of Chronology and History, which ignorance, credulity, superstition, partiality and national pride had altered, blurred, falsified or suppressed.

A Treatise on the art of successfully violating the rules and principles established by past masters in all genres of literary composition.

Accounts of astonishing misfortunes and strange reverses that had led certain men to the peak of felicity; rare examples but appropriate to disillusion the vain minds who attempt to subject events to the laws of a consummate prudence, often confounded by unexpected accidents, which do not render men any wiser or more consequential.

Excessive praise that servile flatters have lavished, in all times, on the Great, of whom posterity abhors the memory: reflections appropriate to save Princes jealous of their glory from the deplorable effects of that deadly poison.

Curious features of different stratagems of war, for the instruction of young soldiers.

Vain systems of several Philosophers carried away by their imagination, knowing well enough what was outside them but not having the slightest idea what was inside their own selves.

---

[254] "I possess Aspasia; Aspasia does not possess me."

An essay on the Reform of Natural History reduced, with few principles, to the bounds of truth.

A collection of the principal features of Practices, Opinions and Customs celebrated in their time and condemned in another, such as Apotheoses,[255] human sacrifices, New Year

---

[255] Author: "Apotheoses were contrived among the Romans, in accordance with a decree of the Senate, by burning the body of an Emperor or some individual celebrated in Arms, Sciences of the Arts. A representation in wax, depicting him as a sick man, was placed on a catafalque for seven days, the pulse of which was taken regularly by Physicians, which they found declining until the seventh day, when it expired in the presence of Knights and Ladies; after which the wax figure was taken to a high building, filled with combustible materials, and draped in gold cloth. The new Emperor set fire to the edifice, and then an eagle emerged from the summit and flew away, presumed to be carrying the soul of the deceased into the heavens. Apotheoses became so frequent among the Romans that they diminished the respect they had for the Gods, with whom they had lived familiarly. 'Should I fear the Gods,' Nero said, 'since I have the power to make them?' Caligula challenged Jupiter to a duel and, hurling stones into the clouds, cried: 'Remove me from the world, or I'll remove you.'

"Horace made a statue of Priapus say: 'I was once the trunk of a fig tree, useless for any kind of purpose, when a carpenter, not knowing at first whether he would make a bench or a God of me, opted to make me a Divinity.' Dionysius the Tyrant added mockeries to the pillages he carried out on the temples of the Gods; he had a massive golden robe removed from Jupiter as too heavy for the summer and too cold for the winter. He took a golden beard from an Aesculapius on the pretext that it was unseemly for the son to wear a beard when Apollo, his father, had none. If a statue was holding out a hand he said that he was authorized to take it away because it would be stupid to make requests of the Gods and not to accept what they offered of their own accord. Vespasian, a natural joker,

277

mistletoe, the Festival of Fools, etc., to serve as a History of the contradictions of the human mind.

Another collection, of petty motives that caused great revolutions and destroyed marvelous aspects of great events, a preservative against the stupid admiration of the Vulgar.

The most remarkable Treatises of Politics uniting narrow laws with honor, probity and truth, models for Negotiators.

A summary of the artifices of the majority of so-called vulgar professions—or, rather, shameful "tricks of the trade"—intended to protect honest souls from the traps and subtleties of rogues and charlatans.

An authentic list of the names of Inventors of useful arts and advantageous discoveries, whose glory had been usurped by others.

A rational catalogue of all useful books, with a plan of the order in which it is appropriate to read them.

A work as useful as necessary for the progress of reason, which destroyed a large number of false axioms that enchain the human mind to the shame of judgment.

Finally, a few indications of the power of habit, the empire of custom and education, the ascendancy of established examples, axioms and precepts, the tyranny of prejudices, the mistakes of the senses, the advantages of philosophy, the

---

sensing that he was reaching his end, said: 'I feel that I'm becoming a God.'

"The Chinese maltreated their Idols when they did not grant them what they requested; they whipped them, dragged them through the mud and mutilated them; if they obtained what they desired during the time of profanation they apologized to them, repaired them, regilded them and, when they took them back to their places they sermonized them on their resistance to doing good. One Chinese Mandarin, having lost his daughter in spite of the offerings and prayers that he had made to a renowned Idol, obtained from the Sovereign Council in Peking that the temple should be razed, the Idol degraded and the priests condemned to pay fines."

charms of verity, the free exercise of reason, the effect of laws, books and studies of the human heart, etc., etc.

What a vast field of morality, scarcely scratched! How many inexhaustible matters lightly brushed by the philosophical mind! I confess, with complaisance, that it is from that source that I have drawn the elements of my own work, which, treated by a skillful hand in its full extent, would be almost limitless.

Those extracts were followed by a few singular examples of freaks of chance, to prepare the soul for all events and to dispose it never to despair of anything.

Jason, abandoned to physicians for an abscess that he has in his chest, seeking an end to his ills, precipitates himself into the midst of his enemies; he is wounded by the thrust of a lance so accurate that the abscess bursts and he is cured.

A Scythian, devoured by a gnawing worm, resolves to deliver himself from it by terminating his life by poison; he only kills the worm and is cured.[256]

A prodigal, fallen into misery and opprobrium by virtue of his dissipations, hangs himself, but, having attached the rope to a ring in the ceiling, draws a trap-door open by his weight, which encloses an immense treasure, of which he is able to take advantage.

Christopher Columbus, seeking a route to China between the tropics and ready to be sacrificed by his companions, stumbles upon the Lucayan Islands and discovers America, the existence of which he had no suspicion.

How many maladies are cured by fortunate errors, which ought to have dragged the invalid to the tomb?

The Collection was terminated by an important Chapter on the consolation of the Human Race. It was filled with incidents from the lives of the greatest men, who had not been exempt from paying a tribute to humanity, by virtue of a few

---

[256] Author: "Père Mabillon was very limited in his youth; a malady caused a great intelligence to develop within him, of penetration and aptitude for the Sciences."

weaknesses, for a few errors or even a few vices, but whose great reputation remains, when the number of virtues far surpasses that of the faults; thus one observes spots on the sun, which do not tarnish its light.

Alexander and Caesar were excessively superstitious. Alexander was cruel and intemperate, Caesar the wife of all husbands and the husband of all wives.

Cicero was vain and pusillanimous, impious and cowardly.

Turenne confided State secrets to a woman, who abused them.

Kepler, the celebrated astronomer, gave the Sun a vegetating, active soul; he believed that the planets were attracted by the star when presenting their friendly side to it and repulsed by the hostile side.

A famous Danish physician attributed to comets the production of monsters and considered them as the abscesses of Heaven.[257]

Heliodorus, Bishop of Treca in Thessaly in the fourth century, preferred to renounce his bishopric than the paternity of his Romance of *Theagenes and Chariclea*.[258]

Pico della Mirandola, who had written against Judiciary Astrology, was its dupe and martyr.

One Scholar has claimed that the Book of Job was only an Opera, a religious poem made to be sung by the People of God.[259]

---

[257] Thomas Bartholin (1616-1680) in *De Cometa* (1665).

[258] Author: "The translation of that Romance was worth an Abbey to Amyot." The romance is also known as *Aethiopica*; Jacques Amyot's French translation appeared in 1547. The identification of its author, Heliodorus of Emesa, with the similarly named Bishop of Trikka is uncertain, to say the least

[259] The scholar in question is cited at length, but not named, in John Garnett's *Dissertation on the Book of Job* (1749)

A Jew celebrated for his writings would only admit in the New Testament the Apocalypse, because he thought he would find the philosopher's stone therein.

Etienne de Pleutre, Canon of St. Victor, found the Life of Jesus Christ in Virgil's *Aeneid*.[260]

The immortal Newton thought he had discovered in the Apocalypse that the Pope is the Antichrist.

Derham, in his Astronomical Theology, thought he saw the Empyrean in that immense space, brighter than the Sky, which is commonly known as the Milky Way.[261]

The military virtue of Hannibal foundered in the delights of Capua.

Hercules spun for Omphale.

Socrates, declared the wisest of men by the Oracle of Apollo, loved Alcibiades and Archelaus; he had two wives and lived with all the courtesans.

Trajan was subject to wine and the *Mollitici peccatum*.[262]

The divine Plato was a libertine.

One of the most virtuous Romans, after having killed his two sons and murdered his benefactor in a cowardly fashion, ended up putting virtue to the question.[263]

Two wise and enlightened Republics, Athens by the Law of Ostracism and Syracuse by that of Petalism, dared to attach penalties to eminent merit, punish pure mores by exile and banish living examples of virtue from their Government.

Finally, one cannot cite any Conqueror, not even excepting Titus or Trajan, who did not soil his glory with some action of inhumanity.

---

[260] This datum is taken from Gilbert Le Gendre's *Traité historique et critique de l'Opinion* (1741).

[261] William Derham, the Rector of Upminster, published his *Physico-Theology; or, A Demonstration of the Being and Attributes of God from His Works of Creation* in 1723.

[262] The tender sin.

[263] Author: "'O Virtue,' said Brutus, 'to whom I have sacrificed, were you not a vain phantom and a pure chimera?'"

Chapter XIII
Discoveries to be made on Earth

"If there is a happy people in the Universe," I said to Arzame one day, "it is doubtless the Selenites, who, with the aid of a sixth sense, have succeeded in disengaging themselves from so many prejudices that confuse reason, in forming a flourishing Empire, and in sagely regulating everything that can contribute to the happiness of humanity. Everything here seems to me to be worthy of envy; the Sciences and the Arts cannot attain a higher degree of perfection."

"We are very far from thinking," Arzame replied, "that our century, superior as it is to the one that preceded it, cannot be surpassed. Although there are still a few imbeciles among us capable of believing that one cannot go any further, the saner party thinks very differently. Presumption is the prerogative of ignorance. The more enlightened one is, the more there still remains to learn and to do.

"Perhaps there will come a time when one cannot conceive how, in obscurity and the privation of so many things that will then be commonplace, our century—not that I am not separating the Earth and the Moon here—had the vanity to think itself advanced.

"Let us imagine a new member of the twenty-fourth century, who, in his reception speech at the Academy, will cry enthusiastically: 'Messieurs, can we, without injustice, draw a parallel between the eighteenth century and ours? People had, in truth, made useful discoveries, a little progress in Philosophy; the Sciences and the Arts flourished then with a certain degree of improvement; Analysis had been fortunately applied to Geometry, Physics and Mechanics, but quite improperly in Metaphysics and Medicine; the two diameters of the Earth had been measured; and, finally, the great Newton had discovered the true system of the Universe. But what did they know about Metaphysics? How limited Geography was! Did they know the interior of Africa, or the Austral lands, that vast fifth of the globe? Did they suspect the possibility of the immense discoveries that our fortunate century has made in the Sciences and the Arts?

"'Do we not have reason to be astonished that our Ancients, instead of consuming so much time in the vain research of longitudes, exposing themselves to terrible shipwrecks, and ruining themselves with excessive expenditure on navigation, had not sought instead, and found, like us, the art of traveling freely in the air and of remaining motionless in the atmosphere against the movement of direction that draws us with the Earth, by means of which, placidly allowing the earth to turn beneath our feet, we can, without moving, go around the world in twenty-four hours, transporting ourselves from Paris to Rome in forty-eight minutes, or to Japan in sixteen or seventeen hours.

"'That they had not thought, following the example of various divers, who can remain under water for a considerable time, of perfecting the means of remaining there at will—means by which we have succeeded in extracting treasures useless to the stupid inhabitants of that terrible element to decorate our cabinets of natural history and restitute to the land immense riches buried in the sea for so many centuries, while people limited themselves to improving the sterile art of Navigation.

"'That people were occupied, for such a long time, in futile arts like spinning wool, byssus cloth, flax and silk, in order to produce works of temporary duration, from materials so scarce and difficult to harvest, when the secret of rendering glass ductile and malleable has furnished us with manufactured items of eternal duration, with all the more facility because the raw material of glass, which is trampled disdainfully underfoot, is in such great abundance on the earth.

"'That people limited themselves to opening up the surface of the earth in order to extract vile metals like gold and silver, when, by digging down to greater depths, we have extracted some so precious that the former no longer have any considerable value, useful at the most for building stones in buildings, paving the roads, making canals, covering roofs and making door-frames, boundary-markers, chains, barriers, etc.

"'That means had not been found of establishing subterranean communications between volcanoes, to ensure the earth against the quakes that compressed air and vapors cause certain regions to suffer so cruelly.

"'That instead of the Thermoscope, of which our Ancients made use, which only indicates the change of heat or cold in the atmosphere, they had not invented the simple machine that is the true Thermometer, with which we measure exactly the relationship of one degree of heat to another.

"'That their Geometrico-Metaphysicians had not succeeded in rendering the mathematical point, which was only conceived by abstraction, sensible, by which means we can demonstrate that a straight line of a foot is no longer than one of an inch, the hypotenuse than one of the other sides of the triangle, the diagonal than one of the sides of the square, etc.

"'That they made such limited use of the substances of asbestos, so easy to whiten with fire, from which we make cloth, paper, perpetual lamp-wicks, etc.

"'That physics and chemistry, in the course of their progress, had so little knowledge of the veritable uses of artificial phosphorus, which was then only the match of philosophers, while we, by means of a mixture capable of conserving the humidity that maintains light in bodies, have succeeded in making it throw a glare into the darkness so bright and soft to the sense of sight that it substitutes so agreeably for the absence of the sun.

"'That they had not imagined the improvement of sign-language, an idiom so natural to humans that one can converse distinctly, without the assistance of articulation, as far as the eye can see. That even less had they thought that the language in question could be written by means of general characters, so that everyone can understand it, without effort, in their own language, like Arabic numbers and algebra, which different Nations understand although each applies different sounds to them; and that Scholars employ that language in order to transmit their productions easily from one hemisphere to the other; that it liberates the mind from the study of foreign languages; that it obviates the obscurity, the blunders and infidelities of translation; and finally, that with its assistance one can easily travel all over the world without needing interpreters.[264]

"'That the vanity of having invented iron horseshoes, in order to hasten the operations of Nature, had not led to the art of conserving the odor of flowers from one spring to the next by retaining, as we do, the particles that they exhale continually in elliptical vases, to the focal points of which the vapors return, after having spread randomly, rendering the flower its natural freshness—a means that we also employ usefully to preserve rare fruits from corruption by a prompt repair.

"'That, at all times, people had wasted time in vain and unjust murmurs against the existence of ferocious beasts, instead of seeking to take advantage of them by studying their virtues, talents and properties. That human industry had been content to tame the horse, the buffalo and the bull, while, with more sagacity, humans would have learned that service can be obtained from all those redoubtable animals; that it was less

---

[264] Author: "This language is all the easier to grasp because almost all people have characteristic signs that have their source in natural needs; that children have them, by which they make themselves understood before the organ of the voice is loosened or they have learned enough words to express themselves intelligibly. Gestures are so natural that they add force to expressions and seem to form part of the discourse of the Theater, the Pulpit and the Bar; that people in conversation, without noticing them, speak as much with the head, the body and the hands as with the glottis. Sign language was doubtless sufficient during the long period before humans, assembled in society and augmenting ideas, need to add sounds to it in order to express themselves with more clarity and extent."

reasonable to occupy themselves with their destruction than to think about familiarizing them by providing their subsistence; that their savage and solitary humor would have been seen to soften by domestic education and their ferocity would be extinguished by the third generation, so that one commonly sees, nowadays, chariots superbly drawn by lions, bears, tigers and leopards, wolves serving as guardians for flocks, foxes watching over the safety of henhouses, red deer drawing fast sleighs, eagles carrying dispatches everywhere, vultures trained among birds of prey, crocodiles procuring abundant catches of fish, etc., so true is it the malevolence is not natural to any animal species, being excited in some by hunger and others by interest, education makes all the difference between them that there is between a Carib and a civilized man.[265]

"'That one only saw, in the menageries of Princes, a few strange animals, instead of their being filled with singular and superb monsters by the coupling of animals entirely opposed in form, color and character, in order to see what results might be obtained from the junction of the most different species, as if one put together the serpent and the parrot, the nightingale and the tortoise, the peacock and the porcupine, the monkey and the eagle, the mole and the canary, etc.[266]

---

[265] Listonai was not to know, although he might perhaps have suspected, that within a matter of decades, the principal difference between the Caribs and civilized men would be that the latter had exterminated the former.

[266] Author: "To destroy what might appear absurd in this proposition, as in the preceding one, it is only necessary to consider that with care, skill and patience, animals commonly made to devour one another, like the cat and the mouse, the ferret and the hen, the fly and the spider, etc., have been accustomed to live together. It is perhaps from the junction of the latter that the flying spider was born. The habit of living together can take inclinations a long way." I have translated the author's *jonction* as "junction" here and in the main text, rather than substituting a more recent term referring to cross-

"'That people went to seek, at great expense, in the most distant climes, simples and plants for the cure of maladies, while disdainfully crushing underfoot the salutary ones that every region produces, which are for us infallible specifics against rabies, discharges, scurvy, calculi, gout, the plague, etc.

"'That, like the magnet before the invention of the compass, electricity was only an object of amusement for the physicist of that century, whereas, by taking experiments much further, it has been possible to obtain marvelous assistance therefrom against paralysis, apoplexy, lethargy and other deadly maladies, which ignorance and incapacity considered incurable; and that the pneumatic machine had not been substituted for suction in drawing off secretions, such a dangerous remedy that it sometimes cost a physician his life.

"'That no one had been able to succeed in music in dividing tones into quarters and eighths, in order to give that art the utmost degree of perfect.

"'That the admirable secret of deflecting and dissipating lightning had only been sketched, prior to being entirely formed and able to terminate the furies of the liquid element without accidents, by which means we preserve our fields from frightful ravages.

"'That a coating of material impenetrable to fire had not been found, in order to cover combustible materials and make them proof against conflagration.

"'That, in those days, when the art of Navigation, useless to us, was so necessary that the secret had not been found of rapidly and cheaply desalinating sea-water, which we do so easily by throwing into a large vessel filed with sea-water a pinch of *slictitz*, which instantaneously precipitates out all the

---

breeding and hybridization, in order to emphasize the simultaneous naivety and ambitious reach of his imagination.

heterogeneous matter and also destroys any infectious germ[267] liable to corrupt it.

"'Ought we not to be surprised that, in the course of so many centuries, art had only been able to add one new order to the four primary orders of architecture, pillaged from two among them?[268] What sterility of imagination! We have found two of them, which have no relationship with the former, and which give our edifices a majesty and a elegance that beautiful antiquity could not approach. And what does the painting of the eighteenth century have in common with ours, which combines the brilliance of coloration with the understanding of chiaroscuro to the greatest perfection of design?

"'Is it conceivable that, in a century so celebrated in its artists, the microscope remained so imperfect that the most powerful lenses only magnified objects sixty-four million times, whereas we, by virtue of the degree of perfection that we have given to that instrument, penetrate the most secret recesses of Nature. We see the air, and all the way to the integral particles of bodies, by means of which we are assured that the particles of water are spherical, those of air branched; that every corpuscle of blood is composed of twelve hundred and ninety-six sanguine globules; that animals, sixty million of which could be covered by a grain of sand, are, like us, afflicted with vermin; and that, finally, we can see plants, fingernails, hair, etc., growing.

---

[267] This reference might seem anachronistic, given that the germ theory of disease would not be popularized in France by François Raspail for nearly a century, and not widely accepted for some time thereafter, but I have merely transcribed the text's *germe infectes* [sic] into the closest English terms parallel at the time, although Listonai could not mean by "infectious" what we do, and it is arguable that "foul germ" would be a fairer translation.

[268] Author: "Strictly speaking, there are only three orders of architecture, the Doric, the Ionian and the Corinthian; they could even be reduced to two."

"'That they had not found, like us, the secret of conserving grain for a century without it being corrupted, and of which provision can be made in abundant years to supplement years of sterility, times in which the rich generously open their granaries in favor of indigents, who, since that admirable invention, only know famine by tradition.

"'I would never finish the enumeration of our useful discoveries, unknown in the eighteenth century, if the limits of this Discourse did not force me to stop, in order to praise ceremoniously my predecessor, your protectors and yourselves, Messieurs, and modestly set fire to the incense that your secretary has prepared for me.'

"If the time comes," said Arzame, "when so many fortunate discoveries have been made, of which we are deprived in spite of the extent of our knowledge, people will then think of us as we do of our ancestors, who, in their capitals, had no fireplaces, no pavements, no lanterns, no aqueducts, no carriages, no bowling greens, no theaters, who had not imagined highways, levees, dykes, canals, postal services, printing, clocks, etc. Enlightened minds will bemoan the indigence and barbarity of our century; their antagonists will say: 'Oh, but one can live without all of that—perhaps, with fewer desires, they were happier than us!'

"When we have succeeded," Arzame said, in terminating his reflections, "in giving body to thought, by the intermediary of mute characters, in conversing with minds separated from us by times that no longer exist, in traversing the Oceans, in measuring the plants, in following the routes of comets, in drawing up the map of the Heavens, I have too high an opinion of human industry to doubt that we can one day make all the discoveries that I sense that we lack, as well as many others that I cannot imagine. If you have the good fortune one day to visit Jupiter or Saturn, as you have the Moon, perhaps you will find that the sublime inventions of which we are so proud are held in very low esteem, that they appear to the inhabitants of those planets to be trivial playthings, by comparison with the advantages that they enjoy naturally."

Chapter XIV
Advertisement for the Next Four Chapters

Any reader who is not led by taste to disentangle the specious from the real in everything, to analyze his own ideas and meditate on those of others, to distinguish in phenomena the effects from the causes; to research the why, the how and the how many of everything that is offered to his eyes and mind; in sum, any reader mechanically habituated to think as others do, for whom a conjecture is a proof and who is frightened by the slightest question, may stop here and skip straight to the final chapter; he will spare himself torments and ennui.

There is nothing in the next four chapters but a host of questions of greater or lesser importance, but all worthy of reflection.

I had already sketched dissertations with regard to many of these questions, whose length frightened me before having concluded anything, when I learned that a General Assembly of all the Academies was held twice a year in Selenopolis, at which everyone had the right to propose doubts and questions on which that respectable Areopage would deliberate and pronounce definitively.

Those Academies, by virtue of a custom different from ours and doubtless better reasoned, instead of proposing themselves questions on which individuals pronounce as best they can, to obtain prizes that are not always merited, make it a duty, by contrast, to provide solutions to questions that are presented to them, and which, in any case, are often merely a game, a source of new doubts, which become a source of enlightenment to that enlightened Tribunal.[269]

I had a mind perpetually embarrassed by questions, which I posed to myself, or proposed to others after having

---

[269] Author: "It is, says Montaigne, for apprentices to enquire and debate, and for the enthroned to resolve them."

mediated fruitlessly.[270] Forced to recognize the insufficiency of our enlightenment, in spite of the extent of our knowledge, I groaned in secret on finding our reason hampered at every step by the most apparently simple matters, and the feeble assistance available to any mind that only yields to demonstration. I therefore seized ardently the opportunity offered by the General Assembly of the Academies, in order to take my doubts there, in the hope of seeing them resolved by such an enlightened Tribunal.

I divided my proposals into four classes: firstly, those trivial in appearance; secondly, those on which we have nothing but conjectures; thirdly, moral and metaphysical questions; and fourthly, those insoluble for any being limited to five senses.

I could have added those of a different order, which the ignorant and the superstitious even in good society, sometime propose gravely, to the shame of their judgment—such as, for instance, why a basilisk kills the human at which it gazes, or whether it dies if it is looked at first; why a drum made from lambskin splits next to a drum made from wolfskin; why in Ocean ports, no one dies during the ebb-tide;[271] how the little fish known as the remora has the strength to stop a vessel; why an angry bull can be calmed down by attaching it to a fig tree; how the amnion, the cowl that remains attached to the heads of a few newborn children, renders them fortunate; how the chameleon can live on air; how a hazel-wand has the virtue of discovering treasures and murderers; why one is heavier after fasting than after having eaten; why a colt that has been chased by a wolf is quicker than another; why hair grows more slowly if it is cut while the moon is waning than when it is

---

[270] Author: "Horace thought differently, saying that, not being able to settle on any opinion, he thought, in that eternal doubt, of rising above all questions instead of submitting to them. (Epistle I.)"
[271] Author: "A very ancient prejudice, since Aristotle mentions it with regard to animals."

waxing;[272] why walnut trees are more likely to be hit by lightning than fig trees; why a heart infected by poison cannot be burned; why children bear the marks of their mothers' cravings during pregnancy, etc., etc., etc., etc.—but such inept questions can be solved by a single response:

None of that is true.[273]

If the quantity of questions that I have assembled revolts frivolous minds, they might perhaps be calmed if they would care to consider that all the questions are natural to any thinking being who frequents all the situations of life. If one collected all of those that have agitated or been proposed by Academies and Periodicals, one could make volumes with them.

Conversations are full of them. The majority of reflections on the practices, mores and ridicule of a century are merely disguised questions, which everyone develops in his own manner, relative to his tastes, his enlightenment or his temperament; Treatises on politics, commerce, finance, medicine and even morality are variegated by them.

All products of the mind are littered with them; they swarm in the Scientific under the name of problems. Illustrious but vain authors such as La B., La R. T. f. D. de P., give highly contestable decisions under the title of reflections.[274] Others more sublime, and consequently more modest, like Bacon, Locke, Newton, Pascal, Montaigne, Bayle, Montes-

---

[272] Author: "In spite of what Pliny affirms in Book II, chapter 19."

[273] Author: "*Transcurramus solertissimas nugas.* Seneca Epistle 117." [Let us skip over these subtle trifles.] Quoted by Montaigne.

[274] Illustrious as the authors cited are said to be, and given that the initials are puzzling in themselves (the f must surely be a misprint, perhaps substituting for an ampersand), it is not easy to suggest probable identifications based on the initials alone, but "La B" is probably Laurent de La Beaumelle (1726-1773), one of Voltaire's most fervent critics.

quieu and *l'Ami des hommes*[275] propose an infinity of questions that are worth as much as decisions.

Questions are the object of Councils that Princes and Generals hold. Trials revolve around questions of fact, subject to contradiction, and the law, balanced by authorities, reefs for the most profound sagacity. Scholars propose great ones, which seem puerile to the ignorant; the latter ask stupid ones, which are sometimes embarrassing for philosophers; some are addressed by the blind, who believe they can see everything, others by those too enlightened not to confess, in good faith, that with their good eyes they can see almost nothing. I ask myself a great many of them, because I desire to see, and to see well, because I believe them useful to anyone who wants to make a sane usage of reason, to enlighten the mind, to provide a basis for its judgments and extend its limits.

I repeat, therefore, that any reader guided by other principles, or who does not want to change, would do well to skip to the conclusion.

The objection will doubtless be raised that in the considerable number of questions that I have assembled, the majority have been agitated, debated and perhaps resolved by celebrated Writers; to which I respond that I am not unaware of that, and that because the most profound reasoning on the majority of these matters only remains probable, I still remain in doubt until the demonstration, if any can be attained.

It ought perhaps to be added that some of these questions, in order to be explored in depth, would require volumes, but that is not my fault; they merit, therefore being presented again, and exercising curious minds and lovers of the truth; thus there will be readers who will find them here with a kind of pleasure.

---

[275] *L'Ami des hommes* was a nickname given to Victor de Riqueti, Marquis de Mirabeau (1715-1789), after the work of that title he published in 1756, subtitled *Traité de la population.*

I presented the following questions to the Assembly of the Academies, and I have been promised that the solutions will be given to me at the next Assembly.[276]

---

[276] Author: "No one should be astonished that the majority of the questions that I took to the Academy only concern the Earth, in preference to everything directly concerning the Moon, if they recall that the inhabitants of that planet have an intimate communication with the Earth, which ought to enable them to satisfy me on matters that interest me more than what happens in other places."

Chapter XV
Seemingly frivolous questions of which it would be curious, and even useful, to know the solution.

Why does the description of a bitter fruit make the mouth water?

How does it come about that a painting of a disgusting object or a medicinal drug induces nausea?

That the idea of milk or honey puts the soul in a tranquil state?

That a threat of being tickled, even the gesture, cases a frisson?

That an account of an act of generosity extracts tears, an account of a cruel action causes a shudder, an account of a disagreeable odor affects the sense of smell?

Why does someone who stammers not stammer while reading, declaiming or singing?

Why does pressure cause milk to coagulate, and further pressure put on curdled milk dissolve it instead of increasing it consistency?

Why does a person yawning cause others to yawn, and even a whole crowd?[277]

Why is it that coral, black marble and every other colored stone become white when they are reduced to powder, while charcoal conserves its black color?

That crayfish, lobsters and other crustaceans turn red when cooked?

That a decoction of roses mixed with chalk produces a dark green?

That a solution of vitriol on the same decoction of roses thickens it and turns it black, and that a few drops of spirit of vitriol thrown into that mixture changes the black to red?

---

[277] Author: "Aristotle says that one can stop a yawn or hiccups by holding one's breath, which is confirmed by experience."

That carp eggs, which are bright yellow, become white when cooked and become yellow again when chilled?

Why can freshwater fish live for some time out of water, while sea fish die as soon as they are landed? Is it because fresh water is more analogous to the nature of the atmosphere than salty water? The atmosphere is, however, charged with salts, of sulfur, niter, etc.

Are fish deaf, as they are mute? Do they sleep?

Are sea-fish subject to epidemic diseases like terrestrial animals?[278] If they are exempt, is it because water is healthier than air?

How is it that musk, which once pleased so much without offending the organ of smell, produce the vapors today, while tobacco, which has an ammoniac odor and a poisonous quality, delight the weakest and most delicate sense of smell? Have the organs changed? Is it an effect of the imagination?

Are odors as harmful to women in childbed as people in France believe? There are countries, including Italy, where women in that condition have their rooms filled with odors, their mantelpieces garnished with pot-pourri and their beds covered with flowers without anyone noticing any accidents ever occurring.

Why do telescopes make stars seem smaller than the naked eye, whereas they magnify less distant objects?

From what organ to we receive the most vivid taste sensation? Is it the palate or the throat?

Why is ice less transparent and whiter than water, of which it is formed?

Why does an ardent piece of charcoal rapidly whirled describe a continuous circle of fire, although the fire only passes through each point of the circle successively, and a wheel painted with all the primary colors, when spun rapidly, only produce the color white?

Why does fire, which hardens mud, soften wax?

---

[278] Author: "Sea-cows, like sea turtles, go to sleep on land and snore like terrestrial animals. Aristotle Book V, chapter 12."

Why does the Sun, which whitens wax, blacken skin?

Why do so many people find themselves uncomfortable, to the extent of fainting, when they travel backwards in a carriage or a boat?

How long could a man with a sound constitution live in a hermetically sealed square room forty feet broad and high, with sufficient food and only the light of a candle?

How does the body deal with things that seem very harmful, such as penetrating odors, varnishes, charcoal vapor, etc.

Why does a table that one scrapes with the blade of a knife, positioned at a right angle, or an unripe fruit unto which someone else has bitten, cause us convulsive movements?

By what mechanism does castration enervate the voice, get rid of the beard or prevent it from growing?

Could one not make use of Dails instead of lamps in apartments at night?[279]

Why do the feathers of ducks and other aquatic birds not get wet in the water, while the fur of dead animals soaks it up?

Why does a field speckled with white flowers seem entirely white at a certain distance, or from an oblique angle?

Why can mules not engender young, although they have the appropriate organs?

What use are wings to ostriches, since they cannot fly, only making use of them to run, but less rapidly than other animals that do not have them?

Why do men go bald so frequently and women so rarely?

Why does one see so few left-handed women by comparison with the number of left-handed men?

Why does a cat that fall from a high place assume its natural stance momentarily, then turn upside-down, and finally land on its four feet?

Is it because a butterfly has no mouth or stomach with which to take nourishment that it only lives for a short time, or is it because it only going to live for a short time that it has no

---

[279] The meaning of "Dails" remains stubbornly obscure.

mouth or stomach? The Ephemera, however, which do not live as long as a butterfly, are conformed for a more extensive life.

In the order of Nature, is a negro less handsome than a white person?

Why does a ball of wax, which floats in cold water, sink to the bottom if the water is heated, and then rise up again if the heat is further increased?

Why does a file, which does not heat up lead or tin, heat iron without warming up itself?[280]

What colors would a prism produce in a dark room by the light of a torch, or that of the moon?

Is it more natural or rational to write, as we do, from left to right, or from right to left, as the Hebrews, the Egyptians, the Arabs, etc., do?[281]

Why does a cross-eyed person not see objects doubled, if it is not for the same reason that well-conformed eyes see them simply? Is the habit of sight guided by touch?

Is it more inconvenient to be deprived of sight or hearing from birth or by accident?

Why do certain portraits seem to be looking at you directly no matter from what angle they are viewed?

What is generally the cause of the repugnance that certain healthy people have for the finest aliments, and, on the contrary, an appetite for the worst?

Why is Champagne wine transparent, while its foam, formed by more rarefied particles, is opaque?

Why do blonde-haired people generally have blue eyes?

Why is fire extinguished by a light wind and augmented by a violent wind?

---

[280] Author: "A little reflection makes one see that the lead and the tin offer very little resistance, while the iron offers a great deal, and that the file cools itself down as it runs over the iron, which suffers a continuous friction."

[281] Author: "The Chinese write from top to bottom, the Mexicans from bottom to top, and sometimes in a circle."

Why does water, which is antagonistic to fire, augment its force when thrown on to it in small quantity, instead of diminishing it?

What produces the filaments that one sees in summer in the country, which are known as maidenhair, and those clusters of exceedingly delicate white threads the points of which, all exactly the same length, meet in a common center?

Why does gum dissolve in water and resin only melt in fire?

Chapter XVI
Questions on which there are only conjectures, mostly plausible but undemonstrated.

Is the Earth motionless at the center of the Universe or does it rotate around the Sun and on its own axis?

Is it the case that until the parallax of a fixed star has been determined relative to the diurnal movement of the Earth, it cannot be demonstrated that it rotates on its axis?

Is light propagated or is it instantaneous? In other terms, is light a fluid spread throughout the Universe that merely waits to be set in motion in order to act, or is it an emanation of the Sun, which reached our eyes in a determined time, as Römer's discovery seems to demonstrate?

Are light and fire the same matter? If so, why is there light that gives no heat and fire that gives no light?

To what degree are flame and light compressible, and by what experiment can that compression be established?

Why do heavenly bodies appear to be larger near the horizon than at the zenith?

Which was created first, the chicken or the egg, the plant or the seed?[282]

To what point can air be condensed, or to what volume can it be reduced by compressing it?

Everyone knows that the elastic force of air can be increased by the heat of boiling water, but how does the air acquire that rigidity?

Does air sometimes cease to be in a fixed state, or does it sometimes cease to be elastic?

---

[282] Author: "This question has been raised since the dawn of reasoning, but has been debased because it is, in the mouths of the Vulgar, one of those that always confounds the most sage, demonstrating the inadequacy of the most profound enlightenment."

Is blood cooled or warmed by the action of the lungs?

Why does the wind, which causes the human body to feel a sensation of freshness or cold, have no effect on a thermometer?[283]

How are crystals and precious stones formed?

What is the apparent location of an object seen in glass or in a mirror?

Is the earth an aliment of plants or a simple agent?[284]

Is it the disposition of the organs of a plant that modifies the nature of the sap, which is probably the same everywhere, in different ways?

How does the sap rise in plants? How does the sap produce flowers and fruits with such different odors and tastes? Do the roots of plants only absorb the parts of the sap that they need, or is sap, similar in nature everywhere, merely a vehicle, which is assimilated to the nature of the plant that it vivifies?

Is what is called sap extremely refined earth, or water and materials that impregnate it?

What are the branches or roots of plants, since, on uprooting a tree and replacing it upside down, the branches become roots and the roots become branches that bear leaves and fruits?

Why do the plants on a slope, or which emerge from a wall, always grow in a line perpendicular to the horizon?

Where do tall trees get their nourishment from after their roots have exhausted the nourishing juices that the earth contains, since, without rain, labor, marl or dung, the earth does

---

[283] Author: "Everyone knows that the cooling sensation that the human body experiences is only relative to the degree of heat that it has, and that the air does not change temperature whether it is agitated or still."

[284] Author: "One can believe the earth to be a simple agent of plants, since they can be seen taking root in walls where there is no earth, and because others vegetate and grow in pure water.

not acquire any more, and the rain does not penetrate to the great enough depth to furnish alimentation to their roots?

Why are certain trees, such as the box, the yew, the green oak, the laurel and the orange tree, green and in leaf all the year round?

What is the true cause of thorns in plants? Of what utility can they be?

Why, in apple trees, pear trees, chestnut trees and others that imitate their bearing, are the crown and roots always level with the plane of the tree?

Why do weak plants that need support in order to grow, like ivy, the broad bean, nasturtiums, etc., always twist from left to right as they rise.

Why do the fruits of a tree sprinkled with scented water, even camphorated, not acquire and odor, when the stalks and tips of the leaves do?

How do fruits change the color of their rind as they acquire a greater degree of maturity, without, in the majority of cases, the interior undergoing any alteration?

How does water rise up above its level in salt, sand, sugar, sponge etc., as well as in capillary tubes?

How does mercury touching a vertically-placed bar of gold rise up to the top more outside than inside?

What is that movement? How does it pass from one body to another? How does the body receive it?

Which of the two is privation, motion or repose?

What is the nature of the aurora borealis and zodiacal light?

What is the productive force of the movement of blood in animals?

Where can a perfectly hard body be found, and a perfectly elastic one, which can serve as types in order to determine the degree of hardness or elasticity of all the others?

Since there is no known body devoid of pores, how can the quantity of matter that one body contains be determined, in order to discover how much the others contain?

How can the measure of a straight line be determined independently of the line of sight?

How can a means be found of engendering an oblique cone?

Of all the occasions when Nature forms grooves in bodies, is there one in which physics is able to take account of the phenomenon?

If the natural state of water is to be frozen, is rest a more natural state than movement?

What utility have physics and society obtained thus far from the mathematics of infinity?

Why are there no tides in the Mediterranean Sea, the Baltic, the Black Sea, the Dead Sea etc., so that one only observes in those seas a simple movement of the waters, which glide over the coasts?

And why are there tides in the Adriatic Sea, which, strictly speaking, is only a gulf or a branch of the Mediterranean, with which it communicates, and which is itself merely a lake?

What is the degree of distance with which the diameter of the pupil of the eye no longer has any sensible relationship?

Why, in obscurity and even with closed eyes, can one see, on pressing the eye on one side, a tiny sun or luminous circle on the opposite side?

How can light penetrate the membrane even in the middle of the night?

What are the true causes of the sympathy and antipathy whose reality cannot be denied even in inanimate bodies?

What is the true cause of the echo?

Is the Milky Way an assembly of stars?

Why does piled-up hay, when it is damp, sometimes heat up to the point of catching fire?

What is the cause of the so-called pleuritic crust, from which the blood can sometimes be recovered, after bleeding, in the basin in which it has been made?

How does the inflammation of gunpowder and the mixture of two liquids produce a sudden and noisy dilatation? If it is by the effort of the air, which, previously compacted, suddenly expands forcefully, as in *larmes de Prusse*,[285] why and how was the air compressed before the explosion?

How does water extinguish fire?

Why does water at rest in tranquil air freeze at a lesser degree of cold than water that is agitated?

Does water freeze in all the different climates at the same degree of cold?

If one admits that *aqua fortis* cannot dissolve gold because its trenchants are not tenuous enough to penetrate its pores, why can *aqua regia*, which does dissolve gold, not dissolve silver?

Why do salts cool ice as they melt it, and why does artificial ice form more rapidly over fire than in very cold open air?

Why do drops of fluid always take on a spherical form?

How did the Romans calculate with their numerals?

How can a few drops of acid, a few drops of alkali, a small quantity of wine-spirit, etc. distribute themselves equally enough and in sufficient proportion in a large quantity of milk to link its parts to the point of losing their fluidity in a very short time?

Can one demonstrate the phenomenon of lime before having a chemical theory of the heat of effervescence?

Why, in congelation, does the ice always form in threads, which constantly attach themselves longitudinally at an angle of sixty degrees—or the hundred and twenty that is its complement—and never at right angles?

Why do the rays of sunlight that produce such an ardent fire when collected by an ardent mirror do not operate at the same focal point when they are reflected by the moon, although they already produce a whiteness five hundred times

---

[285] Although mentioned by various French proto-scientists, including Pierre Massuet and Gibert Le Gendre, in connection with explosions, it remains stubbornly unclear from their references what *"larmes de Prusse* (or *de Hollande*)" are.

more considerable than the light that surrounds them? Is it the distance of ninety thousand leagues? But what is that distance compared with a distance of thirty-three million leagues?

What is the property that dioptric and catroptric instruments have of magnifying objects?

How and of what matter are the resin and gum formed that are found on the trunks of trees?

Do hot fermentations and cold fermentations have the same cause?

If the difference between hot and cold fermentations consists in the fact that in hot fermentations the igneous particles cause the lightest particles of the liquid to evaporate, and in cold fermentations it is the particles of fire that evaporate, how does that happen?

Why are the Americans who inhabit in the torrid zone the same climates as the kaffirs and negroes, instead of being black, paler than some Europeans?

What is the cause of gout and arthritic leaven, and how is that malady hereditary, like pneumonia, phthisis, epilepsy, etc.?

What is the cause of falsetto voices?

Does the planet Mercury rotate on its axis?

How long does Venus take to rotate on its axis?

Does the planet Saturn rotate on it axis?

Is the angle at which the Earth cuts the ecliptic always the same?

How does a magnet communicate its virtue to a needle?

Lighting, it is said, is a composite of greasy, bituminous, sulfurous, nitrous, etc., exhalations elevated and heated by the ardor of the sun, which catch fire; if so, how do those exhalations catch fire?

What is the cause of the meteor that the Ancients called Castor and Pollux, and the Moderns St. Elmo's Fire, which appears at the tops of ships' masts after a tempest at sea?

Why does the not touch certain polished metals on which mists fall?

Do the celestial bodies have any influence on things on earth, or the moon in particular on vegetation and animal economy?[286]

Do humans who are struck by lightning, without it being possible to discover any trace of what might have deprived them of life, die of fright, although they could not have heard the stroke, of the vapor of the ignited sulfur, or of the violent rarefaction of the air that surrounds them, leaving them to perish in the void?

Why are certain liquids fermented by the action of lightning, while others, such as wine and beer, cease fermenting and others, such as milk, are corrupted?

All physicists agree that in order to produce fire, it requires a substance, air and combustible material; however, when one sets fire to red lead in a void by means of a burning glass, it bursts into flame and breaks everything it encounters; and if one pours the strongest spirit of niter on to caraway oil, it catches fire and disintegrates; what, then, is the cause of all these phenomena in which fire is produced without air?

Why is it that salt added to snow or crushed ice produces artificial ice, and that sea water freezes less promptly than pure water?

Do the rays that come from objects fall on the retina or the choroid?[287]

How, after amputation, does one feel pain in the parts of the body that were afflicted and are now separated from the organ of sensation?

Do rivers begin to freeze at the surface or in the depths?

---

[286] Author: "One can neither deny or affirm the fact; at the most one can suspect it by virtue of the mutual and necessary relationship between all the bodies that compose the system of the Universe, of which phenomena are the consequences."

[287] Author: "There is every reason to believe that vision does not have its seat in the choroid, since in depriving the eye of an ox of its sclerotic and choroid, the image of a body presented to the hole of the pupil is distinctly painted on the retina."

What is the cause of the external border and the mass of black or red grains that are almost always found on worm-infested fruits?

What is the cause of the sound, or the sonorous noise, that certain bodies render and others do not?

In what manner does a creature obtain its nourishment in its mother's womb?

How does a fetus begin to be animated?

How are the glow-worm, fish and wood able to emit light?

How is it conceivable that the same animals live at the poles and in the torrid zone, without the uniformity of their natural heat being altered?

Which is the person more to be pitied in old age: one who becomes deaf or one who goes blind?

A person born deaf is necessarily mute, since speech is merely exercising the voice in the repetition of what one hears, with the result that a Parisian would be deaf in Peking; but will a child who loses hearing at the age of three, after having heard and spoken, become mute?

Are all substances hard, or is there any that is not? Are we familiar with enough substances to permit us one or the other assertion?

Are human beings carnivorous or frugivorous animals? Is it only the form of their teeth that cam settle the question? Do carnivorous animals all have teeth placed and formed in the same manner?

Of what matter are coal, slate and the majority of fossils formed?

Could there be another moon to illuminate the Earth in the absence of the one that exists? What should be its diameter? At what distance from the Earth ought it to be set, to produce the required effect?

What is the set of the vegetative soul of plants? Do vegetables have a sensitive soul, like plants? Do not a few sympathies that are observed among some of them, like the palm tree and its female, and the strong antipathies between many others, induce one to think so?

Why does the ardent mirror have less efficacy in great heat than in temperate seasons?

Are the greater number of moving microscopic animals veritable animals? The finest dust particles agitated in the air are not alive.

Why does a rifle bullet, which passes through a board mobile on hinges not communicate any impulsion to it, and why is it hardly disfigured by it, when it flattens out in water and causes a great commotion all along the bank, which can be felt trembling underfoot?

With what instrument can certain tiny worms eat away the hardest oaks, and do they feast on the wood?

Does the air drawn into the lungs travel that path in order to mingle with the blood?

Might there not be in the air a vital and singular unknown substance, in consequence of which that fluid is so necessary to the nutrition of flames and the maintenance of everything that breathes?[288]

What weight do conjectures have for rational minds? For the greater number—which is to say, for superficial minds—are they not equivalent to verities? Are they, for geometrical minds, anything other than what plausibility is to certainty, and probability to evidence?

Observation

The majority of the questions that I have presented in this chapter, the number of which could easily have been increased by millions of others, have remained until now in pro-

---

[288] It was not until 1774 that Joseph Priestly published his observations of what he called "dephlogisticated air", for which Antoine Lavoisier rapidly substituted the term "oxygen," thus providing the answer to this question and confirming Listonai's conjecture.

found obscurity for anyone who only yields to demonstration. If the difficulty of resolving them afflicts pride, they can at least serve to exercise sage minds, which will be able to stop where experiences is refused.

Chapter XVII
Moral and Metaphysical Questions

The general weakness of human beings is to be content with a first response to the most abstract questions; that is why, for the majority of minds, there are so many resolved issues, which, for philosophy, still remain in the class of questions, especially in Metaphysics.

Metaphysics is the Experimental Physics of the soul, but the instruments appropriate to carry out the experiments are so imperfect, and the entities on which they are exercised giving so little purchase to the intelligence, that it is not astonishing, in a state of continual uncertainty, that one is limited to reasoning on what cannot be demonstrated.

People flatter themselves in vain that they make discoveries in abstract matters; everything that belongs to metaphysics has been an object of thought in all times and in all people who cultivate the intellect, but in spite of that, we are still at the stage of first principles. People have thought and reasoned before us; let us, therefore think and reason too; it is the noblest employment that we can make of time, until it has succeeded in giving us knowledge of ourselves, the most sublime kind of knowledge there is, and perhaps the only one necessary to human felicity.

Questions

Does happiness exist absolutely? Is it not rather a phantom, which depends on human beings to create it or annihilate it by their ways of thinking?

Are there sure means of applying one's way of thinking to events, or subordinating them to a way of thinking? Are we free to direct our imagination? Are we not, on the contrary, constrained, as if in spite of ourselves, by the tide of general opinion and forced to think as it pleases all those who surround us?

In other terms, can one render oneself happy in the midst of misery and the maximum of misfortune by one's way of thinking and feeling? I presume so, but does the fashion of thinking and feeling depend on us? I doubt it. Is not the fashion of thinking and feeling the effect within us of organization, of the first impressions received, and of the circumstances that surround understanding? In that case, is it therefore accidental, like birth, beauty, intelligence, etc.?

Can meditation and reflection not triumph over the obstacles that oppose our happiness? That is what the true philosopher experiments every day when he succeeds in overcoming affliction, in contenting himself with little, in not allowing himself to be intoxicated in prosperity or overwhelmed in adversity.[289]

If, therefore, the manner of envisaging things and feeling them has such an influence on judgment that it redresses or bastardizes it, does it not follow that it has the same power over health and the different situations of life, and that the power in question is the fruit of philosophy, the sole instrument of our happiness, the first of all goods, which holds sway over all the others, and which anyone can acquire by study, meditation and the search for the truth?

Is there anything more afflicting than the consolations taken from the necessity of evil, the misfortunes of condition, and the futility of the remedies that employ, with a sort of satisfaction, the melancholy and the atrabiliary? Would it not be better, instead of nourishing those dolorous ideas, to have recourse to means, whatever they might be, of charming our misery, to render ourselves happy at least in the imagination? One would be, in fact, since it is sufficient to believe that one is in order really to be.

---

[289] Author: "The majority of misfortunes and accidents are only extraordinary in the manner in which one feels them."

Is it as difficult as people believe to be moderate, and even humble, in prosperity? Can one even conceive that it is so very rare when one considers that, with modesty, probity acquires glamour and hypocrisy finds a noble means of flattering its pride?

What does one understand, or ought one to understand, by a reasonable animal, if not a being endowed with reason, who may have it, but who does not always have it?

Considering the difficulty of being perfectly happy, and the tyrannical empire that the passions exercise over the human heart, is one not tempted to believe that the honest man, physically, is the one in whom vice and virtue are in equilibrium?

What is it that contributes more to rendering a human being happy: the possession of great wealth, or the art of knowing how to do without it? The necessary is reducible to so very little![290] Some people cannot live on the same income that would comfortable support a numerous community. An infinite number of the things that we have, and of which we are unaware, would each complete the supreme happiness of someone. There are some people whose entire desire is limited to having one eye or two arms.

In spite of the repugnance of any thinking being to end it all, no matter how unhappy they might be, are there many people who would consent to recommence their career on the condition of experiencing all the evils and misfortunes that they have suffered?[291]

---

[290] Author: *"Nam si, quod satis est homini, id satis esse potesset, hoc sat erat:....* Lucilius cited by Ammianus Marcellinus. V. section 98." [For if what is enough for a man could be enough, it would be enough.]

[291] Author: "All things considered, I hold to the negative; as for myself, although the sum of good things has outweighed that of bad, and I have always enjoyed perfect health, and have an agreeable idea of being the last survivor in my class, I say boldly and with verity that I would not want to be reborn."

Is the soul equally satisfied in the enjoyment of a familiar pleasure as in the deprivation of an unfamiliar one? If pleasure is always preceded by desire, which is a dolor, is it, therefore, merely a remedy for an infirmity, which it would have been better not to have experienced?

Is not asking whether a human being would be happier without passions and with desires, than with ills and the means to cure them, asking whether a malady is necessary to make to make us savor the price of health more deliciously, or a long captivity desirable to render the charms of liberty more sensible?

If true happiness consists in abstention from dolor, can it be encountered anywhere else than in perfect indifference? But how can that state be grasped? Does absolute indifference exist?

If calm of mind contributes to human felicity, who would be the happier: an honest Minister or a slave in chains?

If the manner of seeing and feeling proceeds from the constitution of the organs, education and circumstances, there are, in consequence, as many tastes as temperaments, as many opinions as studies, as many judgments as accidents. The continual variation of those three things ensuring that tastes are never exactly the same, at various times, what foundation can there be for the enlightenment of the human mind?

Does not the diversity of opinions come from the form of the heads to which the brain is necessarily adapted?

By virtue of the diversity of opinions, can we not be sure of the diversity of organs, which gives rise to different ways of seeing, as corporeal as they are intellectual, with the result that colors are not the same for all eyes, just as all objects appear yellow to eyes affected by distributed bile; and ought we not agree that we are only in accord with respect to the names of things, not the things themselves?

Are men born wicked, as they are born ferocious, slothful and cowardly? Is it not more reasonable to think that they are weak by nature and wicked by virtue of circumstances?

What is the sentiment known as self-esteem, which, being insufficient in itself, is not a virtue, and is at most the principle of some; which, only having a precarious existence, only lives so to speak, by borrowing, and in the judgment and opinion of others? Is it inherent in the nature of every being? Would it exist outside society? Is it born of it? Engendered by it?

What is the most sublime intelligence worth, since a thrust of a midwife's finger could have made Voltaire an idiot?

Is health, in itself, a very sensible thing? Does it not serve more often to make us experience more sensibly the privation of all the others?

Mademoiselle Scuderi.

Is not honor, that source of so many beautiful actions useful to society, an adroit means that comes down, in the final analysis, to producing the effects of virtue by way of vanity? And what is honor, in its true significance, if not the good opinion that others have of our merit, and a chimera outside the social condition?

Is it easy to love work if one does not love pleasure?

Which is preferable: mediocrity that is placidly enjoyed, or great fortune incessantly agitated by the desire for what one does not have or regret for what one no longer has?

Have the first laborers not been placed in the ranks of the Gods with far more reason than placing those of today beneath other men?

If, in delirium, drunkenness or obscurity, a person can enjoy keen pleasures that become cruel pains when sanity or light is restored, is illusion preferable to reality and imagination to judgment?[292]

---

[292] Author: "Is the condition of human beings such that they can only be happy by anticipation living on projects, chimeras, illusions and hopes?"

Ought someone who does not consult reason in his pleasures to flatter himself that he can expect its help in his pains?

Is the constancy of sage individuals in the face misfortunes and setbacks anything but the art of imprisoning agitation in the heart?

If one removed from the number of virtues those caused by vanity or temperament, would there be many real ones left?

If it were the case that we were not human, but endowed with reason, what would we think of the bizarre species of creatures known as the human race? Could we imagine something that had passions so foolish and reflections so sage; a duration so short and views so long; so much knowledge of almost useless things and so much ignorance of more important things; so much ardor for liberty and so much penchant for servitude; such a strong desire to be happy with such a great incapacity for being so? How could understand all these things be understood if, looking at ourselves objectively, we were able to divine how we are made?

Fontenelle.

Who can be sure that the most heroic actions and the most useful discoveries do not have for a motive some corrupt passion, such as frantic ambition, pride, cupidity, presumption, the fear of dishonor, anger, vengeance, etc.?

Why is the courage of soldiers animated by liquor and surges of anger that make them less than human? Why are the arts stimulated by recompenses, zeal by benefits, virtue of by fear of punishment? Fear or hope then takes the place of virtue.

Do ambition and cupidity produce more evil than good in human society?

What is the monster of vanity or pride that drives humans to persist in recognized error?

Why blush to admit that one has made a mistake? Is it not, on the contrary, appropriate to announce that one is wiser today than one was yesterday?

Would there be so many false minds is there were as many ways to grasp the truth as they are of setting it aside?

Would there be as many awkward people of there were not a thousand ways of doing something badly and only one way to do it well?

Is it by virtue of reason or weakness that one consoles oneself for ills without remedy?

Is not only doing good at the end of one's life a final testimony of avarice, and making use of one's spoils rather than one's gifts?

Is not making restitution by testament taking witnesses to one's avarice or dishonor, and afflicting an heir without obliging a creditor?

Is it really with reason that we take so much vanity from inventions in the Arts? Is the utility that we obtain from them necessarily absolute, and does it balance out the evils that that have followed from them?

How much do we have to complain of the person who, by virtue of a misunderstood delicacy, imagined clothing? Without it, all the infirmities caused by the vagaries of the seasons would not exist; in the coolest climates one does not cover the most tender part of the body, the eyes; the continual need that one has of them has saved them from that blindness. All the other body parts could equally well do without being garroted, smothered, etc.

Is not the first person who imagined taking cover in a hut or forming a shelter out of branches the author of the deaths of all those who have perished in the construction of edifices, beneath the ruins of their houses, in fires, flood and earthquakes?

Has not the compass, by improving communication, considerably augmented the number of shipwrecks?

Was not the first boat, formed from a hollowed-out treetrunk or made of animal skins, invented by reason of avidity, which has caused the destruction of so many individuals whom Nature had not destined to perish in a foreign element?

Has not the deadly invention of *yours* and *mine* engendered cupidity, the source of all the evils that inundate the world: thefts, murders, poisonings, and consequently the death of malefactors, who would have lived tranquilly had they had nothing to covet or to protect?

There is no insult where there is no property. Has not luxury, born of the distinction of ranks and fortunes, delivered to death a considerable number of unfortunates in the working of mines and quarries, and caused one part of the human race to die of hunger and the other of excess? Could one believe, however, that what keeps human in a perpetual state of agitation is the love of repose?

If all our knowledge comes via the senses, and if all our sensations are merely ways of being, how can we see objects outside ourselves? Does it not seem that we should only see our soul, differently modified?

Are there ideas and indifferent sensations except by comparison? Everything is more or less disagreeable, otherwise, would not sensing and not sensing be the same thing?

Because real perfection is a chimera, are human being forever dispensed from reaching for it, and Governments from exciting it? Is the State not on the road of honest citizens, brave soldiers and good Magistrates?

Are there people born fortunately or unfortunately—which is to say, for whom everything succeeds or turns out badly, independently of the most judicious measures that prudence employs? A few examples might make one suspect so, but does not their enlightenment, the cast of their intelligence and their temperament contribute, in large measure to the events whose success or failure they attribute to a blind chance that does not exist?

Is it not to make oneself a slave to renown, affairs and the public to accept a responsibility?

Is it not a strange ambition to sell one's liberty for a shadow of power, and to consent to be no longer one's own master for the frivolous and dangerous pleasure of commanding others?

317

Has there ever been any action or opinion that was universally approved or criticized?

Is it not opinion that measures time and finds it short or long?[293]

Afflictis lentae, celeres gaudentibus, borae.[294]

Is the shortest day less than twenty-four hours? Is the longest any more, in a dungeon as on a throne? It depends on the human imagination to extend or abridge the course of life.

How can life seem so short to the majority of people who find the days so long and seem only to be occupied in the concern of abridging its term? Life is certainly too long for those who are in pain or suffering ennui, and too short for those who enjoy in liberty the benefits of health and fortune. For the sage it is such that he does not desire a longer or a shorter one.

If one only counted the days on which useful employment was made of time, what miscalculations would we not find in the method of estimating human age? How few one would see showing a beautiful maturity in the flower of age, and how many adolescent and stupid young septuagenarians!

If time is the destroyer of all things, is it a bad thing to kill it? And among the different means of killing it, should one not count, with reason, gossip, reading fiction, gambling, parades and French Opera?

If, from the number of thinking beings who inhabit our little planet, one were to remove those insensible to the pleasures of the soul, uniquely occupied in the search for physical pleasure, the avoidance of dolor and the care of their own

---

[293] Author: "*Ut nox longa; quibus mentitur amica, diesque longa videtur opus debentibus, ut piger annus pupillis, quos dura premit custodia matrum; sic mihi tarda fluunt....* Horace, Book I, Epistle I." [As the night is long to the man whose mistress deceives him, and the day long to men obliged to toil, and the year lags for children oppressed by a mother's harsh control, just as sluggish are the passing hours....]

[294] Slow to the afflicted, time is rapid to the happy.

conversation, for whom true philosophy consists of the art of enjoying life, would many reasonable animals remain?

Why does one see in the civilized state so many people complaining of life, desiring death, and even giving it to themselves, while free savages await it so much more tranquilly that they do not fear it? Is the natural state, then, happier than the civilized? If it is happier, is it comprehensible that humans gave it up, and now glorify themselves for having quit it?[295]

What do we understand by the age of reason? At what number of years does it arrive? At seven, at ten, at sixty? How many sexagenarians does one see in whom reason has not yet become manifest?

In what does human beauty consist, as much in the features as the color, since beauties that touch and evoke the admiration of one people serve others as a model to depict ugliness and deformity? Which is the better founded: the European, in depicting the devil as black, or the Ethiopian, in depicting him as white? Have humans really nothing appropriate to them but their opinions?

Is there not injustice in demanding constancy in humans—which is to say, in bodies whose nature is constantly changing, and, in consequence carry souls to which the senses continually give different means of perceiving and judging? Would there be less absurdity in demanding that a person be cheerful while tormented by colic, or sing a comic song in the middle of a mathematical calculation?

Without flattery, praise, dread and superstition, would there still be veritable enchantments?

---

[295] Author: "...*Quos ille timorum Maximus, haud urget lethi metus. Indi ruendi in ferrum mens prona viris, animaeque capaces Mortis....* Lucan, Book I, line 459-62." [Those people whom the fear of death, the greatest of all, never moves; hence their courage, prone to rush on steel, their minds despising death.]

Without the passions, which make and unmake everything, would anything happen on the earth? Would it not be an abode of indolence, slumber and ennui?

In judging the works of intelligence, is sentiment surer than discussion? Ought they not to concur?

Is there nothing marvelous or beautiful except in prospect? Does the human mind ever pass from imagination to reality without loss?

On what is the puerile care to conceal age founded, if Nature is engraving it in the facial features? Is it because of the shame of appearing less sage that one ought not to be a certain age?

What idea should one form of a Nation in which the Highly-placed give their cooks and coachmen a salary ten times that of a tutor; in which a fish can be sold ten times as dearly as an ox; in which well-brought-up young women can walk better than they talk, follow the steps of a dance better than those of their own financial affairs;[296] in which women are accused of falsity if they bend the laws of decency in opposition to those of Nature; in which plays are esteemed and actors stigmatized; in which a very keen humor is adapted to excessively slow music; in which gambling debts are paid in preference to those owed to merchants and workers; in which the charges of judicature are venal and commissions of finance not done; in which individuals incapable of regulating their domestics set themselves up as arbiters of the interests of sovereigns; in which the honor of a husband is tarnished by the behavior of his wife; in which the Great give up the useful

---

[296] Author: "*Motus doceri gaudet Ionicus matura virgo et singitur artibus jam nunc et incestos amores de tenero meditator ungui*. Horace Book III, Ode VI." [Adapted into English (rather freely) by the Earl of Roscommon as: "Behold a ripe and melting maid, Bound 'prentice to the wanton trade. Ionian artists at a mighty price, Instruct her in the mysteries of vice, What nets to spread; where subtle baits to lay, And with an early hand, they form'd the tempered clay.]

professions from which they obtained their origin, with which they are allied and which ought to replace extinct nobilities; in which, very sensitive to the glory of the Nation, people console themselves for a disgrace by means of a song or an epigram; in which, alternately victim to prejudice and frivolity, everyone lays claim to the title of philosopher and citizen, and a work of fiction is more widely read than a treatise on morality, politics, commerce or agriculture; in which, in one part of the State, slavery evokes horror, and in another, people are bought and sold; in which someone who is insulted is dishonored if he obeys the law and punished by death if he infringes it; in which an entire family is covered with opprobrium for the crime of one individual; in which industry is taxed and idleness free from all imposition; and in which, finally, a juggler, a musician or an actor has an easier life than an agricultural worker, and those who make people laugh earn more than those who enable them to live?

Would one not imagine that some enchanter had placed a talisman in that country, which had turned all heads, and forced people to be in constant opposition to themselves?[297]

Which would one prefer in a statesman: a superior genius with an ordinary mind, or an infinite mind with a mediocre genius?

Which is the more difficult art, painting or sculpture?

If there is no greater satisfaction than being alone with a person one loves, why can people, who are so full of self-love, not remain in their own company for long? Is it the fear of knowing oneself that causes that ennui?

Which is more likely to lead to fortune, phlegm or vivacity?

---

[297] Author: "...*Convivae, prope dissentire videntur, poscentes vario multum diversa palate, qui dem? quid non dem?* Horace, Book II, Epistle II."[I have dissenting guests at my feast, each requiring different food to satisfy his taste. Which courses should I choose, and which omit?]

Is there a means of disposing the imagination in such a manner that it separates pleasure from pains and only allows the pleasures to pass?

Has the commerce of the world done more good than harm to men of Letters and artists?

On what is the glory founded, or the vanity obtained therefrom, of counting the illustrious men, scholars and celebrated inventors of one's Nation? What has it got to do with us?

Is the impossibility of finding a remedy for some violent misfortune, such as the loss of someone near, as reason for consolation or eternal affliction?

What is the ascendancy that certain people have over the will of others: intelligence, eloquence over the heart, beauty over all souls? What is the secret force that subjugates and moves others to veneration, respect, love, etc.?

Is public education preferable to public education?

Is it permissible to kill animals, except in self-defense or the absolute necessity of nourishing oneself?

If it is true that the passions of animals circulate in their blood, should one not abhor meat; ought the hunter not dread that the ferocity of the wild boar might pass into his soul?

Is it preferable to be governed by common sense or genius? It is not dubious which is preferable to be for human beings in general.

Is the multiplicity of literary Academies advantageous or harmful to progress in Science and Letters?

Is luxury necessary, or at least tolerable in a great Monarchy that reaps all the primary necessities?

If one asked a thousand people, selected at random, which is the most fortunate condition in the established order, or what they would choose for preference, with the reasons for their choice, can one be sure that two would be found in perfect agreement?

Is it permissible to forget equity in order to save the Fatherland, or to sacrifice one's century to the fortune of posterity?

Since we have discovered the art of reading the past in hieroglyphs, writing and printing, and thus representing events very distant from us, can we be sure that we will never find one that unveils the future?

After what lapse of time can an absentee by presumed dead?

Is fire a more honorable sepulcher for the dead than earth, and why is fire, which was once employed only for emperors, today reserved for malefactors?[298]

If the senses were not constantly at odds, would tastes change? Would one thing please us or displease us more at one time than another?

Is it easier to pass from hatred to love than from antipathy?

By what means can one discern that which comes from Nature and that which comes from education?

Since the life of plants and insects can be prolonged by keeping plants, which heed heat to grow, in cold places, and, by denying eggs the warmth necessary for their hatching, the life of animals still in embryo can be extended, ought we to despair of discovering some means of extending human life beyond its term?

Is not the concern that produces such an ardent devotion to leaning about past events, such a frantic curiosity to penetrate the future and such great indifference to the present—which is the only one of the three that veritably belongs to humankind—a malady of the mind?

What name can one give to the society formed between the horse, the dog, the hawk and the hunter?

Who can be sure of finding a *juste milieu* between two extremes, between passion and sensuality, superstition and

---

[298] Author: "In Colchis the dead were suspended from trees, the Egyptians embalmed them, the Romans burned them, and the Paeonians threw them in ponds."

incredulity, blasphemy and idolatry, pain and pleasure,[299] cowardice and recklessness, abstinence from forbidden pleasures and the abuse of permitted pleasures, misery and felicity, presumption and pusillanimity, reason and instinct, the vegetable kingdom and the animal kingdom, infection and perfume, geometry and prejudice, sensible movements and imperceptible ones, mind and matter, being and nothingness, etc.?

Who can likewise assign limits to extremities, which are perhaps thus in name only?

In sum, is vice set between two virtues or virtue between two vices?

Is it easy to stop in course of fortune?

Why does love, which so often makes the fortune of all beings, so often make individuals unhappy?[300]

In what do the disagreeable perception of dolor and the agreeable perception of pleasure consist?

Can understanding produce an idea by itself, or is there none that has not been transmitted to it by the senses?

What is the real price of a precious metal that only has value by virtue of human industry, which a tyrant fabricates voluntarily for his own use, and which, by a corruption of reason, he esteems more than himself, since he uses it to buy servants, workmen, courtiers and slaves?

If precious stones have no other merit than their gleam and no other value but rarity, why not substitute for the avarice of nature by a general agreement only to esteem the artificial ones with which so many honest eyes are deceived.

---

[299] Author: "It is a philosophical verity that pain and pleasure are adjacent, and that where the sensation of pleasure ends, that of pain commences; that is what one experiences when one scratches too hard in response to an itch."

[300] Author: "Monsieur de Buffon, who poses this question, replies that in the passion in question there is only physical good, and that the moral aspect is worthless."

Which is preferable in a painter: to combine all the aspects of paining to a high level, or only to possess one, but to a sublime degree?

Cochin.[301]

Can the sense of taste savor itself? Can smell perceive its own scent? Can the eye see itself? Has any man ever seen his own face? Without experience, which is not always reliable, who can judge, when a person blushes, whether it is from shame or anger?

If one is doing nothing when one is not doing anything, and when one is not doing anything one is doing nothing, in the same way that on seeing the wheel of a machine, one cannot judge the machine entire, is it not reckless to judge the fortunes or the lives of people, or to endeavor to cure them? Magistracy and Medicine are, therefore, two very delicate professions.

What is what is vulgarly called homesickness? Is it caused by education, instinct, inconstancy or regret for what one has quit, by virtue of disgust for what one is enjoying?[302]

Why do two men who would have been enemies in their native land suddenly find themselves friends when they meet at the antipodes? Is to a mutual need that they have to hold forth on the mores and practices they regret, or freely to censure those that have before their eyes, that they owe the union of their hearts? Does national instinct increase, then, in proportion to the square of distance?

Is not love of the Fatherland a sentiment exclusive of universal love? Why do the intelligent people, the Scholars, celebrated Artists, Philosophers and Gentlefolk of all lands, esteem themselves independently of the circumstances that alienate States, the particular interests that render entire Nations hostile and the rivalry that engenders hatred between two

---

[301] Charles Nicolas Cochin (1715-1790)

[302] Author: "*Ante oculos errant domus, urbsque et forma locorum.* Ovid, Tristia Book III, iv, line 57." [Before my eyes drift my home, the city and the shapes of places.]

cities of the same order or between societies which, speaking the same language, only differ in costume? Does not love of the Fatherland have limits that can be prescribed? Should it be reduced to the surrounding walls that saw us born? Should the difficult of fixing limits have disabused humans of that chimera of the Ancients?

What is the nature of the temperament most appropriate to form men of genius?

Why are there so many declamations against coquetry, since, without the desire for pleasure that is its driving force, few women would be amiable, few men would be sociable, and there would be very few good books?

If singularity, in productions of the intelligence and of art is not a sign of the instability or decadence of taste, would not the vivid impression that it makes on the mind be preferable to the contemplation of the beautiful, which leads, in time, to ennui?

Which is it more difficult to acquire in society: the title of philosopher or that of good companion? Which ought to flatter a well-made soul more?

Why has Elegy, which was in vogue in the last century, gone out of fashion? Is it because more impetuous passions and coarse appetites have expelled delicacy and tender sentiments from the empire of amour?

Is it not to the indiscreet requests of suitors and the ingratitude of wards, rather than to the insensibility of guardians that one ought to attribute the harshness that is so commonly reproached on the part of the majority of people in positions of responsibility?

Why do so many child prodigies, so marvelous in youth, become mediocre individuals later in life? Does Nature exhaust herself in their favor by excessively violent efforts, like fields from which one attempt to take productions too rapidly?

If people, before taking vanity from something, took care to ensure that it really belonged to them, would there be much vanity in the world?

By virtue of what bizarerrie of custom is the air expelled impetuously from nostrils, in what is known as sneezing, less shocking than that erupting from other places, whose retention is so pernicious to the health? Is an infirmity common to all beings a vice or an indecency, and can one take offense at it without injustice?[303]

Monsters

Are there really monsters, and what is the subtle distinction between monsters by excess and monsters by default?[304]

What is a monster, in the physical sense, except a figure differing from the ordinary form, to which we arbitrarily attach the idea of beauty, propriety or regularity?

Are the individuals that we are pleased to call monsters anything other than creatures—sports of nature if one wishes, but with what does Nature not play?—or extraordinary objects more deformed of bizarre to our eyes than those to which we are accustomed? Although something can be produced that is out of the ordinary, can there be anything outside of Nature, rather than our feeble perceptions? Are all possible forms known to us? Can any enter our ideas beyond the scope of the models we have before our eyes? In sum, do we know all the ways in which Nature operates well enough to dare to pronounce judgment on her irregularities, and treat as bizarreries or caprices what are perhaps the produce of her greatest efforts?

---

[303] Author: "In certain countries, such as Spain, delicacy is not so inhumane. The effects of poor digestion are excused. The Emperor Claudius permitted the relief of flatulence, even in his presence, by an Edict."

[304] Author: "Strictly speaking, there are only monsters in figuration, but there are people of perverse inclinations or false and corrupt ideas led to commit, deliberately, actions harmful to society or the human race."

Is it not with as much reason the botanists call double carnations and anemones monsters?

Is not our judgment even more at fault with regard to the animals we call monsters? In what do they differ from an infinite number of others that attract our admiration by their singularity? What is so horrible or frightening about them, that they cannot cease to appear so by the habit of seeing them?

Who would dare to decide that, in the order of Nature, the barn owl is less beautiful than the parrot, or the bat than the canary?

Does not a hideous face, monstrous in vulgar language please us in a painting, which would disgust or frighten us in reality?

Wishes

Are wishes always the work of reason, as desires always emerge from temperament, and is it not a privative good fortune, for the majority of people, that their wishes are not always granted?[305]

Such is a woman's desire for a beauty, whose humors, caprices, jealousy and infidelity would have made it the torment of her life.

Such is the ardent wish of an heir, whose conduct would have ruined his father and dishonored his father.

Such is the desire of an intriguer for an important position in a Court, in which he would have been persecuted by virtue of envy and cabals, robbed of himself, the object of public hatred in times of calamity, and finally a victim of disgrace that would have thrown him into despair.

---

[305] Author: "*Nam pro jucundis optissima quaeque dabunt Dii. Charior est illis homo quam fibi....* Juvenal Satire X." [The Gods, instead of what is most pleasing, will give what is most proper. Man is dearer to them than he is to himself.]

Such is the ambition of a talent for poetry that would have been paid to write a satire, a scurrilous pamphlet or an epigram.

Such is the desire of a man tranquil in mediocrity for wealth that would have rendered him the victim of the avarice or evils attached to his satisfied passion.

Such is the solicitation of a diplomat who, by virtue of the insufficiency of his enlightenment, would have lost his repose, his reputation and the esteem of his master at the expense of his probity.[306]

In how many cases would one thank heaven for a refusal if one could foresee the evils to which the granting of a wish would have exposed us?

How many wishes are there, the motive for which we would not dare to confess, how, how many requests from heaven that no one would have dared to voice aloud?

How can someone claim to know or to calculate infinity, if the indefinite, which is far less, is incomprehensible to him?

Why should he complain of ignorance of the causes of phenomena that he knows, since only the effects are really important to him?

To what causes can one attribute the great inequality of intelligence that one observes between well-constituted men who have received the same education?

If education, more often than the disposition of organs, contributes to the development of natural faculties, why does one discover so much intelligence and common sense in some rustics and so much imbecility in some Aristocrats?

When one considers how often knowledge harms a person, and how the different aspects of things throw uncertainty

---

[306] Author: "*Jamne igitur laudas, quod de sapientibus altr ridebat, quoties a limine moverat unum protuleratque pedem flebat contrarius alter?* Juvenal. Satire X, line 28." [Nor, therefore, do you approve that one of the wise men laughed, as he had often moved from the threshold and put forward a foot, while the other, contrary, wept?]

into judgments, can one not compare the human mind to an Ocean, which only gains on one coast what it loses on the other?

It is not wiser to occupy oneself with enjoying the world than in judging it?

If life is a dream, is it not important to make it a good one, and to be virtuous, in order to dream at one's ease?

On Symmetry

Is symmetry a real beauty in architecture? Is it not often the cause of a disagreeable uniformity, a fastidious monotony?

Are proportions always true beauties; are they so indispensable that one cannot stray from them tastefully; are they not prejudices of art rather than precepts of reason?

Except in the organization of animals, in which economy demands relationships and harmony for the maintenance and operation of the machine, where does one find proportions in the works of nature, the model of all human productions? Does there not reign, on the contrary, an affected disorder, a rusticity, that charms the eyes? What order does one find in the arrangement and the grandeur of the planets? What symmetry is there in the position and the heights of mountains? One sees only sinuosities in the courses of rivers, only irregularity in the shapes of lakes and seas, and a strange confusion in forests. The Earth is not spherical, it does not rotate on its poles, its orbit is not circular; it is, however that diversity of aspects, that irregularity of scenes, that gives birth to the spectacle of Nature. Is it therefore the case that the beauty of symmetry and proportions, which is not encountered anywhere in Nature, is only an effect of habit, a blind subjection to rules prescribed by austere geniuses, an ideal of convention, and, in consequence, subject to the caprices of fashion, with no empire over the reality of beauty?

On seeing half of a work symmetrically constructed, one can imagine the whole; the other half no longer has anything agreeable, since it cannot cause any surprise. The contrary occurs in the works of Nature, as simple in her means as she is various in her effects. The diversity of aspects, which are not repeated, never harms the charm of what one calls the ensemble.

It is doubtless the same in the works of the mind in which the author only sets forth with compasses; and, T-square in hand, infallibly sows ennui along his route. A drama of which one can foresee the denouement is a failed enterprise, which announces its fall.

Is it not to the form of government, rather than to the nature of the climate and even the principles of education to which one ought to attribute the virtues and vices dominating Nations?

Are not the mores of the Spartans, compared with those of the Athenians, proof of the influence of laws on mores? Is not the difference between the Greeks and Romans of our day and their Ancients another proof, even more convincing? And if one asks why Rome, once so powerful, is so weak today, could one not respond that it is for the reason that everything there that ought to be in cannons is in bells?

Is not punishing theft and murder equally with death putting the lives of citizens in danger, who would have escaped by the sacrificed of a small part of their wealth, which they have a thousand means of repairing by means of their labor or industry?

If experience teaches us that, with a few exceptions, Nature forms humans soundly, can we deny that the majority of the evils they suffer originate from their intemperance, the corruption of their minds and the deadly art of refining their pleasures? In that case, are the understanding and liberty with which humans are endowed, to the exclusion of animals, therefore fatal instruments, with which the fabricate evils and pains, which are transmitted inhumanely to their posterity?

What are the precise limits of necessity in which abuses and scandals ought to be contained?

Is prudence a virtue? Undoubtedly, but if it envisages all the dangers of an enterprise, would not humankind often be deprived of rescue? Would one see so many examples of that fortunate boldness, of which events have justified the cause, vicious in its essence? It is, therefore, useful that human beings do not reason all the time.

Can one be sure that reflection enters into, or that they will plays any part in, the movements that a man makes whose foot vacillates in order to counterbalance a stumble? Could the most skillful anatomist conceive, let alone calculate, the number of contractions and dilatations of fibers, nerves, flexor and extensor muscles that suddenly act to prevent the fall of a body that has lost its center of gravity? Can a musician comprehend how he has given one of the ribbons of the larynx, rather and another, the necessary vibration to produce the sound that he requires of it and which is never anything but an impact on the air?

What necessity is there, it is commonly asked, for there to be ferocious animals[307] on the earth, biting insects, poisonous plants, intemperate seasons, thunderbolts in the air, tempests at sea, etc.? Do the plaints and murmurs regarding these inconveniences have any other foundation than the limits of the human mind and human pride, insensate enough to relate everything in the universe to himself?[308]

---

[307] Author: "The most ferocious animal, in our estimation, is the Tiger; for the insect, it is the sheep."

[308] Author: "There are inconvenient insects and harmful, venomous animals; but they are, so to speak, merely an ephemeral existence. Cleanliness, a little care and a thousand means can provide protection from them. Those which devastate the fields, like caterpillars, rats and locusts, only afflict a few countries; they often encounter antagonists, which destroy them.

"There are ferocious animals that seem, like conquerors, born to destroy human beings, but they rarely attack unless pressed by hunger, while they are assailed by humans for their pleasure or gluttony. By virtue of a sage providence, however, that has judged them to be necessary, since they exist, they are less fecund than useful animals, and the grass is very inadequate for their subsistence. In fact, if lions, tigers, bears, wolves, panthers, crocodiles, etc., pullulated as much as they could, the earth would be covered by them in ten years, every human species would become their prey, human industry could do nothing against their voracity and the greater number of animals would perish. It seems that it did not please the fecund father of the human race to deliver the earth to them. If he did not, it was doubtless in obedience an eternal decree that their species were admitted to the ark.

"There are poisonous plants, which we reject as harmful for want of knowing all their properties. Some of them are both useful and harmful, like the root of the plant known as Lunaria, which contain a poison to which the leaves produce an antidote, in contrast to the leaves of the plant called Mimosa, which are poisonous, and to which the root is the counterpoison. With the Cassava, the juice of which is poisonous, bread is made for the negroes in America, etc. Thus, many plants carry contrary virtues within them.

"The pestilential exhalations that catch fire in mid-air are consumed by the fire. Storms cause some temporary damage, but they bring general good by the dissolution of clouds that, in falling to the earth, fertilize it and render it strength to resist the great ardor of the sun. Excessively violent winds cause tempests at sea, which occasion some disorder, but without the winds, vessels would be unable to sail, the waters of the sea would stagnate at the edges and communication between peoples would be very limited. It is to earthquakes that we owe the discovery of the metals that avidity has rendered so precious to us.

"If, during a single century, only males or females were born, the human race would be annihilated. If no more males than females were born, the population would decline and the human species would become extinct in a few centuries, since navigation, war, difficult labor in quarries and mines, for which men are destined, would remove a considerable num-

333

Is it knowledge or the fear of peril that causes humans not to swim as naturally as the heaviest animals, such as the elephant, the dromedary and the rhinoceros? If it is ignorance of the peril that makes the security of animals, why, in other regards, are some more timid than others? Might courage not be, in humans as in animals, only an effect of clear sight, or an entire ignorance of danger?

Why does one see, almost without paying attention to it, deformed humans, but one is so disturbed on encountering twisted and bizarre minds? Is it because the latter are less

---

ber. Is one not tempted to believe that the wars and misfortunes attached to avidity are necessary in the order of things, since Nature seems to lend herself to them, by compensating for those pretended disorders by the difference she constantly puts into the number of births of either sex?

"If all the acorns that fell from oaks, cones from pines, and the seeds and grains of other plants took root and fructified, the woods would perish for lack of air; a forest would become, in a century, a solid mass like a rock, over which other trees would rise, having become mountains in their turn, heaping up, and the project of Enceladus could be realized; fortunately, there is always such an admirable order that one might believe that there is never a instant when a man, of no matter what age, cannot mate with his companion; that falling acorns only fructify as much as is necessary for the oaks already produce to grow without obstacles, etc.

"The Being endowed with reason, who has the imbecility of making himself the motive and center of everything, would find less to criticize in Nature and the order of things if he put less pride and more philosophy into his reasoning. If he deigned to observe, he would recognize that everything he calls chance is planned, that all is well and doubtless as well as it is possible to be; he would cease to dispute good and evil, of which does not know the ends or the connections. Murmurs are always reckless, and reason, which is submissive, finds subjects of adoration and gratitude everywhere."

common? Experience demonstrates the contrary. Is it because they can be reformed? That is open to question.

If one encounters a warrior decorated with marks of his valor, scarred, deprived of an eye, his temple disfigured by a plaster, one looks at him with a sort of respect and commiseration, excited by the noble subject of his misfortune; why regard with repugnance the man whom Nature has afflicted with similar disgraces?

What is the strange power of habit that makes a hunter whose sleep is disturbed by a crease in his sheet, his head stirred by a slight odor and his breathing intercepted by a draught, confront, in the woods, rain, snow or the ardor of the sun without feeling any discomfort? Ought he not to have turned that power of habitude to his advantage?

What is the significance of the vague and bizarre terms *fate, fortune, hazard, luck, destiny*, etc., except a humiliating confession of the profound ignorance humans are in of primary causes and the established order of Nature, of which all phenomena are merely the necessary consequences?

Is the musical Duo in Nature?

On the supposition to the most widely admitted principle, that memory depends on corporeal impressions in the brain, in which ideas are traced, can one conceive that ides, which are not corporeal can engrave them on the body, and that the impression remains there, in such a manner that the will—another incomprehensible faculty—will find them there at need, and how, subsequently, can new ideas be placed in such a small space without effacing the imprint of those already engraved there, especially when they are antagonistic and can only be established by the destruction of the first?

Is it certain that humans alone have the faculty of laughter and that other animals do not laugh? Are their frolicsome games not signs of pleasure and joy, which excite laughter? Does it always require, in order to design laughter, a movement of the hips and a convulsive erupting of the voice? Perhaps animals are only derived of the laughter caused by surprise and the comparison of disparate ideas or bizarre things, which cannot cause it in a being to which one has refused ideas? In any case, how can one recognize laughter in the features of the visage, since the same movements design both laughter and tears?

What does it matter what principle makes humans act—love of glory or of virtue, self-interest or pleasure—if the duties of society are at least fulfilled? Does the order that Nature has established on the earth subsist any less if folly or reason concurs with it?

Is it not singular that the more a people is lively and gay, the more its music is grave and slow, and vice versa?

Do all the words that compose a language owe their origin to chance, if they are not onomatopoeic? Are there, in consequence, noble and base ones? Are they not were habit has placed them—sublime or trivial, honest or obscene—purely by virtue of convention? Are not some of them honest in one sense and dishonest in another? Are not so-called dirty words more contrary to politeness than to good morals? Are they frightening in the mouths of the populace? What difficulty would there be if "horror" signified tenderness, "debauchery" voluptuousness, "temple" sewer, "rags" pomp, "spectacle" dungeon, or "oyster" Great Lord?

Why should the ear be wounded by one sound rather than another? Are words anything but signs representing ideas? Do they have any relationship with things?

Is there anything base and vile in Nature? Is mud more despicable than diamond? Is lead less valuable than gold? With regard to its utility, is not iron preferable to the most precious metal known?[309]

---

[309] Author: "Esteem and scorn in all things are only relative to our needs, tastes and pleasures. All matter is one; mud can become diamond as diamond can become mud. Gold piled up for a long time changes into water, which becomes foul. Everything is sought out or shunned in accordance with the affection or aversion that it inspires, but is not hateful or estimable in an absolute sense. A broken statue is less valuable than an

Are there vile and despicable conditions among those that contribute honestly to public utility? Is the condition of a cesspit-emptier inferior to that of a noble idler?

Does not the distinction between conditions, holding one lower than another, depend entirely on opinion? In Sparta, was not the haulier more esteemed, with reason, than the dressmaker, the agricultural laborer more than the financier, the pedant more than the poet, the historian more than the romancer, the cowherd more than the coachman, the carpenter more than the sculptor, the manual worker more than the decorator, the physician more than the metaphysician, the blacksmith more than the chemist and the locksmith more than the lapidary?

On Inconsequence

What does one understand by the term inconsequence, with which the majority of human speeches and actions are taxed? Is there inconsequence in any conduct that seems diametrically opposite to the goal that has been set? Does it not exist rather in ignorance of what the goal in question is, or the faulty interpretation of the means and motivations that people employ, which make them act? Speaking absolutely, humans are not inconsequential, nor fickle; they only seems so because they are incessantly seeking happiness, which they cannot grasp, and always hoping to find it by changing routine or system.[310] Their changes do not prove their inconsequence, or

---

intact one, but the matter of one is no more despicable than that of the other. We tread disdainfully on the matter of which palaces, mirrors, paintings and porcelain are made."

[310] Author: "…*dum abest, quod avemus, id exsuperare videtur caetera; post aliud, quum contigit illud, avemus; et sitis aequa tenet vitai semper hiantis.* Lucretius Book III line 1096." [While that which we desire is lacking, it seems to surpass all the rest; when we have got it we want something else; the thirst is always the same.] Quoted by Montaigne.

even their inconstancy,[311] so much as the difficulty of finding any felicity.

Can one think that a man, having deliberated, might take a path that will, or which he believes will take him away from his goal, if he were not deflected by a false judgment, or if he were not carried away by passion and circumstances? Who can boast of having never done anything except what he wanted to do? There are no actions devoid of motives, otherwise there would be effects without causes, which implies contradiction.

Is the miser inconsequential in depriving himself of everything in order to lack nothing, when, insensible to the enjoyment of things, which makes the delight of others, all his pleasure consists of the power of being able to procure them? In what does he differ from a curiosity-seeker who inconveniences his fortune or deprives himself of necessary things in order to acquire, at a high price, an antique medallion, a rare shell, or a colored canvas that only has value in the imagination?

The prodigal, who cannot hide it from himself that he will be unable to sustain a long career in ease, is only occupied with the present, which alone belongs to humans; he pities the miser, who deplores his fate. Can one not conclude from the difference between these two characters, without rigorously criticizing one or the other, that one has too long a vision and the other one too limited?

Is the Alchemist who supposes himself to be more enlightened than those who treat him as a madman less foolish than the mariner, already opulent, who risks his life, more precious than any wealth, to increase a fortune that a thousand accidents might prevent him from enjoying?

The Magistrate who pronounces a judgment opposite to a sentence he has previously rendered in a similar case is not

---

[311] Author: "The Ancients had made Constancy a Divinity with two faces. If an attachment is badly placed, constancy takes the name stubbornness, and inconstancy that of reason."

contradicting himself in the eyes of the man he had condemned; he is not inconsequential; he is showing the public that his way of seeing is more enlightened than it was before. Does true virtue ever blush at the admission that it has been mistaken?

Pleasures are only such when they affect the soul with an agreeable sensation. Depraved tastes and extravagant appetites only have the effect, in the moral as in the physical, of a deteriorated disposition of the organs; that is the cause of the fact that farce pleases some people more than high comedy, and romances please some people more than history; that a small number of people of good taste prefer a French monologue bristling with cadences to the melody of a great Italian aria. How, then, can taste be defined? How can the principles and rules by which it can be defined be prescribed and fixed? Is not that sentiment, always relative, subject to a thousand variations? Is not the taste of once century often ridiculed by the one that follows? Does it not sometimes come back, after having been proscribed? So many routes seem to lead to happiness that nothing is easier than to go astray. One rejects the road that leads to it, another takes the path that deviates from it; each treats the other as inconsequential, because their focus is not the same. Are they not both victims of their prudence and tributaries of error?

How many seemingly blameworthy actions would attract esteem and admiration if their true motive was revealed? On the contrary, how many striking deeds, honored by great eulogies, would only be worthy of scorn and horror is their source were discovered? How many imagined inconsequences there are in actions, and how many real inconsequences in judgments! Humans cannot really judge anything as inconsequential except themselves.

Can absolute consequence exist in a being who is the perpetual victim of events, passions and circumstances?

Is the polite or sociable man inconsequential when, between friends, he seems to lend himself to puerile actions bordering on the ridiculous? Is he doing anything but accommodating himself to human weakness and exercising the regard due to society in the established fashion? It would be all the more indulgent if he were more enlightened. If he applauds a young Muse whose first efforts are feeble, he wants to encourage talent. If he flatters a capricious beauty or coquette, of whom he is fundamentally scornful, decently, it is because, having no right to reform her, he is making himself agreeable at scant expense and saving himself from the hatred or ridicule attached to the character of the Cynic or Misanthrope. Adulation is only shameful when it incenses vices; he prefers, with reason, the reputation of delicate complaisance to that of futile censure.[312]

A man very attached to life, as every being is mechanically, seems to scorn it in crossing the sea. That insensate in the eyes of others, whose passions are tranquil, is often less guided by ambition or cupidity than the noble sentiment of a good father or a generous citizen. Is not sacrificing his happiness to public opinion to be the dupe of reason? Can reason perfect the usage of the senses, or the usage of the senses perfect reason?

Which would be the happier of a man whose reason deadened all pleasures or one who tasted them all equally, without reflection?

If the human body, as Hippocrates says, in a circle, who can say at what point it commences?

What experiments would be necessary to succeed in knowing the natural man, and what are the means of carrying out those experiments in the bosom of society?

Which is the easier to find of an impartial Writer or an equitable Reader, if both of them are only near-reasonable beings?

---

[312] Author: "*Cum tristibus severe, cum remissis jucunde, cum senibus graviter, cum juventute comiter vivere.* Cicero." [(Cicero is speaking of Catiline, saying that) he lived with the sad severely, the cheerful agreeably, the sad gravely, and the young pleasantly]

Can there be universal or invariable principles to judge the beautiful in all genres?

If the beautiful is that which pleases all the time and in all lands, there is really no beauty either in the moral or the physical, without excepting the majority of the works of Nature.[313]

If the eyes are, as is commonly said, the mirror of the soul, and if physiognomy announces character, would one so frequently be the dupe of oaths and hypocrisy?

To what causes can dreams be attributed?

Why are there so many excellent poets and so few good historians?

Is fiction easier to treat than verity, or is judgment rarer than genius?

What is the power of the passions and the imagination over temperament?

What is the reciprocal influence of the opinions of people on their language and of the language on their opinions?

Can the mind, in making comparisons, conceive of two ideas, or understand two propositions, at the same time? If that is impossible, as is claimed, how can the mind make the comparison?[314]

In dramatic works, which is the easier genre to treat, the tragic or the comic?

What is it that attracts us to the theater? The design of correcting our mores? No. That of reforming our ridiculousness? Even less. Pleasure? Yes, undoubtedly. Weeping is,

---

[313] Author: "In Ethiopia and in China, at Tonkin, where the features of beauty are not the same as in Europe, the Venus of the Medicis would appear to be an image rendered ugly by the caprice of the sculptor, to the scorn of beautiful nature, as we see, with horror, their most beautiful idols."

[314] Author: "One can only see objects from the viewpoint that corresponds to the optic axes; only that one sees distinctly; we can see several perceptions at the same time, but confused, only one of which we can distinguish clearly."

therefore, an agreeable sentiment; it is not always a sign of sadness. Thus, dolor sometimes produces pleasure. Is it not singular that one can excite oneself to pleasure by means of tears, and quite bizarre that one can bring oneself to laugh immoderately at an Attelan or other farce, shortly after one has taken so much pleasure in affliction?

Is it certain that every Writer has his own style? If it is, there are as many styles as there are heads. There can therefore be an infinite number of good styles.

Is it as easy as it is commonly thought to recognize an author who has written before by the style of his work? In twenty or thirty years does the style not sometimes change sufficiently to be no longer recognizable? Who can recover in *Cinna* the author of *Clitandre* or *Mélite?*[315]

Is it necessary, in order to depict the passions well, to be keenly penetrated by them? If so, what danger might there be in the society of certain tragic authors?

Is it certain that an author paints himself in his writings in such a way that one can discover his sentiments and his character there, however much care he takes to veil them? Is it not more natural to believe that the heart and the mind each have their own style? Otherwise, what judgment could one make of the character of Rousseau, Aretino and others, who excelled equally in treating the pious and the obscene? Is La Fontaine not an insoluble problem of finesse and simplicity?

Can there be a fixed rule of taste for all peoples and for all individuals?

Would it be very difficult to prove that among books reputed to be well-written there is not one whose style is similar to another?

Would it be difficult to prove that there is not a single well-written book?

If the measured discourse of rhymed Poetry, the origin of which is barbaric among all peoples, was invented to aid the memory with regard to the things most necessary to retain,

---

[315] Pierre Corneille.

who would not believe that the Code ought to be in verse and La Fontaine in prose?

How can it happen that a stupid man when wide awake can show intelligence while dreaming or delirious, and that an imbecile when sober can make quips when drunk?

Would there be as many fathers who complain of their children's defects if they had neglected their education less or they had accompanied their precepts with better examples?

Is it not shame that gives rise to the self-respect that makes it more difficult for educated adults to learn and pronounce foreign languages than it is for children?

If one could be sure of secret emissaries, would it be advantageous for Princes to keep Ambassadors and Ministers in foreign Courts in order to penetrate Treaties that might be made contrary to their interests? If they only received what they gave, would it not be the same as of everyone kept his secret? With simple Agents sufficient for the promptest expedition of affairs, would that reform not at least be a considerable economy for the State? Europe furnishes a few examples.

Are gold and silver, as one Ancient says, a favor of the Gods, or an effect of their anger?

Are there as many ingrates as is commonly published? Are not the majority born of the ridiculous price that benefactors put on their services?

What is the most suitable color to express mourning by way of garments?[316]

Is it not a blatant injustice to judge a man on the first step he takes in Society, or in Letters, since that is the moment when he has least judgment and experience to guide him? Do

---

[316] Author: "In China mourning dress is white. That for the Emperor lasts three years and gives rise to all kinds of charges and magnificence. In Spain it was worn in that color until 1498. In Turkey one wears blue, in Egypt yellow, in Ethiopia gray and in Europe black or violet. It is lightened by mixing black and white. Many peoples content themselves with wearing it in the heart."

the lives of Augustus and Nero not give the lie to that iniquitous maxim? Is there a more striking example in Letters than
the great Corneille?

We have fixed, in the present state of things, the common life of a human being at twenty years and the generations
at thirty; but if human life were equal to that of the Patriarchs,[317] how many years would a generation be, and what
would be the common age? Counting the interest on money at
one twentieth for perpetual returns, which would be the rate of
life annuities and tontines, and on what footing would the
classes be distributed? Finally, what would be the age of majority, and in what space of time would a man be deemed to be
dead?

Would it not be desirable for every man at twenty to
have a duty to forget everything that he had learned and to
learn it all again by examination and reflection, without basing
it on the principles or judgment of others? Would that not be
the surest means of making a sane use of reason and finding
the whole truth?

Is it not gratuitously to exhale the vapors of misanthropy
to degrade the human condition at pleasure, by sustaining
loudly that people are becoming increasingly perverted? Is
that not tacitly to admit that one is worse than one's father,
who was worse than his? Does the spirit of satire never weary
of such vain and false declarations, belied by the History of all

---

[317] Author: "In considering the longevity of the Patriarchs, do
not suppose with the vulgar that they counted a lunar month as
a year; the year has always been an entire revolution around
the sun. If the months had been counted as years, instead of
finding marvels in the long lives of the first men, they would
have had a lifespan less than ours. It is cited as a singular fact
that Sara became pregnant at the age of ninety-seven; according to that false calculation she would only have been eight.
Moses would have commanded the army before the age of
five at the passage of the Red Sea; the youngest soldiers would
not have attained the age of two, etc."

times, and would it be very difficult to prove that, human be-ings having always been fundamentally similar, save for a few nuances, all things considered, our century is better that those which preceded it, and to draw the conclusion that it will be followed by a bettor one?

Should one not believe, on the basis of the Writings of the century, that the virtue exercised by the Romans in the highest degree and so lauded by Historians, *the love of the Fatherland*, of which, in truth, we have very little idea, has been replaced by that of *the love of the Human Race?* Have not so many excellent works on commerce, political and rural economy, navigation, military art, mechanics, morality, the examination of prejudices, etc., proved that? Are they not evi-dent signs of the progress of Reason?

Is not the respectable word *Humanity*, so frequently em-ployed in all these writings, and which evil minds seem to want to put on trial, the eulogy of current sentiments? Is it not the symbol of reigning mores?

Can one call frivolous the century is which the bounty and humanity of the Sovereign have passed into the heart of his subjects? *Regis ad exemplum, totus componitur orbis.*[318] Does it not merit, in every regard, with more reason, the title of the *Human Century*, the *Philosophical Century?*—titles which, to judge by the efforts of some generous citizens, nec-essarily entail that of the *Agricultural Century.*[319]

---

[318] The example of the monarch is the law on earth.

[319] Author: "One might justly call it the Wicked Century if only judged it by the shameful success of some satirical plays and the debit of certain periodicals, but it is the lot of Enlight-ened Centuries to have their Aristophanes and their Zoilus." Zoilus was a grammarian who criticized Homer, thus ruining his own reputation eternally.

Chapter XVIII
Questions insoluble for any Being limited to five senses,
and on which he is free to adopt any Philosophy or to
form a System for his own satisfaction, convinced that it
is not given to the human mind to resolve them.

What is the cause of weight? Is it attraction? In that case, what is the cause of attraction? Is it impulsion? What is the nature of the fluid that causes it?

With what degree of velocity does fire penetrate bodies?

How can the quadrature of the Circle, the duplication of the Cube, the trisection of the Angle, the relationship between the diagonal and one of the sides of the Square, the commensurability of one Cube with another, Perpetual Motion, the Philosophical Stone and the Universal Medicine be found?

Has Light a movement of acceleration, like falling bodies?

What is Oil?

Why do rays of sunlight rebound from the surfaces of bodies without touching the surfaces in question?

Why are Liquids, principally Water, not compressible, although they are elastic, while Metals, which have far fewer pores, including Gold, which has nineteen times more matter than Water are compressible?

In what does the Act of Conception consist in the animals, and how does Generation occur in viviparous and oviparous ones? How does it occur in slugs, aphids and fish, which engender without copulation, and, finally, in polyps and other animals whose severed parts reproduce themselves?

How does Digestion occur in the stomach, where aliments of different nature are equally transformed into milk, chyle, blood, lymph and solid components?

Does any unopposable circumstance exist in Nature?

How does the Will act on some parts of our body, and why does it have no action on the others?

Is there an absolute gravity of all corpuscles? What is their specific gravity?

What constitutes the different configuration of bodies?

If bodies only differ in color, weight, quality and shape by virtue of the different arrangement of the elements that compose them, so that the elements of lead and gold are the same—as is supposed—and finally, if every particle is a body, do those particles have a primitive hardness or does their hardness become fluid under pressure, and if so, what is the cause of that pressure?

What is the nature of the substance known as Gluten? Is it that to which stones, which are only earth of greater consistency, owe that consistency? Is it, in sum, the substance of concretion, petrifaction and crystallization? How is sandstone bound by that gluten, which crumbles to dust at the slightest friction?

Where is the seat of intelligence, memory and judgment?

Are the brightest stars, which appear to us to be the largest, really nearer to us than those which can only be perceived by the best telescopes? Is scintillation a proof that they are as many suns, and, by analogy, all of the same size?

How far does the knowledge of animals extend beyond self-preservation? Do they have a language? Is there a different one for each species? What, in the final analysis is instinct?

Is the Universe maintained by the motion imparted to matter at the commencement of the World, or by a new creation at every instant?

In what proportion does attraction act between light and substance?

What is the mechanism of dissolution, considered in the relation to the dissolving substance—that of salt in water, water in air, etc.? Is it hatred or antipathy? How can inanimate bodies have that faculty?

Is fire an element or a particular substance, or is it only an effect of matter put in motion?

Is it to physical or mechanical causes that one ought to attribute animal heat? In what part of the body is its hearth or principal seat?

Does the heat that one feels at a certain depth underground have its source in a central fire, or is it caused by the agitation of sulfur and minerals that are found in abundance in the entrails of the earth?

What is light? Is it a substance emanated by the sun? Is it an intermediary substance whose existence is independent of that star, a fluid spread throughout the entire Universe, which only awaits, in order to act sensibly upon sight, to be put in motion? What is that phenomenon, and what impression does it make on the sense of sight? Is it only a pressure on the extremities of the nerves? Does it not impart a movement of vibration? Are the nervous threads on which it acts hollow and filled with animal spirits? What are so-called animal spirits? Is it really certain that they exist? If they exist and are susceptible to the impression of external objects, by what mechanism do they transmit their impressions to be brain? Is it by a movement of flow or of vibration? What is their action on the brain? Do they form traces? Do they only cause the fibers to vibrate? Etc.

If light is a substance emanated by the sun, ought not the quantity of corpuscles, which fill space and do not return physically to their source, in spite of their tenuousness, become so prodigious in millions of centuries that space would become compact, and the globes that the sun illuminates augment in volume at its expense to the point that, after having dried up the source, they become suns themselves, formed of the debris of the one that will have transmitted its substance to them? The aliment that comets furnish the sun in their passage is, in truth, a neat and ingenious hypothesis to repair its loss; it only lacks plausibility, and the knowledge of whether the largest comet is in a condition to restore to the sun in a short time, all that it loses continuously.

What are the laws of the union of the soul with the body?[320]

What is that which we call force in bodies, except for the name of something of which we have no idea?

Where is the center of gravitation of the sun with the plant and comets in its vortex?

Finally what is the nature of the substance of the air?

What are the causes of the cohesion of substances?

Of the coagulation of liquids?

Of elasticity?

Of hardness?

Of electricity?

Of ductility?

Of fragility?

Of malleability?

Of fermentation?

Of effervescence?

Of magnetism?

Of the declination of magnetized needles?

Of attraction?

Of impulsion?

Of the contraction and dilatation of muscles?

Of fluidity?

Of sympathy and antipathy, all the way to inanimate bodies?

Of motion?

Of the prolific virtue of seeds and grains?

---

[320] Author: "One Wit has said that the body and soul are two enemies that cannot quit one another, and two friends that cannot abide one another."

Chapter XIX and Last
The End of the Voyage

After six months, the date of the General Assembly of the Academies having been announced, I went in haste to the Secretary, who handed me a considerable packet secured by the seal of the Academy, containing the decisions of that respectable Tribunal on all the questions that I had presented, and which, according to what the Secretary told me, would furnish material for four folio volumes. All that was demanded of me was that I would not open the packet until I had returned to the Earth. I submitted to that condition, with some difficulty, and, proud of such a precious booty, I paid not further heed to anything except my departure.

I employed the little time that I counted on remaining in Selenopolis in carefully writing down all the knowledge that I had acquired and the curious discoveries I had made for the pleasure, utility and benefit of humankind, with the intention of enriching my Fatherland. And, content with the success of my endeavors, I was adding my last period when, by the most fatal accident, the ground suddenly shook beneath me, and, seeing temples and palaces crumble and the ground opening up to bury me in profound abysses, I launched myself precipitately through a window in order to reach the plain.

By an even greater misfortune than the one I was trying to escape, however, I found myself beside my bed, lying on the parquet, my limbs crumpled and almost motionless. I was less sensible, however, to the dolor that I felt from my fall, than the chagrin of realizing that the majority of my doubts would remain without solution, and that all that I had seen and heard was only the effect of a vain dream, a sad but faithful image of the majority of the felicities of life.

Eppue troppo e la vita un Sogno.[321]

---

[321] Approximately: "But then, life is a dream."

SF & FANTASY

Adolphe Alhaiza. *Cybele*
Alphonse Allais. *The Adventures of Captain Cap*
Henri Allorge. *The Great Cataclysm*
Guy d'Armen. *Doc Ardan: The City of Gold and Lepers*
G.-J. Arnaud. *The Ice Company*
Charles Asselineau. *The Double Life*
Henri Austruy. *The Eupantophone; The Olotelepan; The Petitpaon Era*
Barillet-Lagargousse. *The Final War*
Cyprien Bérard. *The Vampire Lord Ruthwen*
S. Henry Berthoud. *Martyrs of Science*
Aloysius Bertrand. *Gaspard de la Nuit*
Richard Bessière. *The Gardens of the Apocalypse; The Masters of Silence*
Albert Bleunard. *Ever Smaller*
Félix Bodin. *The Novel of the Future*
Louis Boussenard. *Monsieur Synthesis*
Alphonse Brown. *City of Glass; The Conquest of the Air*
Emile Calvet. *In a Thousand Years*
André Caroff. *The Terror of Madame Atomos; Miss Atomos; The Return of Madame Atomos; The Mistake of Madame Atomos; The Monsters of Madame Atomos; The Revenge of Madame Atomos; The Resurrection of Madame Atomos; The Mark of Madame Atomos; The Spheres of Madame Atomos; The Wrath of Madame Atomos* (w/M. & Sylvie Stéphan)
Félicien Champsaur. *The Human Arrow; Ouha, King of the Apes; Pharaoh's Wife; Homo-Deus*
Didier de Chousy. *Ignis*
Jules Clarétie. *Obsession*
Michel Corday. *The Eternal Flame*
André Couvreur. *The Necessary Evil*; *Caresco, Superman; The Exploits of Professor Tornada* (3 vols.)
Captain Danrit. *Undersea Odyssey*
C. I. Defontenay. *Star (Psi Cassiopeia)*
Charles Derennes. *The People of the Pole*
Georges Dodds (anthologist). *The Missing Link*
Charles Dodeman. *The Silent Bomb*
Harry Dickson. *The Heir of Dracula; Harry Dickson vs. The Spider*

Jules Dornay. *Lord Ruthven Begins*

Alfred Driou. *The Adventures of a Parisian Aeronaut*

Sâr Dubnotal *vs. Jack the Ripper*

Alexandre Dumas. *The Return of Lord Ruthven*

Renée Dunan. *Baal*

J.-C. Dunyach. *The Night Orchid; The Thieves of Silence*

Henri Duvernois. *The Man Who Found Himself*

Achille Eyraud. *Voyage to Venus*

Henri Falk. *The Age of Lead*

Paul Féval. *Anne of the Isles; Knightshade; Revenants; Vampire City; The Vampire Countess; The Wandering Jew's Daughter*

Paul Féval, *fils. Felifax, the Tiger-Man*

Charles de Fieux. *Lamékis*

Louis Forest. *Someone is Stealing Children in Paris*

Arnould Galopin. *Doctor Omega*; *Doctor Omega and the Shadowmen* (anthology)

Judith Gautier. *Isoline and the Serpent-Flower*

H. Gayar. *The Marvelous Adventures of Serge Myrandhal on Mars*

Léon Gozlan. *The Vampire of the Val-de-Grâce*

G.L. Gick. *Harry Dickson and the Werewolf of Rutherford Grange*

Edmond Haraucourt. *Illusions of Immortality; Daah, the First Human*

Nathalie Henneberg. *The Green Gods*

Eugène Hennebert. *The Enchanted City*

V. Hugo, P. Foucher & P. Meurice. *The Hunchback of Notre-Dame*

Romain d'Huissier. *Hexagon: Dark Matter*

Jules Janin. *The Magnetized Corpse*

Michel Jeury. *Chronolysis*

Gustave Kahn. *The Tale of Gold and Silence*

Gérard Klein. *The Mote in Time's Eye*

Fernand Kolney. *Love in 5000 Years*

Paul Lacroix. *Danse Macabre*

Louis-Guillaume de La Follie. *The Unpretentious Philosopher*

Jean de La Hire. *Enter the Nyctalope; The Nyctalope on Mars; The Nyctalope vs. Lucifer; The Nyctalope Steps In; Night of the Nyctalope; Return of the Nyctalope; The Fiery Wheel*

Etienne-Léon de Lamothe-Langon. *The Virgin Vampire*

André Laurie. *Spiridon*

Gabriel de Lautrec. *The Vengeance of the Oval Portrait*

Alain le Drimeur. *The Future City*

Georges Le Faure & Henri de Graffigny. *The Extraordinary Adventures of a Russian Scientist Across the Solar System* (2 vols.)

Gustave Le Rouge. *The Mysterious Doctor Cornelius* (3 vols.); *The Vampires of Mars; The Dominion of the World* (w/Gustave Guitton) (4 vols.)

Jules Lermina. *Mysteryville; Panic in Paris; To-Ho and the Gold Destroyers; The Secret of Zippeliu; The Battle of Strasbourg*

André Lichtenberger. *The Centaurs; The Children of the Crab*

Jean-Marc & Randy Lofficier. *Edgar Allan Poe on Mars; The Katrina Protocol; Pacifica; Robonocchio; Return of the Nyctalope;* (anthologists) *Tales of the Shadowmen 1-11*

Xavier Mauméjean. *The League of Heroes*

Joseph Méry. *The Tower of Destiny*

Hippolyte Mettais. *The Year 5865; Paris Before the Deluge*

Louise Michel. *The Human Microbes; The New World*

Tony Moilin. *Paris in the Year 2000*

José Moselli. *Illa's End*

John-Antoine Nau. *Enemy Force*

Marie Nizet. *Captain Vampire*

C. Nodier, A. Beraud & Toussaint-Merle. *Frankenstein*

Henri de Parville. *An Inhabitant of the Planet Mars*

Gaston de Pawlowski. *Journey to the Land of the 4th Dimension*

Georges Pellerin. *The World in 2000 Years*

Ernest Pérochon. *The Frenetic People*

Pierre Pelot. *The Child Who Walked on the Sky*

J. Polidori, C. Nodier, E. Scribe. *Lord Ruthven the Vampire*

P.-A. Ponson du Terrail. *The Vampire and the Devil's Son; The Immortal Woman*

Edgar Quinet. *Ahasuerus; The Enchanter Merlin*

Henri de Régnier. *A Surfeit of Mirrors*

Maurice Renard. *The Blue Peril; Doctor Lerne; The Doctored Man; A Man Among the Microbes; The Master of Light*

Jean Richepin. *The Wing; The Crazy Corner*

Albert Robida. *The Adventures of Saturnin Farandoul; The Clock of the Centuries; Chalet in the Sky; The Electric Life*

J.-H. Rosny Aîné. *Helgvor of the Blue River; The Givreuse Enigma; The Mysterious Force; The Navigators of Space; Vamireh; The World of the Variants; The Young Vampire*

Marcel Rouff. *Journey to the Inverted World*

Léonie Rouzade. *The World Turned Upside Down*

Han Ryner. *The Superhumans; The Human Ant*

Pierre de Selenes: *An Unknown World*

Angelo de Sorr. *The Vampires of London*

Brian Stableford. *The New Faust at the Tragicomique;The Empire of the Necromancers (The Shadow of Frankenstein; Frankenstein and the Vampire Countess; Frankenstein in London); Sherlock Holmes & The Vampires of Eternity; The Stones of Camelot; The Wayward Muse.* (anthologist) *News from the Moon; The Germans on Venus; The Supreme Progress; The World Above the World; Nemoville; Investigations of the Future; The Conqueror of Death; The Revolt of the Machines*
Jacques Spitz. *The Eye of Purgatory*
Kurt Steiner. *Ortog*
Eugène Thébault. *Radio-Terror*
C.-F. Tiphaigne de La Roche. *Amilec*
Louis Ulbach. *Prince Bonifacio*
Théo Varlet. *The Golden Rock. The Xenobiotic Invasion; The Casta-ways of Eros; Timeslip Troopers* (w/André Blandin); *The Martian Epic* (w/Octave Joncquel)
Paul Vibert. *The Mysterious Fluid*
Villiers de l'Isle-Adam. *The Scaffold; The Vampire Soul*
Philippe Ward. *Artahe ; The Song of Montségur* (w/Sylvie Miller) *Manhattan Ghost* (w/Mickael Laguerre)

MYSTERIES & THRILLERS

M. Allain & P. Souvestre. *The Daughter of Fantômas*
A. Anicet-Bourgeois, Lucien Dabril. *Rocambole*
A. Bernède. *Belphegor*; *Judex* (w/Louis Feuillade); *The Return of Judex* (w/Louis Feuillade); *The Shadow of Judex*
A. Bisson & G. Livet. *Nick Carter vs. Fantômas*
V. Darlay & H. de Gorsse. *Arsène Lupin vs. Sherlock Holmes: The Stage Play*
Séamas Duffy. *Sherlock Holmes in Paris*
Paul Féval. *Gentlemen of the Night; John Devil; The Black Coats ('Salem Street; The Invisible Weapon; The Parisian Jungle; The Companions of the Treasure; Heart of Steel; The Cadet Gang; The Sword-Swallower)*
Emile Gaboriau. *Monsieur Lecoq*
Goron & Emile Gautier. *Spawn of the Penitentiary*
Rick Lai. *Shadows of the Opera: Retribution in Blood; Sisters of the Shadows: The Curse of Cagliostro*
Steve Leadley. *Sherlock Holmes: The Circle of Blood*

Maurice Leblanc. *Arsène Lupin vs. Countess Cagliostro; Arsène Lupin vs. Sherlock Holmes (The Blonde Phantom; The Hollow Needle); The Many Faces of Arsène Lupin; The Island of the Thirty Coffins*

Gaston Leroux. *Chéri-Bibi; The Phantom of the Opera; Rouletabille & the Mystery of the Yellow Room; Rouletabille at Krupp's*

Richard Marsh. *The Complete Adventures of Judith Lee*

William Patrick Maynard. *The Terror of Fu Manchu; The Destiny of Fu Manchu*

Frank J. Morlock. *Sherlock Holmes: The Grand Horizontals; Sherlock Holmes vs Jack the Ripper*

Jean Petithuguenin. *The Adventures of Ethel King*

Antonin Reschal. *The Adventures of Miss Boston*

P. de Wattyne & Y. Walter. *Sherlock Holmes vs. Fantômas*

David White. *Fantômas in America*

Pierre Yrondy. *The Adventures of Thérèse Arnaud*

Victor Margueritte. *The Bacheloress; The Companion; The Couple*

SCREENPLAYS

Mike Baron. *The Iron Triangle*

Emma Bull & Will Shetterly. *Nightspeeder; War for the Oaks*

Gerry Conway & Roy Thomas. *Doc Dynamo*

Steve Englehart. *Majorca*

James Hudnall. *The Devastator*

Jean-Marc & Randy Lofficier. *Royal Flush*

J.-M. & R. Lofficier & Marc Agapit. *Despair*

J.-M. & R. Lofficier & Joël Houssin. *City*

Andrew Paquette. *Peripheral Vision*

Robert L. Robinson, Jr. *Judex*

R. Thomas, J. Hendler & L. Sprague de Camp. *Rivers of Time*

NON-FICTION

Stephen R. Bissette. *Blur 1-5. Green Mountain Cinema 1; Teen Angels*

Win Scott Eckert. *Crossovers* (2 vols.)

Jean-Marc & Randy Lofficier. *Shadowmen* (2 vols.)

Randy Lofficier. *Over Here*

www.ingramcontent.com/pod-product-compliance
Lightning Source LLC
Chambersburg PA
CBHW060415030726
47495CB00003B/594